SHARPE'S WATERLOO

Bernard Cornwell was born in London, raised in Essex and now mostly lives in the USA. He is the author of the Arthurian series, the Warlord Chronicles; the Starbuck Chronicles, on the American Civil War; *Stonehenge*; the Grail Quest Series; *Gallow's Thief* and *The Last Kingdom*.

For more information, visit:
www.bernardcornwell.net

BERNARD CORNWELL

Sharpe's Waterloo

Richard Sharpe and
the Waterloo Campaign,
15 June to 18 June 1815

HARPER

HarperCollins*Publishers*
77–85 Fulham Palace Road,
Hammersmith, London w6 8jb

www.harpercollins.co.uk

This paperback edition 2007
1

Previously published in paperback by HarperCollins 1993
(reprinted five times)
and by Fontana in 1991 (reprinted three times)

First published in Great Britain by
Collins 1990

Copyright © Rifleman Productions Ltd 1990

isbn 978-0-00-789470-3

Typeset in New Baskerville by
Palimpsest Book Production Limited,
Grangemouth, Stirlingshire

Printed and bound in Great Britain by
Clays Ltd, St Ives plc

Sharpe's Waterloo is for Judy,
with all my love

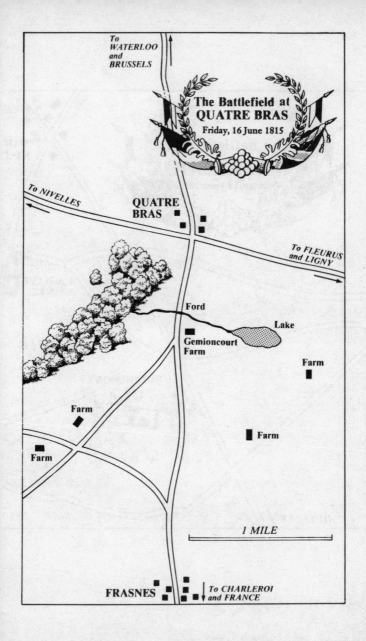

The Battlefield at QUATRE BRAS
Friday, 16 June 1815

To WATERLOO and BRUSSELS

To NIVELLES

QUATRE BRAS

To FLEURUS and LIGNY

Ford

Lake

Gemioncourt Farm

Farm

Farm

Farm

Farm

1 MILE

FRASNES

To CHARLEROI and FRANCE

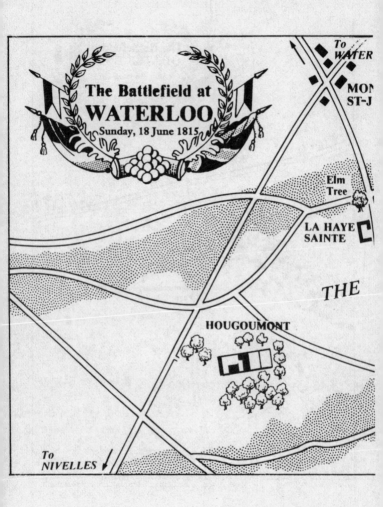

The Battlefield at
WATERLOO
Sunday, 18 June 1815

To WATER

MON
ST-J

Elm
Tree

LA HAYE
SAINTE

THE

HOUGOUMONT

To
NIVELLES

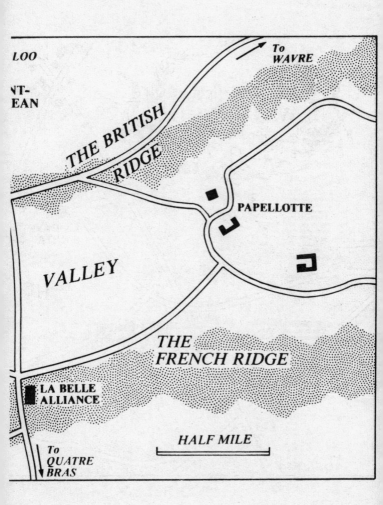

LOO

NT-
EAN

To
WAVRE

THE BRITISH

RIDGE

PAPELLOTTE

VALLEY

THE
FRENCH RIDGE

LA BELLE
ALLIANCE

HALF MILE

To
QUATRE
BRAS

FOREWORD

I remember that when I first began writing this book I attempted – in vain, as it turned out – to insert a plot into the story. It never worked. I spent weeks, probably months, trying to get that story to work, and it always failed. In the end the obvious dawned on me: no plot I could devise could ever rival the sheer drama, the cliff-hanging suspense, of the real thing. The battle of Waterloo was as dramatic as any author could ever wish, and so I abandoned the fifty or sixty thousand words that had tormented me for so long and wrote, 'It was dawn on the northern frontier of France.'

For it was at dawn, on Thursday 15 June 1815, that Napoleon's army crossed the northern frontier of France on its way to a battle on 18 June. The story of those four days is a tremendous one, often retold, yet its ending is still as dramatic as ever. Late on the eighteenth the British army is skinned bare. There are no reserves left. The colours have been sent to the rear to prevent their capture and the men are bone-weary. And Napoleon's finest troops, held back so that they could deliver the crushing blow at the crucial moment, are attacking. True, the Prussians have arrived at last and are engaging the French right wing, but if the French attack on the British right succeeds then Napoleon can still win this battle. No plot of mine could compete with such drama.

It was a famous victory. Napoleon's headquarters

before the battle were at the inn called la Belle Alliance, 'the beautiful alliance', and Blücher, the Prussian commander, suggested to Wellington that the battle should be named for that inn. It was a good idea, for it testified to the undoubted truth that it had been an allied victory: Blücher could not have won without Wellington and Wellington could not have won without Blücher. Wellington, however, wrote his despatch in the nearby town of Waterloo and, prosaically, that became the battle's name and that was a pity because the alternative, the battle of la Belle Alliance, might have served to remind subsequent generations that it was a joint victory. Wellington certainly believed so, as did Blücher, but now, nearly two hundred years after the battle, there is a steady stream of books that set out to 'prove' that Wellington tried to steal the credit from Blücher, or deliberately misled Blücher. As I write this foreword a book is announced with the subtitle 'Waterloo, the German victory'. This is all nonsense. Waterloo was no more a German victory than it was a British victory. It was an allied victory. Wellington bore the brunt of the fighting, but he did that willingly because he knew the Prussians were coming to his aid, and the Prussians marched to his aid because they trusted that Wellington would stand long enough to let them arrive. That truth has been obvious since dusk on 18 June 1815, and it is a pity that so many trees are being cut down to argue the opposite.

The duke did not like authors. He had, he said, been too much exposed to them. He still suffers from them, but this novel, at any rate, tries to give him his due. It was never his proudest achievement on a battlefield; that, he said, belonged to Assaye (*Sharpe's Triumph*), while many have said that his masterpiece was Salamanca (*Sharpe's Sword*), but it was a near run thing and, for me, his finest hour. Relive it with Sharpe.

THE FIRST DAY
Thursday, 15 June 1815

CHAPTER 1

It was dawn on the northern frontier of France; a border marked only by a shallow stream which ran between the stunted trunks of pollarded willows. A paved high road forded the stream. The road led north from France into the Dutch province of Belgium, but there was neither guardpost nor gate to show where the road left the French Empire to enter the Kingdom of the Netherlands. There was just the summer-shrunken stream from which a pale mist drifted to lie in shadowy skeins across the plump fields of wheat and rye and barley.

The rising sun appeared like a swollen red ball suspended low in the tenuous mist. The sky was still dark in the west. An owl flew over the ford, banked into a beechwood and gave a last hollow call, which was lost in the dawn's loud chorus that seemed to presage a bright hot summer's day in this rich and placid countryside. The cloudless sky promised a day for haymaking, or a day for lovers to stroll through heavy-leafed woods to rest beside the green cool of a streambank. It was a perfect midsummer's dawn on the northern border of France and for a moment, for a last heart-aching moment, the world was at peace.

Then hundreds of hooves crashed through the ford, spattering water bright into the mist. Uniformed men, long swords in their hands, rode north out of France. The men were Dragoons who wore brass helmets covered

3

with drab cloth so the rising sun would not reflect from the shining metal to betray their position. The horsemen had short-barrelled muskets thrust into bucket holsters on their saddles.

The Dragoons were the vanguard of an army. A hundred and twenty-five thousand men were marching north on every road that led to the river-crossing at Charleroi. This was invasion; an army flooding across an unguarded frontier with wagons and coaches and ambulances and three hundred and forty-four guns and thirty thousand horses and portable forges and pontoon bridges and whores and wives and colours and lances and muskets and sabres and all the hopes of France. This was the Emperor Napoleon's Army of the North and it marched towards the waiting Dutch, British and Prussian forces.

The French Dragoons crossed the frontier with drawn swords, but the weapons served no purpose other than to dignify the moment with a suitable melodrama, for there was not so much as a single Dutch customs officer to oppose the invasion. There were just the mist and the empty roads, and the far-off crowing of cockerels in the dawn. A few dogs barked as the invading cavalrymen captured the first Dutch villages unopposed. The Dragoons hammered their sword hilts against doors and window shutters, demanding to know whether any British or Prussian soldiers were billeted within.

'They're all to the north. They hardly ever show themselves here!' The villagers spoke French; indeed, they thought of themselves as French citizens and consequently welcomed the helmeted Dragoons with cups of wine and offers of food. To these reluctant Dutchmen the invasion was a liberation, and even the weather matched their joy; the sun was climbing into a cloudless sky and beginning to burn off the mist which still clung in the leafy valleys.

On the main highway leading to Charleroi and Brussels

the Dragoons were clattering along at a fine pace, almost as if this was an exercise in Provence instead of war. A lieutenant of Dragoons was so dismissive of any danger that he was eagerly telling his Sergeant how the new science of phrenology measured human aptitudes from the shape of a man's skull. The Lieutenant opined that when the science was properly understood all promotion in the army would be based on careful skull measurements. 'We'll be able to measure courage and decisiveness, common sense and honesty, and all with a pair of calipers and a measuring tape!'

The Sergeant did not respond. He and his officer rode at the head of their squadron, and were thus at the very tip of the advancing French army. In truth the Sergeant was not really listening to the Lieutenant's enthusiastic explanation; instead he was partly anticipating the Belgian girls and partly worrying when this headlong advance would run into the enemy picquets. Surely the British and Prussians had not fled?

The Lieutenant was somewhat piqued by his Sergeant's apparent lack of interest in phrenology, though the Sergeant's low and scowling brow ridge undoubtedly betrayed the scientific reason for his inability to accept new ideas. The Lieutenant nevertheless persisted in trying to enlighten the veteran soldier. 'They've done studies on the criminal classes in Paris, Sergeant, and have discovered a remarkable correlation between –'

The remarkable correlation remained a mystery, because the hedgerow thirty yards ahead of the two horsemen exploded with musket-fire and the Lieutenant's horse collapsed, shot in the chest. The horse screamed. Blood frothed at its teeth as it lashed frantically with its hooves. The Lieutenant, thrown from the saddle, was kicked in the pelvis by a thrashing hoof. He screamed as loudly as his horse that was now blocking the high road with its flailing death throes. The astonished Dragoons could hear the enemy ramrods rattling in their musket barrels. The Sergeant looked back at the troopers. 'One of you kill that bloody horse!'

More shots hammered from the hedge. The ambushers were good. They had allowed the French horsemen to come very close before they opened fire. The Dragoons sheathed their long swords and drew their carbines, but their aim from horseback was uncertain and the short-barrelled carbine was a weapon of notorious inaccuracy. The Lieutenant's horse still lashed and kicked on the road. The Sergeant was shouting for his men to advance. A trumpet called behind, ordering another troop to file right into a field of growing wheat. A trooper shot the Lieutenant's horse, leaning from his saddle to put the bullet plumb into the beast's skull. Another horse fell, this one with a leg bone shattered by a musket-ball. A Dragoon was lying in the ditch, his helmet fallen into a nettle patch. Horses crashed past the wounded Lieutenant, their hooves spurting mud and road-flints into the air. The Sergeant's long sword shone silver.

More shots, but this time the gouts of white smoke were scattered more thinly along the hedgerow. 'They're retreating, sir!' the Sergeant shouted to an officer far behind him, then, not waiting for any orders, spurred his horse forward. 'Charge!'

The French Dragoons swept past the line of the hedge. They could see no enemy in the long-shadowed landscape, but they knew the ambushers had to be close. The Sergeant, suspecting that the enemy infantry was hiding in the mist-skeined wheat field, turned his horse off the lane, forced it through a ditch and so up into the wheat. He saw movement at the far side of the field, close by a dark-leafed wood. The movement resolved into men running towards the trees. The men wore dark blue uniform coats and had black shakos with silver rims.

6

Prussian infantry. 'There they are!' The Sergeant pointed at the enemy with his sword. 'After the bastards!'

Thirty Dragoons followed the Sergeant. They thrust their carbines into the bucket holsters on their saddles and dragged out their long straight-bladed swords. Prussian muskets pricked flame from the wood's edge, but the shooting was at too long a range and only one French horse tumbled into the wheat. The remaining Dragoons swept on. The enemy picquet that had ambushed the French vanguard was hurrying to the shelter of the wood, but some of them had left their retreat too late and the Dragoons caught them. The Sergeant galloped past a man and cut back with a savage slash of his sword.

The Prussian infantryman clapped his hands to his sword-whipped face, trying to cram his eyes back into their sockets. Another man, ridden down by two Dragoons, choked on blood. 'Charge!' The Sergeant was carrying his sword to the infantry among the trees. He could see Prussian soldiers running away in the undergrowth and he felt the fierce exultation of a cavalryman given a helpless enemy to slaughter, but he did not see the battery of guns concealed in the deep shadows at the edge of the wood, nor the Prussian artillery officer who shouted, 'Fire!'

One moment the Sergeant was screaming at his men to charge hard home, and the next he and his horse were hit by the metal gale of an exploding canister. Horse and man died instantly. Behind the Sergeant the Dragoons splayed left and right, but three other horses and four more men died. Two of the men were French and two were Prussian infantry who had left their retreat too late.

The Prussian gunner officer saw another troop of Dragoons threatening to outflank his position. He looked back to the road where yet more French cavalry had appeared, and he knew it could not be long before the first French eight-pounder cannon arrived. 'Limber up!'

The Prussian guns galloped northwards, their retreat guarded by black-uniformed Hussars who wore skull and crossbone badges on their shakos. The French Dragoons did not follow immediately; instead they spurred into the abandoned wood where they found the Prussian camp-fires still burning. A plate of sausages had been spilt onto the ground beside one of the fires. 'Tastes like German shit.' A trooper disgustedly spat a mouthful of the meat into the fire.

A wounded horse limped in the wheat, trying to catch up with the other cavalry horses. In the trees two Prussian prisoners were being stripped of weapons, food, cash and drink. The other Prussians had disappeared northwards. The French, advancing to the northern edge of the captured wood, watched the enemy's withdrawal. The last of the mist had burned away. The wheels of the retreating Prussian guns had carved lanes of crushed barley through the northern fields.

Ten miles to the south, and still in France, the Emperor's heavy carriage waited at the roadside. Staff officers informed His Majesty that the Dutch frontier had been successfully crossed. They reported very light resistance, which had been brushed aside.

The Emperor grunted acknowledgement of the news then let the leather curtain fall to plunge the carriage's interior into darkness. It was just one hundred and seven days since, sailing from exile in Elba with a mere thousand men, he had landed on an empty beach in southern France. It was just eighty-eight days since he had recaptured his capital of Paris, yet in those few days he had shown the world how an emperor made armies. Two hundred thousand veterans had been recalled to the Eagles, the half-pay officers had been restored to their battalions, and the arsenals of France had been filled.

8

Now that new army marched against the scum of Britain and the hirelings of Prussia. It was a midsummer's dawn, and the Emperor was attacking.

The coachman cracked his whip, the Emperor's carriage lurched forward, and the battle for Europe had begun.

CHAPTER 2

An hour after the French Dragoon Sergeant and his horse had been broken and flensed by the canister another cavalryman rode into the bright midsummer sunshine.

This man was in Brussels, forty miles north of where the Emperor invaded Belgium. He was a tall good-looking officer in the scarlet and blue finery of the British Life Guards. He rode a tall black horse, superbly groomed and evidently expensive. The rider wore a gilded Grecian helmet that was crested with black and red wool and plumed with a white tuft. His bleached buckskin breeches were still damp, for to achieve a thigh-hugging fit they were best donned wet and allowed to shrink. His straight heavy sword hung in a gilded scabbard by his royal blue saddle-cloth that was embroidered with the King's cipher. The officer's black boots were knee-high, his spurs were gilded steel, his sabretache was bright with sequins and with gold embroidery, his short scarlet jacket was girdled with a gold sash, and his tall stiff collar encrusted with bright lace. His saddle was sheathed in lamb's fleece and the horse's curb chains were of pure silver, yet, for all that gaudy finery, it was the British officer's face that caught the attention.

He was a most handsome young man, and this early morning he was made even more attractive by his expression of pure happiness. It was plain to every milkmaid and street sweeper in the rue Royale that this British officer was glad to be alive, delighted to be in Belgium, and that he expected everyone in Brussels to share his evident enjoyment of life, health and happiness.

He touched the black enamelled visor of his helmet in answer to the salute of the red-coated sentry who stood outside an expensive front door, then cantered on through Brussels' fashionable streets until he reached a large house on the rue de la Blanchisserie. It was still early, yet the courtyard of the house was busy with tradesmen and carts that delivered chairs, music stands, food and wine. An ostler took the cavalryman's horse while a liveried footman relieved him of his helmet and cumbersome sword. The cavalry officer pushed a hand through his long golden hair as he ran up the house steps.

He did not wait for the servants to open the doors, but just pushed through into the entrance hall, and then into the great ballroom where a score of painters and upholsterers were finishing a long night's work during which they had transformed the ballroom into a silk-hung fantasy. Shiny swathes of gold, scarlet and black fabric had been draped from the ceiling, while between the gaudy bolts a brand-new wallpaper of rose-covered trellis disguised the damp patches of the ballroom's plaster. The room's huge chandeliers had been lowered to floor level where servants laboriously slotted hundreds of white candles into the newly cleaned silver and crystal holders. More workers were twining vines of ivy around pillars newly painted orange, while an elderly woman was strewing the floor with French chalk so that the dancing shoes would not slip on the polished parquet.

The cavalry officer, clearly delighted with the elaborate preparations, strode through the room. 'Bristow! Bristow!' His tall boots left prints in the newly scattered chalk. 'Bristow! You rogue! Where are you?'

A black coated, white-haired man, who bore the harassed look of the functionary in charge of the ball's preparations, stepped from the supper room at the peremptory summons. His look of annoyance abruptly changed to a delighted smile when he recognized the young cavalry officer. He bowed deeply. 'My lord!'

'Good day to you, Bristow! It's a positive delight to see you.'

'As it is a delight to see your lordship again. I had not heard your lordship was in Brussels?'

'I arrived yesterday. Last night.' The cavalryman, who was called Lord John Rossendale, was staring at the sumptuous decorations in the supper room where the long tables were draped in white linen and thickly set with silver and fine china. 'Couldn't sleep,' he explained his early appearance. 'How many are you seating tonight?'

'We have distributed four hundred and forty tickets, my lord.'

'Four hundred and forty-two.' Lord John Rossendale grinned at Bristow, then, as if he were a magician, produced a letter that he flourished in the elderly servant's face. 'Two tickets, if you would be so kind.'

Bristow took the letter, unfolded and read it. The letter was from Her Grace's private secretary and gladly agreed that Lord John Rossendale should be given a ticket for the ball. One ticket, the letter said, and Bristow gently pointed to the instruction. 'It says just one ticket, my lord.'

'Two, Bristow. Two, two, two. Pretend you cannot read. I insist upon two. It has to be two! Or do you want me to wreak havoc on the supper tables?'

Bristow smiled. 'I'm sure we can manage two, my lord.' Bristow was butler to the Duke of Richmond whose wife was giving the ball in this large rented house. Competition to attend was keen. Much of London society had moved to Brussels for the summer, there were army officers who would be mortified if they were not invited, and there was the local aristocracy who had to be entertained. The Duchess's answer to the eagerness of so many to attend her ball had been to have tickets of admission printed, yet, even so, Bristow expected there to be at least as many interlopers as ticket holders. It was not two days since the Duchess had issued instructions that no more tickets were to be given away, but it was hardly likely that such a prohibition would apply to Lord John Rossendale whose mother was an intimate friend of the Duchess of Richmond.

'Her Grace is already having breakfast. Would you care to join her?' Bristow asked Lord John.

Lord John followed the butler into the private rooms where, in a small sunlit salon, the Duchess nibbled toast. 'I never do sleep before a ball,' she greeted Lord John, then blinked with astonishment at him. 'What are *you* doing here?'

Lord John kissed the Duchess's hand. She was in a Chinese silk robe and had her hair gathered under a mob-cap. She was a quick-tempered woman of remarkable good looks.

'I came to collect tickets for your ball, of course,' Lord John said airily. 'I assume you're giving it to celebrate my arrival in Brussels?'

'What *are* you doing in Brussels?' The Duchess ignored Lord John's raillery.

'I've been posted here,' Lord John explained. 'I arrived last night. I would have been here sooner but one of our carriage horses slung a shoe and it took four hours to find a smith. I couldn't sleep either. It's just too exciting.' He smiled happily, expecting the Duchess to share his joy.

'You're with the army?'

'Of course.' Lord John plucked at his uniform coat as though that proved his credentials. 'Harry Paget asked for me, I begged Prinny's permission, and he finally relented.' Lord John, though a cavalry officer, had never been permitted to serve with the army. He was an aide to the Prince Regent who had resolutely refused to lose his services, but Henry Paget, Earl of Uxbridge, who was another crony of the Prince and who also commanded Britain's cavalry, had successfully persuaded the Prince to give Lord John his chance. Lord John laughed as he went to the sideboard where he helped himself to toast, ham and coffee. 'Prinny's damned jealous. He thinks he should be here to fight Napoleon. Talking of whom, is there any news?'

'Arthur doesn't expect any nonsense from him till July. We think he may have left Paris, but no one's really very sure.' Arthur was the Duke of Wellington. 'I asked Arthur whether we were quite safe having our ball tonight, and he assured me we are. He's giving a ball himself next week.'

'I must say war is an ordeal,' Lord John smiled at the Duchess from the sideboard.

The Duchess shrugged off his flippancy, and instead offered the elegant young man a most suspicious stare. 'Have you come alone?'

Lord John smiled winningly as he returned to the table. 'Bristow is very kindly finding me two tickets.'

'I suppose it's that woman?'

Lord John hesitated, then nodded. 'It is Jane, indeed.'

'Damn you, Johnny.'

The Duchess had sworn in a very mild tone, but her words still made Lord John bridle. Nevertheless he was too much in awe of the older woman to make any voluble protest.

The Duchess supposed she would have to write to Lord John's mother and confess that the silly boy had brought his paramour to Brussels. She blamed the example of Harry Paget who had run off with the wife of Wellington's younger brother. Such an open display of adultery was suddenly the fashionable sport among cavalrymen, but it could too easily turn into a blood sport and the Duchess feared for Lord John's life. She was also offended that a young man as charming and eligible as Lord John should flaunt his foolishness. 'If it was London, Johnny, I wouldn't dream of letting her come to a ball, but I suppose Brussels is different. There's really no saying who half these people are. But don't present this girl to me, John, because I won't receive her, I really won't! Do you understand?'

'Jane's very charming –' Lord John commenced a defence of his slighted lover.

'I don't care if she's as beautiful as Titania and as charming as Cordelia; she's still another man's wife. Doesn't her husband worry you?'

'He would if he were here, but he isn't. At the end of the last war he found himself some French creature and went to live with her, and so far as we know, he's still in France.' Lord John chuckled. 'The poor fool's probably been imprisoned by Napoleon.'

'You think he's in France?' The Duchess sounded aghast.

'He certainly isn't with the army, I made sure of that.'

'Oh, my dear Johnny.' The Duchess lowered her cup of coffee and gave her young friend a compassionate look. 'Didn't you think to check the Dutch army list?'

Lord John Rossendale said nothing. He just stared at the Duchess.

She grimaced. 'Lieutenant-Colonel Sharpe is on Slender Billy's staff, Johnny.'

Rossendale blanched. For a second it seemed that he would be unable to respond, but then he found his voice. 'He's with the Prince of Orange? Here?'

'Not in Brussels, but very close. Slender Billy wanted some British staff officers because he's commanding British troops.'

Rossendale swallowed. 'And he's got Sharpe?'

'Indeed he has.'

'Oh, my God.' Rossendale's face had paled to the colour of paper. 'Is Sharpe coming tonight?' he asked in sudden panic.

'I certainly haven't invited him, but I had to give Slender Billy a score of tickets, so who knows who he might bring?' The Duchess saw the fear on her young friend's face. 'Perhaps you'd better go home, Johnny.'

'I can't do that.' For Lord John to run away would be seen as the most shameful of acts, yet he was terrified of staying. He had not only cuckolded Richard Sharpe, but in the process he had effectively stolen Sharpe's fortune, and now he discovered that his enemy was not lost in France, but alive and close to Brussels.

'Poor Johnny,' the Duchess said mockingly. 'Still, come and dance tonight. Colonel Sharpe won't dare kill you in my ballroom, because I won't let him. But if I were you I'd give him his wife back and find yourself someone more suitable. What about the Huntley girl? She's got a decent fortune, and she's not really ugly.' The Duchess mentioned another half-dozen girls, all eligible and nobly born, but Lord John was not listening. He was thinking of a dark-haired and scarred soldier whom he had cuckolded and impoverished, a soldier who had sworn to kill him in revenge.

Forty miles to the south, the Dragoon Lieutenant who had been kicked by his dying horse haemorrhaged in the nettles beside the ditch. He died before any surgeons could reach him. The Lieutenant's servant rifled the dead man's possessions. He kept the officer's coins, the locket from about his neck, and his boots, but threw away the book on phrenology. The first French infantry butchered the Lieutenant's dead horse with their bayonets and marched into Belgium with the bleeding joints of meat hanging from their belts. An hour later the Emperor's coach passed the corpse, disturbing the flies which had been crawling over the dead Lieutenant's face and laying their eggs in his blood-filled mouth and nostrils.

The campaign was four hours old.

The Prussian guns withdrew north of Charleroi. The artillery officer wondered why no one had thought to blow up the bridge which crossed the River Sambre in the centre of the town, but he supposed there must be fords close to Charleroi which would have made the destruction of the fine stone bridge into a futile and even petulant gesture. Once the guns had gone, the black-uniformed Prussian cavalry waited in the town north of the river, reinforcing the brigade of infantry that ransacked the houses near the bridge for furniture, which they rather half-heartedly made into a barricade at the bridge's northern end. The townspeople sensibly stayed indoors and closed their shutters. Many of them took their carefully stored tricolours from their hiding places. Belgium had been a part of France till just a year before, and many folk in this part of the province resented being made a part of the Netherlands.

The French approached Charleroi on all the southern roads. The inevitable green-coated Dragoons reached the town first, followed by Cuirassiers and Red Lancers. None of the horsemen tried to force a passage across the barricaded bridge. Instead the Red Lancers, many of whom were Belgians, trotted eastwards in search of a ford. On the river's northern bank a troop of black-uniformed Prussian Hussars shadowed the Red Lancers, and it was those Hussars who, rounding a bend in the Sambre Valley, discovered a party of French engineers floating a pontoon bridge off the southern bank. Six of the engineers had swum to the northern bank where they were fastening a rope to a great elm tree. The Hussars drew their sabres to drive the unarmed men back into the river, but French artillery had already closed on the southern bank and, as soon as the Hussars went into the trot, the first roundshot slammed across the water. It bounced a few yards ahead of the Hussars' advance, then slammed into a wood where it tore and crashed through the thickly leaved branches.

The Hussar Captain called his men back. He could see red uniforms further up the river bank, evidence that the Lancers had found a place to cross. He led his men back to Charleroi where a desultory musket fight was flickering across the river. The French Dragoons had taken up positions in the southern houses, while the Prussian infantry in their dark blue coats and black shakos lined the barricade. The Hussar Captain reported to a Prussian brigade commander that the town was already outflanked, which news was sufficient to send most of the Prussian infantry marching briskly northwards. A last derisive French volley smashed splinters from the furniture barricade, then the town fell silent. The Prussian Hussars, left with a battalion of infantry to garrison the northern half of Charleroi, waited as French infantry reached the town and garrisoned the houses on the river's southern bank. Glass crashed onto cobbles as soldiers bashed out window-panes to make crude loopholes for muskets.

A half-mile south of the bridge the first French staff officers were rifling the mail in Charleroi's post office in search of letters which might have been posted by allied officers and thus provide clues of British or Prussian plans. Such clues would add to the embarrassing riches of intelligence which had recently flooded in to Napoleon's headquarters from Belgians who desperately wanted to be part of France again. The bright tricolours hanging from the upper floors of Charleroi's newly liberated houses were evidence of that longing.

A French General of Dragoons found a bespectacled

infantry Colonel inside a tavern close to the river and angrily demanded to know why the barricaded bridge had not been captured. The Colonel explained that he was still waiting for orders, and the General swore like the trooper he had once been and said that a French officer did not need orders when the enemy was in plain sight. 'Attack now, you damned fool, unless you want to resign from the Emperor's service.'

The Colonel, trained in the proper management of war, diagnosed the General's crude enthusiasm as excitement and gently tried to calm the old man by explaining that the sensible course was to wait until the artillery reached the town, and only then to mount an attack on the infantry who guarded the barricaded bridge. 'Two volleys of cannon-fire will clear them away,' the Colonel explained, 'and there'll be no need for our side to suffer any casualties. I think that's the prudent course, don't you?' The Colonel offered the General a patronizing smile. 'Perhaps the General would care to take a cup of coffee?'

'Bugger your coffee. And bugger you.' The Dragoon General seized the Colonel's uniform jacket and dragged the man close so that he could smell the General's garlic and brandy flavoured breath. 'I'm attacking the bridge now,' the General said, 'and if I take it, I'm coming back here and I'm going to tear your prudent bloody balls off and give your regiment to a real man.'

He let the Colonel go, then ducked out of the tavern door into the street. A Prussian musket bullet fluttered overhead to smack against a house wall that was smothered with posters advertising a fair, which was to be held on the feast day of St Peter and Paul. Someone had limewashed a slogan huge across the rash of posters: '*Vive l'Empereur!*'

'You!' The General shouted at an infantry lieutenant who was sheltering in an alley from the desultory Prussian fire. 'Bring your men! Follow me. Bugler! Sound the assemble!' The General beckoned to his orderly to bring his horse forward and, ignoring the Prussian musketry, he pulled himself into his saddle and drew his sword. 'Frenchmen!' he shouted to gather in whatever men were within earshot. 'Bayonets! Sabres!'

The General knew that the town had to be taken and the momentum of the day's advance kept swift, and so he would lead a rag-taggle charge against the Prussian infantrymen who lined the crude barricade. He fancied he could see a lower section at one end of the piled furniture where a horse might be able to jump the obstruction. He kicked his horse into a trot and the hooves kicked up sparks from the cobbles.

The General knew he would probably die, for infantry took pleasure in killing cavalry and he would be the leading horseman in the attack on the bridge, but the General was a soldier and he had long learned that a soldier's real enemy is the fear of death. Beat that fear and victory was certain, and victory brought glory and fame and medals and money and, best of all, sweetest of all, most glorious and wondrous of all, the modest teasing grin of a short black-haired Emperor who would pat the Dragoon General as though he was a faithful dog, and the thought of that Imperial favour made the General quicken his horse and raise his battered sword. 'Charge!' Behind him, spurred on by his example, a ragged mass of dismounted Dragoons and sweating infantry flooded towards the bridge. The General, his white moustaches stained with tobacco juice, spurred on to the bridge.

The Prussian infantry levelled their muskets over the furniture barricade.

The General saw the glitter of sunlight flashing from the brass decorations of the muskets. 'Kill the bastards! Kill the bastards!' he screamed to persuade himself that he was not frightened, and suddenly the barricade dissolved in an explosion of smoke through which the musket flames stabbed like shivers of light and the General's long white moustache was whipped by a bullet that went on to tear away his left ear-lobe, but that was the only injury he took for he had always been a lucky man, and he caught a glimpse of long weeds shivering under the silvery water beneath the bridge, then he kicked his heels hard back, and his awkward ugly horse clumsily jumped the heaped chairs at the right-hand end of the barricade. The horse soared through the foul-smelling smoke and the General saw a bayonet reach towards the animal's belly, but he slashed down with the sword, knocking the bayonet aside, and suddenly the horse had landed safely beyond the furniture and was running free of the smoke. The Prussian Hussars, who had waited fifty yards from the bridge to give themselves room to charge any attacker who broke through the infantry, spurred forward, but the General ignored them. He wheeled his horse back to the barricade and drove the animal hard at the frightened infantrymen.

'Bastards! Bastards!' He killed a Prussian soldier, slicing the sword hard into the man's neck above the stiff black collar. The remaining infantrymen were running. There had not been many Prussians at the bridge, for at best they had only been supposed to delay the French advance. Flames stabbed across the furniture from the French side, and the General shouted at his men to hold their damned fire and to pull the barricade down instead.

The Prussian infantry was running north. The cavalry, seeing that the French had captured the bridge with an insolent ease, turned to follow the foot soldiers. The French General, knowing he had earned his pat on the head from the Emperor, shouted derision at their retreat. 'You lily-livered bastards! You boy-lovers! You lap-dogs! Stay and fight, you scum!' He spat, then sheathed his sword. Blood from his torn ear was soaking his left epaulette with its tarnished chains and gilded eagle.

French infantry began to dismantle the barricade. The single dead Prussian infantryman, his uniform already looted of food and coins, lay by the bridge. A Dragoon sergeant hauled the body aside as more cavalrymen poured across the bridge. A woman ran from one of the houses on the northern bank and was almost knocked down by a clattering troop of Dragoons. The woman carried a bouquet of dried violets, their petals faded almost to lilac. She went to the French General's stirrup and held the pathetic bouquet up to the grim-faced man. 'Is he coming?' she asked.

There was no need for her to say who 'he' was; her eager face was enough.

The bloodied General smiled. 'He's coming, *ma poule*.'

'These are for you.' She offered the General the drooping flowers. Throughout Napoleon's exile the violet had been the symbol of the *Bonapartistes*, for the violet was the flower which, like the deposed Emperor, would return in the spring.

The General reached down and took the little bouquet. He fixed the fragile blossoms in a buttonhole of his braided uniform, then leaned down and kissed the woman. Like her, the General had prayed and hoped for the violet's return, and now it had come and it would surely blossom more gloriously than ever before. France was on the march, Charleroi had fallen, and there were no more rivers between the Emperor and Brussels. The General, scenting victory, turned his horse to search for the infantry Colonel who had refused to attack the bridge and whose military career was therefore finished. France had no need of prudence, only of audacity and victory and of the small dark-haired man who knew how to make glory bright as the sun and as sweet as the violet. *Vive l'Empereur.*

CHAPTER 3

A single horseman approached Charleroi from the west. He rode on the Sambre's northern bank, drawn towards the town by the sound of musketry which had been loud an hour before, but which now had faded into silence.

The man rode a big docile horse. He did not like horses and rode badly.

He was a tall man with a weathered face on which a blade had slashed a cruel scar. The scar gave his face a mocking, sardonic cast except when he smiled. His hair was black, but with a badger's streak of white. Behind his horse a dog loped obediently. The dog suited the man, for it was big, fierce, and unkempt.

The man wore French cavalry boots, much patched, but still supple and tight about his calves. Above the scarred boots he wore French cavalry overalls that had been reinforced with leather where the crutch and inside legs took the saddle's chafing. The red stripes on the overalls' outer seams had long faded to a dull purple. Outside the overalls he wore a faded green jacket that was decorated with the remnants of black piping. The jacket was the uniform of Britain's 95th Rifles, though it was now so threadbare and patched that it might have belonged to a tramp. The man's brown tricorne hat had come from neither the French nor the British army, but had been bought at the market in the Norman town of Caen. The scarlet, gold and black cockade of the Netherlands was gaudy on the hat.

In a holster on the man's saddle was a British-made Baker rifle. Stuck into his snake-clasped belt was a long-barrelled German pistol, while at his left hip was a battered metal scabbard in which there hung a British heavy cavalry sword. The man was a mockery of a soldier, tattered in a medley of a uniform, and sitting his horse with the grace of a sack of meal.

His name was Sharpe, Richard Sharpe, and he was a British soldier. He came from the gutter, the child of a whore, and he had only escaped the gallows by taking the King's shilling and enlisting as a private in the 33rd Regiment of Foot. He became a sergeant and later, because of an act of suicidal bravery, became one of the few men promoted from the ranks to become an officer. He had joined the 95th Rifles and later commanded the red-coated Prince of Wales's Own Volunteers. He had fought in Flanders, in India, in Portugal, in Spain and in France. He had been a soldier for almost all his life, but of late he had been a farmer in Normandy, drawn to the land of his enemies by a woman met by chance in the chaos of peace. Now, by the chaos of war, and because the exiled Napoleon had returned to France and thrust a new period of battle on Europe, Sharpe was a lieutenant-colonel in the 5th Belgian Light Dragoons, a regiment he had never met, had no wish to meet, and would not have recognized if it had formed line and charged him. The promotion was nothing more than a device to give Richard Sharpe some status on the Prince of Orange's staff, but so far as Sharpe himself was concerned he was still a Rifleman.

The rising sun, lancing down the Sambre Valley, dazzled Sharpe. He pulled the tricorne hat low over his eyes. The land he rode was marshy, forcing him to weave an intricate course past the more treacherous patches. He kept glancing north to make certain no enemy troops appeared to pin him against the river. Not that he believed that the firing he had heard had been caused by the French. They were not expected to advance till July, and were certainly not expected in this part of Belgium, so Sharpe suspected that the musketry had been caused by Prussian troops at firing practice, yet a long acquaintance with war's surprises had spurred Sharpe to investigate the sound.

His horse put up waterfowl and once disturbed a whole field of rabbits that scampered in panic towards the hedgerows. His dog, scenting breakfast, took off in pursuit. 'Nosey, you bastard! Heel!' The dog had been named Nosey on the grounds that the Duke of Wellington, 'Nosey' to his men, had spent twenty years giving Sharpe orders, so, when Sharpe had found the dog in peacetime, he had decided to return the compliment.

Nosey reluctantly slunk back to Sharpe, then saw something across the river and gave a bark of warning. Sharpe saw horsemen. For a second he supposed them to be Prussian, then recognized the shape of the cloth-covered helmets. Dragoons. French. His heart quickened. He had thought, after the battle of Toulouse, that his fighting days were over, that an emperor exiled to Elba spelt a Europe at peace, but now, fourteen months later, the old enemy was in sight again.

He spurred the horse into a canter. So the French had ridden into Belgium. Maybe it was nothing but a cavalry raid. The enemy Dragoons had seen Sharpe and ridden to the water's edge, but none tried to cross the deep river. Two of the green-coated horsemen unholstered their carbines and took aim at Sharpe, but their officer shouted at the troopers to hold their fire. The Rifleman was too far away for the short-barrelled, smooth-bore guns to be effective.

Sharpe angled away from the river, guiding the horse

beside a field of rye which had grown as tall as a man. The field path led uphill, then, after picking a delicate path through a tangled copse where tree roots gave treacherous footing for the horse, Sharpe slid down an earthen bank on to a rutted road where he was shadowed and hidden from the Dragoons by the trees that arched overhead. From his saddlebag he took out a frayed and crease-torn map. He unfolded it carefully, took a stub of pencil from his ammunition pouch, and marked a cross where he had seen the enemy cavalry. The position was approximate, for he was still not certain how far he was from Charleroi.

He pushed the map away, uncorked his canteen, and took a drink of cold tea. Then he took off his hat which left the mark of its rim indented in his unwashed hair. He rubbed his face, yawned, then crammed the hat back onto his head. He clicked his tongue, urging the horse to the end of the embanked cutting from where there was a distant view across the low hills north of Charleroi. Dust was pluming from a road in the centre of that landscape, but, even with the help of the battered old telescope, Sharpe could not tell what traffic made the dust rise, or in what direction it travelled.

There could have been an innocent explanation for the dust cloud: it could have been caused by a herd of cows being driven to market, by a Prussian regiment on exercise, or even by a work gang hammering cobbles into the highway's bed of chalk and flint, yet the musket-fire Sharpe had heard earlier, and the presence of the enemy Dragoons on the southern bank of the Sambre suggested a more sinister cause.

Invasion? For days now there had been no news from France, evidence that the Emperor had forbidden all traffic over the border, but that silence did not necessarily suggest an immediate invasion, but rather the concealment of exactly where the French forces concentrated.

The best allied intelligence insisted that the French would not be ready till July, and that their attack would advance through Mons, not Charleroi. The Mons road offered the shortest route to Brussels, and if Brussels fell the Emperor would have succeeded in driving the British back to the North Sea and the Prussians back across the Rhine. Brussels, to the French, spelt victory.

Sharpe urged his horse down the rutted lane that dropped into a shallow valley before climbing between two unhedged pastures. He veered to his right, not wanting to betray his presence with dust from the dry mud of the lane. The mare was breathing hard as she trotted up the pastureland. She was accustomed to exercise for, each morning for the past two weeks, Sharpe had saddled her at three o'clock, then ridden her south to watch the dawn break over the Sambre Valley, but this morning, hearing the crackle of musketry to the east, he had ridden the mare much further than usual. The day also threatened to be the hottest of the summer, but Sharpe's fears of the enemy's mysterious appearance made him force the beast onwards.

If this was the French invasion then the news of it must reach the allied headquarters quickly. The British, Dutch and Prussian armies guarded eighty miles of vulnerable Dutch frontier; the Prussians to the east and the British and Dutch to the west. The allied forces were spread like a net to trap an emperor, but as soon as the Emperor touched the net it was supposed to contract and entangle him. That was the stratagem, but the Emperor was as aware of those allied hopes as any British or Prussian officer and he would be planning to slash the net into two pieces and separately tear them apart. Shape's urgent duty was to discover whether this was the Emperor's slashing stroke, or merely a cavalry raid launched deep into the Belgian province.

From the crest of the next hill he saw more French

Dragoons. They were half a mile away, but on Sharpe's side of the river and barring his approach to Charleroi. They saw him and kicked their horses forward so Sharpe turned his tired mare northwards, and spurred her into a gallop. He crossed the road, thumped across a pasture, then dropped into a small valley where a tangle of thorns grew either side of a trickling brook. Sharpe forced his horse through the bushes, then turned east again. He could see a wood far ahead of him. If he could make the shelter of the trees he thought there might be a chance of watching the high road from the wood's far side.

The French Dragoons, content with having chased the lone horseman away, did not follow him. Sharpe slapped the mare's neck which was wet with sweat. 'Come on, girl! Come on!' She was a six-year-old hunter, docile and strong; one of the horses that Sharpe's friend Patrick Harper had fetched from Ireland.

It was cooler and very quiet in the wood that was tangled with old huge trees. Nosey trotted close at the mare's heels. Sharpe went slowly, threading the horse between the ancient trunks and past fallen, moss-covered logs. Long before he reached the edge of the wood he knew this was no mere cavalry raid. He knew because he heard the distinctive, never-forgotten thump and jangle of artillery on the move.

He curbed the horse, dismounted, and tied her reins to a low branch of oak. From his saddlebag he took a length of rope that he knotted as a leash round Nosey's neck, then he drew his rifle out of the saddle holster, cocked it, and went silently forward. He held the dog's rope in his left hand, the rifle in his right.

The wood ended at a wheat field that sloped downhill to the unhedged road from which the dust was rising to hang in the hot air. Sharpe, his telescope open, stared down at the old, familiar enemy.

French infantry, in their blue coats, were marching

in the trampled wheat either side of the road so as to leave the harder road surface for the artillery. The guns were twelve-pounders. Every few minutes the guns would halt as some obstruction worked its way down the long column. Staff officers galloped fine horses down the road's wide verges. On the far slope of the valley a troop of Red Lancers cantered through a wheat field, each horse leaving a straight trail of crushed plants.

Sharpe had no watch, but he estimated that he stayed at the edge of the wood for two hours during which time he counted twenty-two guns and forty-eight supply wagons. He also saw two carriages that might have been carrying senior officers, and he flirted with the idea that one of the carriages might have belonged to the Emperor himself. Sharpe had fought the French for over twenty years, yet he had never seen the Emperor and, all unbidden, a sudden and childish image of a man with cloven tail, sharp horns and demonic fangs stalked Sharpe's fears that were made worse by the Emperor's real reputation as a soldier of genius whose presence on a battlefield was worth a whole corps of men.

Still the French marched north. Sharpe counted eighteen infantry battalions and four squadrons of cavalry, one of which, composed of Dragoons, rode very close to his hiding place at the wood's edge, but none of the French troopers glanced left to see where the Englishman and his dog lay in the shadows. The French horsemen were close enough for Sharpe to see their *cadenettes*, the pigtails which framed each man's face as a mark of distinction. Their equipment looked good and new, and their horses were well fed. In Spain the French had whipped and ridden their horses to destruction, but these troops were freshly mounted on strong and healthy animals.

Newly mounted cavalry, eighteen battalions of infantry and twenty-two cannon did not constitute an army, but they certainly added up to a threat. Sharpe knew he was seeing much more than a cavalry raid, though he was not certain whether this was the real invasion. It was possible that these men were nothing but a strong feint designed to draw the Allies towards Charleroi while the real French thrust, fuelled by the Emperor's presence, attacked twenty-five miles to the west at Mons.

Sharpe slithered back from the treeline and climbed wearily into the saddle. His job now was to let the allied headquarters know what he had seen: that the French had crossed the frontier and that the campaign had therefore begun. Sharpe remembered that Lucille, who had loyally left France to stay at his side, had been invited to some fashionable and expensive ball that was supposed to take place in Brussels this night. The expense would all go for nothing now because the Emperor had just rewritten the social calendar. Sharpe, who hated dancing, smiled at the thought, then turned and spurred the horse towards home.

Two miles away, in the streets of Charleroi, the Emperor sat outside the Belle Vue inn. His coach had been parked out of sight while his white saddle horse had been tethered to a post at the roadside so that the passing soldiers would think their Emperor was riding to war instead of being carried in upholstered comfort. The men cheered their monarch as they marched past him. '*Vive l'Empereur! Vive l'Empereur!*' The drummers, tediously beating the rhythm of the march, broke into joyous flurries when they realized their Emperor was so close. The troops could not reach their idol, for he was protected by bear-skinned guardsmen, but some men broke ranks to kiss the Emperor's pale horse.

Napoleon showed no reaction to his men's adulation. He sat motionless, swathed in a greatcoat despite the day's oppressive heat, and with his face concealed by the peak of his hat that he had turned fore and aft to shadow his eyes. He sat in the low chair with his head bowed, looking for all the world like a genius deep in contemplation, though in fact he was fast asleep.

Beyond the captured bridge a French gunner officer kicked the body of the dead Prussian infantryman into the River Sambre. For a few moments the corpse was trapped on a half-sunken log, then an eddy loosed the dead man and carried him westwards.

And the campaign was six hours old.

Sharpe emerged from the wood and turned the mare north-west. The tired horse faced a journey of at least twenty miles across heavy country so he kept her at a sedate trot. The sun was high and as harsh as on any day Sharpe remembered from the long campaigns in Spain. The dog, seemingly tireless, roamed eagerly ahead.

It was a good five minutes before Sharpe noticed the French Dragoons who followed him. The enemy horsemen were silhouetted on the southern skyline and Sharpe suspected they must have been trailing him ever since he had emerged from the trees. He cursed himself for his carelessness, and dug his heels back to speed the weary mare. He hoped the Frenchmen would be content to drive him away from the high road rather than pursue and capture him, but as he quickened the mare's pace, so the Frenchmen spurred their own horses.

Sharpe turned westwards away from the Brussels road which he supposed the Dragoons were guarding. For thirty minutes he pressed the horse hard, always hoping that his flight would persuade the Dragoons to abandon their pursuit, but the Frenchmen were stubborn, or else the chase was a welcome break in their day's tedium. Their horses were fresher, and gradually closed on Sharpe who, to spare the mare's strength, tried to avoid the worst hills, but he eventually found himself trapped in a long valley and was forced to put the mare at a steep grass slope which led to a bare skyline.

The mare plunged gallantly at the hillside, but even the long rest in the dark cool wood had not restored her full strength. Sharpe spurred her into a clumsy gallop that made his heavy sword flap in its slings and crash its disc hilt painfully onto his left thigh. The Dragoons were bunched like steeplechasers as they reached the foot of the slope. One Frenchman had taken his carbine from his holster and now tried a long shot at Sharpe, but the bullet fluttered harmlessly overhead.

The mare's breath was roaring as she reached the crest. She wanted to check, but Sharpe pushed her through a gap in a straggling hedgerow and spurred her across an undulating pasture which, years before, had been under the plough and old furrows still formed corrugations that faced Sharpe like waves of pale grass. Sharpe was riding across the grassy waves and the mare took the hard, uneven ground heavily, jarring him with every step. Nosey raced ahead, circled back, barked happily, then ran alongside the labouring horse. Sharpe twisted to look behind and saw the first Dragoons reach the skyline. They had spread out and were racing to capture him. The ridged pasture was falling away in front of Sharpe, sloping down to a long dark oak wood from which a cart track ran north towards a big stone-walled farm that looked like a miniature fort. Sharpe looked behind again and saw the closest Dragoons were now just fifty yards away. Their long swords were drawn and their horses' teeth bared. Sharpe tried to draw his own sword, but the moment he took his right hand off the reins he almost fell and the mare immediately tried to check. 'Go on!' he shouted at the mare and scraped his spurs hard down her flanks. 'Go on!'

He glanced right and saw another half-dozen Dragoons racing to cut him off from the cart track. He swore viciously, turned the mare a touch westward again, but that merely gave the pursuers a better angle to close on him. The wood was only a hundred paces away, but the sweat-streaked mare was blown and slowing. Even if she reached the trees, the Dragoons would soon ride Sharpe down in the tangle of undergrowth. He swore silently. If he lived he would be doomed to spend the war as a prisoner.

Then a distant trumpet blared a challenge, making Sharpe turn with astonishment to see black-coated horsemen streaming pell-mell from the fortress-like farm buildings. There must have been at least twenty cavalrymen rowelling their horses down the cart track. Sharpe recognized the cavalry as Prussians. Dust spurted and drifted from their hooves and the bright sun flashed cruel and beautiful from their drawn sabres.

The Dragoons closest to the Prussians immediately turned and galloped back up the slope towards their comrades. Sharpe gave the mare a last despairing hack with his heels, then ducked his head as she crashed through a stand of ferns and thus into the wood's cool margin. She would go no further, but just pulled up under the trees, shivering and sweating and blowing. Sharpe dragged the big sword free.

Two green-uniformed Dragoons followed Sharpe into the trees. They came at full speed, the leading man aiming to Sharpe's left, the other pulling to his right. Sharpe had his back to the attackers and the mare was too exhausted and too obstinate to turn. He slashed across his body to parry the attack of the man on the left. The Frenchman's blade rang like a bell on Sharpe's sword, then scraped down the steel to be stopped by the heavy disc hilt. Sharpe threw the Dragoon's blade off then desperately backswung the long sword to meet the second man's charge. The swing was so wild that it unbalanced Sharpe, but it also terrified the second Dragoon who swerved frantically away from the blade's hissing reach. Sharpe grabbed a handful of his mare's mane to haul himself back upright. Both Dragoons had galloped past Sharpe and were now trying to turn their horses for a second attack.

In the pasture behind Sharpe the Prussian horsemen were making a line to face the remaining Dragoons who, outnumbered, had cautiously pulled back towards the skyline. That confrontation was none of Sharpe's business; his concern was with the two horsemen who now faced him in the wood. They glanced past Sharpe, judging how best to rejoin their comrades, though it was clear they wanted Sharpe's life first.

One of them began to tug his carbine out of its holster. 'Get him, Nosey!' Sharpe shouted, and at the same time he raked his spurs back so savagely that the exhausted and astonished mare jerked forward, almost spilling Sharpe out of his tall Hussar's saddle. He was screaming at the two men, trying to frighten them. The dog leaped at the closest man who, encumbered with carbine and sword, could not cut down at the beast, then Sharpe's mare slammed into the Frenchman's horse and the big sword slashed down at the Dragoon. The blade hit the peak of the man's cloth-covered helmet, ringing his ears like the knell of doom. The beleaguered Frenchman screamed desperately for help from his comrade who was trying to circle behind Sharpe to get a clear thrust at the Englishman's back.

Sharpe hacked again, this time landing a blow on the back of the helmet. The sword ripped the canvas cover to reveal a flash of scarred brass. The Dragoon dropped the carbine and fumbled for his sword which hung from its wrist strap. He was clumsy and could not make his grip. Sharpe lunged, but Nosey had frightened the Frenchman's horse which twisted away and so carried the Dragoon out of Sharpe's reach. Sweat was stinging Sharpe's eyes. Everything seemed awkward. He spurred forward, sword raised, then a shout from his rear made him twist in the saddle. He saw two German troopers spurring at the second Frenchman. There was the clash of sword on sabre and a scream that was abruptly silenced. Sharpe looked again for his own enemy, but the first Dragoon had taken enough and was holding out his sword in meek surrender.

'Nosey! Down! Leave him!'

The second Dragoon was dead, his throat sliced by a Hussar's sabre. His killer, a toothless Prussian sergeant, grinned at Sharpe, then cleaned his curved blade by running it through a handful of his horse's mane. The Sergeant wore a silver skull and crossbones on his black shako, a sight that made Sharpe's prisoner even more nervous. The other Frenchmen were retreating up the slope, unwilling to give battle to the greater number of black-uniformed Hussars. The Hussar officer was ahead of his men, taunting the French officer to a duel, but the Frenchman was too canny to risk his life for such vain heroics.

Sharpe reached over and took the reins of the Dragoon's horse. 'Get down,' he spoke to the man in French.

'The dog, *monsieur*!'

'Get down! Hurry!'

The prisoner dismounted, then stumbled out of the wood. When he took off his dented helmet he proved to have bristly fair hair above a snub-nosed face. He reminded Sharpe of Jules, the miller's son from Seleglise, who used to help Sharpe with Lucille's flock of sheep and who had been so excited when Napoleon returned to France. The captured Dragoon shivered as the German cavalry surrounded him.

The Prussian Captain spoke angrily to Sharpe in German. Sharpe shook his head. 'You speak English?'

'*Nein. Français, peut-être?*'

They spoke in French. The Hussar Captain's anger had been prompted by the French refusal to fight him. 'No one is allowed to fight today! We were ordered out of Charleroi. Why do we even come to the Netherlands? Why don't we just give Napoleon the keys to Berlin and have done with it? Who are you, *monsieur*?'

'My name is Sharpe.'

'A Britisher, eh? My name's Ziegler. Do you know what the hell is happening?'

Ziegler and his men had been driven westwards by a whole regiment of Red Lancers. Like the Dragoons on the pasture, Ziegler had retreated rather than face unequal odds. He and his men had been resting in the farm when they saw Sharpe's ignominious flight. 'At least we killed one of the bastards.'

Sharpe told Ziegler what he knew, which merely confirmed what the Prussian Captain had already discovered for himself. A French force was advancing northwards from Charleroi, probably aiming at the gap between the British and Prussian armies. Ziegler was now cut off on the wrong side of the Brussels road, but that predicament did not worry him. 'We'll just ride north till there are no more damned French, then go east.' He turned baleful eyes on the captured Dragoon. 'Do you want the prisoner?' he asked Sharpe.

'I'll take his horse.'

The terrified young Frenchman tried to answer Sharpe's questions, but either he knew very little or else he was cleverly hiding what he did know. He said he believed the Emperor was with the troops on the Brussels road, but he had not personally seen him. He knew nothing of any advance further to the west near Mons.

Ziegler did not want to be slowed down by the prisoner, so he ordered the Frenchman to strip off his boots and coat, then ordered his Sergeant to cut the man's overall straps. 'Go! Be grateful I didn't kill you!' The Frenchman, in bare feet and clutching his overalls, hurried southwards.

Ziegler gave Sharpe a length of cold sausage, a hard-boiled egg, and a piece of black bread. 'Good luck, Englishman!'

Sharpe thanked him. He had mounted the Dragoon's horse and was leading the tired mare by her reins. He assumed that by now the allied Generals must be aware of the French advance, but it was still his duty to report what he had seen and so he kicked back his heels, waved farewell to the Prussians, and rode on.

CHAPTER 4

Clouds were showing in the west. The vapour, rising over the North Sea, drifted slowly eastwards to heap white and grey thunderheads above the coast. The farmers feared heavy rain that would crush their ripening crops.

No such worries crossed the mind of the Prussian Major who had been sent to Brussels with news of the French advance and details of the Prussian response. The despatch told how the Prussian garrison at Charleroi was falling back, not on Brussels, but north-east to where the main Prussian army was assembling. The Major's news was vital if the British and Dutch troops were to join the Prussians.

The Major faced a journey of thirty-two miles. It was a sunny and very hot day, and he was tired and monstrously fat. The exertions of the first five miles when he had thought the Dragoons might burst from behind every hedgerow or farmhouse had exhausted both the Major and his horse, so once he felt safe he sensibly slowed to a contemplative and restoring walk. After an hour he came to a small roadside inn that stood on the crest of a shallow hill and, twisting in his saddle, he saw that the inn gave him a good view of the road right to the horizon so that he would see any French pursuit long before it represented any danger. Nothing moved on the road now except for a man driving eight cows from one pasture to another.

The Major eased himself out of the saddle, slid heavily

to the ground, and tied his horse to the inn's signpost. He spoke passably good French and enjoyed discussing food with the pretty young serving girl who came out to the table by the roadside, which the Major had adopted as his vantage point. He decided on roast chicken and vegetables, with apple pie and cheese to follow. He requested a bottle of red wine, but not of the common kind.

The sun shone on the long road to the south. Haymakers scythed steadily in a meadow a half-mile away, while much further off, far beyond the blur of fields and woods, dust whitened the sky. That was the artificial cloud kicked up by an army, but no troops threatened the Major's peaceful rest and so he saw no reason to make undue haste, especially as the roast chicken proved to be excellent. The chicken's skin was crisped nicely and its yellow flesh was succulent. When the girl brought the Major his pie, she asked him if Napoleon was coming.

'Don't you worry, my dear! Don't you worry.'

Far to the Major's north, in Brussels, a detachment of Highland soldiers had been ordered to the Duke of Richmond's house, where they were shown into the dazzling ballroom hung with the Belgian colours. Before supper was served the Highlanders would offer the guests a display of their dancing.

The Highlander Lieutenant asked that one of the unlit chandeliers be raised from floor level so he could make certain there would be adequate room for his dancers' crossed swords. The Duchess, intent that every particular of her ball should be arranged to perfection, insisted on a demonstration. 'You are bringing pipers tonight?' the Duchess demanded.

'Indeed, Your Grace.'

Which only gave the Duchess a new detail to worry over: how would the orchestra leader know when to stop his men playing so that the pipers could begin?

Her husband averred that doubtless the orchestra and

the pipers would arrange things to their own satisfaction, and further opined that the Duchess should leave the ball's arrangements to those who were paid to worry about the details, but the Duchess was insistent on voicing her concerns this afternoon. She earnestly asked her husband whether she should request the Prince of Orange not to bring Lieutenant-Colonel Sharpe?

'Who's Sharpe?' the Duke asked from behind his copy of *The Times*.

'He's the husband of Johnny Rossendale's girl. She's coming, I'm afraid. I tried to stop him bringing her, but he's clearly besotted.'

'And this Sharpe is her husband?'

'I just told you that, Charles. He's also an aide to Slender Billy.'

The Duke grunted. 'Sharpe's clearly a fool if he lets an idiot like Johnny Rossendale cuckold him.'

'That's precisely why I think I should talk to the Prince. I'm told this Sharpe is an extremely uncouth man and is more than likely to fillet Johnny.'

'If he's uncouth, my dear, then doubtless he won't wish to attend your ball. And I certainly wouldn't mention the matter to Orange. That bloody young fool will only bring Sharpe if he thinks it'll cause trouble. It's a sleeping dog, my dear, so let it lie.'

But it was not in the Duchess's nature to let anything remain undisturbed if it was amenable to her interference. 'Perhaps I should mention it to Arthur?'

The Duke snapped his newspaper down to the table. 'You will not trouble Wellington about two damned fools and their silly strumpet.'

'If you say so, Charles.'

'I do say so.' The rampart of newspaper was thrown up, inviting silence.

The other English Duke in Brussels, Wellington, would have been grateful had he known that Richmond had spared him the Duchess's worries, for the Commander-in-Chief of the British and Dutch armies already had more than enough worries of his own. One of those worries, the smallest of them, was the prospect of hunger. Wellington knew from bitter experience that he would be required to make so much conversation at the Duchess's ball that his supper would inevitably congeal on its plate. He therefore ordered an early dinner of roast mutton to be served in his quarters at three o'clock that afternoon.

Then, noting that clouds were building to the west, he took his afternoon walk about the fashionable quarter of Brussels. He took care to appear blithely unworried as he strolled with his staff, for he knew only too well how the French sympathizers in the city were looking for any sign of allied defeatism that they could turn into an argument to demoralize the Dutch-Belgian troops.

The quality of those troops was at the heart of the Duke's real worries. On paper his army was ninety thousand strong, but only half of that paper force was reliable.

The core of the Duke's army was his infantry. He had thirty battalions of redcoats, but only half of those had fought in his Spanish campaigns and the quality of the other half was unknown. He had some excellent infantry battalions of the King's German Legion, and some enthusiastic troops from Hanover, but together the German and British infantry totalled less than forty thousand men. To make up the numbers he had the Dutch-Belgian army, over thirty thousand infantrymen in all, which he did not trust at all. Most of the Dutch-Belgians had fought for the Emperor and still wore the Emperor's uniforms. The Duke was assured by the King of the Netherlands that the Belgians would fight, but, Wellington wondered, for whom?

The Duke had cavalry too, but the Duke had no faith in horsemen, whether Dutch or English. His German cavalry was first class, but sadly few in numbers, while the Duke's English cavalrymen were mere fools on horseback; expensive and touchy, prone to insanity, and utter strangers to discipline. The Dutch-Belgian horsemen, for all the Duke cared, could have packed their bags and ridden home right now.

He had ninety thousand men, of whom half might fight well, and he knew he would likely face a hundred thousand of Napoleon's veterans. The Emperor's veterans, fretting against the injustices of Bourbon France, had welcomed Napoleon's return and flocked to the Eagles. The French army, which the Duke still thought was massing south of the border, was probably the finest instrument that Napoleon had ever commanded. Every man in it had fought before, it was freshly equipped, and it sought vengeance against the countries that had humbled France in 1814. The Duke had cause for worry, yet as he strolled down the rue Royale he was forced to put a brave face on the desperate odds lest his enemies took courage from his despair. The Duke could also cling to one strong hope, namely that his scratch army would not fight Napoleon alone, but alongside Prince Blücher's Prussians. So long as the British and Prussian armies joined forces, they must win; separately, the Duke feared, they must be destroyed.

Yet twenty-five miles to the south the French were already pushing the Prussian forces eastwards, away from the British. No one in Brussels knew that the French had invaded; instead they prepared for a duchess's ball while a fat Prussian major paid for his roast chicken, finished his wine, then ambled slowly northwards.

At one o'clock in the afternoon, eight hours after the first shots had been fired south of Charleroi, Sharpe met more cavalrymen; this time a patrol in red-faced dark blue coats who thundered eagerly across a pasture to surround

Sharpe and his two horses. They were men from Hanover, exiles who formed the King's German Legion that had fought so hard and well in Spain. Now the German soldiers stared suspiciously at Sharpe's strange uniform until one of the troopers saw the Imperial 'N' on the horse's saddle-cloth and the sabres rasped out of their metal scabbards as the horsemen shouted at Sharpe to surrender.

'Bugger off,' Sharpe snarled.

'You're English?' the KGL Captain asked in that language. He was mounted on a fine black gelding, glossy coated and fresh. His saddle-cloth bore the British royal cipher, a reminder that England's King was also Hanover's monarch.

'I'm Lieutenant-Colonel Sharpe, of the Prince of Orange's staff.'

'You must forgive us, sir.' The Captain, who introduced himself as Hans Blasendorf, sheathed his sabre. He told Sharpe his patrol was one of the many that daily scouted south to the French border and beyond; this particular troop had been ordered to explore the villages south and east of Mons down as far as the Sambre, but not to encroach on Prussian territory.

'The French are already in Charleroi,' Sharpe told the German.

Blasendorf gaped at Sharpe in shocked silence for a moment. 'For certain?'

'For certain!' Tiredness made Sharpe indignant. 'I've just been there! I took this horse off a French Dragoon north of the town.'

The German understood the desperate urgency of Sharpe's news. He tore a page from his notebook, offered it with a pencil to Sharpe, then volunteered his own patrol to take the despatch to General Dornberg's headquarters in Mons. Dornberg was the General in charge of these cavalry patrols which watched the French frontier, and finding one of his officers had been a stroke of luck for Sharpe; by pure accident he had come across the very men whose job was to alert the allies of any French advance.

Sharpe borrowed a shako from one of the troopers and used its flat round top as a writing desk. He did not write well because he had learned his letters late in life and, though Lucille had made him into a much better reader, he was still clumsy with a pen or pencil. Nevertheless, as clearly as he could, he wrote down what he had observed – that a large French force of infantry, cavalry and artillery was marching north out of Charleroi on the Brussels road. A prisoner had been taken who reported a possibility that the Emperor was with those forces, but the prisoner had not been certain of that fact. Sharpe knew it was important for Dornberg to know where the Emperor was, for where Napoleon rode, that was the main French attack.

He signed the despatch with his name and rank, then handed it to Blasendorf who promised it would be delivered as swiftly as his horses could cross country.

'And ask General Dornberg to tell the Prince's Chief of Staff that I'm watching the Charleroi road,' Sharpe added.

Blasendorf nodded an acknowledgement as he turned his horse away, then, realizing what Sharpe had said, he looked anxiously back. 'You're going back to the road, sir?'

'I'm going back.'

Sharpe, his message in safe hands, was free to return and watch the French. In truth he did not want to go, for he was tired and saddle-sore, but this day the allies needed accurate news of the enemy so that their response could be certain, fast and lethal. Besides, the appearance of the French had spurred Sharpe's old excitement. He had thought that living in Normandy would make him

44

ambivalent towards his old enemy, but he had spent too many years fighting the Crapauds suddenly to relinquish the need to see them beaten.

So out of habit as much as out of duty, he turned his captured horse and rode again towards the enemy. While to the north Brussels slept.

Major General Sir William Dornberg received the pencil-written despatch in the town hall at Mons which he had made into his headquarters, and where he had transformed the ancient council chamber into his map room. The panelled room, hung with dusty coats of arms, suited his self-esteem, for Dornberg was a very proud man who was convinced that Europe did not properly appreciate his military genius. He had once fought for the French, but they had not promoted him beyond the rank of colonel, so he had deserted to the British who had rewarded his defection with a knighthood and a generalship, but even so, he still felt slighted. He had been given command of a cavalry brigade, a mere twelve hundred sabres, while men he thought less talented than himself commanded whole divisions. Indeed, the Prince of Orange, a callow boy, commanded a corps!

'Who was this man?' he asked Captain Blasendorf.

'An Englishman, sir. A lieutenant-colonel.'

'On a French horse, you say?'

'He says he captured the horse, sir.'

Dornberg frowned at the message, so ill-written in clumsy pencilled capitals that it could have been scrawled by a child. 'What unit was this Englishman, Sharpe? Is that his name? Sharpe?'

'If he's the Sharpe I think he is, sir, then he's quite a celebrated soldier. I remember in Spain –'

'Spain! Spain! All I hear about is Spain!' Dornberg slapped the table with the palm of his hand, then glared with protruding eyes at the unfortunate Blasendorf. 'To listen to some officers in this army one would think that no other war had ever been fought but in Spain! I asked you, Captain, what unit this Sharpe belonged to.'

'Hard to say, sir.' The KGL Captain frowned as he tried to remember Sharpe's uniform. 'Green jacket, non-descript hat, and Chasseur overalls. He said he was on the Prince of Orange's staff. In fact he asked that you tell the Prince's headquarters that he's gone back towards Charleroi.'

Dornberg ignored the last sentences, seizing on something far more important. 'Chasseur overalls? You mean French overalls?'

Blasendorf paused, then nodded. 'Looked like it, sir.'

'You're an idiot! An idiot! What are you?'

Blasendorf paused, then, in the face of Dornberg's overwhelming scorn, sheepishly admitted he was an idiot.

'He was French, you idiot!' Dornberg shouted. 'They seek to mislead us. Have you learned nothing of war? They want us to think they will advance through Charleroi, while all the time they will come towards us here! They will come to Mons! To Mons! To Mons!' He slammed a clenched fist onto the map with every reiteration of the name, then dismissively waved Sharpe's despatch in Captain Blasendorf's face. 'You might as well have wiped your arse with this. You're an idiot! God save me from idiots! Now go back to where you were ordered. Go! Go! Go!'

General Dornberg tore up the despatch. The Emperor had touched the net spread to contain him, but the British half of the trap was unaware of its catch, and so the French marched on.

South-west of Brussels, in the village of Braine-le-Comte, His Royal Highness the Prince William, Prince of Orange, heir to the throne of the Netherlands, and Duke, Earl,

Lord, Stadtholder, Margrave and Count of more towns and provinces than even he could remember, leaned forward in his chair, fixed his gaze at the mirror which stood on the dressing-table and, with exquisite care, squeezed a blackhead on his chin. It popped most satisfyingly. He squeezed another, this time provoking a small spurt of blood. 'Damn. Damn, damn, damn.' The bloody ones always left a livid mark on his sallow skin, and Slender Billy particularly wanted to look his best at the Duchess of Richmond's ball.

'*Eau de citron*,' the girl on his bed said lazily.

'You're mumbling, Charlotte.'

'*Eau de citron*. It dries the skin and shrivels away the spots.' She spoke in French. 'You should use it.'

'Shit,' the Prince said as another blackhead burst bloodily. 'Shit and damn and bugger!'

He had been educated at Eton College so had an excellent command of English. After Eton he had gone to Oxford, then served on Wellington's staff in Spain. The appointment had been purely political, for Wellington had not wanted him, and the exiled Prince had consequently been kept well away from any fighting, though the experience had nevertheless convinced the young man that he had a fine talent for soldiering. His education had also left him with a love for all things English. Indeed, apart from his Chief of Staff and a handful of aides, all his closest friends were English. He wished the girl on the bed were English, but instead she was Belgian and he hated the Belgians; to the Prince they were a common, ox-like race of peasants. 'I hate you, Charlotte.' He spoke to the girl in English. Her name was Paulette, but the Prince called all such girls Charlotte, after the English Princess who had first agreed to marry him, then inexplicably broken off the engagement.

'What are you saying?' Paulette spoke no English.

'You stink like a sow,' the Prince continued in English,

'you've got thighs like a grenadier, your tits are greasy, and in short you are a typical Belgian and I hate you.' He smiled fondly at the girl as he spoke, and Paulette, who in truth was very pretty, blew him a kiss before lying back on the pillows. She was a whore fetched from Brussels and paid ten English guineas a day to bed the Prince, and in her opinion she earned every ounce of the precious gold. Paulette thought the Prince disgustingly ugly: he was obnoxiously thin, with a bulbous round head on a ridiculously long neck. His skin was sallow and pitted, his eyes bulged, and his mouth was a slobbering frog-like slit. He was drunk as often as he was sober and in either condition held an inflated opinion of his abilities, both in bed and on the battlefield. He was now twenty-three years old and commander of the First Corps of the Duke of Wellington's army. Those who liked the Prince called him Slender Billy, while his detractors called him the Young Frog. His father, King William, was known as the Old Frog.

No one of any sense had wanted the Young Frog to be given a command in the Duke's army, but the Old Frog would not hear of the Netherlands joining the coalition unless his son held high command, and thus the politicians in London had forced the Duke of Wellington to concede. The Old Frog had further insisted that his son command British troops, on which point the Duke had also been forced to yield, though only on condition that reliable British officers were appointed to serve on the Young Frog's staff.

The Duke provided a list of suitable, sober and solid men, but the Young Frog had simply scrawled out their names and replaced them with friends he had made at Eton and, when some of those friends declined the honour, he found other congenial officers who knew how to leaven war's rigours with riotous enjoyment. The Prince also demanded a few officers who were experienced in

48

battle and who would exemplify his own ideas of how wars should be fought. 'Find me the most audacious of men!' he ordered his Chief of Staff who, a few weeks later, diffidently informed the Prince that the notorious Major Sharpe was on the half-pay list and evidently unemployed. The Young Frog had immediately demanded Sharpe and sweetened the demand with a promotion. He flattered himself that he would discover a twin soul in the famous Rifleman.

Yet somehow, and despite the Prince's easy nature, no such friendship had developed. The Prince found something subtly annoying about Sharpe's sardonic face, and he even suspected that the Englishman was deliberately trying to annoy him. He must have asked Sharpe a score of times to dress in Dutch uniform, yet still the Rifleman appeared in his ancient, tattered green coat. That was when Sharpe bothered to show himself at the Prince's headquarters at all; he evidently preferred to spend his days riding the French frontier which was a job that properly belonged to the pompous General Dornberg, which thought reminded the Prince that Dornberg's noon report should have arrived. That report had a special importance this day for, if any trouble threatened, the Prince knew he could not afford to go dancing in Brussels. He summoned his Chief of Staff.

The Baron Jean de Constant Rebecque informed His Highness that Dornberg's report had indeed arrived and contained nothing alarming. No French troops troubled the road to Mons; it seemed that the Belgian countryside slept under its summer heat.

The relieved Prince grunted an acknowledgement, then leaned forward to gaze critically in the mirror. He twisted his head left and right before looking anxiously at Rebecque. 'Am I losing too much hair?'

Rebecque pretended to make a careful inspection,

then shook his head reassuringly. 'I can't see that you're losing any, sir.'

'I thought I'd wear British uniform tonight.'

'A very apt choice, sir.' Rebecque spoke in English because the Prince preferred that language.

The Prince glanced at a clock. It would take his coach at least two hours to reach Brussels, and he needed a good hour to change into the scarlet and gold finery of a British major-general. He would allow himself another three hours to enjoy a private supper before going to the Duchess's ball where, he knew, the food would be cold and inedible. 'Has Sharpe returned yet?' he asked Rebecque.

'No, sir.'

The Prince frowned. 'Damn. If he gets back, tell him I expect his attendance at the ball.'

Rebecque could not hide his astonishment. 'Sharpe? At the Duchess's ball?' Sharpe had been promised that his duties to the Prince were not social, but only to provide advice during battle.

The Prince did not care what promises had been made to the Englishman; forcing Sharpe to dance would demonstrate to the Rifleman that the Prince commanded this headquarters. 'He told me that he hates dancing! I shall nevertheless oblige him to dance for his own good. Everyone should enjoy dancing. I do!' The Prince laughingly trod some capering steps about the bedroom. 'We shall make Colonel Sharpe enjoy dancing! Are you sure you don't want to dance tonight, Rebecque?'

'I shall be Your Highness's eyes and ears here.'

'Quite right.' The Prince, reminded that he had military responsibilities, suddenly looked grave, but he had an irrepressibly high-spirited nature and could not help laughing again. 'I imagine Sharpe dances like a Belgian heifer! Thump, thump, thump, and all the time with that gloomy expression on his face. We shall cheer him up, Rebecque.'

'I'm sure he'll be grateful for it, sir.'

'And tell him he's to wear Dutch uniform tonight!'

'Indeed I will, sir.'

The Prince left for Brussels an hour and a half later, his carriage escorted by an honour guard of Dutch Carabiniers who had learned their trade in the French Emperor's service. Paulette, relieved at the Prince's departure, lay cosily in his bed while Rebecque took a book to his own quarters. The clerks laboriously copied out the orders listing which battalions the Prince would visit in the coming week, and what manoeuvres each battalion should demonstrate for the Prince's approval.

Clouds heaped higher in the west, but the sun still shone on the village. A cat curled up by the boot-scraper at the front door of the Prince's headquarters where the sentry, a British redcoat, stooped to fondle the animal's warm fur. Wheat and rye and barley and oats ripened in the sun. It was a perfect summer's day, shimmering with heat and silence and all the beauty of peace.

The first news of French activity reached the Duke of Wellington while he ate his early dinner of roast mutton. The message, which had originated in Charleroi just thirty-two miles away, had first been sent to Marshal Blücher at Namur, then copied and sent on to Brussels, a total journey of seventy miles. The message merely reported that the French had attacked at dawn and that the Prussian outposts had been driven in south of Charleroi.

'How many French? It doesn't say. And where are the French now? And is the Emperor with them?' the Duke demanded of his staff.

No one could tell. The mutton was abandoned on the table while the Duke's staff gathered about a map pinned to the dining-room wall. The French might have advanced into the country south of Charleroi, but the

Duke, as ever, brooded over the left-hand side of the map which showed the great sweep of flat country between Mons and Tournai. That was where he feared a French advance that would cut the British off from the North Sea. If the French took Ghent then the Duke's army would be denied its supply roads from the North Sea, as well as its route home.

Wellington, had he been in the Emperor's boots, would have chosen that strategy. First he would have pushed a strong diversionary force at Charleroi, then, when the allies moved to defend Brussels from the south, he would have launched the real attack to the west. It was by just such dazzling manoeuvres that the Emperor had held off the Russian, Prussian and Austrian armies in the spring of 1814. Napoleon, in the weeks before his abdication, had never fought more brilliantly, and no one, least of all Wellington, expected anything but the same cleverness now.

'We've heard nothing from Dornberg?' the Duke snapped.

'Nothing.'

The Duke looked back at the Prussian message. It did not tell him how many French had crossed the frontier, nor whether Blücher was concentrating his army; all it told him was that a French force had pushed back the Prussian outposts.

He went back to the dinner-table. His own British and Dutch forces were scattered across five hundred square miles of countryside. They had to be thus dispersed, not only to guard every possible French invasion route, but also so that the mass of men and horses did not strip any one locality of food and grazing. Now, however, he knew the army must begin to shrink towards its battle order. 'We'll concentrate,' the Duke said. Every division of the army had a prearranged town or village where it would gather and wait for further orders. 'And send a good man to Dornberg to find out what's happening in front of him.'

The Duke frowned again at Blücher's message, wondering whether he had over-reacted to its small news. Surely, if the French incursion was serious, the Prussians would have sent a more urgent messenger? No matter. If it turned out to be a false alarm then the army's concentration could be reversed next day.

Nine miles to the south, in the little village of Waterloo, the hugely fat Prussian Major had stopped his plodding horse at a small inn opposite the church. The wine he had taken for lunch, together with the oppressive afternoon heat, had quite tired him out. He asked for a little restorative brandy, then saw a baker's tray of delicious cakes being carried into the inn's side-door. 'And some of those pastries, I think. The ones with the almond paste, if you'd be so kind.'

He slid out of the saddle and gratefully sat on a bench that was shaded by a small chestnut tree. The despatch which would have told Wellington of the loss of Charleroi and the further French advance lay in the Major's saddlebag.

The Major leaned against the chestnut's trunk. Nothing much stirred in the village. The paved road ran between wide grass verges where two tethered cows and four goats grazed. A few chickens scratched by the church steps where a dog twitched in its sleep. A small child played tipcat in the archway of the inn's stableyard. The fat Major, pleased with such a scene of rural innocence, smiled happily, then, as he waited for his snack, dozed.

Sharpe's horses limped into the Prince of Orange's headquarters just ten minutes after the Prince had left for Brussels. Aggressive French patrols had prevented Sharpe getting close to the road a second time, but he had ridden near enough to see the dust clouds drifting away from the boots, hooves and wheels of an army on the march. Now, flinching at the soreness in his thighs, he eased himself out of the saddle. He shouted for an ostler, tied Nosey to a metal ring on the stableyard wall and gave the dog a bowl of water before, carrying his map and weapons, he limped into the silent house. Dust floated in the beams of light that flooded through the fanlight over the front door. He looked into the map room, but no one was there.

'Duty Officer!' Sharpe shouted angrily, then, when no one answered, he hammered his rifle butt against the wooden panelling in the hallway. 'Duty officer!'

A bedroom door opened upstairs and a face appeared over the banister. 'I hope there's a good reason for this noise! Oh, it's you!'

Sharpe peered into the gloom and saw the affable face of the Baron Jean de Constant Rebecque. 'Who's on duty?'

'Colonel Winckler, I think, but he's probably sleeping. Most of us are. The Prince has gone to Brussels, and he wants you there as well.' Rebecque yawned. 'You're required to dance.'

Sharpe stared upwards. For a few seconds he was too shocked to speak and Rebecque assumed that the silence merely expressed Sharpe's horror at being ordered to a ball, but then the Rifleman exploded with his news. 'Haven't you heard? My God, Rebecque, the bloody French are north of Charleroi! I sent Dornberg a message hours ago!'

The words hung in the hot still air of the stairwell. It was Rebecque's turn to stare silently. 'Sweet God,' he said after a few seconds, then began buttoning his blue coat. 'Officers!' His shout echoed through the house. 'Officers!' He ran at the stairs, taking them three at a time. 'Show me.' He pushed past Sharpe into the map room where he threw back the heavy wooden shutters to flood the tables with sunlight.

'There.' Sharpe placed a filthy finger on the map just north of Charleroi. 'A mixed force; infantry, cavalry and guns. I was there this morning, and I went back this afternoon. The road was crowded both times. I couldn't see much this afternoon, but there must have been at least one whole corps on that road. A prisoner told me he thought Napoleon was with them, but he wasn't certain.'

Rebecque looked up into Sharpe's tired and dust-stained face and wondered just how Sharpe had taken a prisoner, but he knew this was no time for foolish questions. He turned to the other staff officers who were crowding into the room. 'Winckler! Fetch the Prince back, and hurry! Harry! Go to Dornberg, find out what in God's name is happening in Mons. Sharpe, you get some food. Then rest.'

'I can go to Mons.'

'Rest! But food first! You look exhausted, man.'

Sharpe obeyed. He liked Rebecque, a Dutchman who, like his Prince, had been educated at Eton and Oxford. The Baron had been the Prince's tutor at Oxford and was living proof to Sharpe that most education was a waste of effort, for none of Rebecque's modest good sense had rubbed off on the Prince.

Sharpe went through to the deserted kitchens and found some bread, cheese and ale. As he was cutting the bread the Prince's girl, Paulette, came sleepily into the room. She was dressed in a grey shift that was loosely belted round her waist. 'All this noise!' she said irritably. 'What's happening?'

'The Emperor's crossed the frontier.' Sharpe spoke in French.

'Good!' Paulette said fiercely.

Sharpe laughed as he cut the mould off a piece of cheese.

'Don't you want butter on your bread?' the girl asked.

'I couldn't find any.'

'It's in the scullery. I'll fetch it.' Paulette gave Sharpe a happy smile. She did not know the Rifleman well, yet she thought he was by far the best-looking man on the Prince's staff. Many of the other officers considered themselves good-looking, but this Englishman had an interestingly scarred face and a reluctant but infectious smile. She brought a muslin-covered bowl of butter from the scullery and good-naturedly pushed Sharpe to one side. 'You want an apple with your cheese?'

'Please.'

Paulette made a plate of food for herself, then poured some ale out of Sharpe's stone bottle into one of the Prince's Sèvres teacups. She sipped the ale, then grinned. 'The Prince tells me your woman is French?'

Sharpe was somewhat taken aback by the girl's directness, but he nodded. 'From Normandy.'

'How? Why? What? Tell me. I want to know!' She smiled in recognition of her own cheekiness. 'I like to know everything about everyone.'

'We met at the end of the war,' Sharpe said as though that explained everything.

'And you fell in love?' she asked eagerly.

'I suppose so, yes.' He sounded sheepish.

'That's nothing to be ashamed of! I was in love once. He was a *dragon*, but he went off to fight in Russia, poor boy. That was the last I saw of him. He said he would marry me, but I suppose he was eaten by wolves or killed by cossacks.' She sighed in sad memory of her lost Dragoon. 'Will you marry your French lady?'

'I can't. I'm already married to a lady who lives in England.'

Paulette shrugged that difficulty aside. 'So divorce her!'

'It's impossible. In England a divorce costs more money than you can dream of. I'd have to go to Parliament and bribe them to pass a law specially for my divorce.'

'The English are stupid. I suppose that's why the Prince likes them so much. He feels at home there.' She laughed. She had thick brown hair, slanting eyes, and a cat-like face. 'Were you living in France with your woman?'

'Yes.'

'Why did you leave?'

'Because the Emperor would have put me in prison if I'd have stayed, and because I needed my half-pay.'

'Your half-pay?'

Sharpe was both amused and irritated by her questioning, but it was harmless, so he indulged her. 'I received a pension from the English army. If I'd have stayed in France there would have been no pension.'

Hooves sounded loud in the yard as Colonel Winckler took off after the Prince. Sharpe, glad that he was not having to ride anywhere, began tugging at his tight boots. Paulette pushed his hands away, put his right foot on her lap, tugged off the boot, then did the same for his other foot. 'My God, you smell!' She laughingly pushed his feet away. 'And Madame left France with you?' Paulette's questioning had the guileless innocence of a child.

'Madame and our baby, yes.'

Paulette frowned at Sharpe. 'Because of you?'

He paused, seeking a modest answer, but could think of nothing but the truth. 'Indeed.'

Paulette cradled her cup of ale and stared through the open door into the stableyard where chickens pecked at oats and Sharpe's dog twitched in exhausted sleep. 'Your French lady must love you.'

'I think she does, yes.'

'And you?'

Sharpe smiled. 'I love her, yes.'

'And she's here? In Belgium?'

'In Brussels.'

'With the baby? What sort of baby? How old?'

'A boy. Three months, nearly four. He's in Brussels too.'

Paulette sighed. 'I think it's lovely. I would like to follow a man to another country.'

Sharpe shook his head. 'It's very hard on Lucille. She hates that I have to fight against her countrymen.'

'Then why do you do it?' Paulette asked in an outraged voice.

'Because of my half-pay again. If I'd have refused to rejoin the army they'd have stopped my pension, and that's the only income we have. So when the Prince summoned me, I had to come.'

'But you didn't want to come?' Paulette asked shrewdly.

'Not really.' Which was true, though that morning, as he had spied on the French, Sharpe had recognized in himself the undeniable pleasure of doing his job well. For a few days, he supposed, he must forget Lucille's unhappiness and be a soldier again.

'So you only fight for the money.' Paulette said it wearily, as though it explained everything. 'How much does the Prince pay you for being a colonel?'

'One pound, three shillings and tenpence a day.' That was his reward for a brevet lieutenant-colonelcy in a cavalry regiment and it was more money than Sharpe had ever earned in his life. Half of the salary disappeared in mess fees and for the headquarter's servants, but Sharpe still felt rich, and it was a far better reward than the two shillings and ninepence a day that he had been receiving as a half-pay lieutenant. He had left the army as a major, but the clerks in the Horse Guards had determined that his majority was only brevet rank, not regimental, and so he had been forced to accept a lieutenant's pension. The war was proving a windfall to Sharpe, as it was to so many other half-pay officers in both armies.

'Do you like the Prince?' Paulette asked him.

That was a sensitive question. 'Do you?' Sharpe countered.

'He's a drunk.' Paulette did not bother with tact, but just let her scorn flow. 'And when he's not drunk he squeezes his spots. Plip plop, plip plop! Ugh! I have to do his back for him.' She looked to see whether her words had offended Sharpe, and was evidently reassured. 'You know he was going to marry an English princess?'

'I know.'

'She couldn't stand him. So now he says he will marry a Russian princess! Ha! That's all he's good for, a Russian. They rub butter on their skins, did you know that? All over, to keep warm. They must smell.' She sipped her ale, then frowned as her mind skittered back over the conversation. 'Your wife in England. She does not mind that you have another lady?'

'She has another man.'

The evident convenience of the arrangement pleased Paulette. 'So everything is all right?'

'No.' He smiled. 'They stole my money. One day I shall go back and take it from them.'

She stared at him with large serious eyes. 'Will you kill the man?'

'Yes.' He said it very simply, which made it all the more believable.

'I wish a man would kill for me,' Paulette sighed, then stared in alarm because Sharpe had suddenly raised a hand in warning. 'What is it?'

'Sh!' He stood and went in his stockinged feet to the open stableyard door. Far off, like a crackling of burning thorns, he thought he heard musketry. He could not be certain, for the sound was fading and tenuous in the small warm breeze. 'Do you hear anything?' he asked the girl.

'No.'

'There it is! Listen!' He heard the noise again, this time

it sounded like a piece of canvas ripping. Somewhere, and not so very far off, there was a musket fight. Sharpe looked up at the weathercock on the stable roof and saw the wind had backed southerly. He ran to the kitchen door which opened into the main part of the house. 'Rebecque!'

'I hear it!' The Baron was already standing at the open front door. 'How far off?'

'God knows.' Sharpe stood beside Rebecque. The small wind kicked up dust devils in the street. 'Five miles?' Sharpe hazarded. 'Six?'

The noise faded to nothing, then any chance of hearing it again was drowned in the clatter of hooves. Sharpe looked down the high street, half expecting to see French Dragoons galloping into the small village, but it was only the Prince of Orange who had abandoned his carriage and taken a horse from one of his escort. That escort streamed behind him down the street, together with the aide who had fetched the Prince back.

'What news, Rebecque?' The Prince dropped from the saddle and ran into the house.

'Only what we sent you.' Rebecque followed the Prince into the map room.

'Charleroi, eh?' The Prince chewed at a fingernail as he stared at the map. 'We've heard nothing from Dornberg?'

'No, sir. But if you listen carefully, you can hear fighting to the south.'

'Mons?' The Prince sounded alarmed.

'No one knows, sir.'

'Then find out!' the Prince snapped. 'I want a report from Dornberg. You can send it after me.'

'After you?' Rebecque frowned. 'But where are you going, sir?'

'Brussels, of course! Someone has to make sure Wellington has heard this news.' He looked at Sharpe. 'I particularly wanted you in attendance tonight.'

Sharpe suppressed an urge to kick His Royal Highness in the royal arse. 'Indeed, sir,' he said instead.

'And I insist you wear Dutch uniform. Why aren't you in Dutch uniform now?'

'I shall change, sir.' Sharpe, despite the Prince's frequent insistence, had yet to buy himself a Dutch uniform.

Rebecque, sensing that the Prince still intended to dance despite the news of a French invasion, cleared his throat: 'Surely there'll be no ball in Brussels tonight, sir?'

'It hasn't been cancelled yet,' the Prince said petulantly, then turned back with specific instructions for Sharpe. 'I want you in evening dress uniform. That means gold lace, two epaulettes with gold bullion on each and blue cushions. And a dress sword, Sharpe, instead of that butcher's blade.' The Prince smiled, as if to soften his sartorial orders, then gestured at one of his Dutch aides. 'Come on, Winckler, there's nothing more to do here.' He strode from the room, leaving Rebecque thin-lipped and silent.

The sound of the hooves faded in the warm air. Rebecque listened again for the sound of musketry, but heard nothing, so instead tapped the map with an ebony ruler. 'His Royal Highness is quite right, Sharpe, you should be wearing Dutch uniform.'

'I keep meaning to buy one.'

Rebecque smiled. 'I can lend you something suitable for tonight.'

'Bugger tonight.' Sharpe twisted the map round so that it faced him. 'Do you want me to go to Mons?'

'I've already sent Harry.' Rebecque went to the open window and stared into the heat haze. 'Perhaps nothing is happening in Mons.' He spoke softly, almost to himself. 'Perhaps we're all wrong about Mons. Perhaps Napoleon is just swinging open the front doors and ignoring the back gate.'

'Sir?'

'It's a double-leafed front door, Sharpe, that's what it is!' Rebecque spoke with a sudden urgency as he strode back to the table and tapped the map. 'The Prussians are the left-hand door and we're the right, and when the French push in the middle, Sharpe, the two leaves will hinge apart. Is that what Bonaparte's doing to us?'

Sharpe stared down at the map. From the Prince's headquarters a road ran eastwards through Nivelles to meet the Charleroi highway at an unnamed crossroads. If that crossroads was lost, then Napoleon would have successfully swung the two doors apart. The British and Dutch had been worrying about Mons, but now Sharpe took a scrap of charcoal and scrawled a thick ring round the crossroads. 'That's the lock on your doors, Rebecque. Who are our closest troops?'

'Saxe-Weimar's brigade.' Rebecque had already seen the importance of the crossroads. He strode to the door and shouted for clerks.

'I'll go there,' Sharpe offered.

Rebecque nodded acceptance of the offer. 'But for God's sake send me prompt news, Sharpe. I don't want to be left in the dark.'

'If the French have taken that damned crossroads, we'll all be in the dark. Permanently. I'm borrowing one of the Prince's horses. Mine's blown.'

'Take two. And take Lieutenant Doggett with you. He can carry your messages.'

'Does that crossroads have a name?' That was an important question, for any messages Sharpe sent had to be accurate.

Rebecque searched the table to find one of the larger scale maps that the Royal Engineers had drawn and distributed to all the army headquarters. 'It's called Quatre Bras.'

'Four arms?'

'That's what it says here, Quatre Bras. Four Arms. Just what you need for opening double doors, eh?'

Sharpe did not respond to the small jest. Instead he shouted for Lieutenant Doggett, then went to the kitchen where he sat and tugged on his boots. He yelled through the open stableyard door for three horses to be saddled, two for himself and one for Lieutenant Doggett. 'And untie my dog!'

The orders for Prince Bernhard of Saxe-Weimar, sealed with Rebecque's copy of the Prince of Orange's personal seal, came ten minutes later. Rebecque brought the orders himself and handed them up to Sharpe who was already mounted. 'Remember you're supposed to be dancing tonight,' Rebecque smiled at Sharpe.

Paulette had come into the stableyard and was leaning against a sun-warmed wall. She smiled at Sharpe as he twisted the Prince's horse towards the archway. 'Go carefully, Englishman,' she called.

The courtyard was filling with horses as staff officers, all alerted by the distant musketry, arrived from the various brigade headquarters to seek information and orders. Sharpe blew the Prince's whore a kiss, then rode to find a crossroads.

CHAPTER 5

The bedroom of the hotel on Brussels' rue Royale stank of vinegar which Jane Sharpe's maid had sprinkled onto a red-hot shovel to fumigate the room. A small metal bowl of sulphur powders still burned in the hearth to eradicate whatever pestilential airs the vaporizing vinegar might have missed. It was, Jane had complained, a foul little suite of rooms, but at least she would make sure they held no risk of contagion. The previous occupant had been a Swiss merchant who had been evicted to make way for the English milord and his lady, and Jane had a suspicion that the Swiss, like all foreigners, harboured strange and filthy diseases. The noxious stench of the scorched vinegar and burning sulphur was making Jane feel ill, but in truth she had not felt really well ever since the sea crossing from England.

Lord John Rossendale, elegantly handsome in white breeches and silk stockings, black dancing shoes, and a gold-frogged cut-away coat with a tall blue collar and twin epaulettes of gold chain, stood at the bedroom's window and stared moodily at the Brussels rooftops.

'I don't know whether he'll be there or not. I just don't know.' It was the twentieth time he had confessed such ignorance, but for the twentieth time it did not satisfy Jane Sharpe who sat naked to the waist at the room's small dressing-table.

'Why can't we find out?' she snapped.

'What do you expect me to do?' Lord John ascribed Jane's short temper to her upset stomach. The North Sea crossing seemed to have disagreed with her, and the journey in the coach to Brussels had not improved her nausea. 'Do you expect me to send a messenger to Braine-le-Comte?'

'Why not, if he can provide us with the answer.'

'Braine-le-Comte is not a person, but the village where the Prince has his headquarters.'

'I cannot think,' Jane paused to dab her cheeks with the *eau de citron* which was supposed to blanche the skin of her face and breasts to a fashionable death-mask whiteness, 'I cannot think,' she resumed, 'why the Prince of Orange, whoever in hell he is, should want to appoint Richard as a staff officer! Richard doesn't have the manners to be a staff officer. It's like that Roman Emperor who made his horse into a consul. It's madness!' She was being unfair. Jane knew just what a good soldier her husband was, but a woman who has deserted her man and stolen his fortune soon learns to denigrate his memory as a justification for her actions. 'Don't you agree that it's madness?' She turned a furious damp face on Rossendale who could only shrug mute agreement. Lord John thought Jane looked very beautiful but also rather frightening. Her hair was splendidly awry because of the lead curling strips which, when removed, would leave her with a glorious gold-bright halo, but which now gave her angry face the fierce and tangled aspect of a Greek Fury.

Jane turned back to the mirror. She could spend hours at a dressing-table, gravely staring at her reflection just as an artist might gaze on his work in search of a final gloss that might turn a merely pretty picture into a masterpiece. 'Would you say there's colour in my cheeks?' she asked Lord John.

'Yes.' He smiled with relief that she had changed the

subject away from Richard Sharpe. 'In fact you're looking positively healthy.'

'Damn.' She glowered at her reflection. 'It must be the hot weather.' She turned as her maid appeared from the anteroom with two dresses, one gold and one white, which were held up for Jane's inspection. Jane pointed to the pale gold dress then returned her attention to the mirror. She dipped a finger into a pot of rouge and, with exquisite care, reddened her nipples. Then, obsessively, she went back to blanching her face. The table was crowded with flasks and vials; there was bergamot and musk, *eau de chipre, eau de luce*, and a bottle of Sans Pareil perfume that had cost Lord John a small fortune. He did not resent such gifts for he found Jane's beauty ever more startling and ever more beguiling. Society might disapprove of the adulterous relationship flaunted so openly, but Lord John believed that Jane's beauty excused everything. He could not bear to think of losing her, or of not wholly possessing her. He was in love.

Jane grimaced at herself in the mirror. 'So what happens if Richard is at the ball tonight?'

Lord John sighed inwardly as he turned back to the window. 'He'll challenge me, of course, then it will be grass before tomorrow's breakfast.' He spoke lightly, but in truth he dreaded having to face Sharpe in a dawn duel. To Lord John, Sharpe was nothing but a killer who had been trained and hardened to death on innumerable battlefields, while Lord John had only ever brought about the death of foxes. 'We needn't go tonight,' he said hopelessly.

'And have all society say that we are cowards?' Jane, because she was a mistress, rarely had an opportunity to attend the more elegant events of society, and she was not going to miss this chance of being seen at a duchess's ball. Not even Jane's tender digestion would keep her from tonight's dancing, and nor did she have any real fear of meeting her husband, for Jane well knew Sharpe's reluctance to dance or to dress up in a frippery uniform, but the possibility of his presence was an alarming thought that she could not resist exploring.

'I shall just try to avoid meeting him,' Lord John said helplessly.

Jane dabbed a tentative finger to test whether her rouged nipples had dried. 'How soon before there's a battle?'

'I'm told the Peer doesn't expect the French to move till July.'

Jane grimaced at the implied delay, then stood with her slender arms raised high to allow her maid to drop the gauzy dress over her head. 'Do you know what happens in battle?' she asked Lord John from under the cascading cloth of gold.

It seemed a rather broad question, and one for which Lord John could not think of a specific answer. 'Rather a lot of unpleasantry, I imagine,' he said instead.

'Richard told me that in battle a lot of unpopular officers are killed by their own men.' Jane twisted herself to and fro in front of the mirror to make sure the dress hung properly. The dress was high waisted and low-breasted; a fashionably filmy screen through which her brightly coloured nipples showed as enticing shadows. Other women would doubtless be wearing such dresses, but none, Jane thought, would dare to wear one without any petticoat as she herself intended. Satisfied, she sat as her maid began to untwist the lead strips from her hair and tease the ringlets into perfection. 'He told me that you can't tell what happens in a battle because there's too much smoke and noise. A battle, in short, is an ideal place to commit a murder.'

'Are you suggesting I should kill him?' Lord John

was genuinely shocked at the dishonour of the suggestion.

Jane had indeed been hinting at the opportunity for her husband's murder, but she could not admit as much. 'I'm suggesting,' she lied smoothly, 'that he may not wish to risk his career by fighting a duel, but instead might try to kill you during a battle.' She dipped her finger in scented black paste that she applied to her eyelashes. 'He's a man of excessive pride and extraordinary brutality.'

'Are you trying to frighten me?' Lord John attempted to pass the conversation off lightly.

'I am trying to make you resolute. A man threatens your life and our happiness, so I am suggesting that you take steps to protect us.' It was as close as Jane dared go to a direct suggestion of murder, though she could not resist one more enticement. 'You're probably in more danger from a British rifle bullet than you are from any French weapon.'

'The French', Lord John said uneasily, 'may take care of him anyway.'

'They've had plenty of chances before,' Jane said tartly, 'and achieved nothing.'

Then, ready at last, she stood. Her hair, ringleted, bejewelled and feathered, crowned an ethereal and sensuous beauty that dazzled Lord John. He bowed, kissed her hand, and led her down to the courtyard where their carriage waited. It was time to dance.

His Serene Highness Prince Bernhard of Saxe-Weimar took one look at Rebecque's orders, grunted his acceptance, and tossed the paper to his Brigade Major. 'Tell the Prince we'll be at the crossroads in one hour,' he told Sharpe.

Sharpe did not reveal that the Prince of Orange knew nothing of the orders. Instead he thanked His Serene

Highness, bowed his way out of the inn which was Prince Bernhard's headquarters, and remounted his horse. Lieutenant Simon Doggett, who had been charged with keeping Nosey from killing the chickens that pecked in the inn yard, followed Sharpe out to the road. 'Well, sir?' he asked Sharpe, but in a nervous voice which suggested that he expected his temerity in asking to be met with a savage reproof.

'He'll be at the crossroads in one hour with four thousand men. Let's hope the bastards can fight.' Saxe-Weimar's men were mostly German troops in Dutch service who had fought for Napoleon in the previous wars, and not even Saxe-Weimar himself was certain whether they would now fight against their old comrades.

Doggett rode eastwards beside Sharpe. Like so many of the Englishmen who served the Prince of Orange, Doggett was an old Etonian. He was now a lieutenant in the First Foot Guards, but had been seconded to the Prince's staff because his father was an old friend of the Baron Rebecque. Doggett was fair-haired, fair-skinned and, to Sharpe's eyes, absurdly young. He was in fact eighteen, had never seen a battle, and was very nervous of the notorious Lieutenant-Colonel Sharpe who was thirty-eight years old and had lost count of all his battles.

Sharpe now anticipated another battle; one for a crossroads that linked two armies. 'If the French already hold Quatre Bras, you'll have to go back and warn Saxe-Weimar,' Sharpe told him. 'Then go to Rebecque and tell him the bad news.'

'Yes, sir.' Doggett paused, then found the courage to ask a question. 'And what will you be doing, sir? If the French have captured the crossroads, I mean?'

'I'll be riding to Brussels to tell the Duke to run like hell.'

Doggett glanced to see whether the Rifleman was smiling in jest, and decided he was not. The two men fell silent as they cantered their horses between low hedgerows that were bright with the early spears of foxgloves. Beyond the hedges the cornfields were thick with poppies and edged with cornflowers. Swallows whipped low across the fields, while rooks flew clumsily towards their high nests. Sharpe twisted in his saddle to see that the western sky was still clouded, though there were great gaps between the heaping clouds through which the sun poured an incandescent flood of light. It was evening, but there were still four hours of daylight left. In a week's time it would be the longest day of the year when, in these latitudes, a gunner could accurately sight a twelve-pounder at half-past nine of an evening.

They passed a great dark wood that grew southwards from the road and, quite suddenly, the pale strip of the paved high road stretched stark across the landscape ahead. Sharpe instinctively reined in his horse as he stared at the small cluster of buildings that marked the crossroads called Quatre Bras.

Nothing moved at the crossroads, or nothing that threatened a soldier's life. There were no troops at the crossroads and the highway was empty, just a pale dusty strip between its vivid green verges. Sharpe tapped his heels to start his horse moving again.

Wisps of smoke revealed that the cottagers were cooking their evening meals at the hearths of the small hamlet which lay to the north of the crossroads. There was one large stone farmhouse, outside which a small dark-haired girl was playing with some kittens by an empty farm-cart. Three geese waddled across the road. Two old women, bonneted and shawled, sat tatting lace outside a thatched cottage. A pig rooted in an orchard, and milk cows lowed from the farmyard. One of the shawled women must have seen Sharpe and Doggett approaching for she suddenly called the small girl who ran nervously towards the thatched cottage. Beyond the tiny hamlet the smaller unpaved road climbed a shallow hill before disappearing eastwards in a stand of dark trees.

'You understand the importance of this road?' Sharpe pointed at the smaller road on which he and Doggett travelled.

'No, sir,' Doggett replied honestly.

'It's the road that joins us and the Prussians. If the French cut it, we're on our own, so if we lose these crossroads, the Crapauds have won the damned campaign.' Sharpe spurred down to the crossroads, touched his hat to the old ladies who were staring with alarm at the two horsemen, then he turned to gaze down the long southwards road that led to Charleroi. The highway stretched pale and deserted in the evening sun, yet this was the very same road on which Sharpe had seen a French corps marching that morning. That sighting had been only twelve miles south of this crossroads, yet now there was no sign of any Frenchmen. Had they stopped? Had they retreated? Sharpe felt a sudden fear that he had raised a false alarm and the force he had seen had been nothing but a feint. Or maybe the French had marched past this crossroads and were already nearing Brussels? No. He dismissed that fear instantly, because there was no sign of an army's passing. The tall rye in the fields either side of the road was untrampled, and the road's crude paving of cobbles on impacted chalk and flint had no deep ruts like those made by the passage of heavy guns. So where the hell were the French?

'Let's go and find the bastards,' Sharpe grunted, and once he had said it he marvelled at how easy it was to slip back into the old ways of speaking about the enemy. He had lived in Normandy for seven months, he had learned the French language and come to love the French countryside, yet now, just as if he had never met

Lucille, he spoke of the French as a hated enemy. The strangeness of that thought suddenly made him miss the château. Lucille's home was very grandly called a château, though in truth it was nothing more than a large moated farm with a crenellated tower to remind passers-by that the building had once been a small fortress. Now the château was Sharpe's home, the first home he had ever truly known. The estates had been neglected in the war and Sharpe had begun the laborious task of repairing the years of neglect. At this time of the year, if Napoleon had not returned, Sharpe should have been thinning the apple crop, stripping away basketloads of the young fruit to give the remaining crop a better chance of ripening in the autumn, but instead he was riding a dusty road in Belgium and searching for an enemy that had mysteriously disappeared.

The road dropped gently down to a ford. To Sharpe's left the stream flowed into a lake, while ahead of him, beyond the shallow ford, a farm with an arched gateway stood on the left-hand side of the road. A woman stared suspiciously from the farm's arch at the two soldiers, then stepped back into the yard and slammed the heavy gate. Sharpe had stopped at the ford to let the horses drink. Bright blue dragonflies hovered and darted in the reeds. The evening was warm; a gentle quiet dusk in which the only sounds were the rippling water and the slight clatter of the rye stalks moving in the breeze. It seemed impossible that this might become a battlefield, and perhaps it would not, for Sharpe was already beginning to doubt what he had seen that same morning. Where the hell had the French gone?

He touched the horse's flanks, splashed through the ford and began to climb the gradual slope beyond. Dogs barked in the farmyard, and Nosey howled in reply till Sharpe snapped at him to be quiet. The familiar homely stink of a dungheap wafted across the highway. Sharpe rode slowly, as though hurrying might spoil the calm of this perfect summer's evening. The road was unhedged, running between wide strips of rank grass in which wood garlic, foxgloves, columbine and yellow archangel grew. Elder and blackthorn bushes offered patches of shade. A rabbit thumped the verge in alarm at the horsemen's approach, then scurried into the rye stalks. The evening was fragrant, warm and rich, lit by the great wash of gold light that flooded through the cloud chasms in the western skies.

Off to Sharpe's left, about a mile away, he could see the roofs of two more farmhouses, while to his right the wood gave way to rolling cornfields intersected by a farm track that twisted between the crops. Nothing untoward moved in the landscape. Had he come to the wrong crossroads? He had a sudden fear that this was not the Charleroi to Brussels road. He took out his map, which indeed suggested that he was riding on the main Brussels highway, but maps were notoriously inaccurate. He looked for a milestone, but none was in sight. He stopped again and listened, but could hear neither musketry nor the sounds of marching men. Had he imagined the enemy this morning? Or the musketry this afternoon? But Rebecque had heard the musketry too. So where were the French? Had they been swallowed into the warm fields?

The road bent slightly to the right. The rye was growing so tall that Sharpe could not see what lay around the bend. He loosened his rifle in its holster and called Nosey to heel. Simon Doggett, riding alongside Sharpe with the spare horse, seemed to share the Rifleman's nervousness. Both men were instinctively curbing their horses.

They edged round the road's bend. Ahead now was a road junction shaded by two big chestnut trees. The highway bent to the left, while a smaller track went off to the right. Far beyond the junction, and half-obscured by the tall rye, was a village. The map tallied with what Sharpe saw, so the village had to be Frasnes.

'We'll go as far as the village,' Sharpe said.

'Yes, sir.'

The sound of their voices broke the nervous spell and both men dug in their heels to make their horses trot. Sharpe had to duck under a low chestnut branch as he turned the next corner to see, five hundred yards ahead of him, the wide village street.

He stopped again. The street seemed empty. He pulled out the battered sea captain's telescope that he had bought in Caen to replace the expensive glass that he had lost after Toulouse. He trained the awkward heavy instrument on the village's single street.

Three men sat outside what must be the village inn. A woman in thick black skirts led a donkey laden with hay. Two children ran towards the church. The image of the church wavered, Sharpe checked the glass's tremor, then froze. 'Jesus Christ!'

'Sir?' Doggett asked in alarm.

'We've got the bastards!' Sharpe's voice was filled with satisfaction.

The French had not disappeared, and he had not imagined them. They were in Frasnes. At the far end of the village street, just coming into sight and foreshortened by distance and the ancient lens, was a battalion of French infantry. They must have been singing for, though Sharpe could hear nothing, he could see their mouths opening and closing in unison. This battalion wore darker blue coats than most French infantry and had very dark blue trousers. 'They're a battalion of Voltigeurs,' Sharpe told Doggett. 'Light infantry. Skirmishers. So where the hell are their Dragoons?' He panned the telescope left and right, but no horsemen showed in the evening sunlight.

Doggett had taken out his own glass and was staring at the French. They were the first enemy troops he had ever seen and the sight of them had made him go pale. He could hear the beat of his bloodstream echoing fast in his ears. He had often imagined seeing the enemy for the first time, but it was strange how very commonplace and yet how exciting this baptism was. 'How many of them are there?' he asked.

'Six hundred?' Sharpe guessed. 'And they're cocksure bastards to march without a cavalry screen.' The only horsemen he could see were ten mounted French officers, but he knew the cavalry and guns could not be far behind. No General pushed unsupported skirmishers too far ahead of the main force. He turned to Doggett. 'Right! You go back to Quatre Bras. Wait there for Saxe-Weimar. Give him my compliments and tell him there's at least one battalion of French skirmishers coming his way. Suggest he advances as far as the stream and stops them there, but make it a tactful suggestion. Take Nosey and the spare horse, then wait for me at the crossroads. Understand?'

'Yes, sir.' Doggett turned his own horse and awkwardly led the spare horse round in a circle. 'What will you do, sir?'

'I'll keep an eye on these bastards. If you hear shooting, don't worry. That's just me playing games. Give Nosey a good kicking if the bastard gives you any trouble.'

Doggett spurred away, followed by a reluctant Nosey, while Sharpe dismounted and led his horse back to the chestnut trees which grew at the road's fork. Just beyond the chestnuts, in the long grass of the verge, a heavy wooden brush harrow had been abandoned. Sharpe tied the horse's reins to the harrow's stout frame, then slid his rifle out of its saddle holster. He checked that the weapon was loaded, then that the flint was firmly seated in its leather-padded jaws.

He went back past the chestnuts, keeping in the shadows of the tall rye on the western side of the road. He ran steadily, getting ever closer to the village and to the approaching enemy. The French troops had not stopped in Frasnes, but were marching doggedly on towards Sharpe who supposed that their orders were to seize the crossroads at Quatre Bras before nightfall. If Saxe-Weimar could reach the crossroads first, and if his men would fight, the French would fail, but it would be a very close race.

Sharpe wanted to slow the French advance. Even a few minutes would help. He dropped in a shallow scrape by the roadside, half hidden by a hazel bush which had been invaded by pink dog roses. None of the approaching enemy seemed to have noticed him. He slid his rifle through the thick grass, then pushed his tricorne hat back so that its peak would not catch on the weapon's doghead.

He waited. The pistol in his belt dug into his belly. The grass of the road's verge was warm and dank. There had been rain earlier in the week and the soil under the thick vegetation was still damp. A ladybird crawled up a dry stalk, then stepped delicately across to the oiled and battered stock of the rifle. The enemy marched careless and unsuspecting. The shadows stretched long over the road. It was a summer's evening as beautiful as God had ever blessed on a wicked world.

A hare appeared on the opposite verge, quivered for a second, then ran swiftly up the road only to leap sideways out of the path of the approaching French infantry. The enemy was three hundred yards away now and marching in a column of four ranks. Sharpe could hear their strong singing. An officer rode ahead of the column on a grey horse. The officer had a red plume on his blue shako and a tall red collar on his unbuttoned blue coat. The red plume was nodding to the rhythm of the horse's steps. Sharpe aimed at the plume, suspecting that at this extreme range the bullet would drop to hit the horse.

He fired. Birds squawked and exploded out of the crops.

Smoke banged from the pan by Sharpe's right eye and the burning scraps of powder flayed back to his cheek. The rifle's heavy brass butt crashed back into his shoulder. He moved even before the singing stopped, rolling into the thick rye stalks where, without bothering to see what damage his shot had done, he began reloading. Prime the pan, close it, pour the cartridge powder down the smoking barrel, then ram in the cartridge's paper and the ball. He slid the ramrod out, jammed it down the long barrel, then pulled it free. No one had shot back. He rolled again into the shadow of the hazel bush where his foul-smelling powder smoke still lingered.

The column had stopped. The officer had dismounted from the grey horse which was skittering nervously at the road's edge. Birds wheeled overhead. The officer was unhurt, and none of the men seemed to have been hit. Perhaps the horse was wounded? Sharpe took the loaded pistol from his belt, cocked it, and laid it beside him. Then he aimed the rifle again, this time at one of the men in the front rank.

He fired. Within seconds he fired again, this time emptying the pistol towards the Frenchmen. The second shot would do no damage, but it might persuade the Frenchmen that there was a group of enemy in front of them. Sharpe rolled right again, this time plunging deeper into the rye stalks before reloading the rifle. He pushed the pistol into his belt.

French muskets banged. He heard the heavy lead balls flicking through the stalks of rye, though none went near him. Sharpe was loading fast, going through the drill he had first learned twenty-two years before. Another volley of musketry hammered from the French who were firing blind into the tall crops.

Sharpe did the same, simply aiming the rifle in the direction of the column, and pulling the trigger so that the bullet whipped off through the stalks. He tap-loaded the next cartridge, not bothering to use the cumbersome ramrod, but just slamming the rifle's butt hard on the ground in hope that the blow would jar the ball down to the loose charge. He fired again, and felt the lesser kick which told him the ball had only lodged half-way down the barrel. That bullet would be lucky to go a hundred yards, but that was not the point. The point was to fire fast to persuade the French that they had run into a strong picquet line.

He fired one more tap-loaded bullet, then ran back parallel to the road. He forced his way through the rye till he was past the chestnuts, then turned to his right. He ran across the road and heard the French shout as they saw him, but by the time they had pulled their triggers, he was already in the shelter of the tall trees. The nervous horse rolled its eyes white and flicked its ears towards the crackling sound of the muskets.

Sharpe reloaded the rifle, this time ramming the bullet hard down against the charge, then released the horse. It was a big black stallion, one of the best in the Prince's stable and Sharpe hoped the beast was battle trained. Men had died because an untrained horse had taken fright at the sound of musketry. He pulled himself into the saddle, settled his sore thighs, and pushed the rifle into its holster. He pulled the horse round to face east-wards, then spurred it into the tall field of rye. So far the French had been fired on from the field on their left, now they would see an officer on the right of their advance.

A shout told Sharpe he had indeed been seen. The rye hid him from the French rankers, and only those officers on horseback could see the Rifleman over the tall crop. Sharpe waved his right arm as though he was beckoning a skirmish line forward. For all the French officers knew the thick rye might have concealed two whole battalions of Greenjackets.

A trumpet sounded from the French. Sharpe trotted in a semi-circle, going to the enemy's flank to suggest an enfilading attack, then he turned and spurred back towards Quatre Bras. A wasteful volley was shot towards him, but the range was far too long and the balls spent themselves among the thick stalks. Three mounted officers rode into the field after the volley, but Sharpe had spurred well clear of any threat from the three men. He just trotted northwards, thinking to fire some more rifle shots from the farm by the ford.

Then hoofbeats pounded to Sharpe's left and he saw another French officer galloping furiously down the high road. Sharpe urged the black stallion on, but the footing under the rye was treacherous; the soil was damp and still held the shape of the plough furrows, and the stallion could not match the Frenchman's speed on the paved road. The stallion stumbled and Sharpe almost fell, and when he recovered himself he saw that the Frenchman had swerved off the road and, with drawn sabre, was charging straight for him. The man was young, probably a lieutenant.

Damn the bloody man. In all armies there were officers who needed to prove their bravery by single combat. The duel could also help a career; if this young French Lieutenant could take Sharpe's horse and weapons back to his battalion he would be a hero. Maybe he would even be made into a captain.

Sharpe slowed his horse and dragged his big unwieldy sword out of its scabbard. 'Go back!' he shouted in French.

'When you're dead, *monsieur*!' The Frenchman spoke cheerfully. He looked as young as Doggett. His horse, like Sharpe's, had been slowed by the plough furrows in the rye field, but the Frenchman rowelled it on as he got close to Sharpe.

Sharpe stood his ground, his right arm facing the attack. The Lieutenant, like all French skirmishing officers, carried a light curved sabre; a good slashing weapon, but not the most accurate blade for the lunge. This man, eager to draw first blood, swerved as he neared Sharpe, then leaned out of his saddle to give a gut-slicing sweep with the glittering blade.

Sharpe simply parried the blow by holding his own heavy sword vertically. The clash of steel jarred up his arm, then he kicked his heels back to force the stallion towards the road. The Frenchman had swept past him, and now tried to turn in the clinging rye.

Sharpe only wanted to reach the road. He had no need to prove anything in single combat. He glanced over his left shoulder and saw the three other officers were still two hundred yards away, then a shouted challenge from his right revealed that the French Lieutenant had succeeded in turning his horse and was now spurring back to make a new attack. He was approaching from behind and slightly to the right of Sharpe. That was foolish, for it meant the Frenchman would have to make his sabre cut across his own and his horse's body. 'Don't be stupid!' Sharpe called back to him.

'Are you frightened, Englishman?' the Lieutenant laughed.

Sharpe felt the anger then; the cold anger that seemed to slow the passage of time itself and make everything appear so very distinctly. He saw the Frenchman's small moustache above the bared teeth. The man's shako had a red, white and blue cockade, and some of the shako's overlapping brass plates were missing from its leather chin-strap. The Lieutenant's horse was tossing its head, snorting, raising its bright hooves high as it trampled the crop. Husks of rye and scraps of straw were being splintered aside by the charging horse. The Lieutenant's sabre was raised, reflecting the dying sun in its brilliant polish and ready for the downwards cut that was supposed to hack into Sharpe's skull. Sharpe was holding his own sword low beside his stirrup, almost as if he could not be bothered to fight. The long blade was whipped by the rye stalks. Sharpe was deliberately curbing the stallion to take shorter slower steps, thus letting the eager Frenchman overtake him, but, just a heartbeat before the sun-bright sabre whipped hard down, Sharpe jerked the long sword back and upwards.

The heavy blade smashed brutally hard into the mouth of the Lieutenant's horse. The beast reared up on its hind legs, screaming, with blood showing at its lips and teeth. Sharpe was already turning the stallion across its front. The Lieutenant was desperately trying to stay in his saddle. He flailed for balance with his sabre arm, then screamed because he saw the heavy sword coming at his throat. He tried to twist away, but instead his horse plunged back onto its forefeet and threw the Lieutenant's weight fast forward.

Sharpe held his straight-bladed sword pointed at the Lieutenant's throat and locked his elbow as the Frenchman fell onto the blade. There was an instant's resistance, then the sword's point punctured skin and muscle to tear into the great blood vessels of the Frenchman's neck. His scream of fear was silenced instantly. He seemed to stare at Sharpe as he died; offering the Englishman a look of mingled surprise and remorse, then a gout of blood, bright as the sun itself, slashed out to soak Sharpe's right arm and shoulder. Specks of the blood spattered his face, then the Frenchman was falling away and his dying weight ripped his body clear of the long steel blade.

Sharpe twisted the stallion away. He thought briefly of taking the Lieutenant's horse, but he did not want to be encumbered by the beast. He saw the other three French officers check their advance. He flourished the bloody sword at them in a mocking salute, then trotted back to the road.

He stopped there, wiped the blade on his overalls, and sheathed the sword. His right arm was soaked with the Frenchman's blood that had saturated the flimsy green sleeve of his old uniform. He grimaced at the smell of fresh blood, then pulled the loaded rifle from its holster. The three officers watched him, but none tried to come close.

He watched the turn in the road by the chestnut trees. After a minute the first French skirmishers ran into sight. They stopped when they saw him, then dived right and left, but at fifty yards the rifle was lethal and Sharpe saw his bullet lift a man clean off the ground.

But at fifty yards the French muskets were almost as accurate as the Baker rifle. Sharpe slammed back his heels and took off down the road as if the demons of hell were at his heels. He counted to eight, then swerved hard left into the tall rye, just as the French volley whipped through the dust cloud left by the stallion's hooves.

The small volley missed. Sharpe rode on down the slope till he reached the stream where, as the stallion drank, he reloaded the rifle and shoved the weapon into its holster. Then, satisfied that the French would check their advance till they were certain no picquet line waited in ambush, he stared westwards towards the clouds and let out a long heavy breath.

He was measuring the fear he had just felt. For months he had been haunted by his memories of the battle of Toulouse; reliving the bowel-loosening terror he had felt at that last conflict of the last war. There had been no horror particular to Toulouse to explain that extraordinary fear; the battle had been less threatening than a half-dozen of the Spanish engagements, yet Sharpe had never forgotten the awful fear, nor his relief when peace had been declared. He had hung the battered sword over the spice cupboard in Lucille's kitchen, and had claimed to be glad that he would never again have to draw the war-dulled blade from its metal scabbard. Yet, ever since Toulouse, he had wondered whether his nerve had gone for ever.

Now, holding his blood-soaked right hand to the evening light, he found his answer. The hand was motionless, yet at Toulouse that hand had shaken like a man afflicted with the palsy of St Vitus's dance. Sharpe slowly closed the hand into a fist. He felt an immense relief that his nerve had come back, but he also felt ashamed that he had enjoyed the discovery.

He looked up at the clouds. He had assured Lucille that he fought only because his pension would be jeopardized if he refused, but in truth he had wanted to know whether the old skills were still there or whether, like a cannon fired too fast and too often, he had simply worn himself out as a soldier. Now he knew, and it had all been so damned easy. The young Lieutenant had ridden on to the blade, and Sharpe had felt nothing. He doubted if his pulse had even quickened as he killed. Twenty-two years of war had honed that skill to near perfection, and as a result a mother in France would soon be weeping.

He looked southwards. Nothing moved among the tall crops. The French would be collecting their casualties, and their officers would be staring northwards in search of a non-existent picquet line.

Sharpe patted the stallion, then walked him downstream until he reached the ford where, once more, he waited for the enemy's advance. The woman had come back to the farm's archway from where she and two men stared nervously up the road towards Frasnes. A horsefly settled on the stallion's neck. Sharpe slapped it bloody, then unsheathed the rifle and held it across his saddle. He would give the French one more shot before retreating back to the crossroads.

Then, from behind him, from the north, he heard the thump of heavy drums and the jaunty thin notes of a flute playing. He twisted in the saddle to see a column of infantry at the crossroads of Quatre Bras. For a second Sharpe's heart leapt, thinking that a battalion of Riflemen had arrived, then he saw the yellow crossbelts over the green coats and he knew he was seeing Prince Bernhard of Saxe-Weimar's force of Nassauers. The German brigade officers were already spurring down the road towards Sharpe.

Saxe-Weimar had arrived at the very nick of time. On the long slope above Sharpe the French battalion had spread into skirmish order. They were invisible in the tall rye, yet their purposeful advance could be traced by the disturbance of the crop through which they moved. The Nassauers' battalion was doubling down the road, while their officers spurred towards the stream to mark the place where the infantry would form a line.

Sharpe rode back behind the advancing troops. Some of the men gave him curious looks because of the blood that had sheeted his right side. He uncorked his canteen and took a long drink of water. More Nassauer infantry were running down the road, their heavy boots stirring a thick dust. Small drummer boys, their lips caked with the road's dust, beat a ragged advance as they ran. The troops seemed eager enough, but the next few seconds would be the acid test of their willingness to fight against their old master, Napoleon.

The first Nassauer battalion was formed in a line of four ranks on the left-hand side of the road. The battalion's Colonel stared at the thrashing of unseen men in the rye field on the stream's far bank, then ordered his men to make ready.

The muskets were lifted to the men's shoulders.

The Colonel paused. 'Fire!'

There was a split second's silence, then the volley crashed hugely loud in the still evening air. The musket-balls slammed across the small stream and bent the rye crop as though a squall of wind had struck the stalks. Rooks protested the disturbance by flapping angrily up from the roadside.

'Reload!' To Sharpe's eyes the battalion's musket drill was lamentably slow, but it did not matter; they were fighting.

A few French skirmishers returned the fire, but they were massively outnumbered and their shooting was wild. Another Nassauer battalion had formed a line to the right of the stream. 'Fire!' Again a volley hammered at the evening's perfection. A bank of smoke, thick and vile smelling, rolled across the stream.

'Fire!' That was the first battalion again. Yet more men were coming from the crossroads and deploying left and right beyond the first two units. Staff officers were gallop-ing busily behind the lines where the battalion's colours were bright in the dusk. The drummers kept up their din.

'How many of them?' The Brigade Major, who spoke English with a thick German accent, reined in beside Sharpe.

'I only saw one battalion of skirmishers.'

'Guns? Cavalry?'

'None that I saw, but they can't be far behind.'

'We'll hold them here as long as we can.' The Brigade Major glanced at the sun. It was not long now till nightfall, and the French advance would certainly stop with the darkness.

'I'll let headquarters know you're here,' Sharpe said.

'We'll need help by morning,' the Brigade Major said fervently.

'You'll get it.' Sharpe hoped he spoke the truth.

Lieutenant Simon Doggett waited at the crossroads and

frowned when he saw the blood on Sharpe's arm. 'Are you hurt, sir?'

'That's someone else's blood.' Sharpe brushed at the bloodstain, but it was still wet. 'You're to go back to Braine-le-Comte. Tell Rebecque that the crossroads at Quatre Bras are safe, but that the French are bound to attack in greater strength in the morning. Tell him we need men here; as many as possible!'

'And you, sir? Are you staying here?'

'No. I'll take the spare horse.' Sharpe slid out of the saddle and began unbuckling its girth. 'You take this horse back to headquarters.'

'Where are you going, sir?' Doggett, seeing the flicker of irritation on Sharpe's face, justified his question. 'The Baron's bound to ask me, sir.'

'Tell Rebecque I'm going to Brussels. The Prince wants me to go to a bloody ball.'

Simon Doggett's face blanched as he looked at Sharpe's frayed and blood-drenched uniform. 'Like that, sir? You're going to a ball dressed like that?'

'There's a bloody war on. What does the Young Frog expect? Bloody lace and pantaloons?' He handed Doggett the stallion's bridle, then carried the saddle over to the spare horse. 'Tell Rebecque I'm riding to Brussels to see the Duke. Someone has to tell him what's happening here. Go on with you!'

Behind Sharpe the firing had died away. The French had retreated, presumably back to Frasnes, while Saxe-Weimar's men had begun to make their bivouacs. Their axes sounded loud in the long wood as they cut the timber for their cooking fires. The people of the hamlet, sensing what destruction would follow the coming of these soldiers, were packing their few belongings into the farm cart. The small girl was crying, looking for her lost kittens. A man cursed at Sharpe, then went to help harness a thin mule to the cart.

Sharpe wearily mounted his fresh horse. The cross-roads were safe, at least for this one night. He clicked his fingers for Nosey to follow him, then rode northwards in the dusk. He was going to a dance.

CHAPTER 6

Lucille Castineau stared gravely at her reflection in the mirror which, because it was only a small broken sliver, was being held by her maid, Jeanette, who was forced to tilt the glass up and down in an effort to show her mistress the whole dress. 'It looks lovely,' Jeanette said reassuringly.

'It's very plain. Oh, well. I am plain.'

'That's not true, madame,' Jeanette protested.

Lucille laughed. Her ball gown was an old grey dress which she had prettified with some lengths of Brussels lace. Fashion dictated a filmy sheath that would scarcely cover the breasts and with a skirt slit to reveal a length of thigh barely disguised beneath a flimsy petticoat, but Lucille had neither the tastes nor the money for such nonsense. She had taken in the grey dress so that it hugged her thin body more closely, but that was her sole concession to fashion. She would not lower its neckline, nor would she have dreamed of cutting the skirt.

'It looks lovely,' Jeanette said again.

'That's because you haven't seen what anyone else will be wearing.'

'I still think it's lovely.'

'Not that it matters,' Lucille said, 'for I doubt whether anyone will be looking at me. Or will even dance with me.' She well knew Richard Sharpe's reluctance to dance, which was why she had been surprised when the message came from the Prince of Orange's headquarters informing her that Lieutenant-Colonel Sharpe would be attending His Royal Highness at the Duchess of Richmond's ball, in anticipation of which His Royal Highness took pleasure in enclosing a ticket for Madame la Vicomtesse de Seleglise. Lucille herself never used her title, but she knew Sharpe was perversely proud of it and must have informed the Prince of its existence.

The reluctant Vicomtesse now propped the broken mirror on a shelf and poked fingers at her hair which she had piled loosely before decorating with an ostrich feather. 'I don't like the feather.'

'Everyone's wearing them.'

'I'm not.' Lucille plucked it out and tickled the sleeping baby with its tip. The baby twitched, but slept on. Henri-Patrick had black hair like his father, but Lucille fancied she already saw her own family's long skull in the baby's wrinkled face. If he had his father's looks and his mother's brains, Lucille liked to say, Henri-Patrick should be well blessed.

She was unfair, at least to herself. Lucille Castineau had lived all her twenty-seven years in the Norman countryside and, though she came from a noble family, she proudly considered herself to be a farm woman. The rural life had denied her Jane Sharpe's fashionable pallor; instead Lucille's skin had the healthy bloom of country weather. She had a long, narrow and strong-boned face, its severity softened by her eyes which seemed to glow with laughter and sense. She was a widow. Her husband had been an elegant officer in Napoleon's cavalry, and Lucille had often wondered why such a handsome man had sought to marry her, but Xavier Castineau had thought himself most fortunate in his wife. They had been married for only a few weeks before he had been hacked down by a sabre. In the peace after the wars, when Lucille had found herself alone in her family's Norman château, she had met Sharpe and become his lover. Now she was the mother of his son.

Loyalty to her man had brought Lucille to Brussels. She had never been a Bonapartist, yet that distaste had not made it any easier for her to leave France and follow an army that must fight against her countrymen. Lucille had left France because she loved Sharpe, whom she knew was a better man than he thought himself to be. The war, she told herself, would end one day, but love was timeless and she would fight for it, just as she would fight to give her child his father's company. Lucille had lost one good man; she would not lose a second.

And tonight, surprisingly, she had an opportunity to dance with her good man. Lucille took a last look in the mirror, decided there was nothing that could be done to make herself any more elegant or beautiful, and so picked up her small bag that contained the precious pasteboard ticket. She kissed her child, gave her hair one last despairing pat, and went to a ball.

A tall man waited at the stable entrance of the lodging house where Lucille Castineau had rented two attic rooms. He was a man whose frightening appearance commanded instant respect. His height, four inches over six feet, was formidable enough, yet he also carried the muscles to match his inches and this evening he looked even more threatening for he hefted an oak cudgel and had a long-barrelled horse-pistol thrust into his belt and a British army rifle slung on one shoulder. He had sandy hair and a flat hard face. The man was in civilian clothes, yet, in this city thronged with soldiers, he had a confidence that suggested he might well have worn a uniform in his time.

The tall man had been leaning against the stable's open gates, but straightened up as Lucille appeared from the house. She looked nervously at the western sky, tumultuous with dark clouds that had so hastened the dusk that the first lamps were already being lit in the city's archways and windows. 'Shall I bring an umbrella?' she asked.

'It's not going to rain tonight, ma'am.' The tall man spoke with the harsh accent of Ulster.

'You don't have to walk me, Patrick.'

'And what else would I be doing tonight? Besides, the Colonel doesn't want you walking the streets alone after dark.' Harper took a step back and gave Lucille an appreciative smile. 'You look just grand, so you do!'

Lucille laughed good-naturedly at the compliment. 'It's a very old dress, Patrick.'

In truth Patrick Harper had not really noticed Lucille's dress, but, being a married man, he knew the importance a woman attached to a compliment. Harper's own wife would need more than a few such compliments when he reached home, for she had been adamantly opposed to her husband travelling to Brussels. 'Why do you do this to me?' Isabella had demanded. 'You're not a soldier any more! You have no need to go! Your place is here, with me!'

That place was Dublin, where, at the end of the last war, Harper had gone with a saddlebag full of stolen gold. The treasure had come from the French baggage captured at Vitoria in Spain, a country where Sergeant Patrick Harper had found both wealth and a wife. Discharged from the army, he had intended to return to his beloved Donegal, but he had reached no further than Dublin where he bought a tavern close to the city's quays. The tavern also did a thriving trade in the sale of stolen horses, an activity that provided Harper with an excuse to travel deep into the Irish countryside. The return of the Emperor to France and the subsequent declaration of war had been good for Harper's trade; a good hunter stolen from a Protestant plantation in Ireland would fetch a prime price in England where so many officers equipped themselves for the campaign.

Harper had used the excuse of horse-trading to explain his journey to Isabella, but she knew the real truth of his escapade. It was not horses that fetched Harper to Belgium, but Sharpe. Sharpe and Harper were friends. For six years, on battlefields and in sieges, they had fought side by side and Harper, as soon as he heard of the new war, had waited for a word from his old officer. Instead, and to Isabella's chagrin, Sharpe had come to Dublin himself. At first it had seemed he was only there to sit out the war with his French woman, but then the summons had come from the Dutch army and Isabella had known that her husband would follow Sharpe.

Isabella had tried to dissuade Patrick. She had threatened to leave him and return to Badajoz. She had cursed him. She had wept, but Harper had dismissed her fears. 'I'm only going to trade a few horses, woman, nothing else.'

'You won't be fighting?'

'Now why in the name of all Ireland would I want to be fighting?'

'Because of him,' Isabella knew her man, 'and because you can't resist joining a fight.'

'I'm not in the army, woman. I just want to make a few pennies by selling some horseflesh. Where's the harm in that?'

In the end Harper had sworn a sacred oath on the Holy Mother and on all the bleeding wounds of Christ that he would not go into battle, that he would remember he was a husband and a father, and that if he so much as heard a musket shot he would turn tail and run away.

'Did you hear there was a wee scrap down south today?' Harper's voice had a note of relish as he spoke of the fighting to Lucille.

'A battle?' Lucille sounded alarmed.

'Probably just a skirmish, ma'am.' Harper thrust aside the beggars who shuffled and reached towards Lucille. 'I expect the Emperor's getting bored with the waiting and decided to see if anyone was awake on this side of the border.'

'Perhaps that's why I haven't heard from Richard today.'

'If he's got a choice between a battle and a dance, ma'am, then begging your presence, he'll take the battle any day.' Harper laughed. 'He's never been much of a man for dancing, not unless he's drunk and then he'll dance with the best of them.' Harper suddenly realized that he might be betraying some confidences. 'Not that I've ever seen him drunk, ma'am.'

Lucille smiled. 'Of course not, Patrick.'

'But we'll hear from him soon enough.' Harper raised the cudgel to drive away the beggars who swarmed ever more threateningly the closer they got to the Duke and Duchess of Richmond's rented house. There were beggars throughout Europe. Peace had not brought prosperity, but higher prices, and the normal ranks of the indigent had been swollen by discharged soldiers. By day a woman could safely walk Brussels' streets, but at night the pavements became dangerous. 'Get back, you bastards! Get back!' Harper thrust two ragged men aside. Beyond the gutter shouting children pursued the polished carriages that rattled towards the rue de la Blanchisserie, but the coachmen were experts with their long whips which snapped sharply back to drive the urchins off.

A squadron of British Hussars were on duty in the rue de la Blanchisserie to keep the beggars away from the wealthy. A helpful corporal with a drawn sabre rode his horse in front of Harper to help clear Lucille's passage to the big house.

'I'll wait for you, ma'am,' Harper told Lucille when they were safely in the courtyard.

'You don't have to, Patrick. I'm sure Richard will escort me home.'

'I'll wait here, ma'am,' Harper insisted.

Lucille was nervous as she climbed the steps. A gorgeously dressed footman inspected her ticket, then bowed her into the hallway which was brilliant with candles and thronged with people. Lucille already felt dowdy. She glanced about the hall, hoping against hope that Richard would be waiting for her, but there was no sign of Sharpe, nor of any of the Prince of Orange's staff. Lucille felt friendless in an enemy country, but then was relieved to see the Dowager Countess of Mauberges who, like so many other Belgian aristocracy, thought of herself as French and wanted the world to know it. The old lady was defiantly wearing her dead husband's *Legion d'honneur* about her neck. 'Your husband was a member of the Legion, was he not?' she greeted Lucille.

'Indeed he was.'

'Then you should wear his medal.'

Not that the ball needed an extra medal for, to Lucille, it seemed as though a jewel shop had been exploded into extravagant shards of light and colour. The colour came from the men's uniforms, gorgeous uniforms, uniforms of scarlet and gold, royal blue and saffron, silver and black; uniforms of Hussars, Dragoons, Guards, Jaegers and kilted Highlanders. There were plumes, froggings, epaulettes, aigulettes, and gold-furnished scabbards. There were fur-edged dolmans, silk-lined pelisses, and gorgets of pure gold. There were princes, dukes, earls, and counts. There were plenipotentiaries in court uniforms so decked with gold that their coats seemed like sheets of light. There were jewelled stars and enamelled crosses worn on sashes of brilliant silk, and all lit by the glittering chandeliers which had been hoisted to the ceiling with their burdens of fine white candles.

The women wore paler colours; white or washed yellow

or delicate blue. Those ladies slim and brave enough to wear the high fashion were ethereal in gauzy dresses that clung to their bodies as they moved. The candlelight glinted from pearls and rubies, diamonds and gold. The room smelt of scents – orange water or eau de cologne, beneath which were the sharper smells of hair powder and sweat. 'I don't know', the Dowager Countess leaned close to Lucille, 'why some of them bother to dress at all! Look at that creature!'

The Countess jabbed her walking cane in the direction of a girl with bright gold ringlets and eyes as radiant as sapphires. The girl was undeniably beautiful, and clearly knew it for she was wearing no petticoat and a diaphanous dress of pale gold that did little to hide her body. 'She might as well be stark naked!' the Countess said.

'It's the fashion.' Lucille felt very drab.

'When I was a girl it took twelve yards of cloth just to make an underskirt for a ball gown. Now they simply unfold some cheese-cloth and throw it over their shoulders!' Hardly that even, for most of the women's shoulders were bared, just as most bosoms were almost naked. 'And see how they walk! Just like men.' In the Countess's childhood, before the Revolution, and before Belgium had been liberated from Austrian rule by the French, women had been taught to glide along a floor, their feet hidden by wide skirts and their slippers barely leaving the polished boards. The effect was graceful, suggesting effortless motion, while now the girls seemed not to care. The Countess shook her head with disgust. 'You can tell they're Protestants! No manners, no grace, no breeding.'

Lucille diverted the old lady by showing her the supper room which, like the ballroom, had been draped with the Belgian colours of black, gold and scarlet. Beneath the silk hangings the long tables were covered in white linen and were thick with silver and fine china.

'They'll lose all the spoons tonight!' the Countess said with undisguised satisfaction, then turned as applause greeted the stately polonaise which had progressed from the far side of the house, advanced through the entrance hall and now entered the ballroom to open the dancing formally. Lucille and the Countess sat by the supper room entrance. The uniformed officers and their ladies stepped delicately in the dancing line, they bowed and curtseyed. The music rang sweetly. A child, allowed to stay up and watch the ball's beginning, stared wide-eyed from a balcony, while the Countess tapped her stick on the parquet floor in time to the music.

After the polonaise, the first waltz brightened the room with its jaunty rhythm. The windows were black with night, but sheeted with the reflections of a thousand candles sparkling on ten thousand jewels. Champagne and laughter ruled the room, while the dancers whirled in glittering joy.

Lucille watched the pretty girl in the diaphanous golden dress who danced with a tall and handsome officer in British cavalry uniform. Lucille noted how the girl refused all partners but that one man and she felt a surge of sympathy because she knew the girl must be in love, just as she herself was in love. Lucille thought the girl and the cavalry officer made a very fine couple, but she wished the girl would smile rather than hold her face in such a cold and supercilious expression.

Then Lucille forgot the girl as the ballroom was swamped by a sudden and prolonged applause, which forced the orchestra to pause.

The Duke of Wellington had appeared with his staff. He stood in the ballroom entrance and acknowledged the applause with a small bow. He was not a tall man, but something about his confidence and reputation gave him an impressive stature. He was dressed in the scarlet and gold of a British field marshal with a tactful Netherlands decoration worn on an orange sash.

Lucille, politely applauding with the rest of the room, wondered whether this man truly was the greatest soldier of his time. Many, including Sharpe, insisted that he was. No one, not even the Emperor, had fought so many battles, and no other General had won all the battles he had ever fought, though the Duke, as every person in the ballroom was aware, had never fought the Emperor. In Vienna, where the Duke had travelled as Britain's ambassador to the Congress, society had greeted him with outrageous flattery, calling him '*le vainqueur du vainqueur du monde*', but Lucille guessed that Bonaparte might have other ideas of the Duke's military stature.

Now the conqueror of the world's conqueror gestured to stop the applause. 'He has a good leg,' the Dowager Countess confided in Lucille.

'He's a handsome man,' Lucille agreed.

'And he's not in a corset. You can tell that by the way they bow. My husband never wore a corset, not like some here tonight.' The Countess cast a scathing eye at the dancers who were beginning yet another waltz, then looked back to the Duke. 'He's a young man.'

'Forty-six,' Lucille told her, 'the same age as the Emperor.'

'Generals are getting younger. I'm sure the soldiers don't like it. How can a man have confidence in a stripling?'

The Countess fell into a disapproving silence as a young and handsome British officer offered Lucille a low and evidently uncorseted bow. 'My dear Lucille!' Captain Peter d'Alembord was resplendent in scarlet coat and white breeches.

'Captain!' Lucille responded with a genuine pleasure. 'How nice to see a friendly face.'

'My Colonel received an invitation, didn't know what

to do with such a thing, so gave it to me. I can't believe you've persuaded Sharpe to attend, or have you turned him into a dancing man?'

'He's supposed to be accompanying the Prince.' Lucille named d'Alembord to the Dowager Countess of Mauberges who gave the officer a very suspicious examination.

'Your name is French!' the Countess accused him.

'My family were Huguenots, my lady, and therefore unwanted in *la belle France.*' D'Alembord's contemptuous scorn for France made the Countess bridle, but he had already turned back to Lucille. 'You'll do me the honour of dancing?'

Lucille would. D'Alembord was an old friend who had dined frequently with Sharpe and Lucille since they had come to the Netherlands. Both men had served in the Prince of Wales's Own Volunteers where d'Alembord had succeeded Sharpe to the command of the first battalion's light company. That battalion was now bivouacked in a village to the west of Brussels where d'Alembord had heard no news of any skirmishes on the frontier. Instead his day had been spent indulging the Colonel's passion for cricket. 'I think he plans to kill us all with boredom,' d'Alembord told Lucille as they took the floor.

'Poor Peter.'

'Not at all, I am the most fortunate of men. Except for Sharpe, of course.'

Lucille smiled at the dutiful but pleasing compliment. 'Of course. And how is Anne?'

'Very well. She writes to tell me that her father has found a house that will be suitable for us. Not too large, but with adequate stabling and a few acres of grazing.'

'I'm glad for you.'

D'Alembord smiled. 'I'm rather glad for me, too.'

'So stay alive to enjoy it, Peter!'

'Don't even tempt fate to suggest I won't.' D'Alembord

was newly engaged, and filled with a touching happiness at the prospect of his marriage. Lucille rather envied him, wishing that she could marry Sharpe. That admission made her smile to herself. Who would ever have believed that Lucille, Vicomtesse de Seleglise and widow of Colonel Xavier Castineau, would be mother to a half-English bastard?

She turned lithely to the music and saw that the blue-eyed girl in the golden dress was watching her very coldly. Was it the dowdy grey dress that had earned the girl's scorn? Lucille suddenly felt very shabby and uncomfortable. She turned her back to the girl.

'Good God!' D'Alembord, who was a very good dancer, suddenly faltered. His eyes were fixed on someone or something at the room's edge and Lucille, turning to see what had caught his astonished attention, saw the golden girl returning d'Alembord's gaze with what seemed to be pure poison.

'Who is she?' Lucille asked.

D'Alembord had quite given up any attempt to dance. Instead he offered Lucille his arm and walked her off the floor. 'Don't you know?'

Lucille stopped, turned to look at the girl once more then, intuitively, she knew the answer and looked for confirmation into d'Alembord's worried face. 'That's Richard's wife?' She could not hide her astonishment.

'God only knows what she's doing here! And with her damned lover!' D'Alembord steered Lucille firmly away from Jane and Lord John Rossendale. 'Richard will kill him!'

Lucille could not resist turning one more time. 'She's very beautiful,' she said sadly, then she lost sight of Jane as the Duke of Wellington's party moved across the ballroom floor.

The Duke was offering bland reassurance about the scanty news of the day's skirmishes. Brussels was full of rumours about a French attack, rumours that the Duke was scarcely able to correct or deny. He knew there had been fighting about Charleroi, and he had heard of some skirmishes being fought in the villages south of the Prince of Orange's headquarters, but whether the French had invaded in force, or whether there was an attack coming in the direction of Mons, the Duke still did not know. Some of his staff had urged that he abandon the Duchess's ball, but such an act, he knew, would only have offered encouragement to the Emperor's many supporters in Brussels and could even have prompted the wholesale desertion of Belgian troops. The Duke had to appear confident of victory or else every waverer in his army would run to be with the Emperor and the winning side.

'Is Orange here?' the Duke asked an aide.

'No, sir.'

'Let's hope he brings news. My dear Lady Mary, how very good to see you.' He bowed over her hand, then dismissed her fears of an imminent French invasion. Gently disengaging himself he walked on and saw Lord John Rossendale waiting to present himself and, with him, a young, pretty and under-dressed girl who somehow looked familiar.

'Who in God's name brought Rossendale here?' the Duke angrily asked an aide.

'He's been appointed to Uxbridge's staff, sir.'

'Damn Harry. Haven't we enough bloody fools in the cavalry already?' Harry Paget, Earl of Uxbridge and commander of the British cavalry, was second in command to the Duke. Uxbridge had eloped with the wife of the Duke's younger brother, which did not precisely endear him to the Duke. 'Is Harry here?' the Duke now asked.

'No, Your Grace.'

'He's sent Rossendale as deputy adulterer instead, eh?'

The Duke's jest was grim, then his face froze into a chill smile as Rossendale ushered Jane forward.

'Your Grace.' Lord John bowed. 'May I name Miss Jane Gibbons for you?' He deliberately used Jane's maiden name.

'Miss Gibbons.' The Duke found himself staring down her powdered cleavage as she curtseyed. 'Have we not met, Miss Gibbons?'

'Briefly, Your Grace. In southern France.'

He had her now. Good God! Wellington stiffened, remembering the details of the gossip. This was Sharpe's wife! What in hell's name did Rossendale think he was doing? The Duke, realizing that the introduction had been made in order to give the adulterous liaison the appearance of his approval, icily turned away without another word. It was not the adultery that offended him, but the stupidity of Lord John Rossendale risking a duel with Sharpe.

The Duke turned abruptly back, intending to inform his lordship that he did not permit duelling among his officers, but Rossendale and Jane had been swallowed up in the crowd.

The Duke forced a smile and airily denied to a lady that he had any fear of an imminent French attack. 'It takes longer to push an army up a road than you might think. It's not like herding cows, madam. We'll have good warning when Bonaparte marches, I do assure you.'

Another burst of applause announced the arrival of the Prince of Orange, who had come with a handful of staff officers. The Young Frog waved happily to the dancers and, ignoring his hostess, made straight for the Duke. 'I knew you wouldn't cancel the ball.'

'Should I have done?' the Duke asked tartly.

'There have been rumours,' the Prince said airily, 'nothing but rumours. Isn't this splendid?' He stared eagerly about the room in search of the prettiest faces, but instead caught sight of Lieutenant Harry Webster, one of his own British aides, who was hurrying across the dance floor. Webster offered the Prince a perfunctory bow, then offered him a despatch.

Most of the ballroom saw the despatch being given, and could tell from Webster's dust-stained boots that he must have ridden hard to bring the paper to Brussels, but the Prince merely thrust the despatch into a pocket of his coat and went back to his scrutiny of the younger women. Webster's face showed alarm. The Duke, catching the expression, smiled thinly at the Prince. 'Might I know the contents of the despatch, Your Highness?'

'If you wish. Of course.' The Prince carelessly handed over the sealed paper, then sent one of his Dutch aides to enquire about the identity of the girl in the diaphanous gold dress.

The Duke tore the despatch open. Rebecque, in Braine-le-Comte, had news both from the Prussians and from Dornberg in Mons. The French had advanced north from Charleroi, but had turned eastwards to attack Blücher and had halted for the night at a village called Fleurus. General Dornberg reported no activity at all on the roads leading to Mons. His cavalry patrols had ridden ten miles into France and had met no enemy troops.

The Prince, his eyes more bulbous than ever, had seized Webster's arm. 'You see that girl? Do you know her?'

'Lieutenant Webster,' the Duke's voice was as cold as a sword in winter, 'four horses instantly to the Prince of Orange's carriage. Your Highness will return immediately to your headquarters.'

The Prince blinked in surprise at his Commander-in-Chief, then offered a small laugh. 'Surely it can wait till –'

'Instantly, sir!' The Duke did not raise his voice, but there was something quite terrifying in his tone. 'Your corps will concentrate on Nivelles now. Go, sir, go!'

The Prince, aghast, stayed a half-second, then fled. A thousand eyes had watched the brief altercation, and now the whispers began in earnest. Something must have happened; something alarming enough to send the Prince scurrying from the ball.

The Duke and Duchess of Richmond sought an answer, but the Duke of Wellington merely smiled and blithely proposed that the company should proceed to supper. He offered the Duchess his arm and the orchestra, seeing the gesture, stopped their playing to allow the Highland pipers to begin their sword dance.

The pipes wailed and squealed into life, then caught their air to fill the room with a martial sound as the company, two by two and slow as an army's progress up a country road, went in to supper.

There were quails' eggs served on scrambled eggs and topped with caviar which the Duchess's chef obscurely called *les trois oeufs de victoire.* They were followed by a port-wine jelly and a cold soup.

The Duke of Wellington was happily seated between two attractive young ladies, while Lucille found herself between d'Alembord and a Dutch gunner colonel who complained about the victory eggs, refused the soup, and said the bread was too hard. Lucille had seen the Prince's arrival and hasty departure, and had resigned herself to Sharpe's absence. In a way she was glad, for she feared Sharpe's violence if he discovered Lord John Rossendale at the ball.

Lucille, a Norman, had been raised on stories of the merciless English pirates who lived just across the Channel and who, for centuries, had raided her homeland to kill and burn and plunder. She loved Sharpe, yet she saw in her lover the embodiment of those ghouls who had been used to scare her into childhood obedience. In the last few months, as the soldier had tried to become a farmer, Lucille had tried to educate her Englishman. She had convinced him that sometimes diplomacy was more effective than force, that anger must sometimes be tamed, and that the sword was not the clinching argument of peace. Yet, Lucille knew, he would remember none of those pacifist lessons if he saw Lord John. The big sword would scrape free. Peter d'Alembord, who shared her fears, had promised to restrain Sharpe if he appeared.

Now, it seemed, he would not be coming, for the Prince had fled the ball. No one knew why, though the Dutch gunner Colonel opined that the reason for the Prince's hasty departure could not have been of great importance, or else the Duke would surely have left with the Prince. The most reasonable assumption was that the French had pushed a cavalry raid across the frontier. 'I'm sure we'll discover the cause by morning,' d'Alembord said, then turned to Lucille to offer her a glass of wine.

But Lucille had gone quite white. She was staring wide-eyed and frightened at the supper room's open doorway which, like a proscenium arch, framed the Highland dancers and, quite suddenly, now also framed her lover.

Sharpe had come to the ball after all. He stood, blinking in the sudden candlelight, a shabby Rifleman among the dancing Scotsmen.

'Good God Almighty!' D'Alembord stared in awe at his friend.

Silence spread slowly across the supper tables as the hundreds of guests turned to stare at the Rifleman who, in turn, searched the supper tables for a particular person. A woman gasped in horror at the sight of him, and the pipes groaned a last uneasy note before the dancers froze above their swords.

Sharpe had come to the ball, but drenched in blood. His face was powder-stained and his uniform darkened with gore. Every other man in the room wore white breeches and silk stockings, yet here, looking like the ghost in the Scottish play, came a soldier from a battle-field; a soldier bloodied and marked, grim-faced as slaughter.

Jane Sharpe screamed; the last sound before the room went wholly silent.

Lucille half stood, as if to reveal herself to Sharpe, but he had seen the Duke and, seemingly oblivious of the effect his entrance had caused on the ball's guests, now strode between the tables to the Duke's side.

Wellington's face seemed to shudder in reaction to the stench of powder, blood, sweat and crushed grass that wafted from Sharpe's uniform. He waved the Rifleman down to a crouch so that their conversation could be more private. 'What is it?' the Duke asked curtly.

'I've just come from a crossroads called Quatre Bras, sir. It's north of Charleroi on the Brussels road. The French attacked there at sunset, but were checked by Saxe-Weimar's men. Prince Bernhard is certain the enemy will make a much stronger attack in the morning.' Prince Bernhard had said no such thing, but Sharpe had decided it would be more efficacious to assign the opinion to the Prince than to confess that it was his own view.

The Duke stared at Sharpe for a few seconds, then flinched at the blood which was caked on the Rifleman's jacket. 'Are you wounded?'

'A dead Frenchman, sir.'

The Duke dabbed his mouth with a napkin, then, very casually, leaned towards his host. 'You have a good map in the house?'

'Upstairs, yes. In my dressing-room.'

'Is there a back staircase?'

'Indeed.'

'Pray let us use it.' Wellington looked to an aide who was seated a few places down the table. 'All officers to their regiments, I think.' He spoke quite calmly. 'Come with us, Sharpe.'

Upstairs, in a room filled with boots and coats, the two Dukes leaned over a map while Sharpe amplified his report. Wellington moved a candle across the map to find the village of Fleurus where the Prussians now faced the French. That had been the first news this night had brought the Duke – that Napoleon's army had branched off the Brussels road to drive the Prussians eastwards away from the British. That news had been serious, but not disastrous. The Duke had planned to assemble as much of his army as possible, then march at dawn on to the French flank to help Blücher's Prussians, but now Sharpe had brought much worse news. The French had closed on Quatre Bras, effectively barring the Duke's planned march. Now, before he could help the Prussians, the Duke must thrust the French aside. The gap between the British and Prussian armies was still very narrow, yet Sharpe's news proved that the Emperor had his foot between the two doors and, in the morning, he would be heaving damned hard to drive the doors apart.

Wellington bit his lower lip. He had been wrong. Napoleon, far from manoeuvring about the Duke's right flank, had rammed his troops into the seam between the allied armies. For a second the Duke's eyes closed, then he straightened up and spoke very quietly. 'Napoleon has humbugged me, by God! He has gained twenty-four hours!' He sounded astonished, even hurt.

'What do you intend doing?' The Duke of Richmond had gone pale.

'The army will concentrate on Quatre Bras,' the Duke of Wellington seemed to be speaking to himself as though he groped towards a solution of the problem Napoleon posed, 'but we shan't stop him there, and if so,' Wellington's gaze flicked across the map, then settled, 'I must fight him,' he paused again to lean over the map for a few final seconds, 'here.' He pressed his thumbnail into the map's thick paper.

Sharpe stepped a pace forward to look down at the map. The Duke's thumbnail had forced a small scar into the map at another crossroads, this one much closer to Brussels and just south of a village with the odd name of Waterloo.

'He's humbugged me!' the Duke said again, but this time with a grudging admiration for his opponent.

'Humbugged?' Richmond was worried.

'It takes our armies two days to assemble,' Wellington explained. 'They're not assembled, yet the Emperor's army is already on our doorstep. In brief he has humbugged us. Sharpe.' The Duke turned abruptly on the Rifleman.

'Sir?'

'You might have dressed for the dance.' It was a gloomy jest, but softened with a smile. 'I thank you. You'll report to the Prince of Orange, I assume?'

'I was going back to Quatre Bras, sir.'

'Doubtless he'll meet you there. I thank you again. And good-night to you.'

Sharpe, thus dismissed, made a clumsy bow. 'Good-night, sir.'

The Duke of Richmond, when Sharpe had gone, grimaced. 'A menacing creature?'

'He came up from the ranks. He saved my life once,' Wellington somehow managed to sound disapproving of both achievements, 'but if I had ten thousand like him tomorrow then I warrant we'd see Napoleon beat by midday.' He stared again at the map, seeing with sudden and chilling clarity just how efficiently the Emperor had forced the allied armies apart. 'My God, but he's good,' the Duke spoke softly, 'very good.'

Outside the dressing-room, Sharpe found himself surrounded by anxious staff officers who waited for Wellington. The Rifleman brushed aside their questions, going instead to the main staircase which led down into the brightly lit chaos of the entrance hall where a throng of officers demanded their horses or carriages. Sharpe, suddenly feeling exhausted, and reluctant to force his way through the crowd, paused on the landing.

And saw Lord John Rossendale. His lordship was standing at the archway that led into the ballroom. Jane was with him.

For a second Sharpe could not believe his eyes. He had never dreamed that his enemy would dare show his face in the army, and Lord John's presence seemed evidence to Sharpe of just how the cavalryman must despise him. The Rifleman stared at his enemy just as many of the crowd in the entrance hall stared up at the blood-soaked Rifleman. Sharpe translated the crowd's attention as the derision due to a cuckold and, in that misapprehension, his temper snapped.

He impulsively ran down the last flight of stairs. Jane saw him and screamed. Lord John turned and hurried out of sight. Sharpe tried to save a few seconds by vaulting the banister. He landed heavily on the hall's marble flagstones, then thrust his way through the press of people. 'Move!' Sharpe shouted in his best Sergeant's voice, and the sight and sound of his anger was enough to make the elegant couples shrink away from him.

Lord John had fled. Sharpe had a glimpse of his lordship running through the ballroom. He ran after him, clear of the crowd now. He dodged past the few remaining couples who still danced, then turned into the supper room. Lord John was hurrying round the edge of the room, making for a back entrance, but Sharpe simply took the direct route which meant jumping from table to table straight across the room. His boots smashed china, ripped at the linen, and cascaded silver to the floor. A drunken major, finishing a plate of roast beef, shouted a protest. A woman screamed. A servant ducked as Sharpe jumped between two of the tables. He kicked over a candelabra, upset a tureen of soup, then leaped from the last table to land with a crash in Lord John's path.

Lord John twisted round, running back towards the ballroom. Sharpe pursued him, kicking aside a spindly gilt chair. A group of scarlet-coated cavalry officers appeared in the supper room entrance and Lord John, evidently encouraged by these reinforcements, turned to face his enemy.

Sharpe slowed to a walk and drew his sword. He dragged the blade slowly through the scabbard's wooden throat so that the sound of the weapon's scraping would be as frightening as the sight of the dulled steel. 'Draw your sword, you bastard.'

'No!' Lord John, as white faced as any of the fashionable women at the ball, backed uncertainly towards his friends who hurried towards the confrontation.

Sharpe was just a few paces from his enemy. 'Where's my money? You can keep the whore, but where's the money?'

'No!' That was Jane, screaming from the supper room's entrance.

'Stop, I say! Stop!' One of the cavalrymen, a tall captain in Life Guard's uniform, hurried to Lord John's side.

Sharpe, though he was still far out of sword's reach, suddenly lunged and Lord John, in utter fear, stepped hurriedly backwards and tripped on his spurs. He flailed for balance, snatched at the closest tablecloth and dragged a cascade of smashing china and chinking silver to the floor as he fell. There was a second's silence after the last shard of china had settled.

'You shit-faced, yellow-bellied bastard,' Sharpe said to the sprawling Lord John.

'Enough!' Lord John's leading rescuer, the Life Guards Captain, drew his own sword and stood above his lordship.

'You want to be filleted?' Sharpe did not care. He kept

walking forward, ready to hack down all the high-born, long-nosed bastards.

The Captain held his sword blade upright, almost at the salute, to show that he was neither menacing Sharpe nor trying to defend against him. 'My name is Manvell. Christopher Manvell. You and I have no quarrel, Colonel Sharpe.'

'I've got a quarrel with that piece of yellow shit at your feet.'

'Not here!' Captain Manvell warned. 'Not in public!' Duelling had been forbidden to serving officers, which meant that any duel would have to be fought in secret. Two other cavalry officers stood behind the Captain.

Lord John slowly climbed to his feet. 'I tripped,' he explained to his friend.

'Indeed.' Manvell kept his eyes fixed on Sharpe, half fearing that the Rifleman might still attack.

'You can keep the whore,' Sharpe said again to Lord John, but this time loud enough for Jane and the other spectators to hear, 'but I want my money.'

Lord John licked his lips. He knew that Sharpe's insults were more than mere anger, but a deliberate provocation to a duel. No man could hear his woman described as a whore and not fight, yet Lord John was truly terrified of the Rifleman and had no doubt who would win a duel, and so, despite the insults and despite the people who witnessed his humiliation, he nodded his acceptance of Sharpe's demand. 'I'll send you a note tomorrow,' he said humbly.

Captain Manvell was plainly astonished at Lord John's swift collapse, even disgusted by the cowardice, but had no choice but to accept it. 'Does that satisfy you, Colonel Sharpe?'

Sharpe was just as surprised at his sudden victory. He felt oddly cheated, but sheathed his sword anyway. 'You can bring the note to me at the Prince of Orange's headquarters.'

He had spoken to Lord John, but Manvell chose to answer. 'I shall act for his lordship in this matter. You have a second to whom I can present the note?'

'He does!' Peter d'Alembord spoke up from the crowd which listened from the supper room's wide entrance. Lucille, her face paled by fear, held d'Alembord's arm as he walked a few paces into the room and bowed primly to Christopher Manvell. 'My name is d'Alembord. I can be found with the Prince of Wales's Own Volunteers who are a part of Sir Colin Halkett's brigade.'

Manvell gave the smallest nod to acknowledge d'Alembord's bow. 'I shall serve you a promissory note tomorrow, Captain d'Alembord. Is that agreeable?'

'Entirely.'

Manvell thrust his own sword home, then took Lord John's elbow and led him away. Jane, watching from the entrance, had a hand over her mouth. Sharpe caught her eye for a second, then turned away as Lucille ran to him.

'I should have killed the bastard,' Sharpe growled.

'You're a fool.' Lucille brushed at the blood on his jacket, then touched his cheek.

D'Alembord, behind Lucille, waited until the spectators had drifted away. 'What happened?' he asked Sharpe.

'You heard for yourself, didn't you? The bastard collapsed.'

D'Alembord shook his head. 'What happened with Wellington? What was the news?'

Sharpe had to drag his thoughts back to the earlier events of the night. 'Napoleon's stolen a march on us. His army's just a day away from here, and ours is still scattered over half Belgium. We've been humbugged, Peter.'

D'Alembord smiled very wanly. 'Oh, my God.'

'So it's time to see how an emperor fights,' Sharpe said grimly, then he put an arm round Lucille's shoulders and steered her towards the ballroom where, because the orchestra had been engaged till dawn, the music still played and a few last couples still danced. The Highland dancers had left, taking their swords for other employment. A few girls, their escorts already gone to join their regiments, wept. The windows had been opened wide and a small breeze fluttered the candles. The remaining dancers, holding each other very close, slowly circled the floor, which was littered with discarded flowers and dance-cards and even a pair of silk gloves. A pearl necklace had broken and two liveried servants scrabbled on hands and knees to retrieve the jewels.

The music was winsome. Like the wind that guttered and blew out the candles, a bloodied man had broken through the dancers' joy to break the glittering ball into dark fragments, yet still some few couples could not bear to relinquish the last moments of peace. A young infantry major danced with his wife of just three weeks. She wept softly, while he held her and believed in the augury that this happiness could not possibly end in death on a battlefield, for such an end would be against all that was good and sweet and lovely in the world. He would live because he was in love. He clung to the thought until, reluctant, and with tears in his eyes, it was time to draw away from his love. She held his hands tight, but he smiled, freed his hands, then reached for the grey ostrich feathers she wore in her hair. The Major plucked one of the grey feathers, kissed his wife's hand, then went to find his regiment.

The Emperor had humbugged them all, and the killing would begin.

THE SECOND DAY
Friday, 16 June 1815

CHAPTER 7

At one in the morning, in the heart of the brief night, Lucille shivered in the courtyard of her Brussels lodging house. Two horses trampled nervously on the cobbles by the yard's arched entrance. The only light came from a lantern which hung in the stable doorway. Her child slept upstairs.

'Take this.' Lucille thrust a bundle towards Sharpe. 'It belonged to Xavier.'

Sharpe shook the bundle loose to reveal that it was a dark blue woollen cloak lined with scarlet silk, a luxury that had belonged to Lucille's husband. 'It's beautiful.' He felt awkward, not certain that he was worthy of the gift. He folded the cloak over his arm, then touched Lucille's cold cheek. 'I'll see you late tomorrow.'

'Maybe.' Lucille absently brushed at the dried blood on Sharpe's threadbare jacket. 'How can you tell?'

'One day to hold them,' he said lightly, 'and one day to beat them.'

'Maybe,' she said again, then, looking up into his eyes, 'and what if you lose?'

'Take a canal barge to Antwerp. I'll find you there. If it's really bad, make your way to Ostend and cross to England.'

Lucille's despondency was caused by a fear of Sharpe's death, not a British defeat, but she dared not articulate such a thought. She sensed a difference in her man; there was a remoteness in Sharpe this night which, though he tried to hide it, was very obvious to Lucille. She knew he had killed one of her countrymen the previous evening, and she supposed he was now preparing himself for all the others he would fight. She also detected a certain relief in Sharpe. Instead of wrestling with the imponderables of land and trees and drainage and crops, he was back where his skills gave him a harsh certainty. She glanced through the open gateway, her attention caught by the tramp of boots. A Scottish battalion was marching down the street, its pace dictated by the soft beat of a muffled drum. 'Maybe I should go home,' she said almost despairingly, 'to Normandy.'

Sharpe put his hands on her shoulders. 'The quickest way home for both of us is to get rid of Napoleon.'

'So you say.' She rested her cheek on his jacket. 'I love you.'

He awkwardly stroked her hair. 'I love you.'

'I don't know why you do.' She pulled away slightly. 'I'm not beautiful like Jane.'

Sharpe traced a finger down Lucille's long nose. 'She has no beauty inside herself.'

Lucille scorned that compliment with a grimace, then gave Sharpe a warning look. 'Her eyes are full of hate. Be careful.'

'There's nothing she can do now, and her man didn't dare face me in a duel.'

'Be careful, though,' Lucille insisted.

Sharpe bent and kissed her. 'Till tomorrow night, my love. Nosey will look after you till then.' He let go of her shoulders and took a pace backwards. 'Let's be moving, Patrick!'

'Whenever you're ready.' Harper, tactfully waiting just inside the stable door, appeared with his weapons and pack. He was wearing his old Rifleman's uniform, less its sergeant's stripes. He had insisted on accompanying

Sharpe to Quatre Bras, not to fight, he said, but just for the chance of glimpsing the Emperor.

'You take care of yourself, Patrick!' Lucille called in English.

'You'll not catch me anywhere near the fighting, ma'am. I've got too much sense for that, so I have.' He had all his old weapons about him, all of them lovingly cleaned and oiled and ready.

Lucille reached up and touched Sharpe's cheek. 'Go with God.'

'And with your love?'

'You know you have that.'

He hated such a parting. Words were hopeless. Sharpe suddenly feared the loss of Lucille and he thought how love made a man fearful and vulnerable. His throat felt thick, so he just turned away and took the reins that Harper held ready. He gripped the pommel, pushed his left boot into the cold stirrup iron, and heaved up into the Hussar saddle with its high spoon that offered support during long hours of riding. His sore thighs complained at being back on a horse. He fiddled his right boot into its stirrup, touched the rifle stock superstitiously, pushed the sword into a comfortable position, then rolled the cloak into a bundle that he jammed under the rifle holster's strap. He looked for a last time at Lucille. 'Kiss the child for me.'

'I'll see you tomorrow night.' She forced a confident smile.

The dog whined a protest as Sharpe rode away. The Rifleman ducked under the arch, then waited as Harper closed the two heavy gates. The Irishman swung himself into the saddle, then followed Sharpe in the footsteps of the Highlanders.

Sharpe and Harper were going back to war.

In the same short darkness of that midsummer night

Lord John Rossendale took a road leading west from Brussels towards a rendezvous with the Earl of Uxbridge and the British cavalry. Lord John did not ride his horse, but rather drove in a gleaming open cabriolet that he had brought from London. Harris, his coachman, was up on the driving box, while Lord John's groom and valet were bringing on the saddle horses behind. Captain Christopher Manvell had ridden on ahead. Lord John had hoped that his friend would accompany him, but he sensed how much Manvell despised him for so easily surrendering to Sharpe's threat.

Rossendale closed his eyes and silently cursed. He was in turmoil, trapped between honour and beauty. It was not Manvell's displeasure that worried him, but Jane's anger. She had lacerated Lord John for his cowardice. He remembered a time when Jane had feared a duel as much as he, but now she seemed more eager to protect her money than Lord John's life.

'And you have no right to promise him any money!' Jane had reminded Lord John when they had regained the privacy of their hotel suite. 'It is not your money, but mine!'

In truth, if the money belonged to anyone, it was the property of the Emperor's brother, Joseph Bonaparte, erstwhile King of Spain and the Indies, who had lost his fortune with the battle of Vitoria. King Joseph had fled and the British had swarmed over his supply wagons where some men, Sharpe and Harper among them, had become rich. Sharpe had taken a royal fortune off the battlefield, and it was that fortune which Jane had stolen from him, and much of which she had already spent on a London house and on silks and on furniture and on jewels and on Lord John's debts, and on silverware and gold plate and Chinese wallpaper and on lapdogs and satin and on the cabriolet in which Lord John now rode towards the cavalry and battle. It was that same fortune which, to save his life, Lord John had promised to return to Sharpe.

'You will not!' Jane had said after the shameful confrontation at the ball.

'You'd have me fight him?' Lord John had asked.

'If you were a man,' Jane had sneered, 'you would not ask the question.'

Lord John, recognizing the horrid truth in her mockery, had wondered why love's happiness was so easily soured. 'I can fight him, if you insist.'

'I don't insist!'

'I can fight him, though.' Lord John had sounded hopeless for he knew he would lose a duel against Sharpe.

Jane had suddenly staunched her anger and melted Lord John with a smile. 'All I want', she had said, 'is the chance to marry you. And once we are married the money will be yours by right. But we cannot marry until . . .'

She did not need to go on. Lord John knew that litany. They could not marry while Sharpe lived. Therefore Sharpe must die, and if he was not to be killed in a duel, then he must be taken care of in another way and, in the darkness as Lord John had said his farewells, Jane had urged him to the other way.

'Harris?' Lord John now called to his coachman.

'I can hear you, my lord!' Harris shouted from the cabriolet's driving seat.

'Did you ever hear of officers being murdered in battle?'

Harris, who had been a cavalry trooper before a French cannonball had crushed his left foot at the battle of Corunna, laughed at the naïvety of the question. 'You hear about it all the time, my lord.' Harris paused for a few seconds while he negotiated the cabriolet over some deep ruts in the high road. 'I remember a major who begged us not to kill him, my lord. He knew we couldn't abide his ways, and he was sure one of us was going to take a hack at him, so he begged for the honour of being killed by the enemy instead.'

'Was he?'

'No. A mucky little devil called Shaughnessy shoved a sword into his back.' Harris laughed at the memory. 'Clean old job he made of it, straight out of the drill book!'

'And no one saw?'

'No one who was going to make a malarkey out of it, my lord. Why should they? No one liked the Major. Not that you need worry, my lord.'

'I wasn't concerned for myself, Harris.'

Harris plucked a bugle from the seat beside him and sounded a blaring note of warning. A battalion of infantry that was marching towards the cabriolet shuffled onto the grass verge. The men, their faces sallow in the small light of the cabriolet's twin lamps, stared reproachfully at the wealthy officer whose carriage clipped by so smartly behind its matched pair of bays. The battalion's officers, under the misapprehension that such an equipage must contain a senior officer, saluted.

Lord John said nothing more of murder. He knew he had behaved badly this night, that he should have faced Sharpe and accepted the challenge. He had lost face, he had lost honour, yet now he flirted with the thought of murder, which was beyond all honour, and he did it solely for a woman.

Lord John leaned his head back on the cabriolet's folded leather hood. Some of his friends said he was bewitched, but if he was, it was a willing enthralment. He remembered how fondly Jane had said farewell after her anger had abated, and the memory made him lift his hand to see, in the first creeping light of dawn, the small smear of rouge that still remained on his forefinger. He kissed it. Marriage, he thought, would solve everything. No more deception, no more circumspection, no more begging Jane for funds, and no more disdain from society for a golden girl who surely deserved the rewards of marriage. Jane's happiness would take just one death; one death on a field of slaughter, one more corpse among the battalions of the dead.

And if it was done properly, no one need ever know.

And if, in the morning, Lord John withdrew his promise to repay the money and accepted the challenge of a duel, then the world would accept him as a man of brave honour. And if Sharpe was to die in battle before the duel could be fought, then the honour would be untarnished. Lord John had behaved badly this night, but he knew that all could be repaired, all won, and all made good, and all for a girl of winsome, heart-breaking beauty.

Behind Lord John the first beam of sunlight struck like a golden lance across the world's rim. It was dawn in Belgium. Clouds still heaped in the west, but over the crossroads at Quatre Bras, and above a stream just north of Fleurus, the sky was clear as glass. Larks tumbled in song above the roads where three hundred and thirty-eight thousand men, in the armies of Prussia, Britain and France, converged on death.

'God save Ireland.' Harper reined in at Quatre Bras. In front of him, and smeared across the southern sky, was the smoke of thousands of camp-fires. The smoke betrayed an army encamped. The French troops were hidden by the folds of ground and by the woods and high crops, but the smoke was evidence enough that thousands of men had closed on Frasnes in the night to support the battalion of French skirmishers who had been baulked the previous evening.

Closer to Sharpe and Harper, around the crossroads of Quatre Bras, more men had gathered; all of them Dutch-Belgians of the Prince of Orange's Corps. There was a smattering of musket-fire from far beyond the stream, evidence that the rival picquet lines of skirmishers were bidding each other a lethal good morning. The Baron Rebecque, waiting with a group of the Prince's aides at the crossroads, seemed relieved to see Sharpe. 'We're concentrating the corps here, instead of at Nivelles.'

'Quite right, too!' Sharpe said fervently.

Rebecque unfolded a sketch map he had made. 'The French are in Frasnes, and we're holding all the farms beyond the stream. Except this one by the ford. We'll only garrison that if we're forced back to it.'

'I'd garrison it now,' Sharpe recommended.

'Not enough men.' Rebecque folded his map. 'So far only eight thousand infantry have arrived, with sixteen guns and no cavalry.'

Sharpe cast a professional eye at the smoke of the French cooking fires. 'They've got twenty thousand, Rebecque.'

'I was hoping you wouldn't tell me that.' Rebecque, accepting Sharpe's experienced estimate without question, smiled grimly.

'So if I can make a suggestion?'

'My dear Sharpe, anything.'

'Tell our skirmishers to hold their fire. We don't want to provoke the Crapauds into nastiness, do we?' There was no sense in inviting battle from a much stronger enemy; it was better to delay any fighting in the hope of more allied troops arriving to even the numbers who faced each other south of Frasnes.

The sky above Quatre Bras was dirtied by the camp-fires, but to the east the rising sun betrayed a much vaster quantity of rising woodsmoke. That larger smear in the sky showed where the Prussian army faced the main force of the French and where the day's real battle would be fought. The French would be trying to defeat the Prussians before the British and Dutch could come to their aid, while the Prussians, to be certain of victory, needed Wellington's troops to march from Quatre Bras and assault the Emperor's left flank. But that rescue mission had been stopped dead by the presence of the twenty thousand Frenchmen encamped in Frasnes who had been sent by the Emperor to make sure that the allied armies did not combine. All that the French needed to do was take the crossroads at Quatre Bras. Sharpe reckoned it could not take the enemy longer than an hour to overrun the fragile line of Dutch-Belgian troops, and in one further hour they could have fortified the crossroads to make them impassable to the British.

The French were thus one hour from victory; just one hour from separating the allied armies, yet as the sun climbed higher and as the smoke of the dying fires thinned, the French made no move to advance on the crossroads. They did not even follow the retreating Dutch skirmishers, but seemed content to let the morning's skirmish die to nothing. Sharpe looked to the north and west, searching for the tell-tale drifts of dust that would speak of reinforcements hurrying towards the threatened crossroads. No dust showed above the roads yet, evidence that the French had plenty of time to make their attack.

The Prince of Orange arrived three hours after dawn, excited at the prospect of action. 'Morning, Sharpe! A bright one, isn't it! Rebecque, all well?'

Rebecque attempted to tell the Prince how his troops were deployed, but the Prince was too restless merely to listen. 'Show me, Rebecque, show me! Let's go for a gallop. All of us!' He gestured to his whole staff who dutifully fell in behind Rebecque and the Prince as they spurred away from the crossroads towards the south. The Prince waved happily at a party of soldiers who drew water from the stream, then twisted in his saddle to shout at Sharpe. 'I expected to see you at the ball last night, Sharpe!'

'I arrived very late, sir.'

'Did you dance?'

'Regrettably not, sir.'

'Nor me. Duty called.' The Prince galloped past the deserted Gemioncourt farm, through a bivouacked Dutch brigade, and did not rein in till he had passed the forward Dutch picquets and could see clear down the paved highway into the village of Frasnes. There had to be some enemy skirmishers close by, yet the Prince blithely ignored their threat. His staff officers waited a few yards to the rear as the young man stared towards the enemy encampment. 'Sharpe?'

Sharpe walked his horse forward. 'Sir?'

'How many of the devils are facing us, would you say?'

Very few enemy troops were actually in sight. A battery of guns stood at the edge of the village, some cavalry horses stood unsaddled in the street beyond, and a battalion of infantry was bivouacked in a field to the right of the guns, but otherwise the enemy was hidden, and so Sharpe stuck with his earlier estimate. 'Twenty thousand, sir.'

The Prince nodded. 'Just what I'd say. Splendid.' He smiled genially at Sharpe. 'And just when are you going to appear in a Dutch uniform?'

Sharpe was taken aback. 'Soon, sir.'

'Soon? I've been requesting that small courtesy for weeks! I want to see you in proper uniform today, Sharpe, today!' The Prince shook an admonishing finger at the Rifleman then took out his telescope to stare at the battery of French guns. It was hard to see what calibre the cannon were for the air was already hot enough to shimmer and blur the details of the far guns. 'It's going to be a hot day,' the Prince complained. His yellowish skin glistened with sweat. He was in a blue uniform coat that was thickly encrusted with gold loops and edged with black astrakhan fur. At his hip hung a massively heavy sabre with an ivory hilt. The Prince's vanity had made him dress for a winter's campaign on what threatened to be the summer's hottest day yet.

The sultry air pressed heavily on the men who guarded the farms that marked the perimeter of the Dutch position. If that perimeter was broken, there was still the Gemioncourt farm by the ford which could be an anchor to a defensive line, but once Gemioncourt was captured there was nothing between the French and the crossroads. Sharpe prayed that the French would go on waiting, and that the British troops who were marching desperately to reinforce the outnumbered defenders at Quatre Bras reached the crossroads in time.

By eight o'clock the French had still not attacked. At nine o'clock the Dutch troops still waited. At ten the Duke of Wellington reached the crossroads and, content that nothing yet threatened the Dutch troops, galloped eastwards to find the Prussians.

The morning inched onwards. It seemed impossible that the French still hesitated. At intervals an enemy horseman might appear at the edge of the village to gaze through a spyglass at the Dutch positions, but no attacks followed such reconnaissances, no skirmishers wormed their way through the fields, and no cannon crashed shell or roundshot at the fragile Dutch lines.

At midday the French still waited. The heat was now oppressive. The western clouds had thickened and the old wounds in Sharpe's leg and shoulder began to ache; a sure prophecy of rain. He lunched with the Prince of Orange's staff in the remains of an orchard behind the farm at the crossroads. Harper, of whose status none of the Dutch was quite certain, shared the princely cold chicken, hard-boiled eggs and red wine. The Prince, momentarily forgetting his orders for Sharpe to change into Dutch uniform, dominated the luncheon conversation as he eagerly expressed his wish that the French would attack before the Duke returned from his meeting with the Prussians, for then the Prince could defeat the enemy with only the help of his faithful Dutch troops. The Prince dreamed of a great Netherlands victory, with himself as its hero. He saw pliant girls offering him the laurels of victory before they fainted before his conquering feet. He could not wait to begin such a triumph, and prayed that the French would offer him the chance of glory before the arrival of any British reinforcements.

And in the early afternoon, and before the hurrying British reinforcements could reach the crossroads, the Prince's wish was granted. An enemy cannon banged its signal.

And the French, at last, were advancing to battle.

'Was that a gun? I swear that was a gun. Would you say that was a gun, Vine?' Lieutenant-Colonel Joseph Ford, commanding officer of the Prince of Wales's Own Volunteers, twisted in his saddle and stared anxiously at his senior Major who, because he was deaf, had heard nothing. Major Vine, thus unable to confirm or deny the sound which had so alarmed his Colonel, merely offered a bad-tempered scowl as a reply, so Colonel Ford looked past him to seek the opinion of the Captain of his light company. 'Was that a gun, d'Alembord? Would you say that was a gun?'

D'Alembord, his head aching with hangover, still wore his white dancing breeches and buckled shoes from the night before. He did not want to speak to anyone, let alone Ford, but he made an effort and confirmed that the Colonel had indeed heard a cannon's report, but very far away and with its sound much muted by the humid air.

'We're going to be late!' Ford worried.

Just at this moment d'Alembord did not care how late they would be. He just wanted to lie down somewhere very dark and very cool and very silent. He wished the Colonel would go away, but he knew Ford would keep pestering until he received some reassurance. 'The brigade marched on time, sir,' he told the worried Ford, 'and no one can expect more of us.'

'There's another gun! D'you hear it, Vine? There! And another! 'Pon my soul, d'Alembord, but it's begun, it's begun indeed!' Ford's eyes, behind their small thick spectacles, betrayed excited alarm. Ford was a decent man, and a kind one, but he had a worrying nervousness that aggravated d'Alembord's patience. The Colonel fretted about the opinions of senior officers, the diligence of his junior officers, and the loyalty of his non-commissioned officers. He worried about the spare ammunition, about the ability of the men to hear orders in battle, and about the morality of the wives who followed the marching column like a gypsy rabble. He agonized about losing his spectacles, for Ford was as short-sighted as a mole, and he worried about losing his battalion's colours, and about losing his hair. He was ever anxious about the weather and, when he could think of nothing else to be anxious about, he became worried that he must have forgotten something important that should have been causing him worry.

The ever-anxious Ford had been appointed to replace Major Richard Sharpe as commanding officer of the battalion, which of itself was cause for the Colonel to worry, for Joseph Ford was keenly aware that the Rifleman had been a most competent and experienced soldier. Nor did it help Ford that many of his junior officers and a good third of his rankers had seen far more fighting than he had himself. Ford had been appointed to the battalion in the dying weeks of the last war, and he had only experienced a few skirmishes, yet now he must lead the Prince of Wales's Own Volunteers against the Emperor's field army, a realization that naturally occasioned Ford constant trepidation. 'But at least', he comforted his officers, 'it's a veteran battalion.'

'It is that, Colonel, it is that.' Major Vine, a small, strutting, dark-eyed, bad-tempered stoat of a man, always agreed with the Colonel when he managed to hear what the Colonel had actually said.

Ford, distrusting such easy agreement, would seek support for his views from the more experienced officers of the battalion, but those officers, such as Peter d'Alembord, doubted whether the Prince of Wales's Own Volunteers could truthfully be called a veteran battalion. A third of its men were new recruits who had seen no fighting, almost another third had seen as little as the Colonel, while only the rest, like d'Alembord, had actually faced a French army in open battle. Still, that experienced third was the battalion's backbone; the men whose voices would stiffen the ranks and give the Colonel the victory he needed in his opening engagement. And that was all d'Alembord prayed for at this moment, that Ford would learn success fast and thus calm his worried fears.

D'Alembord also prayed for a swift and overwhelming victory for himself. He wanted to return to England where a bride and a house and a secure civilian future waited for him. His bride was called Anne Nickerson, the daughter of an Essex landowner whose reluctant consent to an army marriage had turned to wholehearted approval when Peter d'Alembord had put up his captaincy for sale.

Then, just as d'Alembord was about to sell his commission and retire to one of his prospective father-in-law's farms, Napoleon had returned to France. Colonel Ford, worried that he was losing his veteran Captain of skirmishers, had begged d'Alembord to stay for the impending campaign and implicit in the Colonel's plea was a promise that d'Alembord would receive the next vacant majority in the battalion. That enticement was sufficient. The captaincy would sell for fifteen hundred pounds which was a good enough fortune for any young man contemplating marriage, but a majority would fetch two thousand six hundred pounds, and so d'Alembord, with some misgivings, but reassured by the prospects of a fine marriage portion, had agreed to Ford's request.

Now, ahead of d'Alembord, the gun-fire rumbled like dull thunder to remind him that the two thousand six hundred pounds must be earned the hard way. D'Alembord, contemplating how much happiness he now stood to lose, shivered with a premonition, then told himself that he had always feared the worst before every battle.

Joseph Ford, frightened because he was about to fight his first real battle, worried that either he or his men might not do their duty and, as ever when worry overwhelmed him, he snatched off his spectacles and polished their lenses on his sash. He believed that such a commonplace action expressed a careless insouciance, whereas it really betrayed his fretting nervousness.

Yet, this day as they marched towards the gun-fire, the men of the Prince of Wales's Own Volunteers were oblivious of their Colonel's fears. They trudged on, breathing the dust of the dry summer road that had been shuffled up by the boots ahead, and they wondered if there would be an issue of rum before the fighting began, or whether they would be too late for the fighting and would instead be billeted in some soft Belgian village where the girls would flirt and the food would be plentiful.

'It's sounding bad,' Private Charlie Weller spoke of the distant gun-fire, which did not really sound so very awful yet, but Weller was feeling a flicker of nervousness and wanted the relief of conversation.

'We've heard worse than that, Charlie,' Daniel Hagman,

the oldest man in the light company, said, but he spoke tiredly, dutifully, unthinkingly. Hagman was a kind man, who recognized Charlie Weller's apprehension, but the day was too hot, the sun too fierce, and the dust too parching for kindness to have much of a chance.

Major Vine curbed his horse to watch the ten companies march past. He snapped at the men to pick up their feet and straighten their shoulders. They took no notice. They did not like Vine, recognizing that the Major despised them as a lumpen, dull ugly mass, but the men themselves knew better; they were Wellington's infantry, the finest of the best, and they were marching east and south to where a pall of gun-smoke was forming like a dark cloud over a far crossroads and to where the guns cleared their throats to beckon men to battle.

The French attack began with a cannonade which punched billows of grey-black smoke into the hazing dancing air above the village of Frasnes. The Prince of Orange, unable to resist the lure of danger, galloped from the crossroads to be with those troops closest to the enemy, and the Prince's staff, their luncheon brutally interrupted by the French gun-fire, hurried after him.

Sharpe was among the staff officers who trotted their horses down the Charleroi road, past the Gemioncourt farm by the ford, and so on up the shallow hill until they reached the infantry brigade which guarded against any frontal attack up the high road.

The French guns were firing at the flanks of the Prince's position; aiming at the farmhouses to east and west. Nothing seemed to be moving on the road itself, though Sharpe supposed the French must have some skirmishers concealed in the fields of long rye.

'They'll be coming straight up the middle, won't they?'

Sharpe turned to see that Harper had joined him. 'I thought you were staying well away from any danger?'

'What danger, for God's sake? No one's firing at us now.' Harper had rescued the cold carcass of a roast chicken from the Prince's interrupted lunch, and now tossed Sharpe a leg. 'They look bloody strange, don't they?'

He was referring to the brigade of Dutch-Belgian infantry that was spread in four ranks either side of the road to block a direct attack from Frasnes. The strangeness lay in the men's uniforms which were the standard French infantry uniforms. Only the eagle badge on their shakos had been changed, replaced by a 'W' for King William of the Netherlands, but otherwise the Dutch-Belgians were dressed exactly like the men they were doubtless about to fight.

'You know what to do?' the Prince asked the brigade commander in his native French.

'If we can't hold them, sir, we fall back on Gemioncourt.'

'Exactly!' The farm by the ford was the last bastion before the vital crossroads. Loopholes had already been made in the stone walls of Gemioncourt's huge barns which, like the buildings of so many of the isolated farms in the low countries, were joined together and protected by a high stone wall, making the whole farm into a massively strong fortress.

'Something's stirring, eh?' The Prince, reverting to English, was elated by an outburst of musket-fire which sounded from somewhere in front of the Dutch line. The musketry was not the huge eruptions of platoon fire, but rather the smaller sporadic snapping of skirmishers which betrayed that the French Voltigeurs were closing on the Dutch light troops, but both sets of skirmishers were well hidden from the Prince and his staff by the tall crops.

'Funny to hear that sound again, isn't it?' Harper commented drily.

'Did you miss it?'

'Never thought I would,' the Irishman said sadly, 'but I did.'

Sharpe remembered the familiar skill with which he had killed the French Lieutenant in this very rye field. 'It's the thing we're good at, Patrick. Maybe we're doomed to be soldiers forever?'

'You maybe, but not me. I've a tavern and a horse-thieving trade to keep me busy.' Harper frowned at the Belgians in their French uniforms. 'Do you think these buggers will fight?'

'They'd bloody better,' Sharpe said grimly. The brigade, with its supporting artillery, was all that lay between the French and victory. The Dutch-Belgians certainly looked prepared to fight. They had trampled down the rye ahead of their line to make a killing ground some sixty yards deep and, judging by the sound of their musketry, the Dutch-Belgian skirmishers were fighting with a brisk energy.

The two wings of the Dutch-Belgian brigade stretched a half-mile on either side of the highway while, athwart the road itself, was a battery of six Dutch nine-pounder cannons. The gunners had parked their limbers and ammunition wagons in the field behind Sharpe. The guns were loaded, their portfires smoking gently in readiness for the French.

'Four-legged bastards, off to the right,' Harper said warningly, and Sharpe turned to see a troop of enemy cavalry trotting towards the Dutch right flank. The horsemen were green-coated Lancers with high helmets topped with forward sweeping black plumes. They were still a good distance off, at least a half-mile, and were not yet any threat to the Prince's troops.

The Prince had positioned himself just behind the six guns of the Dutch battery. Rebecque, staying close to his master, gravely inspected one of the cannon almost as if he had never seen such an object before, then, suddenly afflicted by hay fever, he sneezed. The Prince muttered, 'Bless you,' then stood in his stirrups to gaze at the Lancers through a telescope. The French cannons abruptly ceased fire. The only sounds now were the intermittent crackle of the skirmishers' muskets and the ragged music of a Dutch band. The Prince's horse whinnied. Rebecque's pawed at the trampled rye stalks. This was the silence before battle.

'Stand ready!' The Prince, unable to bear the quiet, spurred his horse towards the closest Belgian battalion. 'You'll see the enemy infantry soon!' he shouted at the men. 'A few volleys will see them off, so stand firm!'

'The bloody gunners are just changing their aim,' Harper said scathingly after Sharpe had translated the Prince's words.

'Probably,' Sharpe said. He patted his horse's neck.

Rebecque suddenly sneezed again and, as if it had been a word of command, the French batteries resumed their cannonade. Harper had been right, they had merely been changing their aim, and now the French gunners concentrated their shots at the centre of the field. There were more enemy guns firing than before. Sharpe counted twenty-four gouts of smoke in the first salvo.

The French gunners were masked by the rye, but some of their balls struck home in the waiting Dutch battalions. One roundshot bounced cleanly between two of the Dutch guns and somehow missed every single horseman surrounding the Prince. The artillery Colonel asked for permission to return the fire, but the Prince ordered him to wait till the enemy infantry was in sight.

The French batteries fired another volley. Sharpe saw the blossoming smoke a fraction before the sound punched the air. More men were struck in the Dutch battalions, but most balls went overhead for the French gunners were firing a fraction too high. Sharpe saw one cannon-ball's passage marked by the flickering of the rye stalks in a darkening line that shot at extraordinary speed across the field behind him. Another roundshot went close enough to Sharpe to sound like a sudden harsh whip-cracking wind. If the balls had been fired higher still the sound would have rumbled like a cask being rolled over floorboards.

'You should go back to the crossroads,' Sharpe told Harper.

'Aye, I will.' Harper did not move.

The Prince cantered towards the Dutch-Belgian battalions on the right-hand side of the road. He had drawn his massive sabre. He called for Rebecque to accompany him. The Baron, his eyes streaming with the hay fever, sneezed once more and the French guns magically ceased fire.

Men wounded by the cannon-fire were screaming and the band was playing, but it seemed like a rather ominous quiet.

Then the French drums began.

'I never thought I'd hear Old Trousers being played again,' Harper said wistfully. It was the sound of French infantry being drummed to the attack. A mass of drums was being beaten, but the drummers, like the approaching infantry, were hidden by the tall crop of rye. There was something curiously menacing in the repetitive drumbeats that seemed to come from nowhere.

Then Sharpe saw the far crops being trampled flat and he knew that each patch of collapsing rye betrayed the advance of a French column. He counted three formations directly to the front. Each column was a solid formation of men aimed like a battering ram at the Dutch line. A crash of musketry off to the right flank betrayed that the farms to the west were under attack, but here in the centre, where the road led enticingly to the crossroads, the enemy was still hidden. Hidden but not silent. The drums suddenly paused and the columns shouted their great war cry. '*Vive l'Empereur!*' The sound of that cheer stopped the Dutch band cold. The musicians lowered their instruments and stared into the concealing field where the rye seemed to move as though an invisible giant's footsteps crushed it down.

The French gunners opened fire again, this time using short-barrelled howitzers that fired shells in a high arc over the heads of their own columns, and which exploded in small dirty gouts of flame and smoke.

The first French skirmishers were appearing at the edge of the trampled area. The Dutch skirmishers had yielded the field, retreating to their battalions, so now the scattering of enemy Voltigeurs could kneel unmolested at the rye's edge and fire at the waiting defenders. Men began to fall. Others screamed. Some died. The main enemy attack was still nothing but a sound of blended menace; a crashing noise in the rye, a thump of drums and a deep-throated cheer.

Rebecque galloped back towards the Dutch battery, shouting at its Colonel to open fire on the concealed columns, but the Colonel was staring at one of his officers who had been killed by a skirmisher's bullet. The officer lay on the chalky road where his blood showed remarkably bright against the white dust. Other gunners were falling. A bullet clanged monstrously loud on a brass barrel and ricocheted up into the sky.

'Fire!' Rebecque shouted angrily at the gunners.

The artillery Colonel jerked round, stared at Rebecque for an instant, then bellowed his own orders, but instead of ordering a killing volley into the tall rye, he commanded his men to retreat. The drivers whipped the horse teams onto the road while the gun crews man-handled the weapons back to hook them on to their limbers. The huge ammunition wagons set off for the crossroads, their massive iron-rimmed wheels digging great gouges into the road's surface. The gun teams began to follow, but two teams collided, their limber wheels locked, and there was a sudden tangle of cursing drivers, stalled cannon and frightened horses.

Sharpe had spurred forward. 'Where are you going?' he shouted in French across the chaos.

'Back!' the gunner Colonel shouted over the noise of an exploding howitzer shell.

'Stop at the farm! Stop at Gemioncourt!' Sharpe knew the panic could not be controlled here, where the French columns filled the air with menace, but perhaps the sturdy walls of Gemioncourt would give these gunners some necessary reassurance.

'Back! Back the gun away!' The Colonel slashed with his riding crop as he tried to disentangle the trapped limbers. Another volley of French howitzer-fire miraculously missed the mêlée of gunners and horses which, stung by the shells' threat, magically disentangled itself. The fleeing Dutch guns crashed up onto the road, their chains and buckets swinging. Those gunners who had no riding place on the guns or limbers were running down the verges in an undisciplined retreat.

'Stop at the farm!' Sharpe bellowed after the gunner Colonel.

A howitzer shell screamed down to smash the wheel of the last gun limber. For a second the shell lay with a smoking fuse amidst the wreckage of the wheel, then it crashed apart in a deafening explosion. One horse died instantly, its guts flung red and wet across the road. Another screaming beast collapsed on broken hind legs. The rest of the team, panicking, tried to gallop free and only slewed the broken limber round. A gunner fell off his seat on the ammunition box and was crushed by the limber's scraping violence. He clawed at the broken wheel that first dragged him across, then pinned him to the road. The other gunners ignored him; instead they slashed at the traces with swords or knives, eventually freeing the four live horses which galloped wild-eyed towards Gemioncourt. The dying horse was mercifully shot by an officer who then took off after his men, abandoning the gun.

The man under the limber was also abandoned. He was left screaming in a terrible wailing sob that made the nearest infantry look nervously round. Harper rode up to the man and saw the broken wheel spokes impaled in his belly and groin. He took the rifle off his shoulder, aimed it, and shot once.

The French skirmishers cheered their victory over the panicked gun teams, then turned their muskets on the nearest Belgian battalions. The Prince of Orange was shouting at his men to stand fast, to wait, but the attrition of the skirmishers was fraying their nerves. They began to edge backwards.

'They'll not stand!' Harper warned Sharpe.

'The buggers bloody well will.' Sharpe spurred towards the nearest Belgians, but before he could even get close to the battalion a French column burst out of the rye and the Belgians, without even firing a volley, turned and ran. One moment they were a formed battalion and the next they were a mob. Sharpe reined in. Two howitzer shells exploded a few paces from his horse, both blasts beginning small fires among the rye. The French were cheering. The Prince was hitting at the running men with the flat of his sabre, but they feared an emperor far more than they feared a prince and so they kept on running. The other battalions were infected by the panic and also fled. The French skirmishers turned their force on the Prince's staff.

Rebecque, his eyes red and swollen from hay fever, reined his horse alongside Sharpe. 'This isn't a very impressive beginning, is it?'

'Get out of here, sir!' Sharpe could hear the hiss and whiplash of musket bullets all around them.

'Can you find out what's happening to Saxe-Weimar?' Rebecque asked.

Sharpe nodded. 'I will, sir! But you go! Now!' The first French skirmishers were running forward but, instead of tackling the staff officers who still lingered close to the Dutch position, they laid their hands on the abandoned gun, the first trophy of their attack.

A trumpet sounded behind the column and a Dutch aide shouted a warning of enemy cavalry. The Prince turned his horse and galloped north towards Gemioncourt and Quatre Bras. Rebecque galloped after the Prince, while Sharpe and Harper rode west. All along the centre of the position the Dutch had collapsed, leaving a great inviting hole into which the French could swarm, yet from the far right flank there still came the sound of reassuring volleys, proof that Saxe-Weimar's men were defending staunchly.

Prince Bernhard's battalions, which had held the crossroads the night before, now protected it again. They were retreating from the French attack, but they were not running. Instead they were marching backwards and pausing every few steps to fire steady and effective volleys at their French attackers. Those Frenchmen, Sharpe noticed, had deployed from column into a line that overlapped and outnumbered Saxe-Weimar's brigade, yet the Nassauers were fighting well. Better still, instead of retreating back to the crossroads, they were going to the cover of the dark wood which ran like a bastion down the left flank of the French route to Quatre Bras. If the Prince could hold the wood, and the centre was somehow saved, there was still a chance.

It was a very slight chance, a mere wisp of straw snatched against an overwhelming disaster, for Sharpe could not see how any general, let alone a pimpled prince, could reform the broken troops of the centre and stop the French from sweeping forward to take the crossroads. And once the crossroads were taken, then no British troops could reach the Prussians and thus the armies would be irrevocably split and the Emperor would have won his campaign.

'We're going back!' Sharpe shouted at Harper.

They turned their horses away from Saxe-Weimar's men who were now edging the treeline with deadly musketry. Sharpe and Harper trotted northwards, staying a few hundred yards ahead of the advancing French. To their left was the long forbidding wood with its tangle of trees and stubborn defenders. In the centre was Gemioncourt farm which should have been a fortress to hold up the French, but was now empty because the Belgian guns and infantry had fled straight past the farm, thus yielding its strong walls and loopholed barns to the enemy. Far ahead of Sharpe was the crossroads itself where the dark mass of fugitives was milling in confusion, while to the right, and acting somewhat as another bastion, was a smaller wood and a handful of cottages.

'Look! Look!' Harper was standing in his stirrups, pointing and cheering at the smaller wood to the right. 'God bless the bastards! Well done, lads!' For in that far wood, which protected the road that ran towards the Prussian army, were Riflemen. Greenjackets. The best of the Goddamn best. The British reinforcements had started to arrive.

But behind Sharpe and Harper the victorious French marched on, and between them and the crossroads there was nothing.

CHAPTER 8

The Prince of Orange, blithely disregarding that nearly half of his troops had fled the field, greeted the Duke of Wellington with good news. 'We're holding the woods!' he announced in a tone that implied victory was thereby guaranteed.

The Duke, returning from Ligny where the Prussians waited for Napoleon's attack, cast a cold eye on the fugitives who streamed northwards towards Brussels, then turned a grave face on the excited Prince. 'The woods?' The Duke's polite request for a more precise report was icy.

'Over there.' The Prince pointed vaguely towards the right flank. 'Isn't that so, Rebecque?'

Rebecque deferred to Sharpe, who had actually visited the right flank. 'Prince Bernhard's brigade retreated into the woods, sir. They're holding the treeline.'

The Duke nodded curt acknowledgement, then urged his horse a few paces forward so he could survey the ruin he had inherited from the Prince of Orange. The Belgian troops had been driven from all the forward farms and, even more disastrously, had failed to garrison Gemioncourt. French cavalry, artillery and infantry had already advanced as far as the stream and it could only be a matter of moments before they thrust a strong attack at the vital crossroads. The only good news was that Prince Bernhard of Saxe-Weimar's men held the woods on the right, thus denying the French the shelter of the trees as they attacked the crossroads, but that slim advantage would count for nothing unless the Duke could construct another defensive line to protect the highway.

The materials for that line were at last arriving. The Riflemen that Harper had seen were the vanguard of Sir Thomas Picton's Fifth Division. The rest of that division was now marching through the crossroads and past the remnants of the dispirited Belgians.

'I promised Blücher we'd march to his aid,' the Duke greeted Sir Thomas Picton, 'but only if we weren't attacked here.' A French gun fired a ranging shot from Gemioncourt and the ball skipped off the road, past the Duke and crashed into a wall of the farm at the crossroads. 'It seems the Prussians will have to fight without us today,' the Duke said drily, then gestured towards the fields which lay to the left of Quatre Bras. 'Your men to line the road there, Sir Thomas, with your right flank in front of the crossroads.'

Lieutenant-General Sir Thomas Picton, a burly and bad-tempered man who had fought gallantly through Spain, glared at the Duke. 'I'll not take orders from that bloody little Dutch boy.'

'You will take orders from me, Picton, and not from His Royal Highness. I quite agree. May I trouble you now to obey those orders?'

Picton, dressed in a top hat and a civilian coat that looked like a farmer's cast-off, obeyed. His infantry marched through the disorganized Dutch battalions and took their station just south of the Nivelles road. Closest to the crossroads was the 92nd, a Highland battalion in kilts, cath-dath hose and black plumed bonnets. Next to them were more Highlanders, the 42nd or Black Watch, who wore a dark plaid and red hackles, and whose officers flaunted vultures' feathers in their caps and carried lethal broadswords. Next to them were the 44th, the East Essex, placid country men in coats of yellow-faced scarlet. All three battalions were veterans, immune to French drums and French cheers, and content to smoke their short clay pipes as they waited to see what the day would bring from the long fields of rye.

The French batteries had been moved forward from Frasnes to the slopes above Gemioncourt. Their gunners now made the last adjustments to their cannons' elevating screws, while the infantry, which had taken the battle-field's centre with scarce a scratch to themselves, rested in the rye. The French seemed to have no sense of urgency, perhaps believing the battle for Quatre Bras already won. Seven miles to the east another and larger battle had begun, evidenced by the sudden and overwhelming sound of cannon salvos that rolled and punched across the intervening countryside. The Emperor had launched his attack on the Prussians.

The first batteries of British artillery reached Quatre Bras and were ordered to unlimber at the crossroads. Almost immediately the gunners came under strong musket-fire from French skirmishers who had crept forward in the long rye. The enemy Voltigeurs were especially thick in the wedge of field between the highway and the woods where Saxe-Weimar's men kept up their stubborn resistance. The Highlanders sent their light companies forward to beat back the French.

Sharpe was a skirmisher himself and he watched the light companies' battle with a professional eye. The job of the skirmisher was simple enough. A battle line was a mass of close-packed men who could fire a deadly weight of metal in disciplined volleys, but to upset those men and thin their ranks, the skirmishers were sent ahead like a swarm of wasps to sting and unsettle them. The best way to defeat the skirmishers was with other skirmishers, the two swarms meeting in a private battle between the lines. It was a battle that the British were accustomed to winning against the French, but today the French seemed to have deployed far more skirmishers than usual. The Highlanders made a spirited attack, but were held up at the field's margin by the sheer weight of French musket-fire that smoked and flickered out of the rye.

'There's thousands of the buggers!' Harper had never seen a French skirmish line so overwhelming in numbers.

'I thought you were staying out of trouble?' Sharpe had to raise his voice over the sound of the French fire.

'I am.'

'Then get back!'

Even more French skirmishers were pushing forward so that all along the line of Picton's division the redcoats were falling and the Sergeants had begun their litany of battle. 'Close up! Close up!' The light companies were helpless against such a horde of enemy skirmishers. Twice the Duke sent whole battalions forward in line to sweep the French Voltigeurs away, but as soon as the British battalion resumed its station the enemy skirmishers crept back and their musket smoke blossomed again from the rye's margin. The cartridge wadding from the French guns had begun small fires in the dry crops. The flames crackled palely in the strong sunlight, adding yet more smoke to the thickening cloud of powder smoke.

Cavalry reached the crossroads. They came down the Nivelles road in a cheerful jingle of curb chains. The horsemen were Dutch-Belgians and Brunswickers. The black-coated Brunswickers were commanded by their own Duke who led a charge into the wedge of field that lay to the west of the highway. The French skirmishers fled the Duke of Brunswick's sabres like mice fleeing a scourge of cats, but then the death's head horsemen came across a French infantry brigade that was concealed in the tall crops beyond the stream. The brigade had formed squares and blasted the German horsemen with volleys of musket-fire so that the cavalry milled about in confusion, men and horses dropping, until, bleeding and baulked, they were forced to retire. Some galloped for safety into the wood, others retreated through the rye to the crossroads. The Duke of Brunswick was dead.

The Prince of Orange had been inspired by the success of the Brunswickers. He galloped past Sharpe. 'Come on, Sharpe! Come on! That's the way to clear them off!'

'Stay here,' Sharpe warned Harper, then kicked his heels back to follow the Prince who was eagerly ordering his own newly arrived cavalry into two ranks. The black-coated Brunswickers, some with bloodied sabres, reinforced the Dutch-Belgians who followed their Prince out into the wide expanse of field where the French skirmishers still raked the redcoats with musket-fire. The Prince had drawn his ivory-hilted sabre which he now waved above his head as a signal for the two lines to quicken into a trot.

The horses plunged into the smoking rye. The French skirmishers, rightly terrified of the curved blades, fled precipitately and the British infantry cheered as their tormentors were driven away.

Sharpe rode with Rebecque and the other staff officers between the two Dutch ranks, while the Prince cantered ahead of the horsemen. The Prince was happy. This was war! He had been cheered by the redcoats, proof that his heroism was appreciated. His horse curvetted prettily and the sun reflected off his sabre's polished blade. The French skirmishers were running in terror from him, fleeing like game from the beaters, and in a moment he would order the full gallop and he imagined the thrill of breaking through the enemy lines, then sabring the gunners and pouncing on the French baggage. Europe would learn that a new military power had risen: William, Prince of Orange!

Still the swarm of French skirmishers retreated before

the Prince. A few Frenchmen stopped to fire at their pursuers, but they dared not pause long for fear of the sabres and thus their wild shooting did no damage. The fleeing Frenchmen splashed through the stream and ran past Gemioncourt farm. There seemed to be no French columns ahead, just the inviting field of rye climbing to the low crest where the French gunners waited to be cut down by the Prince's sabres. Lieutenant Doggett, riding next to Sharpe, nervously drew his sword. 'I've never fought on horseback.'

'Just concentrate on staying in the saddle, and try not to chop your horse's ears off.'

'Yes, sir.' Doggett gave his horse's ears a rather speculative look.

'Don't chop with your sword,' Sharpe continued his last minute tuition, 'but stab with it. And keep your horse moving! If you stand still in a mêlée, you'll be dead.'

'Yes, sir.'

The Prince seemed to have no fear, but trotted through the ford straight towards the French guns, which stood silent on the skyline. He was wondering why he had not thought to have had a huge banner of orange silk made; a banner that would follow him on a battlefield to terrify the enemy. He turned to look for Rebecque, intending to order the Chief of Staff to have just such a banner made, but instead he saw that the entire first rank of his horsemen had come to an ignominious halt at the far bank of the stream.

'Come on!' the Prince shouted at them. 'Follow me!'

Not a man nor a horse moved, and the second rank of horsemen stopped a few paces behind the first.

The Prince turned back to his front and saw why. A brigade of French light cavalry had appeared beside the enemy guns. The enemy horsemen were Lancers and Hussars, gaudy in green, scarlet and blue, who now spread ahead of the cannons to make their own two lines of attack. The French standard bearers carried guidon flags, while each Lancer had a small red and white swallow-tailed flag attached just beneath his weapon's slender blade. The French cavalry were outnumbered by the Prince's force, but they still advanced with a jaunty confidence. It would be sabre against sabre and sabre against lance.

The French came to a halt two hundred yards from the immobile Dutch cavalry. The Lancers formed the front rank while the Hussars reined in fifty paces behind. For a few seconds the two bodies of cavalry just stared at each other, then the Prince raised his heavy sabre high over his head. 'Charge!'

He shouted it in a fine loud voice. At the same instant he spurred forward and lowered his sabre's point, but then realized that his men had not moved from the streambank. The staff officers had dutifully begun to follow the Prince, but the Belgian horsemen had stayed obstinately still.

'Charge!' the Prince shouted again, but again no one moved. Some officers tried to urge their men forward, but those few who were forced ahead soon pulled aside and stopped again.

'Bloody hell.' Sharpe drew his sword, then looked at Simon Doggett. 'In a few seconds, Lieutenant, this is going to be a Goddamned bloody shambles. Ride like hell for the crossroads when it starts. Don't look back, don't slow down, and don't try and play games with Lancers.'

'Yes, sir.'

Doggett glanced left and right, but the Belgians would not close on the Frenchmen. Just a year ago these Belgians had been a part of the French army, and they had no wish to kill their old comrades. Some of the Belgian horsemen pulled their horses' heads round to demonstrate their unwillingness to charge.

The French horses snorted, tossed their heads and trampled the rye. The Lancers held their eight-foot-long weapons vertically so that the red and white flags made a brave show against the sky. Sharpe hated lances. He had been captured at lance point in India and still bore the scar on his chest. Some men preferred fighting lances to sabres, claiming that once the lance point was evaded, the Lancer was dead meat, but Sharpe had never felt easy facing the razor-sharp and narrow-bladed spears.

Then, with a deliberate slow menace, and apparently without any order being given, the whole front rank of the French cavalry swung their lance points down into the charge.

The sight of the blades dropping was enough for the Belgian horsemen. They wrenched their horses about, rammed back their spurs, and fled. The staff officers tried to rally the nearest horsemen, but it was hopeless.

Sharpe pulled Doggett's bridle round. 'Get out of here! Ride!'

The Prince had already fled. Rebecque was staring at the enemy through eyes made swollen and watery by hay fever. A French bugle sounded loud and mocking, starting the Lancers on their pursuit.

'Come on, Sharpe!' Rebecque shouted.

Sharpe had already turned his horse. He saw the Prince ahead of him, head down and galloping. He spurred his own horse, hearing the crash of the galloping enemy horses behind. The enemy's trumpet calls filled the sky with threat.

It was a race. The quickest of the French horses swiftly overtook the slower Belgians. Lances were drawn back and thrust forward into unprotected backs. Men screamed, arched their spines, and fell. Hooves drummed up great chunks of soil. A Dutchman cut blindly at a Lancer and, to his own surprise, knocked the man backwards from his saddle. A bleeding horse limped.

A Brunswicker tumbled from his saddle, scrambled to his feet, and was immediately cut down by a Hussar's sabre. The Hussars were catching up with the slower Dutch-Belgian horsemen now and their sabres slashed into necks and laid open ribs. Blood slicked the rye straw. Hundreds of broken Dutch-Belgian horsemen streamed northwards towards the crossroads and the enemy rode among them, screaming to keep the panic bubbling, killing and slashing when they could.

The Duke of Wellington rode forward to stop the rout, but the Dutch-Belgian cavalry ignored him, parting about his staff in a flood of sweating horses and frightened men. The French were racing up behind and on the flanks.

'Get back, sir!' a staff officer shouted at the Duke who still swore and shouted at the panicked Belgians. All the Duke could see was a chaos of dust, burning rye, blood and frightened horsemen, until, clear in the panicked swirl, he suddenly saw the bright gleam of French helmets and lance blades. The Duke turned his horse and spurred hard. There was no escape on the road, for that was crowded with fugitives, so instead he galloped straight towards the solid ranks of the 92nd. There were Frenchmen to his left and right, trying to cut ahead of the Duke. Two Lancers were behind, rowelling their horses' flanks bloody in an attempt to reach him. Copenhagen, the Duke's horse named for one of his early victories, stretched out his neck. The Highlanders were in four standing ranks that bristled with bayonets. No horse would charge home into such a thickly packed formation, but the Duke was shouting at the Scotsmen, 'Down! Down! Down!'

Four files of men dropped to the ground. Copenhagen gathered himself, jumped, and the Duke sailed safely over the sixteen crouching men.

'Fire!' a Highlander officer shouted, and a volley of musketry slashed into the French pursuers. The two

Lancers died instantly, their horses flailing bloodily along the ground almost to the feet of the front rank. 'Reload!' The officer who shouted the fire orders had been one of the men dancing above the crossed swords in the Duchess's ballroom the night before. 'Fire!' A Hussar's face disappeared in blood as his wounded horse reared. Man and beast fell screaming into the path of a galloping Lancer. The Lancer's horse tumbled, legs breaking, while its rider sprawled unhurt. The lance, driven deep into the soil, quivered. 'Reload!' the Scots officer shouted.

A mixture of French and Dutch-Belgian cavalry galloped at the infantry line. The Belgians, desperate for safety, spurred through the gaps between the battalions and the French horsemen rode with them. The redcoats suddenly realized that there were enemy horsemen in their rear.

The Black Watch was ordered to form square. The wings of the battalion curved backwards and inwards, but the enemy Lancers were already behind the line and spurring into the space between the wings. They saw the Scottish colours and rammed their lances forward at the men who protected the great silk banners. Two Scottish officers faced them on horseback. One Lancer went down under a claymore's strike, his skull split down to his coat collar. Colonel Macara was shouting at his flanks to close and, by sheer brute strength, the two ends of the line forced themselves inwards to make a crude square. A dozen enemy Lancers were trapped inside the formation. One lunged at the Colonel, but Macara knocked the lance aside then rammed his claymore forward. 'Platoon, fire!' he shouted while his sword was still killing the Lancer. Other Lancers were being dragged from their saddles by vengeful Scottish soldiers who stabbed down with bayonets. Outside the square the horsemen veered away from the platoon volleys, while inside the square the trapped Lancers were butchered.

The colours were safe, and the pipes had never stopped playing.

The neighbouring battalion, the East Essex, stayed in their line. They, like the Scots, had been in four ranks, but their Colonel simply turned his rear rank about and opened fire front and rear, killing Dutch-Belgians and French horsemen indiscriminately. One band of determined French cavalry spurred hard from the rear in a furious attempt to capture the battalion's colours. The spears chopped down two British sergeants, a sabre slashed a redcoat aside, then a Lancer rammed his long blade into the eye of the Ensign carrying the regimental flag. Ensign Christie fell, but he held tight to the big yellow silk banner as he collapsed. Two Hussars attacked the fallen Christie, leaning down from their saddles to hack at the sixteen-year-old with their sabres.

Redcoats scrambled forward, climbing over their own dead and wounded. A Lancer tried to pick up the colour with his weapon's point, but Christie hung on grimly. The two Hussars grunted as they chopped at him with their sabres. A musket shot killed one Frenchman, the other parried a bayonet thrust, then stabbed down at Christie a last time.

Another musket hammered and the Hussar was plucked out of his saddle like a puppet jerked on strings. A knot of red-coated officers and men surged over the prone Christie, driving the last enemy away. A Lancer had speared a corner of the flag and now jerked his lance up to tear a fragment of the yellow silk away, but even that trophy was denied the French. Three muskets flamed and the Lancer toppled backwards from his horse.

'Close up! Close up!' the Sergeants shouted. A crashing volley cleared a space in front of the battalion. The air was thick with the foul powder smoke, rank with the stench of blood, and loud with the noise of screaming horses and men. A loose horse galloped wildly across the face of the line, streaming blood. A Lancer staggered away on foot and was dropped by a musket bullet. The French horsemen were turning and riding away, trying to escape the musket volleys.

Ensign Christie was alive, still with the colour gripped to his body that had been slashed with more than twenty sabre and lance wounds. His men made a litter of muskets and blankets and carried him back to the surgeons who had set up for business in the barn by the crossroads. The colour, its bright yellow silk slashed by steel and stained with Christie's blood, was raised again. The French cavalry, like an ebbing tide of blood, reformed a quarter mile away. The crossroads had held.

The Black Watch dragged the dead Lancers from inside their square and dumped the bodies as a kind of rampart to trip any more charging horses. Men reloaded their muskets. The wounded limped back to the surgeons. One man fell to his knees, vomited blood, then collapsed.

The French had come perilously close to breaking the British line apart. Some of the Hussars and Lancers, who had ridden to the rear of the red-coated battalions, had galloped along the road they were trying to capture, and had only retreated back through the intervals between the battalions because there were not enough horsemen to hold the temporarily captured road. It now seemed to the French that one more effort would surely succeed, and that the red-coated infantry would break just like the Dutch-Belgian horsemen had broken. The trumpets screamed for that second effort which, to ensure success, was strengthened with eight hundred Cuirassiers; the *gros frères*, big brothers, of the French army. The Cuirassiers wore steel breastplates, helmets and backplates, and rode the heaviest horses of all the

French cavalry. A big brother, his armour and his horse weighed more than a ton. The *gros frères*, their armoured steel reflecting the sun like silver fire, would lead the second charge and crush the infantry by sheer weight and terror.

But the infantry, expecting the charge, was ready. The musket volleys crashed smoke and flame, and punched their bullets clean through the armour plate. The Cuirassiers were tumbled down to the crushed rye as the musket volleys settled into their killing rhythm. Dying horses quivered on the compacted rye, while wounded Cuirassiers struggled to unburden themselves of helmets and armour before limping away. The Lancers and Hussars, seeing the slaughter of the armoured horsemen, did not press their own charge home.

'Cease fire! Reload!' the officers and sergeants called to the British squares. The regimental bands played on, while in the squares the colours hung heavy in the humid and smoke-stained air. The enemy cavalry, bloodied and beaten, pulled back to the stream. From the east came the sound of cannon, proof that the Prussians still fought their battle.

Then the French skirmishers crept forward and opened their galling fire again, and from beyond Gemioncourt the French twelve-pounder cannons opened fire on the British ranks. The enemy cavalry was still in sight, and not so very far off, and so the infantry was forced to stay in their squares as prime targets for the heavy French cannon.

It was time for the infantry to suffer.

On the roads leading to Quatre Bras from the west and north the hurrying British troops saw the growing canopy of smoke, and heard the incessant punch of the heavy guns. Carts were already travelling back to Brussels carrying wounded men who groaned in the afternoon heat while their blood dripped through the bottom-boards to stain the white road red. Other wounded men walked away from the battle, staggering in the sun towards their old bivouac areas. In Nivelles the townspeople huddled at their doors, listened to the noise of battle, and stared wide-eyed at the foully wounded soldiers who limped past. Some unwounded Belgian soldiers spread the news that the British were already beaten and that the Emperor was already on his way to Brussels.

The clouds thickened in the west, climbing ever higher and darker.

Twelve miles to the north of Quatre Bras, in the orchard of a farm called Hougoumont which, in turn, was close to the small village of Waterloo, some men were busy thinning the apple crop. They plucked the unripe fruit and tossed it into baskets, thus ensuring that the remaining apples would grow big and juicy. The discarded fruit would be fed to the pigs that lived in the yard of the château of Hougoumont.

It was a hot day, and as the men worked they could hear the percussive thumping of the guns to the south. From the top of their ladders they could see the growing cloud of dirty smoke that climbed over the battlefield. They chuckled at the sight, relieved that it was not they who were being shot at, nor their homes being invaded by soldiers, and not their land being ridden ragged by cavalry.

The château windows were open and white curtains stirred in the small breeze that offered a slight measure of relief from the stifling heat. A plump woman came to one of the upstairs windows where she rested her arms on the sill and stared at the strange conical smoke canopy that grew in the far southern sky. On the main highway that ran through the valley east of the château she could see a stream of soldiers marching south. The men wore red, and even at this distance she could see they were hurrying. 'Better them than us, eh, ma'am?' one of the apple pickers shouted.

'Better them than us,' the woman agreed, then crossed herself.

'We'll get rain tomorrow,' one of the men remarked, but the others took no notice. They were too busy picking apples. Tomorrow, if it did not rain, they were supposed to finish the haymaking down in the valley's bottom, and there was a flock of sheep to be sheared as well, while the day after tomorrow, thank the good Lord, they would have a day off because it was Sunday.

More British troops arrived at Quatre Bras, but they had to be sent to the flanks which were under increasing pressure from the French. Sharpe, after scraping home in front of the French cavalry, had been sent through the wood to find Prince Bernhard of Saxe-Weimar. The Prince, a dour tough man, had been holding his position, but his ammunition was running low and his men were being killed by the ever-present skirmishers. Newly arrived British infantry were sent to support him, while yet more redcoats were sent to help the Rifles on the left flank who were also under heavy attack from a brigade of French infantry.

'Why don't they attack our centre with infantry?' Doggett asked Sharpe, who had rejoined Harper behind the crossroads.

'Because they're being led by a cavalryman.' A Hussar prisoner had revealed that it was Marshal Ney who led the French troops at Quatre Bras. Ney was called 'the bravest of the brave', a red-haired cavalryman who would have ridden through the pits of hell without a murmur, but who had yet to launch an infantry attack against the battered defenders at the crossroads.

'You have to understand something about cavalrymen, Mr Doggett,' Harper explained. 'They look very fine, so they do, and they usually take all the credit for any victory, but the only brains they've got are the ones they keep in their horses' heads.'

Doggett blushed. 'I wanted to be a cavalryman, but my father insisted I joined the Guards.'

'Don't worry,' Harper said cheerfully, 'the Guards aren't our brightest lads either. God save Ireland, but just look at those poor boys.'

The poor boys were the Highlanders beyond the crossroads who could only stand and be slaughtered by the French guns. They were in square, which made them a tempting target for the French artillerymen, and they dared not relinquish the formation for fear of the French cavalry that watched them like hawks. The Scotsmen could only stand while the roundshot slammed into the files, and each shot that struck home killed two or three men, sometimes more. Once Harper saw a roundshot strike the flanking face of a square and ten men went down in a single bloody smear. The British artillery at the crossroads was being saved for any French infantry attack, though once in a while a gun would try to hit a French cannon. Such counter-battery fire was almost always wasted, but as the infantry's suffering dragged on the Duke ordered more of it simply to help the morale of the redcoats.

'Why don't we do something?' Doggett asked plaintively.

'What's to do?' Harper asked. 'The bloody Belgians won't fight, so we haven't got any cavalry. It's called being an infantryman, Mr Doggett. Your job is to stand there and get slaughtered.'

'Patrick?' Sharpe had been staring up the Nivelles road. 'Do you see what I see?'

Harper twisted in his saddle. 'Bloody hell, sir, you're right!' A further brigade of British infantry was arriving, and among the troops was the Prince of Wales's Own

Volunteers. Sharpe and Harper spurred towards their old battalion.

Sharpe stood his horse beside the road and took off his hat as the leading company came abreast. It was his old company, the light, led by Peter d'Alembord. The men's faces were pale with dust, through which the rivulets of sweat had driven dark trails. Daniel Hagman raised a cheer as Sharpe tossed them a full canteen of water. D'Alembord, his white dancing breeches stained from the wax with which his saddle had been polished, reined in beside the two Riflemen and looked dubiously towards the smear of smoke that marked the battlefield. 'How is it?'

'It's stiff work, Peter,' Sharpe admitted.

'Is Boney here?' It was the same question that nearly every newly arriving officer had asked, as though the presence of the Emperor would dignify the day's death and dismemberment.

'Not so far as we know.' Sharpe saw that his answer disappointed d'Alembord.

The brigade halted while Sir Colin Halkett, its commander, discovered where his four battalions were wanted. Lieutenant-Colonel Ford and his two Majors, Vine and Micklewhite, walked their horses up the road until they came close to where Sharpe, d'Alembord and Harper chatted. Ford, myopically peering towards the cannon smoke, realized too late that he had come close to Sharpe, whose presence made him feel so uncomfortable and inadequate, but he put a brave face on the chance meeting. 'It sounds brisk, Sharpe, does it not?'

'It's certainly hard work, Ford,' Sharpe said mildly.

No one seemed to be able to find anything else to say. Ford smiled with a general benignity which he thought fitting to a colonel, while Major Vine scowled at the men of the Prince of Wales's Own Volunteers who had slumped on the roadside, and Major Micklewhite pretended to be enthralled by the enamel picture on the lid of his snuff-box. A sudden explosion was loud enough to penetrate the half-deaf ears of Major Vine who twisted round to see that a British gun limber, crammed with ready ammunition, had been struck by a French shell and was now spewing a thick skein of smoke and flames into the sky.

Colonel Ford had jumped at the sudden violence of the explosion, and now he gazed through his thick spectacles at the rest of the battlefield, which appeared as a threatening blur of trampled corn, blood, smoke, and the lumped bodies of the dead. Cannon-balls were ploughing through the slurry of rye and soil, spewing gouts of earth before bouncing into the bloody lines of Highlanders. 'Dear God,' Ford said with rather more feeling than he had intended.

'Watch out for their skirmishers,' Sharpe advised drily. 'They seem to have more of the bastards than usual.'

'More?' The tone to Ford's voice betrayed the Colonel's fear of taking his battalion into the cauldron beyond the crossroads.

'You might like to think about deploying an extra company as skirmishers,' Sharpe, well aware of Ford's uncertainty, offered the advice as forcefully as he could without sounding patronizing, 'but warn the lads to keep an eye open for the cavalry. They're never very far away.' Sharpe pointed across the highway to where the stream fed a small lake behind Gemioncourt farm. 'There's a fold in the ground over there and it's swarming with the evil buggers.'

'Quite so, quite so.' Ford took off his spectacles, cleaned them on the tasselled end of his red sash, then hooked the earpieces back into place. He stared through the newly cleaned glass but could see neither a fold in the ground nor any cavalry. He wondered whether Sharpe was deliberately trying to frighten him, and so, to show that he was quite equal to the prospect of fighting, Ford straightened his shoulders and turned his horse away. Vine and Micklewhite, like obedient hounds, followed their Colonel.

'He won't take a blind bit of notice,' d'Alembord sighed.

'Then you watch out for the cavalry, Peter. They're in something of a murderous bloody mood. There's about three thousand of the bastards: Hussars, Lancers, and the Heavies.'

'You do cheer me up, Sharpe, you really do.' D'Alembord superstitiously touched the breast pocket which bulged with his fiancée's letters. 'Have you had your note from that bloody man yet?'

It took Sharpe a second or two to realize that d'Alembord was talking about Lord John Rossendale. He shook his head. 'Not yet.'

'Oh, God. I suppose that means we'll have to arrange a duel in the morning?'

'No. I'll just find the bugger and cut his balls off.'

'Oh, splendid!' d'Alembord said in mock seriousness. 'That should satisfy everyone's honour.'

Orders came back to the battalion. The newly arrived brigade was to take up positions in the wedge of field in front of Saxe-Weimar's wood, from where their musket-fire could rake across the flank of any French attack down the road. Sir Thomas Picton's staff brought the orders which insisted that the four battalions were to form square in the rye.

Sharpe shook d'Alembord's hand. 'Watch those skirmishers, Peter!' He waved to Captain Harry Price who had once been his Lieutenant. 'It's hot work, Harry!'

'I'm thinking of resigning, sir.' Harry Price, too poor to own a horse, was sweating from the exertions of his long day's march. 'My father always wanted me to take holy orders, and I'm beginning to think I rejected his views too quickly. Good God, it's Mr Harper!'

Harper grinned. 'Good to see you, Mr Price.'

'I thought the army had discharged you.'

'It did.'

'You're as mad as a bloody bishop! What are you doing here?' Harry Price was genuinely puzzled. 'You could get hurt, you damned fool!'

'I'm staying well out of any trouble, so I am.'

Price shook his head at Harper's foolishness, then had to hurry away as the battalion was ordered into the wood. The companies filed through the trees and so out into the sunlit rye field where, like the other three battalions in Halkett's brigade, they formed square.

Sharpe and Harper walked their horses back to the crossroads where the Prince of Orange was fidgeting with the ivory hilt of his sabre. He was frustrated by the day's setbacks. He had seen his infantry crumple at the first French attack, then watched his cavalry flee at the drop of a lance point, yet he blamed the day's lack of success on anyone but himself or his countrymen. 'Look at those men, for instance!' He pointed towards the four battalions of Halkett's brigade which had just formed their squares on the flank of the wood. 'It's a nonsense to form those men in square! A nonsense!' The Prince turned irritably, looking for a British staff officer. 'Sharpe! You explain it to me! Why are those men in square?'

'Too many cavalry, sir,' Sharpe explained gently.

'I see no cavalry!' The Prince stared across the smoke-shrouded battlefield. 'Where are the cavalry?'

'Over there, sir.' Sharpe pointed across the field. 'There's a lake to the left of the farm and they're hidden there. They've probably dismounted so we can't see them, but they're there, sure enough.'

'You're imagining it.' Since losing his Belgian cavalry the Prince had been given nothing to do, and he felt slighted. The Duke of Wellington was ignoring him, reducing the Prince to the status of an honoured spectator. Well, damn that! There was no glory to be had in just watching a battle from behind a crossroads! He looked back at the newly deployed brigade that stood in its four battalion squares. 'What brigade is that?' he asked his staff.

Rebecque raised an eyebrow at Sharpe, who answered. 'Fifth Brigade, sir.'

'Halkett's, you mean?' The Prince frowned at Sharpe. 'Yes, sir.'

'They're in my Corps, aren't they?' the Prince demanded.

There was a brief silence, then Rebecque nodded. 'Indeed they are, sir.'

The Prince's face showed outrage. 'Then why wasn't I consulted about their placement?'

No one wanted to answer, at least not with the truth which was that the Duke of Wellington did not trust the Prince's judgement. Rebecque just shrugged while Sharpe stared at the smoke of the French guns. Harry Webster, beyond Rebecque, looked at his watch, while Simon Doggett slowly moved his horse back till he had left the group of embarrassed staff officers and was next to Harper's horse. The Prince drew his sabre a few inches then rammed it back into its scabbard. 'No one gives orders to my brigades without my permission!'

'When I was in the ranks, Mr Doggett, we had a way of dealing with young gentlemen like His Royal Highness,' Harper said quietly.

'You did?'

'We shot the little buggers.' Harper smiled happily.

Doggett stared into the battered and friendly face. 'You did?'

'Especially buggers like him.' Harper nodded scornfully towards the Prince. 'He's nothing but a silk stocking full of shit.'

Doggett stared in horror at Harper. Doggett's sense of

propriety, as well as his natural respect for royalty, were outraged by the Irishman's words. 'You can't say things like that!' he blurted out. 'He's royalty!'

'A silk stocking full of shit with a crown, then.' Harper was quite unmoved by Doggett's outrage. 'And if the little bugger doesn't watch out, Mr Sharpe will feed his guts to the hogs. It wouldn't be the first time he's done it.'

'Murdered someone?' Doggett blurted out the question.

Harper turned innocent eyes on the Guards Lieutenant. 'I know for a fact he's rid the world of some bad officers. We all have! Don't be shocked, Mr Doggett! It happens all the time!'

'I can't believe it!' Doggett protested, but too loudly, for the sound of his voice made the Prince turn irritably in his saddle.

'Is something offending you, Mr Doggett?'

'No, sir.'

'Then get back here, where you belong.' The Prince looked back to the four battalions of Halkett's brigade which were an itch to his wounded self-esteem. Closest to the crossroads, and just forward of the Highlanders across the highway was a battalion of Lincolnshire men, the 69th, who were unknown to Sharpe. They had never fought in Spain, instead they had been a part of the disastrous expedition that had failed to free the Netherlands at the end of the previous war. Beyond them was the 30th, the Three Tens, a Cambridgeshire battalion which, like the 33rd next in line, had also been a part of the Dutch débâcle. Furthest south was the Prince of Wales's Own Volunteers, the only veterans of the Spanish campaign in the brigade.

'So who ordered them to form square?' the Prince demanded petulantly.

No one knew, so Harry Webster was sent to discover

the answer and came back after ten minutes to say that Sir Thomas Picton had deployed the brigade.

'But they're not in Picton's division!' The Prince's pique had turned to a real anger that flushed his sallow face.

'Indeed not, sir,' Rebecque said gently, 'but –'

'But nothing, Rebecque! But bloody nothing! Those men are in my corps! Mine! I do not give orders to brigades in Sir Thomas Picton's division, nor do I expect him to interfere with my corps! Sharpe! My compliments to Sir Colin Halkett, and instruct him to deploy his brigade in line. Their task is to give fire, not cower like schoolboys from non-existent cavalry.' The Prince had taken a sheet of paper from his sabretache and was scribbling the order in pencil.

'But the cavalry –' Sharpe began to protest.

'What cavalry?' The Prince made a great fuss of pretending to stare across the battlefield. 'There is no cavalry.'

'In the dead ground over –'

'You're frightened of unseen horsemen on the left? But this brigade is on the right! Here, take this.' He thrust the written order at Sharpe.

'No, sir,' Sharpe said.

The bulbous eyes swivelled to stare in amazement at Sharpe. Rebecque hissed a warning at the Rifleman, while the other staff officers held their breath. The Prince licked his lips. 'What did you say, Sharpe?' His voice was filled with horror and revulsion.

'I'm not taking that order, sir. You'll kill every man jack of that brigade if you insist on it.'

For a second the Prince literally shook with rage. 'Are you refusing to obey an order?'

'I'm refusing to take that order, sir, yes.'

'Rebecque! Suspend Colonel Sharpe from his duties. Have this order sent immediately.'

'You can't –' Sharpe began, but Rebecque seized Sharpe's bridle and tugged his horse out of the Prince's reach. 'Rebecque, for God's sake!' Sharpe protested.

'He's entitled!' Rebecque insisted. 'Listen, by tomorrow he'll have forgotten this. Give him an apology tonight and you won't be suspended. He's a good-hearted man.'

'I don't give a damn for his heart, Rebecque. It's those men I care about!'

'Rebecque!' The Prince turned petulantly in his saddle. 'Has that order gone!'

'Immediately, sir.' Rebecque shrugged at Sharpe, then turned away to find another officer to carry the Prince's command.

The order was sent. Sir Colin Halkett rode back to the Prince's command post vehemently to protest the command, but the Prince would not be denied. He insisted that there was no danger of a French cavalry attack and that, by deploying in square, the brigade was sacrificing three-quarters of the firepower that might be needed to rake the flank of a French infantry attack.

'We mustn't be cautious!' the Prince lectured the experienced Sir Colin. 'Caution won't win battles! Only daring. You will form line! I insist you form line!'

Sir Colin rode unhappily away while Sharpe, goaded beyond endurance by the Prince's crowing voice, spurred forward. 'Sir,' he said to the Prince.

The Prince ignored him. Instead he looked at Winckler, one of his Dutch aides, and deliberately spoke in English. 'I can't think why the Duke called his men the scum of the earth, Winckler. I think he must have meant his officers, don't you?'

'Yes, sir,' Winckler, a sycophantic man, smiled.

Sharpe ignored the provocation. 'Permission to rejoin my old battalion, sir.'

The Prince gave the smallest, curtest nod.

Sharpe turned his horse away and spurred it forward.

Hooves sounded loud behind him, making him twist in his saddle. 'I thought you promised Isabella you'd stay out of trouble?'

'There isn't any trouble yet,' Harper said. 'When there is I'll get the hell out of it, but till then I'll keep you company.'

Harper followed Sharpe down the bank onto the Nivelles road where Sharpe exploded in rage. 'Bastard! What a cretinous dirty-minded little Dutch bastard! I'd like to ram his poxed bloody crown up his royal arse.' Instead Sharpe snatched the tricorne hat off his head and ripped the black, gold and scarlet cockade of the Netherlands from its crown. He hurled the silken scrap into a patch of nettles. 'Bastard!'

Harper just laughed.

They scrambled up the bank into the trampled field of rye. To their right the trees were heavy with leaf, though here and there a splintered branch showed where a French cannon-ball or shell had struck high. There was not much litter in this part of the field; merely the corpses of two dead Voltigeurs, a scatter of dead horses, and a discarded and undamaged Cuirassier's breastplate that Harper dismounted to retrieve. 'Useful, that,' he said as he tied the polished piece of armour to the strap of a saddlebag.

Sharpe did not reply. Instead, he watched as Sir Colin Halkett's brigade staff ordered the four battalions out of square and into line. The regimental bands played behind the brigade. Sharpe saluted the colours of the 69th, the 30th and the 33rd. He felt a particular fondness for the 33rd, the Yorkshire regiment which he had joined as a sullen youth twenty-two years before. He wondered if their recruiters still carried oatcakes pierced on a sword, the curious symbol he'd seen as Sergeant Hakeswill had expounded to the sixteen-year-old Sharpe the benefits of an army life. Hakeswill was long dead, as were almost all the other men Sharpe remembered from the battalion, except for the Lieutenant-Colonel who had led the 33rd when Sharpe had first joined and who was now His Grace the Duke of Wellington.

The six hundred men of the Prince of Wales's Own Volunteers were deployed the furthest south, a full half-mile from the crossroads. Peter d'Alembord's skirmishers were fifty yards in front of the battalion and having a hard time with the greater number of Voltigeurs. It seemed that Ford had not taken Sharpe's advice to send out extra skirmishers, but was leaving d'Alembord's men to cope as best they could. Sharpe, not wanting to interfere with Ford, reined in a good thirty yards behind the battalion, close to the treeline where the battalion's band was playing. Mr Little, the rotund bandmaster, first greeted Sharpe with a cheerful grin, then with a quick and cheerful rendition of 'Over The Hills and Far Away', the marching song of the Rifles. Colonel Ford, who had just finished dressing his newly formed line, turned as the music changed. He blinked with surprise to see the two Riflemen, then nervously took off his spectacles and polished their round lenses on his red sash. 'Come to see us fight, Sharpe?'

'I've come to see you die.' But Sharpe said it much too softly for anyone but Harper to hear. 'Can I suggest you form square?' he said more loudly.

Ford was clearly confused. He had only just been ordered to form the battalion into line, and now he was being asked to revert to square? He put his spectacles back into place and frowned at Sharpe. 'Is that an order from brigade?'

Sharpe hesitated, was tempted to tell the lie, but he had no written authority to prove the order, so he shook his head. 'It's just a suggestion.'

'I think we'll manage quite well by following orders, Mr Sharpe.'

'A pox on you, too.' Again Sharpe spoke too softly for anyone but Harper to hear.

Mr Little's bandsmen played merrily on while Colonel Ford took his place behind the battalion's colours and Sharpe slowly drew his long sword which he rested on his pommel.

The Prince, waiting behind the gun line at the cross-roads, felt that at long last he was beginning to impose his youthful genius on the battle.

On the shallow southern crest above Gemioncourt a French cavalry scout stared in disbelief at the long exposed line of infantrymen that had been stationed in front of the woods. He stared for a long time, seeking the implicit trap in the formation, but he could see none. He could only see men lined up for the slaughter and so, turning his horse, he spurred towards the dead ground.

While Sharpe and Harper, with two thousand two hundred men of Halkett's Fifth Brigade, just waited.

CHAPTER 9

In Brussels the gun-fire sounded like very distant thunder, sometimes fading to a barely perceptible rumble, but at other times swollen by a vagary of wind so that the distinct percussive shocks of each gun's firing could be distinguished. Lucille, troubled by the sound, walked Nosey to the southern ramparts where she joined the crowd who listened to the far-off noise and speculated what it might mean. The majority hoped it signified Napoleon by nightfall, a torchlight parade and dancing. The Empire would be restored and safe, for surely the Austrians and Russians would not dare attack France if Britain and Prussia had been defeated?

The first news from the battlefield gave substance to those Imperial hopes. Belgian cavalrymen, their horses sweating and exhausted, brought tales of a shattering French victory. It had been more of a massacre than a battle, the horsemen said. British corpses were strewn across the landscape, Wellington had been killed, and the troops of the Emperor were even now advancing on Brussels with drums beating and Eagles flying.

Lucille noted that the guns were still firing, which seemed to cast doubt on the Belgian claims of victory, though some of the hundreds of English civilians still in Brussels were more ready to give the news credence. They ordered their servants to load the travelling boxes and trunks onto the coaches that had been standing ready since dawn. The coaches were whipped out of the city on the Ghent road; their passengers praying that they would reach the Channel ports before the Emperor's scavenging and victorious horsemen cut the roads. Others of the English, more cautious, waited for official news.

Lucille, unwilling to flee with her child into an unknown future, walked beside one of the first carts of wounded that reached the city. A British infantry sergeant, his face bandaged and one arm crudely splinted, told her that the battle had not been lost when he left Quatre Bras. 'It was hard work, ma'am, but it weren't lost. And as long as Nosey's alive it won't be lost.'

Lucille went back to her child. She closed the window in the hope that the glass would obscure the sound of the cannons, but the noise drummed on, insistent and threatening. To the west the thunderheads were heaping into a sombre bank that cast an unnaturally dark shadow across the city.

Five streets away from Lucille, in the expensive suite of rooms that had been so thoroughly fumigated, Jane Sharpe vomited.

Afterwards, gasping for breath from the stomach-griping heaves, she went to the window, rested her forehead on the cool glass, and stared at the great ridge of cloud that blackened the western sky. Beneath her, in the hotel yard, a groom whistled as he carried two pails of water from the pump. A flock of pigeons circled, then fluttered down to the stable roof. Jane was aware of none of it, not even of the harsh percussive grumble of gun-fire. She closed her eyes, took a deep, tentative breath, then groaned.

She was pregnant.

She had suspected as much before she and Lord John had left England, but now she was certain. Her breasts were sore and her stomach sour. She ticked the months down on her fingers, reckoning that she would have a January child; a winter's bastard. She swore softly.

She stepped away from the window and crossed to the dressing-table where last night's candles still stood in their puddles of cold wax. She still felt sick. Her skin was prickly with sweat. She hated the thought of being pregnant, of being lumpish and awkward and gross. She rang for her maid, then sat heavily to stare into the looking-glass.

'Has Harris returned?' Jane asked the maid.

'Yes, ma'am.'

'Tell him I shall want him to take a message to his lordship.'

'Yes, ma'am.'

Jane waved the maid out of the room, then drew a heavy sheet of creamy writing paper towards her. She dipped a quill in ink, sat for a moment in thought, then began to write.

The guns fired on.

More troops were arriving at Quatre Bras; troops who had marched till their blistered feet were agony, but who now had to plunge straight into the humid, smoke-thickened air where, unit by unit, the Duke was building the force that would counter-attack the French and drive them back to Frasnes. More and more British guns crashed and jangled off the road and onto the crushed rye stalks. Fires were burning in the crops behind the French skirmishers as British howitzer shells exploded. The battle was not won yet, but the Duke was beginning to feel like a man who had escaped defeat. He knew his Guards Division was close, and there was even a rumour that the British cavalry might reach the crossroads before dark.

A small west wind was stirring the thick smoke. The British skirmishers, reinforced by newly arrived battalions of light infantry, were beginning to blunt the fire of the Voltigeurs. The French artillery was still taking its grievous toll of the infantry by the crossroads, but now the Duke could replace the men who fell. If Blücher held off the Emperor, and if Marshal Ney was thrown back from Quatre Bras, then in the morning the Prussian and British armies would combine and Napoleon would have lost.

The Duke opened his watch lid. It was half-past five of a summer's evening. The battlefield was darkening, shadowed by the huge western clouds and shrouded by its pall of smoke, but plenty of daylight remained for the Duke's counter-stroke. 'Any news of the Guards?' he asked an aide.

It seemed that the Guards were being apprehended by the Prince of Orange who, as company after company of the élite troops arrived, was sending them north through the great wood to reinforce Saxe-Weimar's men. The Duke, muttering that the Prince was a bloody little boy who should be sent back to his nursery, ordered that the Guards were not to be so dispersed in penny packets, but were to be held ready for his orders.

'Your Grace!' an aide called in warning. 'Enemy cavalry!'

The Duke turned to stare southwards. Through the smoke he saw a mass of French cavalry spurring up from dead ground and heading slantwise across the field. They were a half-mile away, and well spread out in four long lines. Their loose formation made them a poor target for artillery, but the British gunners loaded with common shell and did their best. The explosions knocked down a few men and horses, but the vast mass of French cavalry trotted safely through the bursting patches of flame and smoke.

The Duke extended his telescope. 'Where are they going?' He was puzzled. Surely his opponent had learned by now that cavalry could achieve nothing against the stalwart squares which had been reinforced with the newly arrived guns?

'Perhaps they're testing Halkett's men?' an aide suggested.

'Then they're committing suicide!' The Duke had his glass trained on the front line of cavalry that was composed of the heavy Cuirassiers in their steel armour. Behind the Cuirassiers were the light horsemen with their lances and sabres. 'They must be insane!' the Duke opined. 'Halkett's in square, isn't he?'

Almost in unison the telescopes of the Duke's staff officers swept to the right of the field, racing past the patches of smoke to focus on the four battalions of Halkett's brigade which stood in front of the wood. The brigade was obscured by cannon smoke, but there were enough rifts in the dirty screen to show that something had gone terribly wrong. 'Oh, Christ.' The voice spoke helplessly from the Duke's entourage. There was a moment's silence, and then again. 'Oh, Christ.'

'Sir?' Rebecque handed the Prince his telescope and pointed towards Gemioncourt farm. 'There, sir.'

The Prince trained the heavy glass. Thousands of horsemen had appeared from the dead ground and now, in four long lines, swept either side of the farm. Dust spurted from the road as the horsemen crashed across. The enemy cavalry was trotting, but, even as the Prince watched, he saw them spur into a canter. The Cuirassiers had their heavy straight swords drawn. Long horsehair plumes tossed and waved from the steel brightness of their helmets. A Cuirassier was hit by a British roundshot and the Prince involuntarily jumped as, magnified in his lens, the steel clad horseman seemed to explode in blood and metal. The Lancers and Hussars, cantering behind, divided to pass the butcher's mess left on the ground.

'They're going for Halkett's brigade, sir,' Rebecque warned.

'Then tell Halkett to form square!' The Prince's voice

was suddenly high-pitched, almost sobbing. 'They've got to form square, Rebecque!' he shouted, spraying Rebecque with spittle. 'Tell them to form square!'

'It's too late, sir. It's too late.' The French were already closer to the infantry brigade than any of the Prince's staff. There was no time to send any orders. There was no time to do anything now, except watch.

'But they've got to form square!' the Prince screamed like a spoilt child.

Too late.

The French cavalry was led by Kellerman, brave Kellerman, hero of Marengo, and veteran of a thousand charges. In most of those charges he had led his men steadily forward, not going from the canter to the gallop till he was just a few yards from the enemy, for only by such discipline could he guarantee that his horsemen would crash in an unbroken line against the enemy.

But this evening he knew that every second's delay would give the redcoats a chance to form square and that once they were in square his horsemen were beaten. A horse would not charge a formed square with its four ranks bristling with muskets spitting fire and bright with bayonets. The horses would swerve round the square, receiving yet more fire from its flanks, and Kellerman had already lost too many men to the British squares this day.

But these redcoats were in line. They could be attacked from their flank, from their front and from behind, and they must not be given time to change formation and thus Kellerman abandoned the discipline of a slow methodical advance and instead shouted at his trumpeters to sound the full charge. Damn the unbroken line hitting home together; instead Kellerman would release his killers to a bloody gallop and loose them to the slaughter.

'Charge!'

Now it was a race between Cuirassiers, Hussars and Lancers. The Cuirassiers raked their horses' flanks and let their heavy horses run free. The Lancers dropped their points and screamed their war cries. The sound of the charge was like a thousand demented drummers as the hooves beat the earth and churned up a mass of blood and soil and straw that flecked the sky behind the four charging lines, which slowly unravelled as the faster horses raced ahead. A cannon-ball screamed between the horses, ploughed a furrow and disappeared southwards. A Lancer swerved round a dead skirmisher. The Lancer's gloved hand was tight on his weapon's grip which was made from cord lashed about the long ash staff. The lance's blade was a smooth spike of polished steel, nine inches long and sharpened like a needle. A shell erupted harmlessly in front of the leading horsemen; the smoke of its explosion whipping back past the galloping killers. A red-plumed trumpeter played mad wild notes. Ahead, beyond the Cuirassiers, the redcoats seemed frozen in terror. This was a ride to death, to a triumph, to the glory of the best and most lethal cavalry in all the world.

'Charge!' Kellerman bellowed, the trumpeters echoed his call, and the French torrent surged on.

'Oh, God. Dear God!' Lieutenant-Colonel Joseph Ford gazed into the battlefield and saw nightmare. The rye was filled with horsemen and the evening light was glinting off hundreds of swords and breastplates and lance heads. Ford could hear the drumming sound of the earth being beaten by thousands of hooves, and all he could do was stare and wonder what in God's name he was supposed to do about it. A small part of his brain knew he was supposed to make a decision, but he was paralysed.

'Cavalry!' d'Alembord shouted unnecessarily. His skirmishers were racing back to the battalion. D'Alembord, like any good skirmish officer, had abandoned his horse to fight with his men on foot, and now he was running like a flushed hare from the threat of hunters. He could scarcely believe the speed with which the enemy horsemen had erupted from the dead ground beyond the highway.

'We should form square?' Major Micklewhite, his horse next to Ford's, suggested to the Colonel.

'Are they French?' Ford had nervously plucked off his spectacles and was frenetically polishing their lens on his sash.

For a second Micklewhite could only gape at the Colonel. He wondered why on earth Ford should suppose that British cavalry might be charging the battalion. 'Yes, sir. They're French.' Major Micklewhite's voice was edged with panic now. 'Do we form square?'

Sharpe had ridden forward, taking position just behind d'Alembord's men who were hastily ranking themselves on the left of the battalion's line. At the right flank of the line, where the Grenadier Company was nearest to the French, an avalanche of cavalry was storming at the battalion's open flank. More cavalrymen were slanting in to the battalion's front. To Sharpe's left, beyond the 33rd, the 30th were already forming square, though the 33rd, like the Prince of Wales's Own Volunteers, seemed frozen in line.

'We should form square!' Major Vine, the battalion's senior Major, shouted at Ford from the right of the line.

'Get out of here, Dally!' Sharpe called to d'Alembord, then raised his voice so all the men of the battalion could hear him. 'Run! Back to the trees! Run!'

It was too late to form square. There was only one chance of living, and that was to gain the shelter of the wood.

The men, recognizing Sharpe's voice, broke and fled. A few sergeants hesitated. Colonel Ford tried desperately to hook his spectacles into place. 'Form square!' he called.

'Square!' Major Vine yelped at the closest companies. 'Form square!'

'Run!' That was Harper, once Regimental Sergeant-Major of this battalion, and still the possessor of a pair of lungs that could jar a regiment from eight fields away. 'Run, you buggers!'

The buggers ran.

'Move! Move! Move!' Sharpe galloped along the front of the line, slashing with the flat of his sword to hasten the redcoats back towards the treeline. 'Run! Run!' He was racing straight towards the enemy's charge. 'Run!'

The men ran. The colour party, encumbered by the heavy squares of silk, were the slowest. One of the Ensigns lost a boot and began limping. Sharpe slammed his horse between the Sergeants whose long axe-bladed spontoons protected the flags and he grabbed a handful of silk with his left hand and speared his sword into the King's colour on his right. 'Run!' He spurred the horse, dragging the two flags behind him. The first refugees were already in the trees where Harper was shouting at them to take firing positions.

A sergeant screamed behind Sharpe as a Cuirassier stabbed a sword down, but the Sergeant's long spontoon tripped the Frenchman's horse that sprawled down into the path of a Lancer who was forced to rein in behind the thrashing beast. A Hussar galloped in from the left, aiming at the colours, but Major Micklewhite slashed from horseback and the Hussar had to parry. He drove Micklewhite's light sword aside, then thrust with his sabre's point to slice Micklewhite's throat back to bone. The Ensign who had lost his boot was ridden over by a Cuirassier whose heavy horse smashed the boy's spine with its hooves. A lance, thrown like a javelin, ripped the yellow silk of the regimental colour, then hung there to be dragged along the ground. Two more Lancers spurred forward, but their attack came close to the trees where

Patrick Harper lurked with his seven-barrelled gun. His one shot emptied both saddles and the very noise of the huge weapon seemed to drive the other Frenchmen away in search of easier pickings.

Sharpe ducked his head, struck back with his heels, and his horse crashed through a patch of ferns and into the trees. He dropped the one colour and shook the other off his sword, then wrenched the horse savagely about in expectation of French horsemen close behind.

But the French had swerved away. They had caught a handful of the slower men and cut them down, and they had killed many of the mounted officers who had stayed behind to shelter the running redcoats, but now the French horsemen feared becoming entangled in the thick wood where the trees would blunt the force of their charge, and so they spurred on for easier prey. Behind them they left Major Micklewhite sprawled dead in a pool of his own blood. Captain Carline was dead, as were Captain Smith and three lieutenants, but the rest of the battalion was safe in the shelter of the wood.

The 33rd, next in line to the Prince of Wales's Own Volunteers, had also run to the wood while beyond them the 30th had formed a rough square that proved solid enough to stand like an island amidst the torrent of French cavalry that split either side of the redcoats. The cavalry ignored the men of the 30th because beyond their crude square the 69th had neither run nor formed square, but was just standing in line with muskets levelled as the full might of Kellerman's cavalry, cheated of its first three targets, thundered straight for them.

'Fire!' a major shouted.

The muskets crashed smoke. Ten Cuirassiers went down in a maelstrom of blood, steel and dying horses, but there were more Cuirassiers on either flank and a rage of Lancers and Hussars were storming in behind the armoured vanguard.

The Cuirassiers hit the open flank of the 69th. A man lunged up with a bayonet, then died as the sword split his skull. The heavy horses slammed into the red ranks that broke apart like rotten wood. The infantry were scattering, thus making themselves even more vulnerable to the enemy blades. The French were in front, behind and chewing up the battalion's flanks with slashing swords that dripped red with every grunting heave.

Then the Lancers struck into the shattered battalion and the redcoats screamed as the horsemen rode clean over the breaking line. The Frenchmen were shouting incoherently. A Lancer threw a corpse off his spear point, then stabbed again. Some infantrymen had broken free and were running to the woods, but they were easily ridden down by Lancers and Hussars who galloped up behind, chose their spot, then stabbed or sliced or hacked or lunged. For the French it was no more difficult than hacking or lunging at the practice sacks of chaff with which they had been trained at their depots at home.

A knot of redcoats gathered round their battalion's colours. There were sergeants with their long-shafted axes, officers with swords and men with bayonets. The French clawed and hacked at the defenders. Lancers rode full tilt at them, grunting as they drove their spears home. One lance struck home with such force that the red and white flag beneath its long blade was buried in the victim's body. A dismounted Cuirassier hacked at the colours' defenders till he was shot in the face by an officer's pistol. A Hussar's horse reared up, hooves flailing, then lunged forward into the knot of men. Two officers went down under the slashing hooves. The Hussar cut down with his sabre. A bayonet raked his left thigh, but the Frenchman did not feel the wound. His horse bit a man, the sabre hissed again, then the Hussar dropped the blade so that it hung from his wrist by its leather strap and he grabbed the staff of one of the colours. The other colour had disappeared, but the Hussar had his gloved hand round the remaining staff. Two men drove bayonets at him. A spontoon wounded his horse, but the Hussar held on. A burly British sergeant tugged at the staff. A Lancer crashed his horse into the mêlée, trampling wounded and living alike, and lunged his weapon at the stubborn Sergeant. The lance point drove into the Sergeant's back, but still the Englishman hung on, but then a Cuirassier, riding in from the far side, hacked his sword down through the man's shako and into his skull. The Sergeant fell.

The Hussar tugged at the colour's staff. A British major seized the colour's silk and stabbed at the Hussar with a sword, but another Lancer came from the right and his blade caught the Major in his belly. The Major screamed, his sword dropped, and the colour came free. The Hussar was bleeding from a dozen wounds, his horse was staggering and bloody, but he managed to turn the beast and he held the British colour high above his head. The rest of the French cavalry was thundering past, charging at the crossroads where yet more infantry waited to be broken, but the Hussar had his triumph.

The 69th was destroyed. A few men had run to safety, and a few still lived in a pile of bodies so drenched and laced with blood that no cavalryman dreamed that any man could still be alive in the stinking heap, but the rest of the battalion had been broken and cut into ruin. Men had died at lance point, or been slashed open by sabres, or pierced by the long straight swords of the Cuirassiers. The battalion, which moments before had been rigid in its formal line, was now nothing but a scattered mess of bodies and blood. There were hundreds of bodies: dead, creeping, bleeding, vomiting, weeping. The cavalrymen left them, not out of pity, but because there seemed no one left to kill. It was as if a slaughterhouse had been upended on this corner of a Belgian field, leaving cuts of meat and spills of blood that steamed in the warm humid air.

The victorious cavalry charged on to the crossroads where the newly arrived artillery greeted them with double-shotted barrels, and the infantry battalions waited in square, and thus it was the Frenchmen's turn to die. The infantry aimed at the horses, knowing that a dead horse was a dismounted man who could be picked off afterwards. For a few moments the cavalry milled about in front of the guns and volley fire, but then Kellerman's trumpeters called for the retreat and the French, their charge done, turned for home.

Slowly, the few survivors of the 69th crept from their shelter in the trees or pushed the dead away. One man, driven to near madness by the memory of the swords and by his brother's blood that had near choked him as he lay beneath the corpse, knelt in the stubble and wept. A sergeant, holding his guts into his sabre-slashed belly, tried to walk to the rear, but fell again. 'I'm all right, I'm all right,' he told a rescuer. Another sergeant, blinded by a Cuirassier and pierced in the belly by a lance, cursed. A lieutenant, his arm hanging by a shred of gristle, weaved as if drunk as he staggered among the bodies.

Survivors pulled the bodies of the living and the dead away from the King's colour. Next to it was the Major who had made the last despairing effort to save the regimental colour. He was dead, pierced deep through his stomach by a lance that was still embedded in his spine. The Major was wearing white silk stockings and gold-buckled dancing shoes, while stuck in his shako's badge, and strangely untouched by any of the blood which had sheeted and soaked and drenched the pile, was an ostrich feather. A soldier plucked the grey feather loose, decided it was of no value, and tossed it away.

A quarter mile to the south a bleeding French Hussar on a wounded horse rode slowly back to his lines. In his right hand he carried the captured colour which he punched again and again at the smoke-skeined air, and with each triumphant punch he called aloud an incoherent shout of victory. His friends followed and applauded him.

From the trees Sharpe watched the Frenchman ride south. Sharpe had dismounted and was standing at the treeline with his loaded rifle. The Hussar was easily within range. Harper, with his own rifle, stood beside Sharpe, but neither man raised his gun. They had once come off a field of battle with an enemy colour, and now they must watch another man have his triumph.

'He'll be an officer by nightfall,' Harper said.

'Bugger deserves it.'

Behind Sharpe the Prince of Wales's Own Volunteers were white-faced and scared. Even the veterans who had endured the worst of the Spanish battles stood silent and bitter. They were frightened, not of the enemy, but of their own officers' incompetence. Colonel Ford would not go near Sharpe, but just sat his horse under the trees and wondered why his right hand was shaking like a leaf.

D'Alembord, his sword still drawn, walked up to the two Riflemen. He stared past them at the captured colour of the 69th, then shook his head. 'I came to thank you. If you hadn't given the order to run, we'd be dead. And I've just been made a major.'

'Congratulations.'

'I'm pleased too.' D'Alembord spoke with a bitter sarcasm. He had wanted promotion, indeed it was the prime reason he had stayed with the battalion, but he resented the sudden price of his majority.

'You're alive, Peter,' Sharpe consoled his friend, 'you're alive.'

'The bloody man.' D'Alembord stared savagely towards Ford. 'The bloody, bloody man. Why didn't he form square?'

Then, to the north, a bugle sounded. Fresh troops were visible at the crossroads, a mass of men who marched forward to make a new line across the battlefield. The horse artillery was among the infantry and, to their left, there was an impressive mass of horsemen. The British cavalry had at last arrived.

'I suppose we've won this battle!' D'Alembord slowly sheathed his sword.

'I suppose we have,' Sharpe said.

But it felt horribly like a defeat.

Drums sounded, bayonets were levelled, and the newly formed British line marched forward. The infantry trod across the scorched straw, over the smears of blood, and around the dead and the dying bodies of horses and men.

From the southern end of the wood, where Saxe-Weimar's men had held through the day, the Guards division attacked the western farms. The French infantry fought back, but could not hold. In the centre the redcoats marched through the stream, recaptured Gemioncourt farm, and went on up the slope. At the far left of the battlefield the Rifles drove the French back to recapture the eastern farms.

Every inch of ground that Marshal Ney had taken during the afternoon was regained. The British line, supported by guns and cavalry, ground on like a behemoth. The French, suddenly outnumbered, were forced to retreat towards Frasnes. Quatre Bras had held and the road to the Prussians was still open. The battle between Napoleon and Blücher still sounded loud in the summer's evening, but that too faded away as the shadows of the western clouds lengthened dark across the landscape.

Lord John Rossendale, riding behind the British light cavalry, stopped where a Cuirassier's body was sprawled beside the road. The man's guts had been flayed clean from his belly and now lay in a blue-red dribble across fifteen feet of the highway's churned surface. Lord John wanted to vomit, but only choked. He gasped for breath and twisted his horse away. A dead British skirmisher lay in the trampled rye, his skull laid open by a bullet. Flies were thick on the exposed brains. Next to the dead man was a French Voltigeur, blood thick in his belly and lap. The man was alive, but shivering with the trauma of his wound. He stared up at Lord John and asked for water. Lord John felt faint with shock. He turned his horse and galloped towards the crossroads where his servants were preparing supper.

In the barns behind the crossroads the surgeons were at their grisly work with knives and saws and probes. The amputated arms, hands, and legs were tossed into the farmyard. Lanterns were hung from the barn beams to light the operations. A Highlander, his right calf shattered by a French cannon-ball, refused to bite the leather gag and made not a sound as a surgeon took his leg off at the knee.

Sharpe and Harper, knowing they were not welcome to stay near the brooding Lieutenant-Colonel Ford, walked their horses back down the flank of the wood, but stopped well short of the crossroads. 'I suppose I'm out of work,' Sharpe said.

'The bugger'll want you back in the morning.'

'Maybe.'

The two Riflemen tethered their horses in a clearing among the trees, then Sharpe walked out to the bloody patch of ground where the 69th had died. He picked up four discarded bayonets and took the leather bootlaces off two corpses. Back in the wood he made a fire with twigs and gunpowder. He stuck the bayonets into the ground at the four corners of the fire, then pulled the straps off the Cuirassier's breastplate that Harper had scavenged earlier. He threaded the bootlaces into the holes at the shoulders and waist of the breastplate, then waited.

Harper had taken his own knife out to the battlefield. He found a dead horse and cut a thick bloody steak from its rump. Then, the steak dripping in his left hand, he crossed to one of the silent British guns and, ignoring its crew, stooped under the barrel to scrape away a handful of the gun's axle grease.

Back in the wood Harper slapped the axle grease into the upturned breastplate, ripped the pelt off the steak, then dropped the meat into the cold grease. 'I'll water the horses while you cook.'

Sharpe nodded acknowledgement. He fed the fire with branches he had cut and split with his sword. In the morning, before the army marched to join Blücher, he would find a cavalry armourer to put an edge back on the blade. Then he wondered whether he would even be with the army next day. The Prince had dismissed him so he might as well ride back to Brussels and take Lucille to England.

Sharpe tied the breastplate to the four bayonets so that it hung like a steel hammock above the flames. By the time Harper brought the horses back from the stream the steak was sizzling and smoking in the bubbling grease.

Night was falling across the trampled rye. Nine thousand men had been killed or wounded in the fight for the crossroads, and some of the injured still moaned and cried in the darkness. Some bandsmen still searched for the wounded, but many would have to wait till the next day for rescue.

'Rain tomorrow.' Harper sniffed the air.

'Like as not.'

'It's good to smell proper food again.' A dog ranged near the fire, but Harper drove it away by shying a clod of earth at it.

Sharpe burned the meat black, then carefully cut it in halves and speared one piece on his knife. 'Yours.'

They held their meat on knife points, gnawed it down, and shared a canteen of wine that Harper had taken from a dead French Lancer. In the east the first stars pricked pale against a sky still misted by battle smoke. In the west it was darker, made so by the towering clouds. Men sang behind the crossroads while somewhere in the wood a flautist made a melancholy music. The trees sparkled with camp-fires, while to the south, and reflecting against the spreading clouds, a red glow showed where Marshal Ney's troops made their bivouacs.

'Crapauds fought well today,' Harper said grudgingly.

Sharpe nodded, then shrugged. 'They should have attacked with their infantry, though. They'd have won if they had.'

'I suppose we'll be at it again tomorrow?'

'Unless the Prussians have beaten Boney and won the war for us.'

Sharpe fetched a flask of calvados from his saddlebag, took a swig and handed it to Harper. The flute music was plangent. He had once wanted to learn the flute, and had thought to make an attempt this last winter, but instead he had spent the evenings making an elaborate cradle from applewood. He had meant to decorate the cradle's hood with carvings of wild flowers, but he had found their intricate curves too difficult to cut so had settled for the straight stark lines of piled drums and weapons. Lucille had been hugely amused by her baby's martial cot.

'Shouldn't you go and see the Prince?' Harper asked.

'Why the hell should I? Bugger the bastard.'

Harper chuckled. He sat with his back propped against his saddle and stared into the dark void where the battle had been fought. 'It's not the same, is it?'

'What isn't?'

'It's not like Spain.' He paused, thinking of the men

184

who were not here, then named just one of those men. 'Sweet William.'

Sharpe grunted. William Frederickson had once been a friend almost as close as Harper, but Frederickson had tilted a lance at Lucille, and lost, and had never forgiven Sharpe for that loss.

Harper, who disliked that the two officers were not on speaking terms, offered the flask to Sharpe. 'We could have done with him here today.'

'That's true.' Yet Frederickson was in a Canadian garrison, just one of the thousands of veterans who had been dispersed round the globe, which meant that the Emperor must be fought with too many raw battalions who had never stood in the battle line and who froze like rabbits when the cavalry threatened.

Far to the west a sheet of lightning flickered in the sky and thunder grumbled like a far sound of gunnery. 'Rain tomorrow,' Harper said again.

Sharpe yawned. Tonight, at least, he was well fed and dry. He suddenly remembered that he was supposed to have been given Lord John's promissory note, but it had not come. That was a problem best left for the morning, but for now he wrapped himself in the cloak that was Lucille's gift and within a few minutes he was fast asleep.

And the Emperor's campaign was forty-one hours old.

THE THIRD DAY
Saturday, 17 June 1815

CHAPTER 10

More battalions, cavalry squadrons and gun batteries arrived at the crossroads throughout the short night until, at dawn, the Duke's army was at last almost wholly assembled. In the first sepulchral light the newcomers stared dully at the small shapes which lay in the mist that shrouded the hollows of the battlefield. Bugles roused the bivouacs, while the wounded, left all night in the rye, called pitifully for help. The night sentries were called in and a new picquet line set to face the French camp-fires at Frasnes. The British camp-fires were revived with new kindling and a scattering of gunpowder. Men fished in their ammunition pouches for handfuls of tea leaves that were contributed to the common pots. Officers, socially visiting between the battalions, spread the cheerful news that Marshal Blücher had repulsed Bonaparte's attack, so now it seemed certain that the French would retreat in the face of a united Prussian-British army.

'We'll be in France next week!' an infantry captain assured his men.

'Paris by July, lads,' a sergeant forecast. 'Just think of all those girls.'

The Duke of Wellington, who had slept in an inn three miles from Quatre Bras, returned to the crossroads at first light. The Highlanders of the 92nd made him a fire and served him tea. He cupped the tin mug in both hands and stared southwards towards Marshal Ney's positions, but the French troops were silent and unmoving beneath the heavy cloud cover that had spread from the west during the short hours of darkness. One of the Duke's staff officers, heavily protected by a troop of King's German Legion cavalry, was sent eastwards to learn the morning's news from Marshal Blücher.

Officers used French Cuirassiers' upturned breastplates as shaving bowls; the senior officers having the privilege of the water when it was hot and the Lieutenants and Ensigns being forced to wait till the water was cold and congealed. The infantrymen who had fought the previous day boiled yet more water to clean their fouled musket barrels. Cavalry troopers queued to have their swords or sabres ground to a killing edge on the treadled stones, while the gunners filled the shot-cases of their field carriages with ready ammunition. There was an air of cheerfulness about the crossroads; the feeling that the army had survived an ordeal the previous day, but that now, and thanks largely to the victory of the Prussians, it was on the verge of triumph. The only grumble was that in the desperate hurry to reach Quatre Bras the army had left its commissariat wagons far behind so that most of the battalions started their day hungry.

The battlefield was searched for bodies. The wounded who still lived were taken back to the surgeons, while the dead were collected for burial. Most of the dead officers had been buried the previous night, so now the diggers would look after as many rank and file as they could. Sharpe and Harper, waking in the overcast dawn, found themselves just a few yards away from a work party that was scratching a wide and shallow trench in which the slaughtered men of the 69th would be interred. The waiting bodies lay in such natural poses that they almost seemed to be asleep. Captain Harry Price of the Prince of Wales's Own Volunteers found the two Riflemen drinking their morning tea just as the first corpses were being dragged towards the inadequate grave. 'Any tea for a gallant officer?' Price begged.

Harper cheerfully scooped another mug of stewed tea out of the breastplate kettle. The dead, who had been stripped of their uniforms, stank already. It was only an hour after dawn yet the day threatened to be humid and sticky and the grave diggers were sweating as they hacked at the soil. 'They'll have to dig deeper than that,' Harper commented as he handed Price the tin mug.

Price sipped the tea, then grimaced at its sour after-taste of axle grease. 'Do you remember the chaos we made trying to burn those poor buggers at Fuentes de Oñoro?'

Sharpe laughed. The ground at Fuentes de Oñoro had been too shallow and rocky to make graves, so he had ordered his dead cremated, but even after tearing down a whole wooden barn and lifting the rafters off six small houses to use as fuel, the bodies had refused to burn.

'They were good days,' Price said wistfully. He squinted up at the sky. 'It'll pour with bloody rain soon.' The clouds were low and extraordinarily dark, as though their looming heaviness had trapped the vestiges of night. 'A rotten day for a battle,' Price said gloomily.

'Is there going to be a battle?' Harper asked.

'That's what the Brigade Major told our gallant Colonel.' Price told Sharpe and Harper the dawn news of Prussian victory, and how the French were supposed to be retreating and how the army would be pursuing the French who were expected to make one last stand before yielding the frontier to the Emperor's enemies.

'How are our lads feeling about yesterday?' Harper asked Price, and Sharpe noticed how, to the Irishman, the battalion was still 'our lads'.

'They're pleased that Mr d'Alembord's a major, but he's not exactly overjoyed.'

'Why not?' Sharpe asked.

'He says he's going to die. He's got a what do you call it? A premonition. He says it's because he's going to be married.'

'What's that got to do with it?'

Price shrugged as if to demonstrate that he was no expert on superstitions. 'He says it's because he's happy. He reckons that the happiest die first and only the miserable buggers live for ever.'

'You should have been dead long ago,' Harper commented.

'Thank you, Sergeant,' Harry Price grinned. He was a carefree, careless and casual man, much liked by his men, but averse to too much effort. He had served as Sharpe's Lieutenant at one time, and had been perpetually in debt, frequently drunk, yet ever cheerful. Now he drained the vestiges of his tea. 'I'm supposed to be reporting to brigade to discover just when we march off.' He shuddered with sudden distaste. 'That was a bloody horrible mug of tea.'

'It had a bit of dead horse in it,' Harper explained helpfully.

'God damn Irish cooking. I suppose I'd better go and do my duty.' Price gave Harper the mug back and ambled on with a cheerful good morning to the burial party.

'And what are we going to do?' Harper asked Sharpe.

'Use the rest of the tea as shaving water, then bugger off.' Sharpe had no wish to stay with the army. The Prince had relieved him of his duties and, if the rumours were true, the French invasion had been thwarted by Blücher's Prussians. The rest of the war would be a pursuit through the fortress belt of northern France until the Emperor surrendered. Sharpe decided he might as well sit it out in Brussels, then go back to his apple trees in Normandy. 'I suppose I never will get to fight the Emperor.' He spoke wistfully, feeling oddly let down. Yesterday's battle had been an unsatisfactory way to gain victory, but Sharpe was an old enough soldier to take victory whichever way it came. 'Is there more tea?'

A troop of King's German Legion cavalry trotted southwards, presumably going to the picquet line to watch for the beginnings of the enemy's withdrawal. Some Guardsmen were singing in the wood behind Sharpe, while other redcoats moved slowly across the trampled rye collecting discarded weapons. A few mounted officers rode among the debris of battle, either looking for keepsakes or friends. Among the horsemen, and looking very lost, was Lieutenant Simon Doggett who seemed to be searching the wood's edge. Sharpe had an impulse to move back into the shelter of the trees, but lazily stayed where he was, then wished he had obeyed the impulse when Doggett, catching sight of his green jacket, spurred past the 69th's mass grave. 'Good morning, sir.' Doggett offered Sharpe a very formal salute.

Sharpe returned the salute by raising his mug of tea. 'Morning, Doggett. Bloody horrible morning, too.'

'The Baron would like to see you, sir.' Doggett sounded deeply uncomfortable as though he was still embarrassed by his memory of Sharpe's altercation with the Prince. Sharpe may have been right to protest the Prince's order, but a Prince was still a Prince, and the habit of respectful obedience was deeply ingrained in Doggett.

'I'm here if Rebecque wants me,' Sharpe said stubbornly.

'He's waiting just beyond the crossroads, sir. Please, sir.'

Sharpe refused to hurry. He finished his tea, shaved carefully, then buckled on his sword and slung his rifle. Only then did he walk back to the crossroads where the Baron Rebecque waited for him.

The Dutchman smiled a greeting at Sharpe, then gestured up the high road as if suggesting that the two of them might care to take a morning stroll. The fields on either side of the road were thick with the men who had reached Quatre Bras during the night and who were now readying themselves to pursue the beaten French. 'It rather looks like rain, doesn't it?' Rebecque observed mildly.

'It's going to rain like the very devil.' Sharpe glanced up at the bellying dark clouds. 'It won't be any kind of a day for musketry.'

Rebecque stared at the grass verge rather than at the clouds or at the tall Rifleman who walked beside him. 'You were right,' he said at last.

Sharpe shrugged, but said nothing.

'And the Prince knows you were right, and he feels badly.'

'So tell the little bastard to apologize. Not to me, but to the widows of the 69th.'

Rebecque smiled at Sharpe's vehemence. 'One is generally disappointed if one expects royalty to make apologies. He's young, very headstrong, but he's a good man underneath. He has the impatience of youth; the conviction that bold action will bring immediate success. Yesterday he was wrong, but who can say that tomorrow he won't be right? Anyway, he needs the advice of people he respects, and he respects you.' Rebecque, suffering from the day's first attack of hay fever, blew his nose into a huge red handkerchief. 'And he's very upset that you're angry with him.'

'What the hell does he expect after he dismisses me?'

Rebecque waved the handkerchief as though to suggest that the dismissal was a nonsense. 'You're not just a staff officer, Sharpe, you're a courtier as well. You have to treat him gently.'

'What the hell does that mean, Rebecque?' Sharpe

had stopped to challenge the mild Dutchman with a hostile stare. 'That I'm to let him slaughter a brigade of British troops just because he's got a crown on his damned head?'

'No, Sharpe.' Rebecque kept remarkably calm in the face of Sharpe's truculence. 'It means that when he gives you an idiotic order, you say, "Yes, sir. At once, sir," and you ride away and you waste as much time as you can, and when you get back and he demands to know why the order hasn't been obeyed, you say you'll attend to it at once and you ride away again and waste even more time. It's called tact.'

'Bugger tact,' Sharpe said angrily, though he suspected Rebecque was right.

'Yesterday you should have told him that the brigade was going to obey his order and would deploy into line just as soon as there was any enemy movement in front of them. That way he'd have felt his orders were being obeyed.'

'So it's my fault they died?' Sharpe protested angrily.

'Of course it isn't. Oh, damn!' Rebecque sneezed violently. 'I'm just asking you to deal with him tactfully. He wants you! He needs you! Why do you think he specifically requested that you should be on his staff?'

'I've often wondered,' Sharpe said bitterly.

'Because you're famous in this army. You're a soldier's soldier. If the Prince has you beside him then he reflects some of your fame and valour.'

'You mean I'm like one of those decorations he dangles round his skinny neck?'

Rebecque nodded. 'Yes, Sharpe, that is exactly what you are. And that's why he needs you now. He made a mistake, the whole army knows he made a mistake, but it's important that we continue to show confidence in him.' Rebecque looked up into Sharpe's face. 'So, please, make your peace with him.'

'I don't even like him,' Sharpe said bitterly.

Rebecque sighed. 'I do. And he does want to be liked. You'll find him much easier if you flatter him. But if you cross him, or make him feel foolish, he'll just become petulant.' Rebecque offered a ghost of a smile. 'And royalty is very good at being petulant. It is, perhaps, its major talent.'

Sharpe waited while a cart of wounded rumbled noisily past, then looked into Rebecque's eyes. 'So now you want me to apologize to the little bastard?'

'I'm astonished how swiftly you learn our courtly ways,' Rebecque smiled. 'No. I shall apologize for you. I shall say that you deeply regret having caused his Highness any perturbation and wish only to be at his side as an adviser and friend.'

Sharpe began to laugh. 'It's a bloody odd world, Rebecque.'

'So you'll report for duty?'

Sharpe wondered just how much duty would be left in the war now that the Emperor was beaten, but he nodded his acceptance anyway. 'I need the money, Rebecque. Of course I'll report back.'

Rebecque seemed relieved. He offered his snuffbox to Sharpe, who refused the offer. Rebecque, as though he was not sneezing enough already, put a pinch of the powder on his left hand, sniffed it vigorously, sneezed three times, then wiped his eyes with his handkerchief. A file of shirt-sleeved cavalry troopers walked past with canvas buckets of water for their horses.

'So where is the Prince?' Sharpe asked. He supposed the bullet would have to be bitten and he would need to face the bloody boy.

Rebecque gestured northwards, suggesting that the Young Frog was many miles up the road. 'I'm keeping him well out of harm's way. It would be politically disastrous if he was taken prisoner today.'

Sharpe stared with surprise at the kindly middle-aged Dutchman. 'What does that mean? Wasn't there the same danger yesterday?'

'Yesterday,' Rebecque said mildly, 'we weren't retreating. Any minute now, Sharpe, and this whole army could be surrounded and fighting for its very existence.'

'Its existence? I thought we were pursuing the bloody French today!'

It was Rebecque's turn to look surprised. 'Didn't you know? Blücher got beaten. His army wasn't destroyed, thank God, but they took a thrashing and have been forced to retreat.' Rebecque sounded very calm as he delivered the appalling news. 'It seems that their Chief of Staff preferred us to think that they had won. That way, our army stayed here as a temptation for Napoleon. He might prefer to attack us, you see, and let the Prussians escape. It's really quite a clever Prussian ploy, when you think about it, but likely to be damned uncomfortable for us.'

'The Prussians are retreating?' Sharpe sounded disbelieving.

'They went late last night, which means we're stranded here on our own. Marshal Ney is still in front of us and at any minute the rest of the French army will attack our left flank.'

Sharpe instinctively looked to the east, but nothing moved in the cloud shadowed landscape of woods and fields. He tried to understand this new reality. Yesterday's victory at Quatre Bras was all for nothing, because Napoleon had kicked the two doors wide apart and the allies were separated. The Prussians had fled in the night and the British had been left isolated to face the full power of the Emperor's whole army.

'So very soon,' Rebecque continued placidly, 'we're going to retreat. The Duke's not making too much fuss, because he doesn't want to start any panic. There's only this one road we can use, you see, and once the rain starts it's likely to be difficult going.'

Sharpe remembered Wellington leaning over the map in the Duke of Richmond's dressing-room. 'Are we going to Waterloo?' he asked Rebecque.

The Dutchman seemed surprised that Sharpe had even heard of the village, but nodded. 'We're going just to the south of Waterloo, to a place called Mont-St-Jean. We march there today, make a stand there tomorrow, and pray that the Prussians will rescue us.'

'Rescue?' Sharpe bridled at the word.

'Of course.' Rebecque, as ever, was imperturbable. 'Blücher has promised that if we make a stand he'll march to our aid. That's so long as the French don't stop him, of course, and undoubtedly they'll be trying. Yesterday we failed to reach him, so we can only pray that tomorrow he doesn't repay the compliment. We certainly can't beat Napoleon on our own, so if Blücher lets us down we're all beaten.' Rebecque smiled at his catalogue of bad news. 'All in all, Sharpe, things are not good. Are you sure you still wish to serve on His Highness's staff?'

'I told you, I need the money.'

'Of course, we may never reach Mont-St-Jean today. The Emperor must realize that he has us at his mercy, so I've no doubt he's hurrying to attack us even now. Might I suggest that you serve as the Prince's personal picquet on the retreat? If it looks as though the Emperor will break through and destroy us, send word to me. I'd rather His Royal Highness wasn't taken prisoner because it would be politically very embarrassing. Keep young Doggett as a messenger. Did you have any breakfast?'

'Some tea.'

'I've got some bread and cold beef in my saddle-bag.' Rebecque turned back towards the crossroads and offered to shake Sharpe's hand. 'The knack of being right, Sharpe, is not to show it. It embarrasses the incompetent who rule over us.'

Sharpe smiled and took the offered hand. 'Then thank God for the Duke of Wellington.'

'Even he may not be good enough for this predicament. We shall see.' Rebecque walked back to his horse and used a stone wall by the crossroads as a mounting block. He settled himself in the saddle. 'Send word if disaster threatens, otherwise, do your best to keep dry.' He handed the food down to Sharpe, then clicked his tongue and rode northwards.

Sharpe turned to stare east and south. Somewhere under the lowering clouds was the man he had fought against for most of his life, yet had never once seen. The Emperor of France, conqueror of the world, was coming to fight the British at last.

The rain, like the French, held off.

The news of the Prussian defeat spread swiftly. Optimism turned to resignation, then to nervousness as the army realized how precarious was its position. The whole might of the French army was about to be concentrated on Quatre Bras and there was no hope of any help from the Prussians.

The retreat began. One by one the battalions of infantry were despatched towards the crossroads at Mont-St-Jean which lay twelve miles to the north. The men who waited their turn grew increasingly tense; every battalion which escaped north was one battalion less to face the expected French onslaught, which left the rearguard ever more likely to be outnumbered and overwhelmed. Marshal Ney's troops were still just to the south, and the Emperor was presumably hurrying from the east, yet battalion after British battalion slipped away unmolested as the morning passed without any French attack.

The Duke of Wellington pretended insouciance. For

a time he sat on the trampled rye reading a newspaper, and even lay down and slept with its pages over his face. He still slept as the outermost picquets were pulled back, yielding the stream and Gemioncourt farm to the French if they cared to advance. Strangely the French did not move and their camp-fires still burned to drift placid smoke up to the darkening clouds.

By midday those clouds were as looming and threatening as the monsoon skies of India. The windless air was curiously still and heavy, presaging disaster. The last infantry battalions edged towards the road that led northwards out of the unsprung French trap. The horse artillery who, together with the cavalry, would form the British rearguard nervously watched the enemy-held ground, but still no French troops marched from Frasnes or appeared in the east. The only sign of the enemy was their smoke.

'They always used to do that,' Harper commented. The Irishman, with Sharpe and Doggett, waited at the edge of the wood by the half-covered grave of the 69th.

'Do what?' Doggett asked.

'Take a morning off after a battle and cook themselves a meal.'

'Let's hope it's a big meal,' Doggett grinned.

The Guards were the last of the British infantry to march north, leaving only the horse gunners, the cavalry and the staff at the crossroads. That rearguard waited long after the Guards had left, giving the slower infantry a good chance to march well clear of Quatre Bras. Still the French hesitated, and still the rain did not come. The first of the British cavalry trotted north and Sharpe saw the Duke of Wellington at last pull himself into his saddle. 'Time for us to go too,' Sharpe said.

A vagary of the storm-threatening clouds caused a rent somewhere in the churning sky and a leprous shaft of sunlight, yellow and misted, slanted down to shine on the highway beside Gemioncourt farm.

'Dear God!' Doggett was staring at the curiously bright patch of land beneath the sky's unnatural blackness.

In which sunlit patch were Lancers.

There were suddenly thousands of Lancers. Lancers in green coats and Lancers in scarlet coats. The farmland had sprouted a thicket of flag-hung spear points that were touched gold by the errant shaft of sunlight.

'Let's get the hell out of here!' Sharpe settled himself into his saddle.

'No, sir! Look! Look!' An excited Doggett was standing in his stirrups, pointing south. Sharpe turned back, saw nothing, so pulled his telescope from his saddlebag.

The lens slid past the foreshortened Lancers, back through the dust which their hooves were kicking up from the rye fields, and back up the white highway to where, outlined against the sun brightened crops and illuminated by the wash of errant light, was a single horseman. The man was darkly dressed, mounted on a grey horse, and wearing a cocked hat sideways across his scalp. He was slumped in his saddle, as though he rode unwillingly.

'It's him!' Doggett spoke almost reverently.

'My God.' Sharpe's voice was awed. There, in his glass, was the small plump man who had dominated Europe for the past ten years, a man Sharpe had never seen, but whose form and face and posture were familiar from a thousand engravings and a thousand statues. Sharpe handed the glass to Harper who stared at the far Emperor.

'It's Bonaparte!' Doggett sounded as excited as though he saw his own monarch riding towards him.

'It *is* bloody time to get out of here,' Harper said.

The Lancers climbed the shallow slope from the ford and, in greeting, every waiting British gun was fired.

The cannons crashed back violently. The gun wheels jarred up while the ground quivered with dust. Smoke jetted twenty yards in front of each cannon muzzle while, above the trampled crops, the shell fuses left small white smoke trails that arced towards the line of advancing cavalry. There was a pause, then it seemed as though the Lancers plunged into a maelstrom of exploding shells. Smoke and flame billowed as horses screamed. Sharpe saw a lance cartwheeling above a boiling mass of smoke.

Then, as if to show that man was puny, a sudden wind howled from the north-west. The wind erupted so abruptly that Sharpe half twisted in the saddle, fearing an exploding shell behind him, and as he turned there was a booming discharge of thunder that sounded like the end of time itself. The rift in the clouds closed as though a vast door had slammed in heaven, and the reverberation of the door was the horrendous thunder that hammered down at the earth in a deafening cascade. A spear of lightning sliced blue-white into the far woods, and then the rain came.

In an instant the whole battlefield was blotted from sight. It was a cloudburst, a torrent, a seething pelting storm that slashed down to soak the fields and flood the ditches and hiss where it hit the hot barrels of the cannons. Sharpe had to shout to make himself heard over the downpour. 'Let's go! Come on!'

Within seconds the field had been churned into a morass. The rain was even heavier than the great sky-shaking storms Sharpe had seen in India. As he led his companions out from the trees' shelter he had to duck his head against the maniacal force of the wind-whipped torrents that soaked his uniform in seconds. The horses struggled against the gale of rain, their hooves sticking in the glutinous mess of mud and straw. The rainwater sluiced off the fields with its load of precious soil, uncovering the white swollen bodies of the barely buried dead.

Thunder cracked in the sky; a battle of Gods that drowned the man-made sounds of war. The vast explosions rumbled from west to east, rebounded, split the clouds with multiple forks of lightning, and deluged the crouching earth. Sharpe led Harper and Doggett onto the Nivelles road that was now a writhing river of water-carried mud. He could see a troop of cloaked cavalry to his left, and a gun team hitching their weapon to its limber on his right, but any object more than thirty yards away was utterly obscured by the silver shafts of rain that crashed down like shrapnel. Behind Sharpe a gun fired, its sound drowned by the greater violence of the storm.

Sharpe turned onto the main highway. The paved surface was firmer; a causeway out of disaster. The hooves of those cavalry horses who struggled northwards in the flanking fields were clubbed with earth; proof that no gun would escape unless it reached the road.

'Move! Move! Move!' Gunners whipped their horses up from the fields onto the road that was swimming with a chalky white effluent. The horses strained, seemingly sensing their masters' panic caused by the near presence of enemy lancers. Men glanced behind into the storm-blotted landscape, then whipped at the gun teams till at last the horse artillery was clear of Quatre Bras and galloping northwards with blood dripping from the horses' whipped flanks and water spraying silver off the gun wheels. Sharpe, Harper and Doggett raced with them.

Miraculously no gun was lost. The mad charge was checked at the village of Genappe where the road narrowed as it twisted between the thatched cottages. The delay gave the French pursuit a chance to catch the rearmost guns, but a regiment of British Dragoons turned and charged the Lancers. More French cavalry spurred forward and it took an assault by the heavy Life Guards, the sovereign's own escort, to drive the Frenchmen away. The Life Guards, scarlet coated and wearing black and gold Grecian cockscomb helmets, hammered at the enemy with their ungainly heavy swords. The sheer weight of the heavy cavalry drove the lighter French horsemen back, giving the guns time to thread the narrow village street.

North of Genappe the French pursuit seemed to lose its ferocity. The rain also slackened, though it was still heavy. Every mile or so the British guns would stop, unlimber, fire a few rounds at their pursuers, then gallop on. The French were never far behind, but did not press home. The British cavalry, Dragoons and Life Guards, hovered on the flanks. Every few moments, when a French squadron trotted close, the British would advance, but each time the French declined to fight. Sharpe was amused to see that if a Life Guardsman tumbled from a slipping horse the man would remount, then hide his soiled uniform in the rear rank of his troop, just as if he was on parade in Hyde Park.

The French managed to bring up some of their own light eight-pounder cannons that opened fire with roundshot. The small cannon-balls fountained a slurry of mud and water wherever they landed. The mud was saving the retreat, not only soaking up the power of the French roundshot, but forcing the French cavalry to stay close to the high road. If the land had been dry the quick light enemy horse could have raced far round the British flanks to come slashing in with lance and sabre on the struggling column, but the mud and rain held them back.

Another weapon came to the British aid. A sudden crashing hiss made Sharpe twist round to see a rocket being fired. He had fought with rockets in Spain, but familiarity did not blunt his fascination with the odd weapon and he watched enthralled as the ungainly missile hurled itself forward on its pillar of flame that scorched the long stick that gave the rocket its balance. Doggett, who had never seen the new and mysterious weapon, was impressed, but Harper shook his head scornfully. 'They're guaranteed to miss every time, Mr Doggett. You just watch.'

The first rocket arched in fire across the damp valley to leave a serpentine trail of smoke. The missile fell towards the French guns, then the fuse inside its head exploded and a rain of red-hot shrapnel crashed down to slaughter every man in a French gun crew.

'Good God Almighty,' Harper said in astonished wonder, 'the bloody thing worked!'

Encouraged by their success, the rocket artillery fired a whole barrage. Twelve rockets were fired from twelve metal troughs angled upwards on short legs. The rockets' fuses were lit, then the rocketmen ran for cover. The missiles began to spew flames and smoke. For a few seconds they quivered in their firing troughs, then one by one they shot up into the wet air. They wobbled at first, then their acceleration hurled them on. Two streaked straight up into the clouds and disappeared, three dived into the wet meadow where their rocket flames seared the wet grass as the missiles circled crazily, five went vaguely towards the French but dived to earth long before they did any damage, and two circled back towards the British cavalry who stared for a second, then scattered in panic.

'That's more like it,' Harper said happily. 'That's how they always used to be, isn't that so, Mr Sharpe?'

But Sharpe was neither listening, nor watching the barrage. Instead he was staring across the highway to where a group of horsemen had scattered frantically away from the rogue rocket's threat. Lord John Rossendale had been among the small group, but, in his effort to find safety, was now separated from his friends.

'I'll join you up the road,' Sharpe said to Harper.

'Sir?' Harper was startled, but Sharpe had already twisted his horse away. And gone.

Lord John Rossendale could not remember being so wet, elated, frightened, or confused. Nothing made sense to him. He expected a battle – and the retreat seemed like a battle to him – to be something orderly and well managed. Officers should give loud confident orders which the men would smartly obey and to which the enemy would dutifully yield, but instead he was surrounded by disorder. Strangely the actors in that disorder seemed to understand what needed to be done. He watched a battery of horse artillery unlimber and go into action. No orders were given that Rossendale could hear, but the men knew exactly what to do, did it with cheerful efficiency, then limbered up to continue their mad careering gallop through the rain. Once, standing his horse in the pelting flood, Lord John had been shocked to hear a voice yelling at him to bloody well move his arse and Lord John had skipped his horse smartly aside only to see that it was a mere sergeant who had shouted. A second later a gun slewed in a spray of mud to occupy the very place where Lord John's horse had been standing. Ten seconds later the gun fired, appalling Lord John with its sound and the violence of its recoil. In Hyde Park, which was the only place Lord John had ever seen cannons fired before, the polished guns made a decorous bang and, because there was no missile packed down onto the charge, such guns hardly moved at all, but this weapon, dirty, muddy and blackened, seemed to explode in noise and flame. Its wheels lifted clear out of the mud as its trail was driven back like a plough before the tons of metal and wood crashed down and its mud-covered crew ran forward to serve the smoking beast with sponges and rammers.

Yet, curiously, the violence of the discharge seemed

very disproportionate to the gun's effect. Lord John watched the missile's strike and there would be a gout of mud, perhaps an explosion if the gun had fired shell, but so little destruction. Once he had seen a Lancer fall from his horse, but within seconds the man had been on his feet and another Frenchman had quickly rescued the frightened horse.

At Genappe Lord John had been close enough to see the Life Guards charge and he had even spurred forward to join them. He had watched a sword snap a lance shaft like a twig. He had seen a Lancer's skull crushed by a blade. He had watched a Life Guard twisting like a fish on the point of a lance. He had heard the grunt of a man making a killing lunge, and heard the hiss of air from a wounded trooper's lungs. He had smelt the sweet thickness of blood and the acrid drift of pistol smoke in the soaking air. Blood from a dying horse spewed onto the road to be instantly diluted by rain. By the time Lord John had drawn his sword and touched his spurs to his horse's flanks, the French had pulled back leaving a dozen dead and twice as many wounded. It had all been so quick and so confusing, but an acquaintance of Lord John's, a Captain Kelly whom Lord John had often met when he was on royal duty, gave his lordship a happy confident smile. 'Bagged a brace of them!'

'Well done, Ned.'

'Once you're past the lance point it's a bit like killing rabbits.' Captain Kelly began wiping the blood off his blade. 'Too easy, really.'

Lord John tried to imagine slipping past a lance point and found it hard. After the skirmish, riding through the village street, he had seen the fear on the faces of the civilians and he had felt very superior to such muddy drab creatures. Later, north of Genappe, when the French did not pursue so closely, he noticed how nervous both sets of cavalry were of each other. A lot of threats were made, and men would ride belligerently forward as if to provoke the other side, but if there was no clear advantage to be gained for either force, the two sides would disengage without a battle. It was all very odd.

Strangest of all were the rockets. Lord John had heard much of the rocket corps, for they were a pet project of his former master, the Prince Regent, but this was the first time he had seen them fired. The first missile was wonderfully accurate and so lethal that every French gun crew within a hundred yards had fled in panic, but the next salvo was laughable. One rocket had seemed to threaten the group of Lord Uxbridge's staff officers and they had whooped gleefully as they scattered away from its hissing shell. Lord John spurred his horse too hard and it almost bolted with him. He managed to curb the mare after a hundred yards and turned to see the rocket buried in the mud with its stick burning merrily above it. The buried powder charge exploded harmlessly.

Then, looking towards the road to find his friends, he saw Sharpe coming towards him instead.

For a second Lord John knew he must stand and fight. The next second he realized he would be dead if he did.

And so he turned and fled.

Lord John's servants were somewhere ahead with the cavalry's baggage. Harris, the coachman, who had ridden from Brussels with a letter from Jane, had also ridden ahead to find that night's quarters. Christopher Manvell and Lord John's other friends had disappeared in the panic engendered by the rogue rocket. Lord John was suddenly alone in the pelting rain with his one dreadful enemy spurring towards him.

He gave his horse its head. It was a good horse, five years old and trained on the hunting field. It had stamina and speed, and was certainly a faster horse than Sharpe rode, and Lord John had learned on the hunting field how best to ride treacherous country. He must have stretched his lead by an extra hundred yards in the first half mile. There were ironic cheers from the road where the retreating gunners supposed the two officers to be racing.

Lord John was oblivious to the cheers and the rain; indeed to everything but his predicament. He was cursing himself; he should have ridden towards his companions and sheltered under their protection, but instead, in a blind panic, he was racing ever further away from help. He dared not look behind. His horse thundered along a field margin, raced over soaking rows of newly scythed hay, then galloped down a gentle incline towards a hedge, beyond which, and across one more field, a long dark copse of trees offered a concealed path back to the road.

His horse almost baulked at the hedge, not because of the height of the blackthorn, but because the approach to the obstacle was inches deep in mud. Lord John savagely rowelled the beast, and somehow it lumbered and scraped its way over the thorns. It landed heavily, splashing thick mud that soaked Lord John's red coat. He spurred the horse again, forcing it to struggle up from the sticky ground. The pasture was firmer going, but even here the earth was spongy from rain.

He reached the trees safely and, looking back from their shelter, saw that Sharpe had yet to negotiate the deep mud at the hedge. Lord John felt safe. He ducked into the thick and leafy copse which proved a perfect hiding place. The road, along which the guns crashed and jangled, was no more than a quarter-mile away and Lord John would be hidden under the wood's leafy, dripping cover right to the road's verge. There he could wait until his friends offered him support. Sharpe, he was certain, would try nothing violent in front of witnesses.

Lord John slowed his blown horse to a walk, letting it pick a twisting path between oak and beech. The rain spattered on the uppermost leaves and dripped miserably from the lower. A scrabbling sound to his right made him whip round in sudden alarm, but it was only a red squirrel racing along an oak branch. He sagged in the saddle, feeling despair.

He despaired because of honour. Honour was the simple code of the gentleman. Honour said a man did not run from an enemy, honour said a man did not flirt with the temptations of murder, and honour said a man did not show fear. Honour was the thin line that protected the privileged from disgrace, and Lord John, slouched in his wet saddle in a damp wood under a thunderous sky, knew he had run his honour ragged. Jane, in her letter, had threatened to leave him if he fulfilled his promise to return Sharpe's money. How long, she had asked, would Lord John allow Sharpe to persecute her happiness? If Lord John could not settle Sharpe, then she would find a man who would. She had underlined the word 'man' three times.

He stopped his horse. He could hear the gun wheels ahead of him, and closer, apparently on a ride that must have pierced the wood parallel to the road, the sound of hooves as a troop of cavalry splashed northwards.

Another voice nagged at Lord John. He could not bear it if another man was to take Jane. Jealousy racked him. He had persuaded himself that her sudden desperation to marry him was a measure of Jane's passionate love, and to think of that passion being expended for another man's happiness was more than he could endure.

A curb chain clinked. Lord John looked up to see his enemy in front of him. Sharpe must have guessed Lord John would double back under the cover of the trees, and so had ridden slantwise to where the wood met the road, then turned eastwards. Now, just twenty paces off, he sat his horse and stared at Lord John.

Lord John felt oddly calm. A few moments before his nerves had been jangled by a squirrel, but now that his enemy had come, and now that he knew what had to be done, he surprised himself by his calmness.

Neither man spoke. There was nothing to say.

Lord John licked the rainwater from his lips. If he drew his sword then he knew the green-jacketed killer would be on him like a fury, so he kept his hand well away from the silver-wrapped hilt of his sword, and instead, not caring for honour, he drew the long-barrelled pistol that was holstered on his saddle. It was a beautiful gun, a gift from Jane, with a percussion cap instead of a flint. Its elegantly curved pistol-hilt was of chased walnut and its long rifled barrel was blued and gilded. The rifling gave the weapon a deadly accuracy, while the expensive percussion cap made it proof against the worst downpour of rain. He drew back the hammer, exposing the small copper wafer in which the gunpowder was packed. When that wafer was struck a lance of flame would pierce through the touchhole to spark the main charge.

He raised the gun. His right hand shook slightly. Sharpe had made no move to defend himself, neither by flight nor by drawing a weapon of his own. Rainwater beaded the gun's barrel. Its blade foresight wavered. Lord John tried to remember his tuition. He must not be tense. He should take a deep breath, let half the air out of his lungs, momentarily hold his breath and, at the same instant, squeeze the trigger gently.

Sharpe urged his horse forward.

The sudden movement disconcerted Lord John, and the gun shook in his hand as he tried to follow Sharpe's advance. Sharpe seemed utterly oblivious of the pistol's threat, as though he had not even seen the weapon.

Lord John stared into his enemy's eyes. He knew he

should pull the trigger, but he was suddenly paralysed by fear. He could hear voices not very far off in the wood and he felt a dreadful fear that the murder might be witnessed, and Lord John knew it would be murder, and he knew the only mercy shown to him as a lord would be that he would be publicly hanged with a rope made of silk instead of a rope made from hemp. He wanted to pull the trigger, but his finger would not move, and all the time the hooves of Sharpe's horse slurred through the thick wet leaf mould until the Rifleman was so close to Lord John that the two men could have shaken hands without even leaning from their saddles. Sharpe had not once taken his eyes from Lord John's eyes even though the pistol was now just inches from his face.

Very slowly, Sharpe raised his right hand and pushed the pistol away. The movement seemed to startle Lord John from his trance, and he tried to pull the weapon back, but Sharpe had gripped the barrel firmly and now twisted it from Lord John's nerveless fingers. Lord John, expecting death, shivered.

Sharpe made the gun safe by lowering the hammer onto the percussion cap. Then, holding the barrel in his right hand and the curved stock in his left, he began levering the weapon apart. It took all his strength, but suddenly the wooden stock split away from the barrel pins and, when the trigger assembly had been wrenched loose, Sharpe was holding the gun in two useless halves which, still without a word, he dropped into Rossendale's lap. The expensive barrel slid down to thump on the leaves, while the torn walnut stock lodged by his lordship's topboot.

Lord John quivered and shook his head as Sharpe reached towards him, but the Rifleman just took hold of Lord John's sword hilt then, quite slowly, scraped the polished and engraved blade free. Sharpe looked up, thrust the narrow blade into the fork of a branch, and snapped the precious sword with one brutally violent jerk. Nine inches of steel was left with the handle, the rest of the blade slid down to the ground.

'You're not worth fighting.' Sharpe still held the broken sword hilt.

'I –'

'Shut your bloody mouth.'

'I –'

Sharpe's left hand slapped hard across Lord John's face. 'I'll tell you when to speak,' Sharpe said, 'and it isn't now. You listen. I don't care about Jane. She's your whore now. But I've got a farm in Normandy and it needs new apple trees and the barn needs a new roof, and the bloody Emperor took all our horses and cattle for his Goddamned army, and the taxes in France are bloody evil, and you've got my money. So where is it?'

Lord John seemed unable to speak. His eyes were wet, perhaps from the rain or else from the shame of this meeting under the trees.

'Has the whore spent it all?' Sharpe asked.

'Not all,' Lord John managed to say.

'Then how much is left?'

Lord John did not know, because Jane would not tell him, but he guessed that there might be five thousand pounds left. He stammered out the figure, fearing that Sharpe would be angered when he realized how much Jane had squandered.

Sharpe did not seem to care. Five hundred pounds was a fortune that would have restored Lucille's château. 'Give me a note now,' he told Lord John.

Lord John seriously doubted whether a promissory note with his signature had the legal force to produce the money, but if it satisfied Sharpe then Lord John was happy to write a thousand such notes. He snatched open the gilded flap of his sabretache and took out a leather-bound notebook and a pencil. He scribbled the words fast, the pencil's point tearing the paper where the rainwater dripped from his helmet's visor onto the page. He ripped the page out and handed it wordlessly to his tormentor.

Sharpe glanced at the words, then folded the paper. 'Where I come from,' he said in a conversational tone, 'men still sell their wives. Have you ever seen it done?'

Lord John shook his head warily.

'Because the poor can't afford a divorce, you see,' Sharpe continued, 'but if everyone agrees, then the woman can be sold. It has to be done in the market place. You put a rope round her neck, lead her there, and offer her to the highest bidder. The price and the buyer are always fixed in advance, of course, but making it an auction adds a bit of spice. I suppose you prinked up aristocratic bastards don't do that to your women?'

Lord John shook his head. 'We don't,' he managed to say. He was beginning to realize that Sharpe was not going to hurt him, and the realization was calming his nerves.

'I'm not a prinked up bastard,' Sharpe said. 'I'm the real thing, my lord. I'm a whore's bastard out of a gutter, so I'm allowed to sell my wife. She's yours. I've got your money,' Sharpe pushed the promissory note into his pocket, 'so all you need is this.' He fumbled in a saddlebag then drew out the scruffy piece of rope that was Nosey's usual leash. He tossed the dirty scrap of sisal across Lord John's saddle. 'Put the noose round her neck and tell her that you bought her. Among the people I come from, my lord, such a divorce is as good as an act of Parliament. The lawyers and the Church don't reckon it is, but who gives a turd about what those greedy bastards think? She's yours now. You've bought her, so you can marry her, and I won't interfere. Do you understand me?'

Lord John tentatively touched the rope. He knew he was being mocked. The poor might sell their wives, but no respectable man would ever so contract into a woman's second marriage. 'I understand you,' he said bitterly.

'But if I don't get the money, my lord, I'll come back for you.'

'I understand.'

Sharpe still held the broken sword. He held it hilt first towards Lord John. 'Go away, my lord.'

Rossendale took the truncated blade, stared one more time into the dark eyes, then spurred his horse forward. He fled from the trees, the rope still trailing from his saddle, and burst onto the road where the last of the guns were rolling northwards.

Sharpe waited a few moments. He swore silently to himself, for there had been no joy in humiliating the weak. But at least he considered he had made a good bargain. A new roof for the château in return for a faithless wife. He patted the pocket where the note was folded, then turned his horse. He was still somewhat shaken for, until he had actually taken the pistol from Lord John, Sharpe had not realized that it was a rainproof percussion weapon. Otherwise he would never have ridden so slowly to its black muzzle.

Harper waited for Sharpe on the high road. He had seen a shaken Lord John Rossendale burst from the trees, now, with a bemused Doggett beside him, the Irishman watched Sharpe urge his horse up to the paved surface. 'So what happened?' Harper asked.

'He pissed himself, then bought the bitch.'

Harper laughed. Doggett did not like to ask for any explanation. Behind them a gun fired a shell at the threatening Lancers, making Sharpe glance south at the pursuing French.

'Come on.' Sharpe lifted his face to the cleansing rain, then spurred his horse northwards.

Just twelve miles south of Brussels the highway to Charleroi and France became the wide main street of the village of Waterloo. South of the village the road threaded the forest of Soignes where the villagers grazed their pigs and chopped their firewood.

Two miles south of the village the trees gave way to a wide expanse of farmland which lay about the hamlet and crossroads of Mont-St-Jean. A half-mile further south still and the highway crossed a shallow, flat-topped ridge which lay east and west. At the crest of the ridge a solitary elm tree grew beside the highroad, which then descended into a wide and shallow valley that was filled with fields of rye, barley, oats and hay. The road crossed the valley before rising to another low ridge which lay three-quarters of a mile to the south. The crest of the southern ridge was marked by a white painted tavern called La Belle Alliance.

If an army took up a position on the northern ridge that was marked by the lone elm tree, and if an opposing army was to assemble around the tavern, then the gentle valley between would become a battlefield.

Between the elm tree and the tavern the road ran straight as a ramrod. A traveller riding the road would probably see nothing very remarkable in the valley other than the richness of its crops and the solidity of its farmhouses. It was evidently a good place to be a farmer.

In the centre of the valley, hard by the road itself, was a farm called La Haye Sainte. It was a prosperous place with a courtyard bounded by stone barns and a stout wall. To the east, three-quarters of a mile down the valley, was a huddle of cottages about a farm called Papelotte, while to the west there was another large farm with a walled courtyard and an extensive orchard which lay just north of a patch of rough woodland. That western farm was called the château of Hougoumont.

If a man wished to defend the northern ridge against an attack from the south, the château of Hougoumont might serve as a bastion on his right flank. La Haye Sainte would stand as a bulwark in the front and centre of his lines, while Papelotte would guard the left-hand edge of his defences.

All three farmsteads stood in the valley in front of the northern ridge, and as the ridge itself was the position where a soldier would make his stand, so the three farms in the valley would serve like breakwaters standing proud of a beach. If an assault was to come across the valley the attackers would be driven away from the stone-walled farms and compressed into the spaces between where they would be fired on from in front and from either side.

There was worse news still for an attacker. If a man was to gaze north from La Belle Alliance he would be blind to what lay behind the ridge where the elm tree grew. In the far distance, if the battle smoke permitted, he might see rising pastureland leading to the forest of Soignes, but he would see nothing of the dead ground behind the ridge, and would not know that a hidden farm lane ran east and west behind the crest that would allow his enemy to shift reinforcements swiftly to wherever the ridge was threatened most.

But perhaps that blindness did not matter if the attacker was the Emperor of the French, for Napoleon Bonaparte was a man in love with war, a man accustomed to glory, a man confident of victory, and the leader of over a hundred thousand veterans who had already defeated the Prussians and sent the British reeling back from Quatre Bras. Besides, the ridge where the elm tree grew was not steep. A man could stroll up its face without feeling any strain in his legs or any shortening of his breath, and the Emperor knew that his enemy had few good troops to defend that gentle slope. Indeed the Emperor knew much about his enemy for all day long the Belgian deserters had flocked to his colours and told their tales of panic and flight.

Some of the Emperor's Generals who had been defeated by Wellington in Spain advised caution, but the Emperor would have none of their cavils. The Englishman, he said, was a mere Sepoy General, nothing but a man who had learned his trade against the undisciplined and ill-armed tribal hordes of India, while the Emperor was Europe's master of war, blooded and hardened by battles against the finest troops of a continent. Napoleon did not care where Wellington chose to make his stand; he would beat him anyway, then march triumphant into Brussels.

The Duke of Wellington chose to make his stand on the ridge where the solitary elm tree grew.

And there, in the rain, his army waited.

The rain slackened, but did not end. As the last of the retreating British infantry passed La Belle Alliance they could see the great swathes of water sweeping west from the trees about Hougoumont. Not that they cared. They just slogged on, each man carrying his pack, haversacks, pouches, canteen, billhook, musket and bayonet; seventy pounds of baggage for each man. Some of the troops had marched most of the previous night and now they had marched all Saturday through the piercing, chilling rain. Their shoulders were chafed bloody by the wet straps of the heavy packs. Only their ammunition, wrapped in oiled paper and deep in rainproof cartouches, was dry. They had long outstripped their supply wagons, so, apart from whatever food any man might have hoarded, they went hungry.

The supply wagons, which had never reached Quatre Bras, were still struggling on flooded minor roads to reach the crossroads at Mont-St-Jean. The wagons carried spare ammunition, spare weapons, spare flints, and barrels of salt beef, barrels of twice-baked bread, barrels of rum, and crates with the officers' crystal glasses and silver cutlery that added a touch of luxury to the battalions' crude bivouacs. The army's women walked with the supply wagons, trudging through the cold mud to where their men waited to fight.

Those men waited behind the ridge where the elm tree grew. The Quartermasters marked bivouac areas for the various battalions in the soaking fields. Fatigue parties took axes and billhooks back to the forest to cut firewood. Provosts stood guard in Mont-St-Jean, for the Duke was particular that his men did not steal from the local populace, but, despite the precaution, every chicken in the hamlet was soon gone. Men made fires, sacrificing cartridges to ignite the damp wood. No one tried to make shelters, for there was not enough timber immediately available and the rain would have soaked through anything but the most elaborate huts of wood and turf. The red dye from the infantry's coats ran to stain their grey trousers, though gradually, as they settled into their muddy homes, all the men's uniforms turned to a glutinous and filthy brown.

The cavalry straggled in later in the afternoon. Staff officers directed the troopers to their bivouacs behind the infantry. The horses were pegged out in long lines, while their riders used forage scythes to gather fodder and others carried collapsible canvas buckets to the water pumps in Mont-St-Jean. The farriers, who carried a supply of nails and horseshoes in their saddlebags, began inspecting the hooves of the tired beasts.

The gunners placed their cannons just behind the ridge's summit so that, while most of the guns were hidden from an approaching enemy, the barrels still had a clear shot down the gentle slope. In the centre of the ridge, close to where the elm grew beside the high road, the guns were concealed behind hedges.

The artillery park was placed at the forest's edge, well back from the guns, and the infantry sourly noted how the gunners were provided with tents, for the artillery alone of all the army had kept their wagons close. No gun could fire long without its supplies, and a battery of six cannon needed a spare wheel wagon, a forage cart, two general supply wagons, eight ammunition wagons, ninety-two horses and seventy mules. Thus the land between the ridge and the forest was soon crammed with a mass of men and horses. Smoke from the bivouac fires smeared the rainy air. The ditches and furrows overflowed with water running off the fields in which the army must sleep.

Some officers walked forward to stare southwards across the wide valley. They watched the last of the British cavalry and guns come home, then the high road was left empty. The farmers, together with their families, labourers, and livestock, had long fled from the three farms in the valley's bottom. Nothing moved there now except for the rain that sheeted and hissed across the road. The British gunners, standing beside their loaded cannon, waited for targets.

In the early evening the rain paused, though the wind was still damp and cold. Some of the infantry tried to dry out their sopping uniforms by stripping themselves naked and holding the heavy wool coats over the struggling fires.

Then a single cannon fired from the ridge.

Some of the naked men ran to the crest to see that a nine-pounder had slammed a cannon-ball into a troop of French Cuirassiers who had been crossing the valley floor. The gunshot had stopped the advance of the armoured horsemen. One horse was kicking and bleeding in the hay, while its rider lay motionless. A mass of other enemy horsemen was assembling on the far crest about La Belle Alliance. Four enemy guns were being deployed close to the inn. For a few moments the tiny figures of the French gunners could be seen tending to their weapons, then the crews ran aside and the four guns fired towards the lingering smoke of the British nine-pounder's discharge.

Every gun on the British ridge replied. The massive salvo sounded like a billow of rolling thunder. Smoke jetted from the crest and roundshot screamed across the valley to thump in muddy splashes among the enemy cavalry. Staff officers galloped along the British crest screaming at the gunners to hold their fire, but the damage had already been done. The French staff officers, gazing from the tavern, saw that they were not faced by a handful of retreating guns, but by the artillery of a whole army. They could even tell, from the smoke, just where that army had placed its guns.

So now the Emperor knew that the British retreat was over, and that the Sepoy General had chosen his battlefield.

At a crossroads among farmland where the hay was nearly all cut and the rye was growing tall and the orchards were heavy with fruit, and where three bastions stood like fortresses proud of a ridge that next day the French must capture, and the British must hold. At a place called Waterloo.

CHAPTER 11

'Not a day for cricket, eh, Sharpe?' Lieutenant-Colonel Ford shouted the jocular greeting, though his expression was hardly welcoming. The Colonel, with Major Vine beside him, crouched in the thin shelter of a straggly hedge, which they had reinforced against the wet and gusting wind with three broken umbrellas.

Sharpe supposed the greeting expressed forgiveness for his usurpation of command the previous day. Sharpe had brusquely ordered the battalion to run while Ford had still been deliberating what to do, but it seemed the Colonel had no desire to make an issue of the affair. Vine, huddled in the roots of the hedge, scowled with dark unfriendly eyes at the Rifleman.

'I was taking some food to my old company. You don't mind, Ford?' Sharpe still had the cold beef and bread that Rebecque had given him that morning. He did not need Ford's permission to visit the Prince of Wales's Own Volunteer's bivouac, but it seemed polite to ask, especially on a day during which Rebecque had lectured him about the need for tact. Sharpe had sent Lieutenant Doggett on to the village of Waterloo where the Generals had their quarters, but Sharpe had no wish to join the Prince yet. He preferred the company of his old battalion.

Sharpe and Harper found the men of their old light company squatted about some miserable fires made from damp straw and green twigs collected from the hedge.

Major d'Alembord was collecting letters from those few men who could write and who wanted to leave a message for their families should anything happen to them the next day.

It had begun to rain again. The men were cold and miserable, though the veterans of the war in Spain pretended that this was a paradise compared to the ordeals they had suffered in their earlier campaigns. The new men, not wanting to appear less tough than the veterans, kept silent.

The veterans of the company made space for Sharpe and Harper near a fire and Sharpe noted how these experienced soldiers were assembled around one blaze and the newcomers about the other feebler camp-fires. It was as if the old soldiers drew together as an élite against which the newcomers would have to measure themselves, yet even the veterans were betraying a nervousness this rainy night. Sharpe confirmed to them that the Prussians had been beaten, but he promised that Marshal Blücher's army was withdrawing on roads parallel to the British retreat and that the Marshal had promised to march at first light to Wellington's aid.

'Where are the Prussians exactly, sir?' Colour Sergeant Major Huckfield wanted to know.

'Over there.' Sharpe pointed to the left flank. The Prince of Wales's Own Volunteers were on the right side of the British position, almost midway between the elm tree and the track which led down to Hougoumont.

'How far away are they, sir?' Huckfield, an intelligent and earnest man, persisted.

Sharpe shrugged. 'Not far.' In truth he did not know where the Prussians were bivouacked, nor was he even certain that Marshal Blücher would march to help this bedraggled army in the morning, but Sharpe knew he must give these men some shred of hope. The newcomers to the battalion were edging closer to the veterans' fire to listen to the Rifleman. 'All that matters,' he said loudly, 'is that the Prussians will be here and fighting in the morning.'

'If this rain doesn't stop we'll need the bloody navy here, not the bloody Prussians.' Private Clayton looked up at the darkening clouds. The rain was steady and hard, drumming on the black shako tops of the shivering men and running down the old furrows to puddle at the field's bottom where a troop of officers' horses were unhappily picketed.

'This rain will bugger up their harvest.' Charlie Weller, who was allowed to bivouac with the veterans because they liked him, plucked a head of soaking wet rye and shook his head sadly. 'It'll all be black and rotten in a week's time.'

'But it'll be well dunged next year, though. Corn always grows better on dead flesh.' Hagman, the oldest man in the company, grinned. 'We saw that in Spain, ain't that right, Mr Sharpe? We saw oats growing taller than a horse where a battle had been fought. The roots was sucking up all that blood and belly, they was.'

'They don't always bury them, though, do they? You remember that place in Spain? Where all the skulls were?' Clayton frowned as he tried to remember the battlefield over which the battalion had marched some weeks after a fight.

'Sally-Manker,' Harper offered helpfully.

'That was the place! There were skulls as thick as blue-bottles in cowshit!' Clayton spoke loudly to impress the new recruits who were listening avidly to the conversation, nor did he drop his voice as a blue-coated battalion of Dutch-Belgian infantry marched close by towards their bivouac. 'I hope those yellow bastards aren't next to us tomorrow,' Clayton said malevolently.

There were growls of agreement. The officers and men of the Prince of Wales's Own Volunteers might be divided between the experienced and the inexperienced, but they were united in their hatred of all outsiders, unless those outsiders had proved themselves as tough, resourceful and uncomplaining as the redcoats. To these men the battalion was their life, their family and probably their death as well. Properly led they would fight for their battalion with a feral and terrifying ferocity, though ill-led, as Sharpe well knew, they could fall apart like a rusted musket. The thought made Sharpe glance towards Colonel Ford.

Clayton still stared with loathing at the Dutch-Belgians. 'I'll wager those buggers won't go hungry tonight. Bastards can't fight, but they look plump enough. No shortage of bloody food there!'

Daniel Hagman suddenly laughed aloud. 'You remember that ripe ham we sold to the Portuguese? That was you, Mr Sharpe!'

'No, it wasn't,' Sharpe said.

The veterans jeered knowingly and affectionately.

'It was you!' Clayton, a clever and cheeky rogue, pointed an accusing finger at Sharpe, then told the story for the benefit of the newcomers. 'There were these Portuguese boys, right? It was after some scrap or other and the bastards were hungry as hell, so Mr Sharpe here chopped the bums off some French dead and smoked them over a fire, and then sold them to the Portuguese as joints of ham.'

The newcomers grinned nervously towards the grim-faced officer who seemed oddly embarrassed by the tale.

'The Portuguese never complained.' Harper justified the barbarity.

'Did you really do that?' d'Alembord asked Sharpe very quietly.

'Christ, no. It was some other Riflemen. The Portuguese had eaten their pet dog, so they decided to get even with them.' Sharpe was surprised that the story was now ascribed to him, but he had noticed how men liked to attach outrageous stories to his exploits and it was hopeless to deny the more exotic feats.

'We could do with some of them Portuguese tomorrow.' Daniel Hagman lit his pipe with a glowing twig from the fire. 'They were proper little fighters, they were.' The admiration was genuine and earned muttered agreement from the veterans.

'But we'll be all right tomorrow, won't we, Mr Sharpe?' Charlie Weller asked with undisguised anxiety.

'You'll be all right, lads. Just remember. Kill their officers first, aim at the bellies of the infantry and at the horses of the cavalry.' The answer was given for the benefit of the men at the outer reaches of Sharpe's audience; the men who had not fought before and who needed simple rules to keep them confident in the chaos of battle.

Weller put a finger into the can of water and found it still lukewarm. He took a twist of dry kindling that he had stored deep in his clothes and put it onto the flames. Sharpe hoped the boy would survive, for Weller was different from the other men. He was a country boy who had joined the army out of a sense of patriotism and adventure. Those motives had helped make him a good soldier, though no better than most of the men who had taken the King's shilling for altogether less honourable motives. Clayton was a thief, and probably would have been hanged if he had not donned the red coat, but his sly cunning made him a good skirmisher. Most of the other men around the fire were drunkards and criminals. They were the leavings of Britain, the unwanted men, the scum of the earth, but in battle they were as stubborn as mules. To Sharpe's mind they were gutter fighters, and he would not have wanted them any other way. They were not impressive to look at; small, scarred, gap-toothed and dirty, but tomorrow they would show an emperor how a redcoat could fight, though tonight their main concern was when the rum ration would reach them.

'The quartermaster has promised it by midnight,' d'Alembord told the company.

'Bastard wagon drivers,' Clayton said. 'Bastards are probably tucked up in bed.'

Sharpe and Harper stayed another half-hour and left the company discussing the chances of finding the French brothel among the enemy baggage. All British soldiers were convinced that the French travelled with such a brothel; a magical institution that they had never quite succeeded in capturing, but which occupied in their mythology the status of a golden prize of war.

'They seem well enough,' Sharpe said to d'Alembord. The two officers were walking towards the ridge top while Harper went to fetch the horses.

'They are well enough,' d'Alembord confirmed. He was still in his dancing clothes which were now stained and ragged. His proper uniform was lost with the missing baggage. One of his dancing shoes had somehow lost its buckle and was only held in place by a piece of string knotted round d'Alembord's instep. 'They're good lads,' he said warmly.

'And you, Dally?'

Peter d'Alembord smiled ruefully. 'I can't shake off a rather ominous dread. Silly, I know, but there it is.'

'I felt that way before Toulouse,' Sharpe confessed. 'It was bad. I lived, though.'

D'Alembord, who would not have admitted his fears to anyone but a very close friend, walked a few paces in silence. 'I can't help thinking about the wheat on the roads. Have you noticed that wherever our supply wagons go the grain falls off and sprouts? It grows for a season, then just dies. It seems to me that's rather a good image of soldiering. We pass by, we leave a trace, and then we die.'

Sharpe stared aghast at his friend. 'My God, but you have got it bad!'

'My Huguenot ancestry, I fear. I am bedevilled by a Calvinist guilt that I'm wasting my life. I tell myself that I'm here to help punish the French, but in truth it was the chance of a majority that kept me in uniform. I need the money, you see, but that seems a despicable motive now. I've behaved badly, don't you see? And consequently I have a conviction that I'll become nothing but dung for a Belgian rye field.'

Sharpe shook his head. 'I'm only here for the money too, you silly bugger.' They had reached the ridge top and could see the twisting trails of French cooking fires rising beyond the southern crest. 'You're going to live, Dally.'

'So I keep telling myself, then I become convinced of the opposite.' D'Alembord paused before revealing the true depths of his dread. 'For tuppence I'd ride away tonight and hide. I've been thinking of it all day.'

'It happens to us all.' Sharpe remembered his own terror before the battle at Toulouse. 'The fear goes when the fighting starts, Dally. You know that.'

'I'm not the only one, either.' D'Alembord ignored Sharpe's encouragement. 'CSM Huckfield has suddenly taken to reading his Bible. If I didn't like him so much I'd accuse him of being a damned Methodist. He tells me he's marked to die in this campaign, though he adds that he doesn't mind because his soul is square with God. Major Vine says the same thing.' D'Alembord shot a poisonous glance towards the hedge where Ford and his senior Major crouched against the rain. 'They asked me whether I thought we should have divine service tomorrow morning. I told them it was a bloody ridiculous notion, but I've no doubt they'll find some idiot chaplain to mumble inanities at us. Have you noticed how we're getting so very pious? We weren't pious in Spain, but suddenly there's a streak of moral righteousness infecting senior officers. I'll say my prayers in the morning, but I won't need to make a display of it.' He began scraping the mud from his fragile shoes against a tuft of grass, then abandoned the cleaning job as hopeless. 'I apologize, Sharpe. I shouldn't burden you with this.'

'It's not a burden.'

'I was unconcerned till yesterday,' d'Alembord went on as though Sharpe had not spoken. 'But those horsemen completely unnerved me. I was shaking like a child when they attacked us. Then there's the Colonel, of course. I have no faith in Ford at all. And there's Anne. I feel I don't deserve her and that any man who is as fortunate as I is bound to be punished for it.'

'Love makes us vulnerable,' Sharpe admitted.

'Doesn't it just?' d'Alembord said warmly. 'But virtue should give us confidence.'

'Virtue?' Sharpe wondered just what moral claims his friend was making for himself.

'The virtue of our cause,' d'Alembord explained as though it was the most natural thing in the world. 'The French have got to be beaten.'

Sharpe smiled. 'They're doubtless saying the same of us.'

D'Alembord was silent for a few seconds, then spoke in a sudden and impassioned rush. 'I don't count Lucille, of course, and you mustn't think I do, but it is a filthily evil nation, Sharpe. I cannot forget what they did to my family or to our co-religionists. And think of their revolution! All those poor dead innocent people. And Bonaparte's no better. He just attacks and attacks, then steals from the countries he conquers, and all the time he talks of virtue and law and the glories of French civilization. Their virtue is all hypocrisy, their law applies only to benefit themselves, and their civilization is blood on the cobblestones.'

Sharpe had never suspected that such animosity lay

beneath his friend's elegant languor. 'So it isn't just the majority, Peter?'

D'Alembord seemed embarrassed to have betrayed such feelings. 'I'm sorry, I truly am. You must think me very rude. I heartily like Lucille, you know I do. I exaggerate, of course. It is not the French who are essentially evil, but their government.' He stopped abruptly, evidently stifling yet more anti-French venom.

Sharpe smiled. 'Where Lucille and I live they will tell you that France is blessed by God but cursed with Paris. They perceive Paris as an evil place inhabited by the most loathsome and grasping people.'

'It sounds like London.' D'Alembord smiled wanly. 'You won't tell Lucille my thoughts? I would not like to offend her.'

'Of course I won't tell her.'

'And perhaps you will do me one more favour?'

'With pleasure.'

D'Alembord took a creased and damp letter from his pocket. 'If I do become rye dung tomorrow, perhaps you'll deliver this to Anne? And tell her I didn't suffer? No tales of surgeon's knives, Sharpe, and no descriptions of nasty wounds, just a clean bullet in the forehead will do for my end, however nasty the truth will probably be.'

'I won't need to deliver it, but I'll keep it for you.' Sharpe pushed the letter into a pocket, then turned as a spatter of musket-fire sounded from the right of the line, about the château of Hougoumont.

A scatter of French infantry were running back from the orchard where British musket flames sparked bright in the dusk. Sharpe could see redcoats going forward among the trees south of the farm. The French must have sent a battalion to discover whether the farmstead was garrisoned, or else the enemy was merely foraging for firewood, but, whatever their mission, the blue-coated infantry had run into a savage firefight. More redcoats ran from the farm to take their bayonets into the woodland.

'What angers me', d'Alembord was taking no notice of the sudden skirmish, 'is not knowing how it will all end. If I die tomorrow, I'll never know, will I?'

Sharpe shook his head in scornful dismissal of his friend's fears. 'By summer's end, my friend, you and I will sit in a conquered Paris and drink wine. We probably won't even remember a day's fighting in Belgium! And you'll go home and marry your Anne and be happy ever after.'

D'Alembord laughed at the prophecy. 'And you, Sharpe, what happens to you? Do you go back to Normandy?'

'Yes.'

'And the local people won't mind that you fought against France?'

'I don't know.' That worry was never far from Sharpe's thoughts, nor indeed, from Lucille's. 'But I'd like to go back,' Sharpe went on. 'I'm happy there. I'm planning to make some calvados this year. The château used to make a lot, but it hasn't produced any for twenty or more years. The local doctor wants to help us. He's a good fellow.' Sharpe suddenly thought of his meeting with Lord John and of the promissory note that, if it was honoured, would make so many things possible in Lucille's château. 'I met bloody Rossendale today. I took the promissory note off him direct. I hope you don't mind.'

'Of course not,' d'Alembord said.

'Oddly enough,' Sharpe said, 'I rather liked him. I don't know why. I think I felt sorry for him.'

' "Love your enemies",' d'Alembord quoted mockingly, ' "bless them that curse you, do good to them that hate you"? I told you we were getting more pious, even you.'

'But we'll still slaughter the bloody French tomorrow.' Sharpe smiled and held out his hand. 'You'll be safe, Peter. Tomorrow night we'll laugh at these fears.'

They shook hands on the promise.

The musket-fire at Hougoumont died away as the French yielded possession of the woodland to the British. A roll of thunder sounded in the west and a spear of lightning glittered brief and stark on the horizon. Then the rain began to pelt down hard again.

The armies had gathered, and now waited for morning.

The lintel of every house in Waterloo's street bore a chalked inscription, put there by the Quartermaster-General's department to identify which general and staff officers would be billeted inside. The inn opposite the church bore the chalked words 'His Grace the Duke of Wellington', while three doors away a two storey house was inscribed 'The Earl of Uxbridge'. Another substantially built house was marked 'His Royal Highness the Prince William of Orange'. Thatched cottages with dungheaps hard under their windows were this night to be the homes for marquesses or earls, yet such men counted themselves fortunate to be sheltered at all, and not to be enduring the numbing cold misery of the rain that thrashed the ridge.

In the Earl of Uxbridge's house the staff officers crammed themselves about a table to share the Earl's supper of boiled beef and beans. It was an early supper, for the whole staff was on notice to rise long before dawn. In the centre of the table, propped against the single candelabra, was Lord John Rossendale's broken sword. One of the staff officers had discovered the snapped blade after Lord John had tried to throw it away and had demanded to know just how the weapon had been broken. The truth was too painful, and so Lord John had invented a rather more flattering account.

'It was after the rocket explosion,' he explained to the assembled staff at supper. 'The damned horse bolted on me.'

'You should learn to ride, John.'

Lord John waited for the laughter to subside. 'Damn thing ran me into a wood off to one side of the road, and damn me if there weren't three Lancers lurking there.'

'Green or red?' The Earl of Uxbridge, just returned from a conference with the Duke of Wellington, had taken his place at the head of the supper table.

'The green ones, Harry.' That bit was easy for Lord John to invent, for he had watched the green-coated Lancers running from the attack of the Life Guards. 'I shot one with the pistol, but had to throw it down to draw my sword. Damn shame, really, because it was an expensive gun.'

'A Mortimer percussion pistol, with a rifled barrel.' Christopher Manvell confirmed the value of the lost pistol. 'A damn shame to lose it, John.'

Lord John shrugged as though to suggest the loss was nothing really. 'The second fellow charged me, I got past his point and gave him the sword in the belly, then the third one damn nearly skewered me.' He gave a modest smile. 'Thought I was dead, to be honest. I slashed at the fellow, but he was damned fast. He drew a sabre and had a good hack at me, I parried, and that's when my sword broke. Then, damn me, if the fellow didn't just turn tail and run!'

The assembled officers stared at the broken sword which lay like a trophy on the supper table.

'The trick of it', Lord John said, 'is to get past the lance point. Once you're past the spike it's a bit like killing rabbits. Too easy, really.'

'So long as your sword doesn't break?' Christopher Manvell asked drily.

'There is that, yes.'

The Earl frowned. 'So if the fellow ran away, why didn't you pick up the pistol, Johnny? You said it was expensive.'

'I could hear more of the scoundrels among the trees. I thought I'd better give them a run.' Lord John gave a small disarming smile. 'To tell you the truth, Harry, I was frightened! Whatever, I whipped my damn horse and ran like the devil!'

Christopher Manvell, who had seemed somewhat less impressed by Lord John's ordeal than the other officers about the table, at least confirmed the story's ending. 'He came back to the road white as a sheet.'

'You did well, Johnny, damned well.' The Earl of Uxbridge spoke gruffly. 'You killed a brace of the buggers, eh? Damn good.' There was a spatter of applause, then Christopher Manvell asked the Earl what news he had gleaned from his conference with the Duke of Wellington.

The truth was that the Earl had gleaned nothing at all. He was second in command to the Duke and had thought that appointment entitled him to know just what the Duke planned for the next day, but his enquiry had met with a very dusty answer indeed. The Duke had said his plans depended entirely on Napoleon, and as Napoleon had not yet confided in the Duke, the Duke could not yet confide in the Earl, and so good-night.

'I think we'll just let the bugger attack us, then see him off, eh?' the Earl said lazily, as though the events of the next day were really not very significant at all.

'But the Prussians are coming?' Manvell insisted.

'I think we can do the business without a few damned Germans, don't you?' The Earl pushed a box of cigars into the table's centre. 'But one thing's certain, gentlemen. No doubt our cavalry will make England proud!'

'Bravo!' A drunken staff officer pounded the table.

After supper Christopher Manvell found Lord John standing in the open front porch from where he was staring into the wet dusk. 'I wish I'd been there to help you against those Lancers,' Manvell said.

For a few seconds it seemed that Lord John would not reply at all, then he just shrugged the subject away. 'Harry seems very sanguine about our chances tomorrow.'

Manvell blew a stream of cigar smoke into the drizzle. 'It's strange, Johnny. I saw you come out of the wood, then not a moment later I saw Colonel Sharpe in the same place. You were lucky not to meet him.'

Again Lord John was silent for a few seconds, then spoke in a rush of quiet bitterness. 'Of course I met him. And of course there were no bloody Lancers. What was I supposed to do? Admit to Harry and everyone else that I was humiliated by a Rifleman?'

'I'm sorry.' Manvell was embarrassed by the tortured admission he had provoked from his friend.

'I gave him his damned note. Not that it will do me any good. Jane won't give me the money unless I marry her, but Sharpe doesn't know that.' Lord John laughed suddenly. 'He gave me a length of rope and told me it was a peasant divorce. He says I'm free to marry her.'

Manvell smiled, but said nothing. The gutters either side of the paved high road were gurgling and flooding. Across the street a sentry ran cursing through the puddles to open a gate for a mounted officer. An orderly hung a lantern outside the stable entrance of the house where the Prince of Orange was billeted.

'It's a matter of honour.' Lord John was staring into the darkening street.

'I beg your pardon?'

'Tomorrow', Lord John said, 'has become a rather desperate matter of honour.' He was very slightly drunk, and his voice held a hint of hysteria. 'I never realized before today how very simple battle is. There's no compromise, is there? It's victory or defeat, and nothing in between, while real life is so damned complicated. Perhaps that's why the best soldiers are such very simple souls.' He turned in the porch to stare at his friend. 'You see, if I want to keep the woman then I have to kill a man, and I don't have the nerve to face him. And he's done nothing to deserve death! It is his money! But if I do the honest thing to the man, then I lose the woman, and I don't think I can live with that loss –'

'I'm sure you can –' Christopher Manvell interrupted and, in his turn, was cut off.

'No!' Lord John did not even wish to discuss Jane. He frowned in puzzlement at his friend. 'Do you think lost honour can be retrieved on a battlefield?'

'I'm sure it's the very best place to retrieve it.' Manvell felt a surge of pity for his friend. He had never realized till this moment just how Lord John's honour had been trampled and destroyed.

'So tomorrow's become rather important to me,' Lord John said. 'Because tomorrow I can take my honour back by fighting well.' He smiled as if to soften the overdramatic words. 'But to do it I'll need a sword, and my spare blade is in Brussels. I suppose you don't have one you could lend me?'

'With pleasure.'

Lord John stared into the drenching twilight. 'I wish it was over. The rain, I mean,' he added hurriedly.

'I think it's slackening.'

Lightning flickered in the west, followed a few seconds later by thunder that crashed across the far sky like the passage of a cannon-ball. Laughter and singing sounded from a house further up the street, temporarily drowning the ominous and repetitive scraping noise of a stone putting an edge onto a sword. A dog howled in protest at the thunder and a horse whinnied from the stables behind the Earl of Uxbridge's billet.

Lord John turned back into the house. He could retrieve his honour and he could retrieve Jane by becoming a hero. Tomorrow.

CHAPTER 12

Captain Harry Price, commander of the first company of the Prince of Wales's Own Volunteers, climbed onto a makeshift platform constructed from spare ammunition boxes. In front of him, standing in the rain-soaked field, were forty or fifty infantry officers who had assembled from the various battalions bivouacked nearby. The last light was draining in the west, while the rain had slackened to a drizzle.

'Are we ready, gentlemen?' Price called.

'Get on with it!'

Price, enjoying himself, bowed to the hecklers, then took the first article from Colour Sergeant Major Huckfield. It was a silver-cased watch that Harry Price held high into the last vestiges of the light. 'A watch, gentlemen, property of the late Major Micklewhite! The item is only very slightly blood-stained, gentlemen, so a good cleaning will have it ticking in no time. I offer you a very fine fob watch, gentlemen, made by Mastersons of Exeter.'

'Never heard of them!' a voice shouted.

'Your ignorance is of no interest to us. Mastersons are a very old and reputable firm. My father always swore by his Mastersons watch and he was never late for a rogering in his life. Do I hear a pound for Major Micklewhite's ticker?'

'A shilling!'

'Now, come along! Major Micklewhite left a widow and

237

three sweet-natured children. You wouldn't want your wives and little ones left derelict because some thieving bastards weren't generous! Let me hear a pound!'

'A florin!'

'This isn't a dolly-shop, gentlemen! A pound? Who'll offer me a pound?'

No one would. In the end Micklewhite's watch fetched six shillings, while the dead Major's signet ring went for one shilling. A fine silver cup that had belonged to Captain Carline went for a pound, while the top price went for Carline's sword that fetched a full ten guineas. Harry Price had to auction sixty-two articles, all the property of those officers of the Prince of Wales's Own Volunteers who had been killed by the French cavalry at Quatre Bras. The prices were low because the French had caused a glut on the market by killing so many officers; at least four other auctions had already taken place this evening, but this night's glut, Harry Price thought, would be as nothing compared to tomorrow night's supply of goods.

'A pair of Captain Carline's spurs, gentlemen! Gold if I'm not mistaken.' That claim was greeted by jeers of derision. 'Do I hear a pound?'

'Sixpence.'

'You're a miserable bloody lot. How would you feel if it was your belongings I was giving away for tuppence? Let us be generous, gentlemen! Think of the widows!'

'Carline wasn't married!' a lieutenant shouted.

'A guinea for his whore, then! I want some Christian generosity, gentlemen!'

'I'll give you a guinea for his whore, but sixpence for his spurs!'

Micklewhite's effects made eight pounds, fourteen shillings and sixpence. Captain Carline's belongings fetched a good deal more, though all the items had been knocked down at bargain prices. Harry Price, who had always wanted to look like a cavalry officer, bought the spurs himself for ninepence. He also bought Carline's fur-edged pelisse; an elegantly impractical garment that high fashion imposed on wealthy officers. A pelisse was a short jacket that was worn from one shoulder like a cloak, and Harry Price took immense satisfaction in draping Carline's expensively braided foible about his own shabby red coat.

He took the money and the promissory notes to the battalion's paymaster who, after he had taken his share, would send the balance on to the bereaved families.

Harry Price fixed the spurs onto his boots and splashed back to the hedge where the officers shivered in their miserable shelter. He saw Major d'Alembord sitting further up the hedge. 'You didn't bid, Peter?'

'Not tonight, Harry, not tonight.' D'Alembord's tone was distinctly unfriendly, discouraging conversation.

Price took the hint and walked a few paces up the hedgerow before sitting and admiring his newly decorated heels. The spurs should cut a dash with the ladies of Paris, and that was the best reason Harry Price knew for fighting; because the girls could be so very obliging to a foreign soldier, and especially a soldier with a pelisse and spurs.

Men were singing in the bivouacs. Their voices came strongly through the ever-present sound of the rain that had begun to fall harder again. Peter d'Alembord, attempting to stir himself from his misery, saw Harry Price's new spurs and perceived the childish delight which they had evidently given to their new owner. D'Alembord was tempted to start a conversation in the hope that Harry Price's usual foolery would distract him from his fears, but then the terror surged up again, strong and overwhelming, and d'Alembord almost sobbed aloud under its impact. Lightning flickered to the north, and d'Alembord touched the pocket where his fiancée's letters were stored. He was going to die. He knew he was going to die. He closed his eyes so that no tears would show. God damn it, he knew he was going to die, and he was afraid.

It was fully dark by the time Sharpe and Harper reached Waterloo and discovered the Prince's billet. A sentry opened the stable gate and the two Riflemen ducked under the low stone arch which led to the yard.

'I'll look after the horses,' Harper offered when the two men reached the shelter of the stable.

'I'll help you.'

'Go and see your wee Prince. He's probably missing you.'

'Missing his bloody mother, more like.' Sharpe slid down from the saddle and breathed a sigh of relief to be free of it. He tried to remember how much sleep he had had in the last three days, but he was too weary to add the few hours together. He remembered he had promised Lucille that he would see her this night, but the Emperor had changed those plans. He needed to write her a letter. He also needed food and sleep. He wearily rested his head against the saddle and listened to the growing violence of the rain.

'Leave it to me,' Harper insisted.

Sharpe obeyed. The kitchen was crammed with officers' servants and rank with the smell of drying uniforms which were hung on every available shelf or hook. Sharpe edged through the room and into the corridor beyond. He was seeking Rebecque, for he wanted to borrow a pen and some ink.

'He wants you.' A girl's voice spoke from the stairway above Sharpe.

Sharpe was surprised to see Paulette, the Prince's girl, leaning on the balustrade. 'What are you doing here?' he asked.

'He wanted me here. But he's been asking for you all evening. He's drunk.'

'Very?'

'Just happy. The usual.'

'Bugger him,' Sharpe said in English. He pushed open a door at random and found himself in a parlour that was crowded with the Prince's staff. They were embarrassed to see Sharpe, imagining him as a prodigal come home for the Prince's pardon. Doggett alone offered the Rifleman a welcome, as well as surrendering his chair and volunteering to pour Sharpe a glass of wine. The chair was close to the fire in front of which, as in the kitchen, thick wool coats were hung to dry and were filling the room with a malodorous steam. 'Where's Rebecque?' Sharpe asked the room at large.

'With His Highness,' Doggett said. 'Red wine?'

'What I would really like,' Sharpe collapsed into the chair, 'is a cup of tea.'

Doggett grinned. 'I shall arrange it, sir.'

Sharpe stretched out his legs, and flinched as the old wound in his thigh shot a stab of agony up to his hip. He wondered if he would ever be dry again. He knew he should beg or borrow some writing paper and pen a swift letter to Lucille, but he was suddenly too tired to move.

'Sharpe!' The door had opened and Rebecque's scholarly face peered into the candle-lit room. 'You are here! His Highness would like a word with you? Now? If you please?'

Sharpe groaned, flinched, and climbed slowly to his feet. 'Can I get something to eat, Rebecque?'

'Royal commands do not wait on hunger.' Rebecque took Sharpe's elbow and propelled him towards the staircase. 'And remember my admonitions, will you? Be tactful!'

Rebecque led Sharpe upstairs where, without ceremony, he ushered Sharpe into the bedroom where the Prince was writing letters at a small table. The Prince was dressed in a thick woollen gown and had a flask of brandy at his right elbow. He did not acknowledge Sharpe's arrival, but instead concentrated on dripping a puddle of sealing wax onto one of his letters. He carefully centred his signet ring, then pressed it down into the wax. 'I always seem to burn my fingers on sealing wax.'

'Your Highness could buy gummed wafers,' Rebecque suggested.

'I hate common things.' The Prince dropped his ring and turned his glaucous eyes on Sharpe. 'I thought I ordered you to dress in Dutch uniform?'

Tact, Sharpe told himself, tact. 'It's drying out, sir.'

'I think our men have a right to see their officers dressed properly. Don't you agree, Rebecque?'

'Entirely, Your Highness.'

The Prince poured himself brandy. He seemed to hesitate, as though debating whether to offer his Chief of Staff and Sharpe a glass each, but then decided his own need was more pressing and so confined himself to the one glass. 'You've seen tomorrow's battlefield, Sharpe?'

Sharpe had been expecting some reference to their altercation at Quatre Bras and had to hide his surprise at the question. 'Yes, sir.'

'And?' the Prince demanded with an arrogant tilt of his strangely small head.

'It'll do,' Sharpe said laconically.

'Do? It's a ridiculous place to fight! A nonsense. It won't be my fault if there's disaster tomorrow.' The Prince stood and began pacing the floorboards. A wooden pail stood in one corner of the room to catch the drips where the roof leaked. The rain seethed and beat on the windows. The Prince, frowning with thought, suddenly turned accusingly on Sharpe. 'Did you look at the open flank on the right?'

'No, sir.'

'Wide open! Wide open! Napoleon will be round that corner in a trice tomorrow, then we'll all be tumbled

242

backwards like skittles. I've told the Duke! Haven't I told the Duke?' The Prince glared at Rebecque.

'Your views have been most strongly conveyed to His Grace, sir.'

'And are doubtless being ignored.' The Prince offered a very hollow laugh as though to suggest that, like all genius, he was accustomed to his advice being ignored. 'Tomorrow, Sharpe, we will prevent that tragedy.'

'Very good, sir.' Sharpe was suddenly aware that his soaking uniform was dripping water onto the Prince's floor. He was chilled to the bone and edged slightly closer to the small coal fire which warmed the Prince's bedroom.

The Prince, evidently forgetting the threat to the battle-field's right flank, stopped his pacing and pointed with his brandy glass at Sharpe. 'Do you know why I particularly desired your presence on my staff?'

'No, sir.'

'Because you have a reputation for boldness. I like that in a man, Sharpe, I relish it! I value it.' The Prince began pacing again, his small head bobbing on his long and ludicrously thin neck. 'I've been educated as a soldier, isn't that so, Rebecque?'

'Indeed, Your Highness.'

'Educated, Sharpe! Think of that! My whole lifetime has been devoted to the study of warfare, and shall I tell you what is the one lesson I have learned above all others?'

'I should like to know, sir.' Sharpe admired his own tactful restraint, especially as the Prince was just twenty-three years old and Sharpe had been a fighting soldier for twenty-two.

'Boldness wins.' The Prince confided the advice as though it was a secret that had been hidden from genera-tions of military men. 'Boldness wins, Sharpe. Boldness, boldness, boldness!'

All Sharpe wanted to do was get dry, eat, lie down, and sleep, but he dutifully nodded instead. 'Indeed, sir.'

'Frederick the Great once said that the greatest crime in war is not to make the wrong decision, but to make no decision.' Again the Prince gestured at Sharpe with the brandy glass. 'You should remember that axiom, Sharpe!'

Sharpe did not even know what an axiom was, but he nodded respectfully. 'I will, sir.'

'There are times when any officer may perceive a superior's decision as being mistaken,' the Prince was clearly alluding to his behaviour at Quatre Bras, but so delicately that Sharpe, in his weariness, hardly noticed, 'but such an officer should be grateful that his superior has had the boldness to make any decision at all. Isn't that so?' The Prince glared at Sharpe, who just nodded.

Rebecque hastened to offer the Prince the required verbal agreement. 'It's very true, sir, very true.'

The Prince, piqued that Sharpe had not responded, stood very close in front of the Rifleman. 'I also think that the least I can expect from my staff is loyalty. Isn't that so? Loyalty?' The word came in a gust of brandy-stinking breath.

'Indeed, sir,' Sharpe said.

Rebecque cleared his throat. 'Colonel Sharpe has already expressed to me his deepest regrets for causing Your Highness any unhappiness. He has also assured me of his loyalty towards Your Highness. Isn't that so, Sharpe?' The question was almost hissed at the Rifleman.

'Indeed, sir.' Sharpe had fallen back into his old Sergeant's ways, merely saying what an officer wanted to hear. It was always easy to keep bumptious officers happy with a succession of yes, no and indeed.

The Prince, perhaps sensing that he had gained as

much victory as he was going to get this night, smiled. 'I'm grateful we agree, Sharpe.'

'Yes, sir.'

The Prince went back to his chair and slowly sat down as though the cares of Europe were pressing on his spindly shoulders. 'I want you to station yourself on the right flank tomorrow, Sharpe. You're going to be my eyes. The moment you see any French outflanking movement, you're to inform me.'

'Of course, sir.'

'Very good. Very good.' The Prince smiled to show that all was forgiven, then looked at Rebecque. 'You have a spare Dutch uniform, Rebecque?'

'Of course, Your Highness.'

'Provide it to Colonel Sharpe, if you will. And you'll wear it tomorrow, Sharpe, do you hear me?'

'Very clearly, sir.'

'Till the morning, then.' The Prince nodded a good-night to both men. 'And Rebecque? Send my seamstress in, will you?'

Rebecque dutifully ushered Paulette into the Prince's room, then took Sharpe down the small landing to his own bedroom where he offered Sharpe a choice of uniforms from a tin travelling trunk.

'Keep them,' Sharpe said.

'My dear Sharpe –'

'I've fought the damned French for ten years in this jacket, Rebecque.' Sharpe's interruption was bitter. 'I wasn't bloody studying how to fight out of bloody books at bloody Eton, I was killing the bastards. I began killing Frenchmen when that little bastard was still wetting his breeches.' In his frustration and anger Sharpe slammed his fist against the wall, breaking the plaster and laths to leave a ragged hole. 'Why the hell does he still want me on his staff anyway? Hasn't he got enough people to cut up his food?'

Rebecque gave a long-suffering sigh. 'You have a reputation, Sharpe, and the Prince needs it. He knows he made a mistake. The whole army knows. Do you think Halkett hasn't complained bitterly to the Duke? So the Prince needs men to see that you are on his side, that you support him, even that you respect him! That's why he wants you in his uniform. After all, you're not on attachment from a British regiment, like Harry or Simon, but you're his personal choice! Now, please, just take a coat and wear it tomorrow.'

'I'm fighting in Rifle green, Rebecque, or I'm not fighting at all. And what the hell am I doing out on the right flank?'

'You're staying out of his way, Sharpe. You're there so you can't make any trouble. Or would you rather spend the battle tied to His Highness's coat-tails?'

Sharpe smiled. 'No, sir.'

'At least we agree on something. Not that the Prince can do too much damage tomorrow. Wellington's broken up the corps, so his Highness doesn't have a real command, though I imagine he'll find something to do. He usually does.' Rebecque sounded wistful, but then he smiled. 'Have you eaten?'

'No, sir.'

'You look all in.' Rebecque, evidently realizing that the Englishman would not yield on the battle of the uniform, closed the travelling trunk. 'Come on, I'll find you some food.'

The clock in the hallway struck eleven. Sharpe, knowing that he must be at the ridge before dawn, left orders that he was to be called at half-past two, then carried Rebecque's gift of bread and cold lamb out to the stables where Harper had sequestered a patch of comparatively dry straw for a bed.

'So how was His Highness?' the Irishman asked.

'As full of shit as an egg's got meat.'

Harper laughed. 'And tomorrow?'

'God knows, Patrick. I suppose tomorrow we meet the Emperor.'

'There's a thought for you.'

'But you're to stay out of trouble, Patrick.'

'I will!' Harper said indignantly, as though Sharpe's nagging reminded him of his wife's.

'You didn't stay clear yesterday.'

'Yesterday! None of the bastards got near me yesterday! But I'll stay out of harm's way tomorrow, never you mind.'

They fell silent. Sharpe pulled the damp cloak over his wet uniform and listened to the rain smash down on the yard's cobbles. He thought of Peter d'Alembord's awful fears and remembered his own terror at Toulouse and he wondered why this battle was not affecting him in the same way. That very thought raised its own fears; that such a lack of dread was in itself a harbinger of disaster, yet, in the darkness and listening to the horses move heavily behind his bed, Sharpe could not feel any horror of the next day. He was curious about fighting the Emperor, and he was as apprehensive as any man, yet he was not suffering the gut-loosening terror that racked d'Alembord.

He listened to the rain, wondering how the next day would end. Tomorrow night, he thought, he would either be in full retreat to the coast, or else a prisoner, or perhaps even marching southwards to pursue a defeated enemy. He remembered the victory at Vitoria that had broken the French in Spain, and how he and Harper had ridden after the battle into the field of gold and jewels. That had been an answer to the soldier's prayer; God send a rich enemy and no surgeon's knife.

Lucille would be worrying for news. Sharpe closed his eyes, trying to sleep, but sleep would not come. His shoulder and leg ached foully. Harper was already sleeping, snoring loud by the door. Under the stableyard's archway the sentry stamped his feet. The smoke of his clay pipe came fragrant to the stable, helping to fend off the stench of the wet dungheap piled at the back of the yard. Upstairs, in the Prince's room, a candle was blown out, plunging the house into darkness. Lightning flickered silent over the rooftops where the rain crashed and bounced and poured from the tiles.

On the twin ridges, three miles to the south, two armies tried to sleep in the downpour. They wrapped themselves in greatcoats for a little warmth, but the comfort was illusory for the rain had long soaked into their last stitches of clothing. Most of the fires had died and what small fuel might have fed them was being hoarded to heat the water for the morning's drink of tea.

Few men really slept, though many pretended. Some sat in the small hedges, clutching their misery close through the hours of darkness. The picquets on the forward slopes of the ridges shivered, while on the reverse slopes, where the crops had already been trampled into quagmire, men lay in furrows that had become torrents of water. A few men, abjuring sleep, sat on their packs and talked softly. Some British horses, their pickets loosened from the wet ground, broke free and, scared by the ice-blue streaks of far lightning, galloped madly through the bivouacs. Men cursed and ran from the threat of the panicked hooves, then the horses crashed out into the wide valley which was dark and empty under the thrashing rainstorm.

In the three farms forward of the British ridge the garrisons slept under the shelter of solid roofs. Sentries peered from the farm windows at the storm. A few men, eager for superstitions that would tell what the future held, remembered the tradition of British victories following great thunderstorms. The outnumbered men at Agincourt, faced by a vast and mighty French army, had similarly crouched like beasts beneath a storm that had crashed across the night sky before their dawn of battle, and now a new generation of old enemies listened to the thunder rack and thrash across a night sky that was split asunder by the demonic shafts of searing light.

The British picquets shivered. The French army was camped by the southern ridge, yet the enemy's fires had long been extinguished and the only lights in the enemy's line were two dim yellow smears which marked the candle-lit windows of the tavern. Even those lights were dulled and sometimes hidden by the sheer volume of rain. It seemed to the picquets that the rain would never stop. It was a deluge fit for a world's ending; a rain that hammered and swept before the wind to drench the fields and slop through the plough furrows and drown the ditches and crush the crops and flood the farm tracks. It was a madness of wind and water, beating through the darkness to bring misery to a field which, because it lay between two ridges, was marked for yet more misery in the morning.

THE FOURTH DAY

Sunday, 18 June 1815

CHAPTER 13

It stopped raining during the night.

At four in the morning the dawn revealed a valley mist which was stirred by a gusting damp wind. The mist was swiftly thickened by the smoke of the new morning fires. Shivering men picked themselves out of the mud like corpses coming to shuddering life. The long day had begun. It was a northern midsummer's day and the sun would not set for another seventeen hours.

Men on both sides of the shallow valley untied the rags which had been fastened round their musket locks, and took the corks out of the guns' muzzles. The sentries scraped out the grey damp slush which had been the priming in their pans and tried to empty the main charge with a fresh pinch of priming. All they achieved was a flash in the pan, evidence that the powder in the barrel was damp. They could either drill the bullet out, or else keep squibbing the gun with fresh priming till enough of the powder inside the touchhole dried to catch the fire. One by one the squibbed muskets banged, their sound echoing forlornly across the shallow valley.

The staff and general officers in Waterloo rose long before the dawn. Their grooms saddled horses, then, like men riding to their business, the officers took the southern road through the dark and dripping forest.

Sharpe and Harper were among the first to leave. The Prince was not even out of his bed when Sharpe wearily hauled himself into his saddle and shoved his rifle into its bucket holster. He was wearing his green Rifleman's jacket beneath Lucille's cloak and riding the mare which had recovered from her long day's reconnaissance about Charleroi. His clothes were clammy and his thighs sore from the long days in the saddle. The wind whipped droplets of water from the roofs and trees as he and Harper turned south into the village street. 'You'll keep your promise today?' Sharpe asked Harper.

'You're as bad as Isabella! God save Ireland, but if I wanted someone else to be my conscience I'd have found a wife out here to nag me.'

Sharpe grinned. 'I'm the one who'll have to give her the news of your death, so are you going to keep your promise?'

'I'm not planning on being a dead man just yet, so I'll keep my promise.' Harper was nevertheless dressed and equipped for a fight. He wore his Rifleman's jacket and had his seven-barrelled gun on one shoulder and his rifle on the other. Both men had left their packs at the Prince's billet, and neither man had shaved. They rode to battle looking like brigands.

As they neared Mont-St-Jean they heard a sound like the sucking of a great sea on a shelving beach. It was the sound of thousands of men talking, the sound of damp twigs burning, the noise of squibbed muskets popping, and the sound of the wind rustling in the stiff damp stalks of rye. It was also a strangely ominous sound. The air smelt of wet grass and dank smoke, but at least the clouds of the previous day had thinned enough so that the sun was visible as a pale pewter glow beyond a cloudy vapour that was being thickened by the smoke of the camp-fires.

There was one ritual for Sharpe to perform. Before riding on to the ridge's crest he found a cavalry armourer close to the forest's edge and handed down his big sword. 'Make it into a razor,' he ordered.

The armourer treadled his wheel, then kissed the blade onto the stone so that sparks flowed like crushed diamonds from the steel. Some of the nicks in the sword's fore edge were so deep that successive sharpenings had failed to obliterate them. Sharpe, watching the sparks, could not even remember which enemies had driven those nicks so far into the steel. The armourer turned the blade to sharpen the point. British cavalrymen were taught to cut and slash rather than lunge, but wisdom said that the point always beat the edge. The armourer honed the top few inches of the backblade, then stropped the work on his thick leather apron. 'Good as new, sir.'

Sharpe gave the man a shilling, then carefully slid the sharpened sword into its scabbard. With any luck, he thought, he would not even need to draw the weapon this day.

The two Riflemen rode on through the encampment. The battalions' supply wagons had not arrived so it would be a hungry day, though not a dry one, for the quartermasters had evidently arranged for rum to be fetched from the depot at Brussels. Men cheered as the barrels were rolled through the mud. Equally to the day's purpose were the wagons of extra musket ammunition that were being hauled laboriously across the soaking ground.

A drummer boy tightened the damp skin of his drum and gave it an exploratory tap. Next to him a bugler shook the rain out of his instrument. Neither boy was more than twelve years old. They grinned as Harper spoke to them in Gaelic, and the drummer boy offered a reply in the same language. They were Irish lads from the 27th, the Inniskillings. 'They look good, don't they?' Harper gestured proudly at his coutrymen who, in truth, looked more like mud-smeared devils, but, like all the Irish battalions, they could fight like demons.

'They look good,' Sharpe agreed fervently.

They reined in at the highest point of the ridge, where the elm tree stood beside the cutting in which the highway ran north and south. Just to Sharpe's left a battery of five nine-pounder guns and one howitzer was being prepared for the day. The charges for the ready ammunition lay on canvas sheets close to the guns; each charge a grey fabric bag containing enough powder to propel a roundshot or shell. Near the charges were the projectiles, either roundshot or shells, which were strapped to wooden sabots that crushed down onto the fabric bags inside the gun barrels. Gunners were filling canisters, which were nothing but tubular tins crammed with musket-balls. When fired the thin tin canisters split apart to scatter the musket-balls like giant blasts of duckshot. Beside the guns were the tools of the artillerymen's trade: drag-chains, relievers, rammers, sponges, buckets, searchers, wormhooks, portfires and handspikes. The guns looked grimly reassuring until Sharpe remembered that the French guns would look just as businesslike and were probably present on the field in even greater numbers.

The smoke of the enemy's camp-fires lay like a low dirty mist over the southern horizon. Sharpe could see a knot of horsemen close to the inn, but otherwise the enemy was hidden. In the valley itself patches of the tall rye had been beaten flat by the night's rain, leaving the fields looking as though they suffered from some strange and scabrous disease.

There were Riflemen positioned some two hundred paces down the road in the valley, just opposite the farm of La Haye Sainte. Sharpe and Harper trotted towards those Greenjackets, who were occupying a sandpit on the road's left, while the farm on the right was garrisoned by men of the King's German Legion.

'A bad night?' Sharpe asked a Greenjacket sergeant.

'We've known worse, sir. It's Mr Sharpe, isn't it?'

'Yes.'

'Nice to know you're here, sir. Cup of tea?'

'The usual smouch?'

'It never changes, sir.' Smouch was a cheap tea which was rumoured to be made from ash leaves steeped in sheep's dung. It tasted even worse than its alleged recipe sounded, but any hot liquid was welcome on this damp cold morning. The Sergeant handed Sharpe and Harper a tin mug each, then stared through the dawn gloom at the enemy-held ridge. 'I suppose Monsewer will start the ball early?'

Sharpe nodded. 'I would if I was in his boots. He needs to beat us before the Prussians come.'

'So they are coming, sir?' The Sergeant's tone betrayed that even these prime troops realized how precarious was the British predicament.

'They're coming.' Sharpe had still not heard any official news of the Prussians, but Rebecque had been confident the night before that Blücher would march at dawn.

The Sergeant suddenly whipped round, proving he had eyes in the back of his head. 'Not here, George Cullen, you filthy little bastard! Go and do it in the bloody field! We don't want to be tripping over your dung all day! Move!'

A group of the Greenjackets' officers had gathered about an empty artillery canister that they had filled with hot water for their morning shave. One of the men, a tall, cadaverous and grey-haired major, looked oddly familiar to Sharpe, but he could neither place the man's face nor his name.

'That's Major Dunnett,' the Sergeant told Sharpe. 'He was only posted to this battalion last year, sir. Poor gentleman had the misfortune to be a prisoner for most of the last war.'

'I remember now.' Sharpe spurred the mare towards the group of officers and Dunnett, looking up, caught his eye and stared with apparent amazement. Then Dunnett shook the soap off his razor blade and walked to meet Sharpe. They had last met during the disastrous retreat to Corunna when Dunnett had been in charge of a half-battalion of Greenjackets and Lieutenant Sharpe had been his quartermaster. Dunnett had hated Sharpe with an unreasonable and ineradicable hatred. The last glimpse Sharpe had caught of his erstwhile commanding officer had been as French Dragoons captured Dunnett while Sharpe had scrambled to desperate safety with a group of Riflemen. Now, denied promotion by his five years in prison, Dunnett was still a major while Sharpe, his old quartermaster, outranked him.

'Hello, Dunnett.' Sharpe curbed his horse.

'Lieutenant Sharpe, as I live and breathe.' Dunnett patted his face dry. 'I heard that you'd survived and prospered, though I doubt you're still a lieutenant? Or even a quartermaster?'

'A Dutch Lieutenant-Colonel, which I don't think counts for very much. It's good to see you again.'

'It's good of you to say so.' Dunnett, evidently embarrassed by Sharpe's compliment, looked away and caught sight of Harper who was still talking with the Sergeant. 'Is that Rifleman Harper?' Dunnett asked incredulously.

'Ex-Rifleman Harper. He cheated his way out of the army, and now can't resist coming back to see it fight a battle.'

'I thought he'd have died long ago. He was always a rogue.' Dunnett was painfully thin, with deep lines carved either side of his grey moustache. He looked back to Sharpe. 'So were you, but I was wrong in my opinion of you.'

It was a handsome retraction. Sharpe tried to throw it off by saying how terrible the retreat to Corunna had been; an ordeal that had abraded men's tempers and manners till they were snarling at each other like rabid dogs. 'It was a bad time,' he concluded.

'And today doesn't promise to be much better. Is it true that Boney's whole army is over there?'

'Most of it, anyway.' Sharpe assumed that Napoleon had sent some men to keep the Prussians busy, but the thickness of the camp-fires across the valley was evidence that most of the French army was now assembled in front of Wellington's men.

'Damn the bastards however many they might be.' Dunnett buttoned his shirt and pulled on his green coat. 'I won't be taken a prisoner again.'

'Was it bad?'

'No, it was even civilized. We had the freedom of Verdun, but if you didn't have money, that was a dubious privilege. I think I'd rather die than see that damned town again.' Dunnett turned and stared towards the empty slope of the French ridge where the only movement was the ripple of the wind moving the standing patches of damp rye. He stared for a few seconds, then turned back to Sharpe. 'It's oddly good to see you again. There aren't many of that particular battalion still living. You heard they were at New Orleans?'

'Yes.'

'Butchered,' Dunnett said bitterly. 'Why do they make fools into generals?'

Sharpe smiled. 'I think you'll find the Duke's no fool.'

'So everyone tells me, and let's hope it's true. I want the chance of killing some Crapauds today. I've scores to settle with the bloody French.' Dunnett laughed as if to dilute the hatred he had betrayed, then offered his hand. 'Allow me to wish you well of this day, Sharpe.'

Sharpe reached down and took his old enemy's hand. 'And you, Dunnett.' He thought how odd it was that men made peace before they went to war, and it seemed odder still as Dunnett, with apparent pride, introduced Sharpe to the other officers. These Riflemen were cruelly exposed, so far forward of the ridge, but so long as the

Germans held the farm buildings then the Greenjackets were assured of their supporting fire. 'Better here than over there.' A captain pointed towards the left flank where the British ridge was pierced and flattened by a shallow re-entrant and where a battalion of Dutch-Belgian troops was in full view of the enemy. The rest of Wellington's infantry were concealed behind the ridge or sheltered behind thick farm walls, but the one Dutch-Belgian battalion was horribly exposed. Doubtless some troops had to be stationed to block the dangerous re-entrant, but, after Quatre Bras, it seemed futile to expect the Belgians to stand and fight.

'Perhaps the Duke wants the buggers to run away early? No point in feeding the scum if they won't fight.' Five years of imprisonment had done nothing to dull Dunnett's tongue.

Sharpe made his farewells, then he and Harper rode back towards the ridge. 'Strange to meet Dunnett again,' Sharpe said, then he twisted to look at the empty French ridge as he thought of the men he knew in that far army. One or two of those men he counted as friends, yet today he would have to fight them.

Once at the crest of the ridge Sharpe and Harper turned west towards the British right flank which the Prince of Orange had judged to be vulnerable. Some battalions were already formed up behind the ridge's crest. The Prince of Wales's Own Volunteers were paraded in a hollow square that faced inwards towards a chaplain who was trying to make himself heard above the sound of the wind and the buzz of other battalions' voices. Sharpe saw d'Alembord's head bowed, apparently in prayer, though more probably in reverie. Just beyond the Prince of Wales's Own Volunteers an infantry battalion of the King's German Legion was singing a psalm. The Hanoverian voices were strong and full of emotion so that Sharpe had the sudden guilty impression that he eavesdropped upon a very private moment. 'It's Sunday, so it is,' Harper said with a note of surprise, then made the sign of the cross on his uniform jacket.

On the ridge's crest a cheerful and rubicund gunner officer was riding from gun battery to gun battery. 'You will not indulge in counter-battery fire. You will save your powder for the infantry and the cavalry! You will not fire at the enemy guns, but at their infantry and cavalry alone! Good morning, Freddy!' He raised his hat to a friend who evidently commanded one of the batteries. 'Thank God it's stopped raining, eh? Give my compliments to your lovely wife when you write home. You will not indulge in counter-battery fire, but you will save your powder . . .' His voice faded behind as Sharpe and Harper rode further west.

'I've never seen so many guns,' Harper commented. Every few yards there was another battery of nine-pounders while, behind the ridge, the lethal short-barrelled howitzers waited in reserve.

'You can bet your last ha'pence that Napoleon's got more guns than us,' Sharpe said grimly.

'All the same, it'll be bloody slaughter if the Crapauds march straight across the valley.'

'Maybe they won't. The little Dutch boy thinks they might hook round this end of our line.' Sharpe spoke sourly, though in truth the Prince's fear was a genuine and intelligent concern, and Sharpe, suddenly fearing that the Emperor might already have marched and that the French might already be threatening to spring a surprise attack on the British right flank, spurred his mare forward.

He reined in on the ridge above the château of Hougoumont. From here he could see far to the south-west, but nothing stirred in the grey morning. A handful of cavalry picquets from the King's German Legion sat untroubled in the fields, proof that the French had not marched. The château itself buzzed with noise as the Coldstream Guards, who formed its garrison, finished their preparations. Sharpe could hear the sound of pick-axes making yet more loopholes in the thick walls of the barns and house.

A knot of horsemen was galloping along the ridge's crest. The horses' hooves flung up great gobs of mud and water from the soaking ground. The leading horseman was the Prince of Orange who, seeing Sharpe, raised a hand in greeting and swerved towards the two Riflemen. The Prince was elegantly dressed in a gold-frogged coat that was trimmed with black fur. 'You were up early, Sharpe!'

'Yes, sir.'

'Nothing moving on the flank?'

'Nothing, sir.'

The Prince suddenly spotted that Sharpe still wore his Rifle green under the cloak. He was clearly tempted to say something, but just as clearly feared an act of downright disobedience that would betray his own lack of princely authority, so instead he scowled and stared towards the vulnerable open flank where the German horsemen sat like statues in the waterlogged meadows. 'The Emperor will come round this way. You can depend on it!'

'Indeed, sir,' Sharpe said.

'An attack around our right will cut us off from the North Sea and take the French away from the Prussians, Sharpe, that's what it'll do, and that's why the Emperor will attack here. A child could work that out! It's a waste of time putting guns on the ridge. They'll all have to be moved to this flank and it'll be a shambles when the orders are given. But at least we'll be ready for the move!'

'Are the Prussians coming, sir?' Sharpe asked.

The Prince frowned as though he found the question aggravating. 'They're coming.' The answer was grudging.

'Blücher says two of his corps will be here by midday and a third will be hard on their heels. The message came a few minutes ago.'

'Thank God,' Sharpe said fervently.

The Prince, already irritated by Sharpe's refusal to wear Dutch uniform, was galled by the Rifleman's evident relief. 'I don't think we need be too grateful, Colonel Sharpe. I trust we can beat those devils without a few Germans, isn't that so, Rebecque?'

'Indeed, Your Highness.' Rebecque, his horse just behind that of the Prince, said tactfully.

'We can beat them so long as we hold this flank.' The Prince turned his horse towards the château. 'So keep watch here, Sharpe! The future of Europe may depend on your vigilance!'

The Prince shouted the last fine words as he spurred down the farm track, which led off the ridge to the château. Rebecque waited a few seconds until his master's entourage was out of earshot, then added a few cautionary words. 'The roads are very heavy, so I wouldn't expect the Prussians till early afternoon.'

'But at least they're coming.'

'Oh, they're coming, right enough. They've promised it. We wouldn't be fighting here if they weren't.' Rebecque smiled to acknowledge his bald contradiction of the Prince's confidence. 'May I wish you joy of the day, Sharpe?'

'And the same to you, sir.'

They shook hands, then Rebecque trotted after his master who had disappeared into Hougoumont's big courtyard.

Patrick Harper glanced up at the sky to judge the time. 'The Germans will be here by early afternoon, eh? Where will they come from?'

'From over there.' Sharpe pointed to the west, far beyond the elm tree and beyond the left flank of

Wellington's line. 'And I'll tell you something else, Patrick. You were right. It's going to be bloody murder.' Sharpe turned to glower at the empty enemy ridge. 'Napoleon's not going to manoeuvre. He's going to come straight for us like a battering ram.'

Harper was amused at Sharpe's sudden grim certainty. 'With the future of Europe at stake?'

Sharpe did not know why he was suddenly so certain, unless it was an inability to agree with anything the Prince of Orange believed. He attempted a more acceptable justification for his certainty. 'Boney will want to get it done quickly, so why manoeuvre? And he's never cared how many of his men die, so long as he wins. And he's got enough men over there to hammer us bloody, so why shouldn't he just march straight forward and have the damned business done?'

'Thank God for the Prussians then,' Harper said grimly.

'Thank God, indeed.'

Because the Prussians had promised, and were coming.

Marshal Prince Blücher, Commander of the Prussian army, had promised he would march to fight beside Wellington, but Blücher's Chief of Staff, Gneisenau, did not trust the Englishman. Gneisenau was convinced that Wellington was a knave, a liar and a trickster who, at the first sniff of cannon-fire, would run for the Channel and abandon the Prussians to Napoleon's vengeance.

Blücher had scorned Gneisenau's fears and ordered his Chief of Staff to organize the march to Waterloo. Gneisenau would not directly disobey any order, but he was a clever enough man to make sure that his method of obedience was tantamount to disobedience.

He therefore commanded that General Friedrich Wilhelm von Bülow's Fourth Corps should lead the advance on Waterloo. Of all the Prussian corps the Fourth was the furthest away from the British. Making the Fourth march first would inflict a long delay on the fulfilment of Blücher's promise, but Gneisenau, fearing that von Bülow might show a soldier's haste in marching to the expected sound of the guns, further ordered the thirty thousand men of the Fourth Corps to march by a particular road that not only led through the narrow streets of Wavre, but also crossed a peculiarly narrow and inconvenient bridge. The Fourth Corps was also commanded to march through the cantonments of Lieutenant-General Pirch's Third Corps, which was instructed to leave its guns and heavy supply wagons parked on the road. Once von Bülow's thirty thousand men had edged past those obstructions, Pirch was permitted to begin his own march in von Bülow's footsteps. Lieutenant-General Zieten's Second Corps, which was only twelve miles from Waterloo and the closest of all the Prussian Corps to the British, was firmly ordered to stay in its cantonments until the Fourth and Third had passed it by, and then the Second was to take a circuitous northerly route that would still further delay its arrival on the battlefield.

It needed a masterful piece of staff work to create such chaos, but Gneisenau was a master and, proving that fortune will often favour the competent, an extra delay was imposed when a burning house blocked a street in Wavre so that von Bülow's men were stalled almost before their march had begun. The soldiers just grounded their muskets and waited.

Somewhere to the south a French Corps was blundering about in search of the Prussian army, but Gneisenau was not worried by that threat. All that mattered was that the precious Prussian army should not be sucked into the huge defeat that the Emperor was about to inflict on the British, and Gneisenau, confident that his skill had averted such a disaster, ordered his breakfast.

*   *   *

A single horseman rode to the solitary elm tree. The horseman wore a blue civilian coat over white buckskin breeches and tall black boots. About his neck was a white cravat, while on his cocked hat were four cockades, one each for England, Spain, Portugal and the Netherlands. A blue cloak was rolled on the pommel of his saddle. His staff closed in behind as His Grace the Duke of Wellington stared through a spyglass at the tavern called La Belle Alliance. The military commissioners of Austria, Spain, Russia and Prussia attended the Duke, and like him trained their telescopes at the far ridge. Some civilians had also ridden from Brussels to observe the fighting and they too crowded in behind the Duke.

The Duke snapped his glass shut and looked at his watch. Nine o'clock. 'Baggage to the rear,' he said to no one in particular, but two of his aides turned their horses away to carry the order down the line.

The battalions shrugged off their packs which were piled onto the carts that had brought up the extra ammunition. The men were ordered to keep nothing but their weapons, cartridges and canteens. The carts struggled through fetlock-deep mud to carry the baggage back to the forest's edge where it joined the carriages of the military commissioners and the artillery wagons and the portable forges and the farriers' carts, and where the supernumeraries of battle – the shoeing smiths, the wheelwrights, the commissary officers, the clerks, the drivers, the harness makers and the soldiers' wives – would wait for the day's decision.

On the northern slope of the ridge the Duke's infantry waited in columns of companies. The leading battalions were far enough advanced for the men of the forward companies to see over the crest to where a faint and watery glimmer of sunlight shone on the enemy ground. That southern ridge was empty, all but for a few horsemen.

Then, suddenly and gloriously, an army began to show.

The veterans in the Duke's army had seen an enemy prepare for battle, but never like this. Before, in Spain, the enemy would come as a threat, as a smear of dark uniforms advancing across sunlit ground, but here the Emperor paraded his army as though this day was a holiday and the British redcoats were spectators of his gorgeous display. The French did not advance to battle; instead they spread themselves in an arrogant panoply of overwhelming power.

Infantry, cavalry and gunners appeared. They marched or rode as though they were on the *Champ de Mars* in Paris. They were not in their combat uniforms, but dressed for the forecourt of a palace. Their coats glistened with gold and silver lace. There were plumes of scarlet, silver, yellow, red, green and white. There were helmets of brass and of steel; helmets trimmed with leopard's fur or rimmed with sable. There were Cuirassiers, Lancers, Dragoons, Carabiniers, and Hussars. Gunners with dark blue pelisses edged with silver fur ordered their weapons slewed to face the enemy. Trumpeters challenged the valley, their instruments trailing banners of embroidered gold. The red and white Polish swallow-tailed flags of the Lancers made a thicket of colour, while guidons, standards, banners, pennants and gilded Eagles studded the watery sky.

And still they came; regiment after regiment, troop after troop, battery after battery; the might of a resurrected Empire displayed in a massive show of incipient violence. Grecian helmets trailed plumes of horsehair, officers wore sashes thick with gold thread, and the élite of the infantry's élite wore black bearskins. Those were the men of the Imperial Guard, Napoleon's beloved *anciens*, each man with a powdered pigtail, gold ear-rings, and the moustache of a veteran. In front of the Emperor's Guard his *jeunes filles*, his guns, stood wheel to wheel.

Sharpe, watching from the ridge above Hougoumont, stared in utter disbelief. After half an hour the enemy was still filing onto the ridge, the new battalions concealing the first, and those new battalions in turn being hidden by yet more troops who poured from the high road to wheel left or right. The bands were playing while officers with gold and lace-trimmed saddle-cloths galloped bravely in front of the display. It was a sight not seen on a battlefield for a hundred years; a formal display of a glorious threat, overwhelming and dazzling and filling the southern landscape with guns and sabres and lances and swords and muskets.

The British gunners gazed at their targets and knew there was not enough ammunition in all Europe to kill such a horde. The infantry watched the thousands of enemy cavalry who would try and break them as they had broken a brigade at Quatre Bras. The Dutch-Belgian troops just watched the whole vast array and knew that no army in all the world could beat such glory into gore.

'God save Ireland.' Even Harper, who had seen most of what war had to offer, was overwhelmed by the sight.

'God quicken the bloody Prussians,' Sharpe said. The sound of the French bands came clear across the valley; a cacophony of tunes among which, at intervals, the raucous defiance of the *Marseillaise* sounded distinct. 'They're trying to make the Belgians run away,' Sharpe guessed, and he twisted in his saddle to stare at the nearest Belgian regiment and saw the fear on their young faces. This was not their fight. They thought of themselves as French, and wished the Emperor was back as their lord, but fate had brought them to this sea of mud to be dazzled by a master of war.

From one end of the far ridge to the other, across two miles of farmland, the French army paraded. The Emperor's guns seemed wheel to wheel; Sharpe tried to number the enemy's artillery and lost count at over two hundred barrels. He did not even attempt to number the enemy's men, for they filled the ridge and hid each other and still they marched from the high road to fill the far fields. The might of France had come to a damp valley, there to obliterate its oldest enemy.

The enemy's drums and bands faded as a cheer billowed from the line's centre. A small man on a grey horse had appeared. He wore the undress uniform of a colonel of the Imperial Guard's *chasseurs à cheval*; a green coat faced with red over a white waistcoat and white breeches. The man wore a grey overcoat loose on his shoulders like a cloak. His bicorne hat had no cockades. His Imperial Majesty, the Emperor of France, galloped along the face of his army and was greeted by the cheers of men who knew they were on the brink of victory.

The Duke of Wellington had long turned scornfully away from the display. 'Tell the men to lie down.'

The British and Dutch obeyed. Men lying flat in the long grass of the ridge's plateau could not see the overwhelming enemy, nor were they visible to the enemy's gunners.

The Duke rode along the right of his line. He did not gallop like his opponent, but trotted sedately. No one cheered the Duke. His gunners, posted on the ridge's crest, watched the Emperor. One gunner captain, his weapon loaded, squinted along its crude sights then called out to the Duke that in a moment the Emperor would gallop directly into the gun's line. 'Permission to fire, Your Grace?'

'It is not the business of army commanders to fire on each other. Save your ammunition.' The Duke rode on, not even deigning to look towards his opponent.

The Duke and his entourage passed near Sharpe, then angled towards the troops who guarded the open flank beyond Hougoumont. The closest battalion was Dutch-Belgian and the troops, seeing the knot of horsemen come down from the ridge, opened fire. The musket bullets fluttered near the Duke, but did not hit any of his party. The Duke swerved away as the Dutch officers shouted at their men to cease their fire. The Duke, grim-faced, rode back towards the elm tree that would be his command post.

A shower of rain briefly obscured the valley as the French redeployed themselves for battle. The great display was evidently over for most of the enemy troops now retreated from the ridge's crest. The French gunners could be seen charging their barrels with powder and shot.

'What's the time?' Sharpe asked a nearby gunner officer who commanded a battery of howitzers.

'Just on half-past eleven.'

If the Prussians came at one in the afternoon? Sharpe tried to guess how long the British could sustain their defence against the onslaught of the huge force he had just watched parade. One and a half hours? It seemed unlikely.

The French, perhaps certain that they had plenty of time in which to do their work, were in no hurry to begin. More guns were manhandled into their battle line, yet none opened fire. Sharpe gazed eastwards to see if any Prussian cavalry scouts had yet appeared beyond the valley's edge, but nothing moved there. He wished he had a watch so he could see the progress of the minutes that must be bringing the Prussians closer. 'The time?' he apologetically asked the gunner officer again.

The gunner obligingly clicked open the lid of his watch. 'A quarter of twelve.'

Behind the howitzers the nearest British redcoats sat or lay on the wet turf. Some smoked their clay pipes. Their canteens were filled with rum or gin, and their pouches with dry cartridges. The wind was dying. The clouds still stretched across the sky, but they must have been thinning for Sharpe saw yet more gauzy floods of sunlight patching the distant fields with gold. The day was warming, though Sharpe's clothes were still clammy and uncomfortable. The minutes passed. The gunner officer fidgeted with his watch, obsessively opening and closing the silver lid. No one spoke. It was almost as if the whole army held its breath. Patrick Harper was watching a pair of skylarks who tumbled in the lower veil of clouds.

Then a French gun fired.

The barrel of the gun was cold, so the shot did not carry the full distance to the British ridge. Instead the roundshot slammed into the valley, scattering rye, then bounced in a flurry of wet soil to bury itself just below the elm tree. The smoke of the gun drifted grey along the French ridge.

A second gun fired. Its roundshot similarly bounded harmlessly through the empty fields. The Duke opened his watch lid to see the time.

There was a pause equal to that which had separated the first two shots, then a third French gun fired. Its ball screamed towards the exposed Dutch-Belgian troops beyond the sandpit, but fell short and ploughed into a patch of soft ground that stopped the missile dead.

The three shots were the Emperor's signal.

To let loose hell.

CHAPTER 14

The Earl of Uxbridge, quite ready for the moment, had arranged for his servant to bring a tray of silver stirrup cups filled with sherry. As the first gun fired the Earl waved the servant forward and watched as the small cups were handed about to his staff.

The Earl waited for the second gun to fire, then, as though these horsemen were about to ride to hounds, he gravely raised his stirrup cup. 'Today's fox, gentlemen. Allow me to give you today's fox.'

The horsemen drank. Lord John Rossendale had to curb the temptation to gulp the sherry down.

The third gun fired. The fox had broken cover, was running, and the blooding could begin.

Every gun on the French ridge opened fire.

The salvo showed as a volcanic eruption of smoke that blurred the far crest with yellow-grey smoke. In the heart of the smoke were the stabbing flames.

Two heartbeats later the sound slammed across the valley; a thunderclap to tell Europe that the Emperor was at war.

The majority of the guns had been loaded with shell. The cold barrels dropped the missiles fractionally short and most plunged harmlessly into mud that either extinguished the burning fuse or soaked up the force of the explosion. A few, very few, ricocheted on the ridge's forward slope to land a second time among the battalions sheltering beyond the crest. The explosions punched ragged blots of dark smoke and livid flame into the damp air.

The first men were dying, but not many, for a shell had to explode in the very heart of a company if it was to kill. Some shells were defused by quick-witted men who either pinched out the fire or knocked the smouldering fuse clean from the powder charge with a swift blow of a musket butt. The smoke from the French guns rolled down into the valley, then began to be fed as the guns which had reloaded the quickest fired again. The firing became ragged, but constant; jet after jet of smoke and flame pumped from the French-held ridge. The shots screamed higher as the gun barrels warmed. Some shells skimmed across the ridge top to explode far back at the forest's edge while the best aimed shots bounced just below the British crest to plunge down among the men hidden behind. The shells made differing sounds, depending on their distance from the ear. Some hummed like children's tops, some whirred like a bird's wingbeat, while others rumbled like thunder. The sounds were already causing a trickle of Belgian troops to retreat towards the forest; one wounded man was an excuse for ten others to help him to safety.

One shell exploded close to the Earl of Uxbridge's staff who, still bunched together after their toast to the day's fox, split asunder like sheep attacked by a wolf. A small silver cup fell into the mud, but otherwise there was no damage other than to the young men's dignity. They curbed their excited horses and watched as each new shot roiled and twitched the bank of smoke which thickened in front of the Emperor's gun line.

On the British right, where the French guns were close to Hougoumont, the gunners were firing canister to scour the British skirmishers from the woods which lay south of the château. Some of the musket-balls hummed up onto the ridge where they pattered on the wet ground like hail.

A British nine-pounder fired a return shot, and earned a furious reprimand from a mounted staff officer. 'Hold your damned fire! Hold your fire!' The Duke was saving his guns the wear and tear of incessant firing that could blow out touchholes and even split barrels. He would need his guns when the enemy infantry or cavalry advanced.

A shell plunged down to smash a howitzer's wheel before bouncing up to explode harmlessly behind the ridge. The gunners quickly brought up a spare wheel and repaired the gun. The French began to mix more solid roundshot with the shells and one of the iron balls took the head off a staff officer, leaving his bloody body momentarily upright in its saddle before the terrified horse bolted and the headless body toppled to be dragged along by the left stirrup. The corpse was finally shaken loose and a group of redcoats scuttled forward to rifle the dead man's pockets.

A shell landed on the ridge top, bounced, then exploded twenty yards to Sharpe's left. A piece of red-hot casing, trailing smoke, smacked harmlessly against his thigh. 'Go back,' Sharpe told Harper.

'I'm all right here, so I am.'

'You made your wife a promise! So bugger off!'

'Save your breath!' Harper stayed. The cannonade was heavy, but it was not overly dangerous. The French gunners were doubly hampered; first they were being blinded by their own smoke, and secondly their enemy was crouching behind the protection of the low ridge, and so most of their shells were exploding harmlessly if they exploded at all. Too many fuses were being extinguished by mud, yet the artillery was making a deal of noise, enough to terrify the Belgian troops who crouched under the sounds of hissing shells and banging explosions and thundering guns.

Sharpe moved to his right, going to a vantage point from where he could see the empty countryside on the army's right flank. The move took Harper and himself away from the worst of the cannonade and to where another British staff officer was evidently posted on the same duty as Sharpe; to watch for a French outflanking march. The man, who was in the blue coat and fur Kolbak of the Hussars, nodded civilly to Sharpe, then consulted a notebook. 'I made it ten of midday, did you?'

'Ten of midday?' Sharpe asked.

'When Bonaparte opened fire. It's good to be accurate about these things.'

'Is it?'

'The Peer likes to be specific. I'm one of his family by the way.' By which the pleasant-faced young man meant he was one of the Duke's aides. 'My name is Witherspoon.'

'Sharpe. And this is my friend Mr Harper from Ireland.'

Captain Witherspoon nodded genially at Harper, then cocked an eye at the clouds. 'I suspect it might well clear up. I detected a quite definite rise in the mercury this morning. I'm honoured to make your acquaintance, Sharpe! You're with the Young Frog, are you not?'

'Yes, I am.'

'Is he good for anything at all?'

Sharpe smiled at Captain Witherspoon's disingenuous tone. 'Not that I know of.'

The cavalryman laughed. 'I was at Eton with him. He wasn't any good there either, though he had a mighty fine opinion of himself. I remember him as being eternally dirty! But he liked the girls, and had a prolific fondness for wine.'

'What's the time now?' Sharpe asked in apparently rude disregard of Witherspoon's gossip.

Witherspoon hauled his watch from his fob and clicked open the lid. 'Four minutes after midday, save a few seconds.'

'You'd best write down that the French are advancing, then.'

'They're doing what? Oh, my soul! So they are! Thank you, my dear fellow! Good Lord, they advance, indeed they do!' He dashed a note into his book.

French skirmishers were swarming towards Hougoumont. They came in a loose mass of men; running, firing, running again. They were mostly among the trees, which gave cover from the foot of their ridge right up to the walls of the château, but some had overlapped onto the open flank where newly cut hay lay in sopping rows among the stubble. The skirmishers of the red-coated Coldstream Guards were falling back fast, evidently ordered not to make a fight of it among the trees. With the redcoats were some Dutch and German troops, the Germans armed with long-barrelled hunting rifles. Sharpe saw at least two of the blue-coated Dutch-Belgian troops running towards the enemy, presumably seeking shelter.

The Guards skirmishers scrambled back into the farm buildings or into the walled garden and orchard that lay alongside the château. The French skirmishers had advanced to the very edge of the wood and were hidden from Sharpe by the loom of the château's buildings. 'I'm going down there,' he told Harper, pointing to the field where a handful of the French skirmishers sheltered behind the rows of wet hay.

'I'll come with you,' Harper said obstinately.

'Take care!' Captain Witherspoon called after the two Riflemen.

Sharpe cantered his horse down the farm track, past a haystack that stood outside the château's rear gates, and then into the open field to the west. The few French skirmishers who had been sheltering behind the cut hay had gone back to the wood, evidently scoured from the field by muskets fired from loopholes hacked in Hougoumont's barns. Sharpe was only a hundred yards from the fight, but he was as safe from it as if he had been on the moon. The French had only one object, and that was to capture the buildings from where they could rake the British-held ridge behind with close-range cannon-fire. They had taken the woods, and now the mass of blue-coated infantry readied themselves for the final rush at the sprawling farm. Some of the French used axes to chop big holes in the hedge that bordered the wood. More French battalions filed into the trees until the woods were filled with enemy infantry waiting for the bugle, which would throw the attack forward.

The bugle sounded, the French cheered, and the great mass rushed at the gaps in the hedge.

The defenders opened fire.

The Guards were behind ditches and hedges, safe behind walls, or firing from the windows in the château's upper floors. A blast of musketry crashed down on the French attack, and every musket fired was immediately replaced by another loaded weapon that fired and in turn was replaced at the loophole or firing step. The crackle of the muskets was incessant, drowning the cannon-fire from the ridge beyond. Smoke filled the space south of the château's walls; smoke that was twitched and torn by new musket blasts that glowed red and sudden inside the acrid cloud. Somehow enough Frenchmen survived the musket volleys to reach the château's walls where they clawed to drag the British muskets clean out of the loopholes. Instead the muskets fired, hurling attackers back into the faces of the men who advanced behind.

There seemed more hope of capturing the kitchen garden that was protected by a wall only a few inches taller than a man. Some of the French held their muskets over their heads to fire blindly down across the wall's coping. Others fired through the British loopholes, while the bravest tried to climb the wall and some even straddled it to stab down with their long bayonets.

Yet the Guards knew how to defend. For every French musket fired into a loophole a dozen British shots replied, while those brave Frenchmen who gained the wall's top were either shot back or else pulled over to be bayoneted among the broken pea plants or in the trampled rose beds. Outside the garden the foot of the wall became treacherous with the bodies of the dead and dying French. Inside the garden files of men queued to take their turn at the loopholes so that the musket-fire never slackened and the heavy lead balls smashed into the mass of Frenchmen who still ran forward from the trees to be baulked by the wall. Bugles and shouts urged them on.

The château's orchard, beyond the garden, had no walls, but only a thick blackthorn hedge. The Guards fired through and over the hedge, but the French brought up pioneers' axes and defended each axeman with a group of muskets, and it seemed that the Emperor's men would have to win here by sheer weight of numbers. The axes crashed at the thick thorn trunks, ripping and shredding and tugging the obstacle away. A redcoat lunged his bayonet at an axeman, lunged too far, and was dragged screaming over the thorns to be ripped by a dozen bayonets.

Then a shell exploded above the French.

Sharpe looked up. High in the sky was a tangle of arcing smoke trails, evidence that the howitzers on the ridge were firing Britain's secret weapon: the spherical case shell invented by Major-General Shrapnel. The shell was a five-and-a-half-inch sphere packed with musket-balls and a powder explosive that, if its fuse was cut to a precise length, would explode lethally in the air above its target. The difficulty lay in cutting the fuses which were affected by humidity as well as by the exact length of the shell's flight, yet these fuses had been cut by a genius for the salvoes were murderously precise. Common shell burst into a few big fragments, but spherical case showered a killing rain of thin casing and musket-balls, and now caseshot after caseshot was crashing apart above the French infantry and the musket-balls and jagged iron fragments were slashing down to cut swathes of bloody flesh in the French attackers.

'That is pretty work! 'Pon my soul, but that's very well done!' Captain Witherspoon had followed Sharpe and Harper to their vantage point and now applauded the skill of the gunners who were dropping the spherical case exactly in the right place; none falling short on the Guards, but all arcing onto the French attackers.

The musket-fire still hammered from the château's walls. The French were faltering now, assailed from above and from their front. Some edged backwards, seeking the shelter of the trees, but the howitzers seemed to anticipate the move and the shrapnel blasts moved away from the château to flense the oaks in the wood of their leaves and branches. Each shell cracked apart with a sharper bang than common shell. In Spain Sharpe had noticed how the spherical case caused more wounds than deaths, but the sight of wounded men streaming back through the trees would shake the confidence of the French troops advancing in support of the first attack.

British skirmishers ran from the château's northern flank into the field where Sharpe and Harper watched. The skirmishers ran south and added their fire from the corner of the farm buildings. The French were retreating fast now, going deep into the woods to escape the explosions and musketry.

'Opening honours to the Duke, wouldn't you say?'

Witherspoon was scribbling his comments in his notebook.

'It'll be a very long day,' Sharpe warned.

'Not too long, I'm sure. Good old Blücher's coming. He must be here soon. Did you hear about the poor fellow's ordeal?'

'No.' Nor was Sharpe much interested, but Witherspoon was a friendly fellow and it would have been churlish not to have listened.

'Seems he was unhorsed and ridden over by the French cavalry at Ligny. He was lucky to survive at all, and the old boy must be seventy if he's a day! Anyway, he rubbed himself with a liniment of garlic and rhubarb and now he's on his way here. God speed his smelly march, I say.'

'Amen to that,' Sharpe said.

The howitzer-fire ceased, one last shell leaving a wavering trail of smoke from its burning fuse that crashed the charge apart inside the wood. The French attack had failed, leaving the space between the wood and château sifted with smoke above a sprawl of blue-coated bodies. Some of those bodies cried for help. The failed attack had left an overpowering smell of rotten eggs, which was the familiar stench of exploded gunpowder. The smell of blood would follow, mingling with the sweeter scent of crushed grasses and crops.

British skirmishers advanced into the wood again, preparing to challenge the next attack. Beyond the château, in the wide valley that was now hidden from Sharpe, the noise of the French cannonade rumbled and cracked. Sharpe, his ears tuned to the familiar sounds of a battlefield, could tell that nothing there had changed. In battle, once the smoke had shrouded the field, the ears were often more useful than the eyes.

'I do believe', Witherspoon said, 'that we should be departing hence.' He gestured right, to where a battery of French eight-pounder guns was being dragged into the upper end of the hayfield. Other French troops, skirmishers, were filing from the woods into the rows of cut hay. Clearly these troops were destined for the château's next ordeal, and just as clearly it was time to yield the hayfield to them.

Sharpe, Harper and Witherspoon trotted briskly out of the hayfield and up the earthen track to the ridge top. The battery of five-and-a-half-inch howitzers that had caused such damage to the French skirmishers stood with their stubby and blackened barrels elevated steeply upwards. Sharpe congratulated the battery's commander, the same man who had fidgeted with his watch waiting for the battle to begin and who was now clearly pleased by the Rifleman's compliment. A few more scraps of French shell casing smoked in the damp crops, and a few more infantry casualties caused by the shells were being helped back to the regimental surgeons, but otherwise there was no new threat to the ridge. It seemed as if the Emperor was content to keep up his cannonade on the main British line while his infantry struggled to capture the bastion of Hougoumont.

Reinforcements from the 2nd Guards Brigade were posted to the ridge close behind the château. The Guardsmen were a part of the Prince of Orange's dispersed corps and the Prince could not resist galloping forward to watch the battalions deploy in column of companies. They looked a brave sight as they advanced beneath their huge colours and with their bands playing. The Prince returned their salutes and called out his best wishes for a brave day. The Young Frog was in high spirits, elated by the music of the fifes and drums that mingled with the fizzing sound of French shell-fuses and the crash of their explosions. His gloom of the previous night seemed to have been dissipated by battle. He spoke cheerfully with the commander of the Guards, then saw

Sharpe waiting higher on the ridge. 'What are you doing there?' he shouted.

'Obeying your orders, sir. Watching the right flank.'

'I think we can abandon that idea, Sharpe!' The Prince's tone implied utter scorn for anyone who seriously believed the French might attempt a flanking march. 'It's going to be a straightforward mill. You can tell that from their gun placements. From now on it will be toes on the scratch and heavy thumping!' The Prince feinted a punch at Sharpe to illustrate his prize-fighting metaphor, then pointed at the château. 'I want you in Hougoumont.'

'To do what, sir?' Sharpe had ridden close to the Prince whose horse skittered sideways as a shell exploded higher up the slope.

'To report to me, of course. I'll need to know when to send the reserves in.'

Sharpe had assumed that the château's defenders were quite capable of deciding that for themselves, but he recalled Rebecque's lecture on the need for tact, so just nodded. 'Very good, sir.'

The Prince suddenly looked past Sharpe. 'Witherspoon! Is that really you? My dear Witherspoon! We haven't met since Eton! I thought you were destined for the Church, not the army! Or are you a vicar in disguise today? Isn't this a splendid day? Such good sport!'

Sharpe left the happy reunion behind as he spurred towards the château. Harper, despite his sworn promise that he would not expose himself to danger, followed. The two Riflemen could hear the splintering crackle of musketry from the woods beyond the château, evidence that a new attack was gathering force. They galloped past the huge haystack that was built close to the northern entrance and Sharpe shouted at the defenders to open the gates. A startled Coldstreamer sergeant poked his head over the farmyard wall, saw the two men galloping towards him, and hastily shouted for the huge double gates to be unbarred. Once inside the farmyard Sharpe slid out of his saddle and unsheathed his rifle. Harper took the reins of both horses and tied them to a metal ring embedded in the stable wall.

A Coldstreamer captain, alarmed by the Rifleman's sudden arrival, ran from the farmhouse to greet Sharpe. 'You bring orders?'

'Ignore us.'

'Gladly!' The Captain ran back to the house which faced towards the woods where the French infantry was massing for their next rush.

A French roundshot crashed into the farmhouse roof, showering slates and splinters into the yard. Sharpe looked up at the damaged rafters and grimaced. 'God knows what we're doing here.'

'You're keeping the wee boy happy, sir.' Harper looked at the nearest defenders. 'My God, but we're in high and mighty company, so we are. I've never fought with the Coldstreamers before. I'd better polish my boots.'

'You'd better stay out of bloody trouble.' Sharpe rammed the charge down his rifle barrel, then slotted the ramrod back into place. The cobbled yard was long and thin, surrounded by sturdy farm buildings amongst which was a small chapel where the wounded from the first attack were being tended. A dungheap was piled against the chapel's wall, while barrels of unripe apples lay beside a pigsty that had lost its inhabitants, presumably to the Coldstreamers' cooking pots. A cat, clearly sensing that the troubled times could only get worse, was carrying her kittens one by one from a huge barn to the main house. Three bandaged Guardsmen sat outside the chapel. The only other Guardsmen in sight were a lieutenant and his squad of men who were evidently the garrison's reserve, and thus ready to reinforce any part of the château's perimeter that was dangerously threatened by the imminent French attack.

'It's a grand place, so it is.' Harper looked approvingly round the farm buildings. Men had started to fire from the upper rooms of the farmhouse, while a volley of musketry sounded loud from the walled garden beyond the barn. The noise of the fighting forced Harper to raise his voice. 'They must own a lot of land to fill all these barns!'

'It's good land, too!' Sharpe agreed.

Muskets crashed close behind them, coming from the stables which formed the western defences. Sharpe ran into the stables to see Guardsmen taking their turns at the loopholes. Other men were awkwardly perched on the roof beams, firing through holes they had made in the slates. Smoke from the muskets was thick among the empty stalls.

Sharpe climbed onto a manger, then hauled himself to a vacant beam where he punched a hole in the slates. French skirmishers were flooding past the stables, running through the hayfield from where he and Harper had watched the first attack. He levelled his rifle through his makeshift loophole, tracked a man carrying an officer's sword, led him by a few inches, then fired.

The rifle's smoke prevented him seeing whether he had done any damage. He ducked as a deafening crash announced the strike of an eight-pound cannon-ball that splintered viciously through the stable rafters and struck two Guardsmen down in gouts of blood. Another cannon-ball smacked against the stable's outer wall, ringing like a sledgehammer but doing no damage to the thick masonry. Sharpe, too cramped in the roof space to reload his rifle, shouted for Harper to give him his.

There was no answer.

Sharpe twisted round. Harper was standing at the stable entrance, staring towards the northern gate through which he and Sharpe had entered the château.

'Patrick! Give me your rifle!'

Still Harper did not reply. Instead, and without taking his eyes off the gate, he unslung his seven-barrelled gun.

Sharpe dropped from the beam and ran to the stable door.

The northern gates were juddering. The French had somehow reached the rear of Hougoumont and were straining and heaving at the two gates which were held shut by a wooden locking bar slotted into twin iron brackets. The gates were old and rickety, and every heave creaked them further apart. A French musket fired through the crack between the gates, then an axe-blade appeared in the gap. The axe chopped down with massive force, biting into the exposed locking bar. A Coldstreamer lieutenant was leading the garrison reserve towards the gate, but before the squad could reach the danger point, the axe struck again and this time with such brute force that the bar splintered and one end jumped clear out of its bracket so that the double gates scraped back and a flood of screaming Frenchmen charged into the courtyard. The charge was led by a huge Lieutenant who was even taller than Harper. It was the huge Lieutenant who was carrying the massive pioneers' axe that had broken through the gate.

'Fire!' the Coldstreamer Lieutenant shouted, then was swamped by the surge of Frenchmen who swept over his men. Bayonets sliced down and came back red. The axe scythed wickedly to splay open a guardsman's ribs.

Harper levelled the volley gun and fired at the mass of men. Sharpe dropped his empty rifle and drew his sword. Coldstreamers were running from the house, the barn and the stables. Muskets flared and crashed. A Frenchman went down under an officer's sword, then the officer was driven screaming to the cobbles by two French bayonets. Yet more of the blue-coated skirmishers were running through the wide open gates.

Sharpe could see no way of retrieving order from the

chaos. It was simply a time to fight. The French, half confused by the unfamiliar surroundings and by the scattered defenders, searched for ways into the farm buildings. Two of them ran to the chapel where the wounded tried to trip them. The French raised their bayonets to finish the three bandaged men, then turned as they heard a more threatening challenge behind them. Sharpe had charged the two men, his sword swinging in a wild sweep. The taller of the two Frenchmen, a sergeant, stepped back from the swing and jabbed hard forward with his blade. Sharpe's momentum took him past the threat, he half tripped on a wounded Guardsman's broken leg, cannoned off the chapel wall, and lunged with the sword. The Guardsman was screaming in sudden pain, but the sword had ripped a wound in the French Sergeant's belly. The other Frenchman came to his Sergeant's aid, then seemed to fly backwards as a rifle bullet struck his throat. Harper had discarded his volley gun, and now reversed the rifle and slammed the brass butt into the Sergeant's face. The huge French officer with the axe was by the stable wall, slashing and cutting down at the redcoats. Someone had split a barrel of half-ripe apples that were being trampled underfoot by the savagely fighting men. A group of French infantry ran towards the main house, but a volley from its rear windows cut them down. Sharpe's mare, terrified of the noise, reared up and lashed with her hooves.

'Bugger this!' Harper picked up one of the French muskets and lunged with its bayonet to finish the Sergeant. The yard was a chaos of shouting men, but beyond the wild-faced French attackers Sharpe could see a disciplined group of Guardsmen struggling to close the huge gates. God alone knew how the small group of Coldstreamers had reached the gates, but they had and, with the strength of desperation, they were now forcing the two heavy doors shut against a renewed rush of enemy infantry. By a miracle none of the Frenchmen already inside the château's yard saw what was happening behind them. A Coldstreamer sergeant had retrieved the broken bar and dropped it into the brackets as, at last, the doors were rammed shut. Most of the Guardsmen pushing on the gates had been officers who now turned with drawn swords to take the intruders from the rear.

'Now kill the bastards!' A voice with a Scots accent shouted the command. 'Kill them all!'

A French drummer boy ran screaming past Sharpe. A French corporal followed, saw the Rifleman, and turned to fire his musket. The flint fell on an empty pan. The man's eyes widened with fear, Sharpe lunged, the man tried to pull the blade from his ribs, but Sharpe drove it forwards, twisting it, forcing the man down to the cobbles where he kicked the sword free before slamming the blade back into the Frenchman's throat. The armourer who had honed Sharpe's blade had done a good job, for the weapon was wickedly sharp, and it needed to be for none of the men who clawed and stabbed and struggled in the courtyard had been given time to reload their muskets, so this fight would now have to be done with steel alone. The importance of Hougoumont gave the fight an extra and brutal bitterness, for every man knew that whoever held the château held the western flank of the battlefield. The Coldstreamers fought to rescue a battle, while the French under their giant Lieutenant fought for immortal glory.

But their prospect of glory was fading. The closing of the gate had cut the French off from aid, so now, trapped on the yard's cobbles, they retreated into a rally square about the huge Lieutenant who stood with a bloody axe above the bodies of four Guardsmen. Outside the château, and giving the fight the desperation of urgency, volleys of French musket-fire witnessed that the building's perimeter was again under heavy assault.

'Finish them off!' a British officer ordered. The Guardsmen in the yard were desperately needed to defend the château's outer walls so there would be no time now for delicacies like trying to persuade the huge Lieutenant to surrender.

Guardsmen tore into the group of Frenchmen. A redcoat went down beneath a French bayonet, then the Coldstreamers seemed to swarm over the blue-coated enemy. An elegant officer lunged with his sword, kicked a Frenchman in the crutch, then lunged again. The yard echoed with the clang and scrape of blades, the scuff of boots on cobbles, and the screams of men slashed or pierced by blades. Patrick Harper, mindless of the promise made to his wife, shouted a Gaelic war cry as he stabbed his captured bayonet forward in the short savage lunges of a professional soldier. One of the Guards' officers in the front rank of the fight was a colonel; the expensive gold lace of his uniform was sheeted with blood as he stamped his foot forward to lunge his sword with a clinical exactitude.

The huge Lieutenant with the axe saw the Coldstreamer Colonel and shouted at his men to make way. He drove a path through them, the axe glittering above the press of men, then Sharpe saw the axe crash down. The Colonel had stepped safely back, now he lunged. The Lieutenant brushed the sword thrust aside with his free hand as though the blade was no more dangerous than a riding crop. He grunted as he began a backswing with the axe calculated to split the Colonel up from the groin to the breastbone, then gasped as a pain exploded behind his knee. Sharpe had rammed his sword forward to hamstring the Frenchman's leg, now he kicked at the crippling wound to topple the huge man sideways. The Lieutenant's scarred face snarled as he tried to swing the huge axe round at his new attacker, but Sharpe was slicing the sword forward again, this time to split the grimacing face into a bloody and broken mask. The Colonel's sword lunged, taking the Lieutenant in the ribs. Still the Frenchman would not give up. The axe rang on the ground as he dragged the blade forward, then two Guardsmen pushed past the Colonel to stab their bayonets hard down. The huge body jerked for a few seconds, then was still.

The last French intruders were being hunted down. A sergeant was bayoneted on the dungheap, while a corporal, backed against the barn wall and screaming for quarter, received two bayonets in his belly instead.

The yard was foul with blood, crushed apples and corpses. Only the French drummer boy, a wee nipper hardly out of his cradle, had been spared from the massacre. A huge Guardsman stood by the boy, protecting him.

'I don't know who you are, but thank you.'

Sharpe turned to see it was the Coldstream Colonel who had spoken. 'Sharpe,' he introduced himself. 'The Young Frog's staff.'

'MacDonnell.' The Colonel was wiping the blood off a very expensive sword blade with an embroidered linen handkerchief. 'Will you forgive me?' He ran back towards the house from where the sound of musketry was louder than ever.

Sharpe wiped the mess off his own sword, then looked at Harper whose face was speckled with blood. 'I thought you'd promised to stay out of the fighting?'

'I forgot.' Harper grinned, threw down the French musket and retrieved his own weapons. 'I'll say one thing. The Guards may be pretty-boy soldiers, but the buggers can fight when they have to.'

'So can the French.'

'Their tails are up, that's for sure.' Harper breathed a belated sigh of relief. 'And how the hell did the Guards close that gate?'

'God only knows.'

'He must be on our side today.' Harper crossed himself. 'God knows, but that was desperate.'

The second French attack on the château, so close to success in the courtyard, now rolled with an equal menace around the orchard. The howitzers opened fire from the ridge again, but this time the French attack was on a wider front, and a horde of men broke through the orchard's hedges and harried the defenders back towards the walled garden. Some of the Guardsmen, too slow to climb the brick wall, were bayoneted at its foot, but then the relentless musketry erupted from the loopholes and from the wall's coping and the French attack stalled again about the garden's margin.

More men of the Coldstream Guards advanced down from the ridge. They attacked in column, their muskets armed with bayonets, and they drove up through the orchard's northern hedge to scour the French away from the garden wall. The woods to the south were still thick with French infantry, but the Guards lined the broken and torn hedge and opened a killing volley fire that blew great holes in the French lines. No troops fired faster than the British, and now, for the first time that day, the French suffered under the flaying volleys of platoon fire. The Guards reloaded with grim speed, propping their ramrods against the hedge before levelling the heavy muskets and blasting at the smoke-obscured enemy. Each platoon fired a second after its neighbour so that the hedge rolled with flames and the woods echoed with volley after volley.

Gradually the French broke away; more and more men fleeing from the remorseless musketry. 'Cease fire!' a Guards officer shouted in the orchard. The space in front of the woods was thick with the dead and wounded. The French had been hurling men against stone and flames, and suffering for it, but the Guards could see yet more men being formed in the far woods, presumably for yet another assault.

In the walled garden the only civilian left in Hougoumont was almost in tears. He was the château's gardener and he had been running from bed to bed, trying to save his precious plants from the boots of the Guardsmen. Despite his efforts the garden was a shambles. Espaliered pears had been ripped from the wall and rosebuds had been trampled. The gardener made a pathetically small pile of plants he had somehow rescued, then flinched as he watched a French corpse being dragged by its heels through the remains of an asparagus bed.

The second French assault had failed. Colonel Mac-Donnell, his face still smeared with blood, found Sharpe in the courtyard when the last musket shot had faded to silence. 'You could be useful to me,' he spoke diffidently, not wanting to encroach on another man's authority.

'I'll do whatever I can.'

'More ammunition? Can you find a wagon of the stuff and have it sent down?'

'With pleasure.' Sharpe was glad to have a proper job to do.

MacDonnell looked around the courtyard and grimaced at the remnants of the massacre. 'I think we can hold here, so long as we've got powder. Oh good! She's alive.' He had spotted the cat carrying the last of her kittens across the slaughteryard. The captured French drummer boy, his face stained with tears, held one hand over his mouth as he stared wide-eyed at the bodies which were being searched for plunder by the victorious Guardsmen. The boy's instrument was lying smashed beside the chapel door, though he still had his drumsticks stuffed into his belt. 'Cheer up, lad!' MacDonnell spoke to the boy in colloquial and genial French. 'We gave up eating captured drummer boys last year.'

The boy burst into tears again. A big Coldstreamer sergeant with a Welsh accent barked at his men to start clearing the enemy bodies away. 'Pile the buggers by the wall there. Look lively now!'

Sharpe and Harper retrieved their horses which had miraculously survived the fighting in the courtyard unhurt. The gate was swung open and the Riflemen rode to find the cartridges that would hold the château firm.

While on the far ridge the Emperor was turning his eyes away from Hougoumont. He was looking towards the British left, to the enticing and empty gentle slope east of the high road. He assumed that the Sepoy General would already have sent his reserves to help the beleaguered garrison at Hougoumont, so now the master of war would launch a thunderbolt on the British left. Marshal d'Erlon's corps, unblooded so far in the brief campaign, could now have the honour of winning it. And when the corps had smashed through the British line, the Emperor would unleash his cavalry, fresh and eager, to harry the fleeing enemy into offal.

It was half-past one. The day was becoming warmer, even hot, so that the thick woollen uniforms were at last drying out. The clouds were thinning and errant patches of sun illuminated the smoke which drifted across the valley from the French guns, but in the eastern fields, where the Prussians were supposed to be arriving, the intermittent sunlight shone on nothing. Gneisenau had done his work well, and the British were alone.

CHAPTER 15

The French gun-fire suddenly ceased. The smoke from the hot gun muzzles drifted in dirty skeining clumps above the rye and wheat. Muskets still fired at Hougoumont, and the howitzers crashed their shells over the château to explode in the wood beyond, but without the French cannon-fire something that seemed very like silence filled the battlefield with foreboding.

Then a slight wind rippled the crops in the valley and swirled the smoke away from the French crest to reveal that men in blue coats, their white crossbelts bright, were marching down the far slope. The first French infantry were advancing to attack the British ridge. They came in four great columns accompanied by eight-pounder galloper guns drawn by horse teams.

Each column was two hundred men broad; four wide phalanxes that marched stolidly down the slope of the French ridge to leave crushed paths of rye or wheat in their trail. A loose mass of skirmishers ran ahead of each formation. The thousands of trampling boots were given their rhythm by the drummers hidden deep inside each column; the drummer boys were beating the *pas de charge*, the old heartbeat of the French Empire that had driven the Emperor's infantry beyond the Vistula and down to the plains beyond Madrid. The massed drums sent a shiver through the valley. The veterans on the British ridge had heard it before, but for most of Wellington's men it was a new and sinister sound.

The four columns crossed the eastern half of the valley. The column which attacked in the valley's centre advanced up the high road and threatened to envelop the farm of La Haye Sainte. A watery sun gleamed faintly on the fixed bayonets of the column's front rank. The Riflemen in the sandpit opposite the farm were dropping the first French skirmishers who had spread out across the rye fields. Behind the skirmishers the boots of the column trampled the crop, then the drummers paused in unison to let the whole column shout its battle cry, '*Vive l'Empereur!*'

On the ridge above the farm a British gunner officer gave the elevating screw of his nine-pounder a last half twist. The fabric bag of gunpowder was crushed in the breech by its roundshot. A stiff quill stood proud of the touchhole. The quill, which was filled with a finely mealed gunpowder, had been rammed hard down into the fabric bag so that the fire would flash deep down into the charge. The gun was pointing downhill, so the roundshot had to be restrained from rolling out of the barrel by a grommet wad; a circle of rope that had been rammed hard up against the shot. When the gun was fired the rope would be annihilated in the explosion. The officer, satisfied that the roundshot would plunge murderously into the approaching French column, stepped well back. The firer stood with his smoking portfire by the gun's right wheel, while the other six men of the crew waited for the orders to reload.

Red-coated and green-jacketed skirmishers ran over the top of the British ridge, then down the long slope where they spread into the skirmishing chain. Riflemen crouched in the rye and dragged back their weapons' flints. The job of the British skirmishers was to hold the French Voltigeurs away from the vulnerable gun crews. Whistles sounded as the light company officers dispersed their men. The Voltigeurs were wading through the half-crushed crops like men struggling through waist-deep water.

A bugle ordered the men in green jackets to open fire. The Baker rifle, with its seven grooves twisting a quarter turn in the barrel, had both a longer range and a deadlier accuracy than the smoothbore musket. The Emperor had refused to arm his Voltigeurs with rifles, claiming that the far quicker rate of musket-fire more than compensated for the loss of range and accuracy, but his officers now paid for that decision, for they were the Riflemen's target. 'Kill the officers!' the Greenjacket Sergeants ordered their men. 'Don't waste your powder! Find their officers and kill the scum!' The first French officers were falling, flung backwards by the force of the spinning balls.

'Run! Run!' a French officer shouted at his men and the Voltigeurs sprinted forward to shorten the range and overwhelm the Riflemen with the threat of their bayonets.

The redcoats opened fire. The muskets made a heavier coughing sound than the sharper crack of the rifles. The French were firing now; so many muskets crashing on both sides that the skirmish sounded as though a horde of small boys were dragging sticks along park railings. Patches of white smoke drifted and coalesced above the slope. This was the private war of the light infantryman; a bitter war fought in the shrinking gap between the columns and the waiting British guns.

A Rifleman fired, and immediately ran back behind his partner who advanced at a crouch, loaded rifle ready to protect his partner who laboriously rammed the bullet down past the tight-gripping grooves of the rifle's barrel.

'Watch left, Jimmy!' a sergeant shouted in warning. 'There's a Jack Pudding and I want the bastard dead!'

Before the French officer could be killed a group of

his blue-coated skirmishers dashed forward with bayonets fixed to their muskets.

'Back, lads! back!' The Rifles, so slow to reload, were vulnerable to such determined rushes, but they fell back through the crouching figures of a redcoat light company who suddenly rose out of the rye and fired a blast of musketry that threw down a half-dozen of the Frenchmen. A ragged answering volley splintered the thigh of a red-coated lieutenant who swore, fell, and watched in disbelief as his blood soaked his white breeches. Two of his men seized the shoulders of his coat and unceremoniously dragged the Lieutenant back up the slope towards the surgeons.

All across the valley the skirmishers fought, but the French Voltigeurs far outnumbered their opponents and slowly, bitterly, the redcoats and Riflemen retreated. Behind them, beyond the crest of the ridge, the rest of the British infantry waited. They were lying flat, hidden both from the light French guns and from the mass of the four advancing columns. The hidden British battalions were in two ranks; a perilously thin formation that would soon have to stand and face the crashing impact of the advancing columns.

Those columns began to step over the dead and dying skirmishers. The drummer boys, deep in the heart of each column, drove their sticks down as if their youthful fervour could drive this vast assault clear on to Brussels itself.

This was the old way of war, the Emperor's way, the attack in column that relied on sheer weight to smash through the enemy's battle line. Yet the French were not fools, and enough of them had fought against British muskets to know that the old way had never worked against the red-coated lines. The British were just too fast with their guns, and every fast musket in a British line could fire at the attacking column, whereas only the men in the first two ranks of the French formation could return the fire, so every time the British had met the columns, the British had won. The British line looked so very frail, but it overlapped the column and drowned it in fire. Against the troops of other nations the column worked beautifully, but the British had learned to pour a destructive blast of musketry that turned the columns into butchers' messes.

So this time the French would do it differently. This time they had a surprise of their own, something to counter the overlapping line and the overpowering musket-fire.

But that surprise must wait till the two sides were close enough to stare into each other's eyes. That confrontation was still some minutes away for the British lines were still in hiding, and the French columns still had to climb the gentle slope in the face of the waiting guns.

'Fire!' the gunner officers shouted along the ridge.

The portfires touched the fire to the quills of mealed powder that flashed the flame down to the charge in the fabric bags, and the guns crashed back on their trails, their wheels jumping clear out of the mud before smashing down yards back from where they had started.

Smoke instantly blotted the ridge.

The nine-pounder balls screamed down the hill and slashed into the marching files. One ball could kill a score of men. The missiles drove into the massed ranks; flensing, smashing, breaking bones, spattering flesh and blood deep into the heavy masses.

'Close up! Close up!' the French Sergeants shouted.

The marching ranks clambered over the writhing bodies to close the ranks. The drummers beat harder and faster, quickening the bloody moment. The men in the centre raised their bayonet-tipped muskets as they cheered their hero. '*Vive l'Empereur!*'

On the ridge the gun crews worked like whipped

slaves. The spongeman, his rammer tipped with a soaking wet sleeve of fleece, forced the wet material down the smoking barrel. The gun had to be cleared of the scraps of still burning powder and canvas that could ignite and explode the next charge. The sudden compression of air as the rammer thrust with the fleece could explode the residues of unburnt powder that was caked to the breech walls, so a gunner, wearing a leather thumbstall, pressed his thumb over the vent to stop the airflow.

The wet fleece was dragged clear and the loader shoved the new charge bag into the barrel, then topped it with the roundshot and wad grommet. The spongeman reversed his rammer and thrust the shot home, shouting as it reached the breech. The shout alerted the ventsman that the charge was ready. He rammed his spike down the touchhole to pierce the canvas powder bag, then thrust the quill of finely mealed powder into the hole he had made. The rammer was already soaking the fleece in a bucket of water, ready for the next shot as the two remaining gunners of the crew heaved on a handspike to lever the gun's trail round so that the loaded barrel pointed through the smoke of the last shot at the approaching enemy.

'Ready!' a corporal shouted.

'Stand back!' The officer put his hands to his ears. 'Fire!'

The cannon crashed back again. This time it had to be run forward, dragged through the muddy scars of its first two firings. Musket-balls from the French skirmishers were whiplashing close, but the gun's smoke protected the crew as they reloaded.

'Double shot! Double shot!' A gunner officer galloped his horse behind the battery. 'Double shot!' The officer, galloping clear of the smoke, had seen the closest column's inexorable progress up the slope and knew it was time to raise the stakes.

This time, instead of loading with roundshot alone, the gunners rammed a canister of musket-balls on top of the roundshot. Now each blast would spread a halo of deadly bullets about the heavy missile.

'Fire!'

The canister shredded, punched apart by the roundshot, and a great gap was ripped bloody in the nearest French column. The Emperor's men were leaving a trail of blood and bodies now, but the attack was still massive and heavy. The French galloper guns were firing from the valley's floor, seeking the British nine-pounders behind their screen of smoke. French cavalry had advanced onto the flanks of the outermost columns, protecting them from the threat of British horsemen. This was how war should be fought; the three arms supporting each other and victory just a drumbeat away across a ridge top which, to the advancing French, seemed almost empty. They saw the cannons and their smoke, and they saw the flitting silhouettes of the retreating skirmishers, and they saw a handful of mounted officers waiting beyond the crest, but they saw no enemy lines because the redcoats still lay flat, still hidden, still waiting. Some Frenchmen, those who had never fought Wellington, dared to hope that the ridge was only defended by guns, but the veterans of Spain knew better. The Goddamn Duke always hid his men behind a hillcrest if he could. In a moment, those veterans knew, the Goddamns would show themselves. That was what the French called the British soldiers, the Goddamns. It was not an affectionate nickname, but nor was it demeaning like the British name for the French; the Crapauds were the 'toads', but the Goddamns were men who would curse God and there was something chilling in that thought.

The French drums paused. '*Vive l'Empereur!*'

'Fire!' Another double-shotted volley smashed down the slope, and this time a British gunner officer heard the distinctive hailstone rattle as the canister balls struck the infantry's muskets. 'We're hitting them now, boys!' A wet fleece hissed as it plunged into the hot barrel.

On the ridge the British infantry officers watched and waited. The drums were loud, while at the back of the French columns men were singing. The British battalion bands were also playing behind the ridge, making it a cacophonous battle of music that the French were winning as more and more men joined in to sing the Marseillaise, '*Allons, enfants de la patrie, le jour de gloire est arrivé!*' The burnished Eagles were bright over the great marching masses that seemed to soak up the murderous gun-fire. A roundshot would butcher through the files, but the ranks closed up and marched on. The French officers, their swords drawn, urged their men on. They only needed to endure a few more seconds of hell, a few more blasts of the guns, then they would carry their bayonets over the ridge to vengeance.

But first, because Wellington's lines always beat the French columns, the surprise had to be unveiled.

'Deploy!' The French officers shouted the command. The columns were now less than a hundred paces from the crest of the British ridge. The Voltigeurs had fallen back to join the columns' ranks and the British skirmishers had gone to join the line, so from this moment on it would be main force against main force. 'Deploy!'

The rearmost ranks of the columns began to spread outwards. This was the surprise, that the column would suddenly become a line, but a line thicker and heavier than the British. Every French musket would be able to fire, and there would be far more French muskets. The defenders' line would not overlap the column, but would be overwhelmed by it. The French would fire their killing volley, then they would charge home. The day of glory had arrived.

* * *

The easternmost French column advanced on Papelotte, driving Prince Bernhard of Saxe-Weimar's men back to the sturdiest of the farm buildings. The westernmost column, advancing athwart the paved highway, swept either side of La Haye Sainte, driving the Riflemen back from their sandpit.

The Riflemen of the King's German Legion who garrisoned the farm itself were safe enough, for La Haye Sainte's walls were of thick stone, well loopholed, and the column had no intention of assaulting such a makeshift fortress. Yet now the farm proved its deadly worth as the garrison flayed the passing column with rifle-fire. The French ranks were blown ragged; assailed by volleys from the flank and double-shotted cannon from their front. In desperation the French ordered the farm attacked. A swarm of infantry broke down the hedges of the kitchen garden and orchard, forcing the defenders back towards the elm tree on the ridge behind. Not that their retreat mattered, for most of the German garrison was safe behind the stone walls of the farm buildings from where they kept up the stinging volleys that had already stalled and broken the attack of the westernmost column.

Wellington's breakwaters were working. Two of the French columns had been stopped, yet the central two columns were still crashing majestically and seemingly unstoppably up the wide bare slope between Papelotte and La Haye Sainte. The Duke, knowing that those central columns were the real danger, rode to where their attack would strike home.

The Prince of Orange took the Duke's place beside the elm tree and stared in horror at the turmoil that raged about La Haye Sainte. The Prince did not see that the farm had effectively broken one whole column of French infantry; instead he only saw a white-walled building lapped by smoke and ringed by enemies. Worse, he saw a stream of King's German Legion Riflemen running in headlong retreat from the farm. Wellington was nowhere in sight, which meant that fate and history had placed the Prince at this vantage point. He gnawed his fingernails as he stared, then knew he must not hesitate. La Haye Sainte could not fall! And if it had already fallen, then it must be retaken! He turned to see a Hanoverian battalion of his corps not far behind the ridge. The Hanoverian infantry wore British-style redcoats and were known to all the army as the Red Germans. 'Tell the Red Germans to advance!' the Prince snapped at Rebecque.

'Sir?' Rebecque had been flinching from the sight of the double-shotted cannons' execution of the closest Frenchmen, and had no idea what the Prince meant by his order.

'The Red Germans, Rebecque! They are to advance on the farm and recapture it. Tell them to form line and to advance. Now!'

'But, sir, the farm has not fallen and –'

'Do it! Now!' the Prince screamed at his Chief of Staff.

Rebecque silently wrote the order, handed it to the Prince for signature, then sent an aide to the Red Germans. The Hanoverians deployed into line, then, to the tap of a drum, marched forward with fixed bayonets. They came over the ridge top and, with their colours hoisted high behind their centre companies, swept down onto the French who still milled ineffectually about La Haye Sainte's loopholed walls.

'That's how it's done!' the Prince exulted. 'Give them steel! Give them steel!'

'Are you sure the French cavalry are gone, sir?' Rebecque asked very quietly.

'You must be bold! Boldness is all! Oh, well done!' The Prince applauded because the Hanoverians had cleared the kitchen garden and were now working their way down the farm's open flank to the west. They were still in line and were firing steady volleys that drove the French infantry backwards.

The French infantry retreated, but their cavalry advanced. That cavalry had been held deep in the valley's floor, safe from the double-shotted British cannon, but now the left flank guard saw a line of enemy redcoats deployed in the rye. French swords rasped out of scabbards. It seemed that God was smiling on the cavalrymen this day.

The trumpets sounded.

Les gros frères, the Cuirassiers, led the charge while the pigtailed Dragoons rode behind the heavy horsemen. The British gunners were aiming at the remnants of the column's flank and, besides, were too obscured by smoke to see the cavalry's threat. The Hanoverians, firing fast volleys, were blinding themselves with smoke, but then the men of the right-hand companies heard the thudding of the hooves and stared in panic through the powder smoke to see the first glints of steel armour and raised swords.

'Cavalry!'

'Form square!'

It was much too late. The heavy horsemen fell on the open end of the Hanoverian line. The big Klingenthal swords, made of the best steel in Europe, hacked down, driven by the ton weight of man and horse. Grim faces, framed by the steel helmets, were flecked by the infantrymen's blood as the horsemen carved a path into the battalion. The Red Germans broke, fleeing in panic from the thunder of the hooves and the lightning blades. The colour party took refuge in the farm's garden, but most of the Hanoverians were caught in the open field and paid the price. Horsemen rode round the field, chasing the last refugees and cutting them down with merciless efficiency.

The Prince of Orange stared aghast from the elm tree. He saw a sword rise in the air, dripping blood from a death, then hack down to make another butcher's sound. 'Stop them, Rebecque!' he said pathetically. 'Stop them!'

'Pray how, Your Highness?'

In the end the British gunners stopped the grisly business. The charge had brought the horsemen into the killing ground of the cannon and the double-shotted guns scoured the cavalry away from the field, but not before they had broken the Red Germans who lay with dreadful slashes, bleeding and twisting in the rye as they died. The Prince of Orange had struck again.

While to the east, where no farm protected the ridge, the two central columns of the French attack deployed into line, and drove on up to victory.

The Dutch-Belgian infantry at the re-entrant of the ridge took one close look at the nearest column and fled.

The British jeered the running men, but the Belgians did not care. Their sympathies were with the Emperor and so they ran to the forest and there, safe under its trees, waited for a French victory to restore Belgium to its proper throne.

The French drummers beat the *pas de charge* as the columns unfolded into the heavy musket line that would blast the ridge's crest with fire.

'Stand up!' The order was British.

All along the ridge, like men springing full armed from the concealing earth, the redcoats stood. One moment the ridge had appeared empty, and the next it was crowned with a line of muskets.

'Present!'

The French, so very close to the ridge top, had stopped for a heartbeat as their enemy had appeared so suddenly from the earth, but the French officers, seeing how hugely they outnumbered the Goddamns, screamed at the men to advance.

'Fire!'

The first British volley crashed down the gentle slope. It was fired at just sixty paces and it slammed into the unfolding columns to crumple the front ranks back like lead soldiers swept down by a petulant child.

'Reload!'

Men bit bullets from the tip of waxed paper cartridges, poured the powder into their musket barrels, wadded the powder with the cartridge paper, spat the bullets after, then rammed down hard with their ramrods. 'Fire by platoons!' a major ordered. 'Grenadier Company! Fire!'

The rolling volleys began, rippling along the hilltop in flame and smoke. The French fired back. Sir Thomas Picton roared an order and died as a bullet pierced his top hat and crashed into his skull. Highlanders and Irishmen and men from the shires bit the cartridges till their lips were black and their tongues sour with the salty taste of the gunpowder. They fired, scorching their cheeks with the flaming scraps spat from the musket locks.

'Close up! Close up!' The Sergeants dragged the dead and wounded back from the line, letting the men close in where the French bullets had struck.

A cannon fired, its canister splitting in bloody ruin among the deploying French, yet still the French came, more ranks advancing from the mist of smoke to thicken their bleeding dying line.

Redcoats scrabbled at their flints, tearing their finger-nails as they cocked their weapons. The muskets kicked like mules. The French were still spreading into line, still advancing, and the drums were still driving them on. A French galloper gun opened fire, splaying a redcoat colour party into ruin. The French musket volleys were slow, but the Crapauds outnumbered the Goddamns and were clawing their bloody way towards the ridge's crest and victory.

And then a trumpet called.

*　　*　　*

Lord John Rossendale, riding close to the Earl of Uxbridge, had watched the advance of the columns in sheer disbelief. He had heard of such attacks, and he had listened to men describe a French column, yet nothing had prepared Lord John for the way such an attack filled a landscape, or how its music made the skin crawl and stretched the nerves, or how irresistible such an assault seemed; as though each column was not made up of individual men, but instead was some ponderously articulated beast that crawled out of nightmare to ooze across the earth.

Yet, even as the columns filled him with dread, he marvelled at the calm of the men with whom he rode. The calmness, Lord John observed, came from the Duke, to whom men were irresistibly attracted as though his confidence would somehow communicate by proximity. The Duke watched the approaching columns with a keen eye, but still had time to laugh at some jest made by Alava, the Spanish commissioner. The only time Rossendale saw the Duke frown was when a brief shower of rain, gone almost as soon as it arrived, made him shake out his cloak and drape it round his shoulders. 'I cannot bear a drenching, nor will I abide umbrellas,' he spoke to Alava in French.

'You could have a canopy held by four stout men?' Alava, an old and valued friend from the Duke's Spanish battles, suggested. 'Like some Mohammetan potentate?'

The Duke gave his odd horse-neigh of a laugh. 'That would serve very well! I like that notion! A Mohammetan canopy, eh?'

'And a harem, why not?'

'Why not, indeed?' The Duke gently drummed his fingers on the small writing desk that was built onto the pommel of his saddle. To Lord John the gesture did not seem to be a nervous reaction, but rather to express the Duke's impatience at the lumbering French columns. By now the enemy skirmishers were close enough to annoy the Duke's party. Their bullets whiplashed and hummed about the horsemen. Two of the Duke's aides were hit; one fatally just two paces to the Duke's left. The Duke gave the dead man a glance, then frowned towards the French galloper guns. 'They'll never do a damn thing with those light cannon,' he complained, as though his enemy's inefficiency offended him, then, switching into French, he asked Alava whether he did not agree that the French were deploying more skirmishers than usual.

'Definitely more,' Alava confirmed, but with no more excitement in his voice than if he was sharing a day's rough shooting with the Duke.

The Dutch-Belgians ran, which caused a compression of the Duke's lips, but then, knowing what could and could not be mended, he simply ordered a British battalion into the gap. He rode further to his left, cantering his horse behind the waiting redcoats. The Earl of Uxbridge and his staff followed. The Duke frowned again as the French columns began to unfold into line, but the unexpected manoeuvre did not seem to rattle him. 'Now's your time!' the Duke called to the nearest redcoat battalion.

The redcoats stood and the volleys began. Lord John, trailing with his master behind the Duke, saw how the French attempt to form line was never completed because of the destructive British fire. The French flanks would not wheel up the slope into the face of the musket volleys, so instead the whole enemy mass edged uphill in neither line nor column, but in a half-way formation instead. To Lord John's untutored eye, and despite the momentary French confusion, it still looked like a frighteningly unequal battle; a mass of Frenchmen poised just beneath the thin and fragile line of redcoats. The mass was also still advancing. Its leading ranks were being bled and beaten by the flail of the British volleys, but still the French pressed uphill, stepping over their dead, and shouting their war cry. Worse, the Cuirassiers who had just destroyed the Red Germans now rode west of the high road to escape the cannon-fire and threatened to attack the thin British line.

The Duke had seen it all, and understood it all. He turned to Uxbridge. 'Your Heavies are ready, Uxbridge?'

'Indeed they are, Your Grace!'

It took Lord John a moment to understand the elegance of the Duke's solution. The French were poised on the brink of a shattering success. Their columns were inching uphill, and in a moment they would be reinforced by the heavy cavalry that would fall on the redcoat flank like a torrent of steel. The Duke's line would be shattered, the French infantry would pour through, then more cavalry would stream across the valley to finish the rout.

Except that the Duke's counter-stroke was ready. Horse would oppose horse and the British heavy cavalry would be unleashed on the Emperor's *gros frères*. The King's Own Household troops: the Life Guards and King's Dragoon Guards and Blues, together with the Union Brigade of the Royals, the Scots Greys and the Inniskilling Horse would save the army.

Lord John turned his own horse, drew his borrowed sword, and raced after the Earl of Uxbridge. 'Harry! You must let me come!' This was the chance Lord John had prayed and waited for. He saw other staff officers, Christopher Manvell among them, hurrying to join their regiments. 'For God's sake, Harry, let me fight!' Lord John pleaded again.

'You can fight, Johnny! The more the merrier! We'll take their horse, then break their infantry!'

The cream of the British cavalry would go to shatter the French attack. Lord John, his borrowed sword bright in his hand, rode to find his honour again. In battle.

CHAPTER 16

Almost two and a half thousand horsemen assembled just behind the ridge's flat crest. Men pulled on gleaming helmets that were topped with long horsehair plumes. The Scots on their huge white horses wore Grenadier bearskins as memorials of the day they had captured the colour of Louis XIV's household guards at Ramillies. They tightened their chin straps and made the usual small jokes of men facing battle. The air was rich with the smell of horse dung.

An officer raised a gloved hand, held it motionless for a second, then dropped it to point at where the gun smoke hung above the valley. A bugle sounded the advance as the long attack lines moved forward in a jingle of curb chains and creak of leather.

They were the heavy cavalry of Britain; the Sovereign's Guard and the Union Brigade. They were the best-mounted cavalry in all the world, and the worst led.

They rode big strong horses reared on rich English and Irish grassland. The horses were fresh, unblooded and eager. The riders drew their swords and looped the weapons' leather straps round their gauntleted wrists. Each sword blade was thirty-five inches of heavy steel that had been sharpened to a spear point. The bugle called the trot and the long plumes began to undulate behind the ranks. Some men took a last pull of rum from their canteens while others touched their lucky charms.

A horse curled its lips to show long yellow teeth, another whinnied with excitement. A man spat a wad of tobacco, then wrapped his horse's reins round his left wrist. The leading ranks of cavalry were at the crest and they could see, through the scrims of cannon-smoke, that the valley was a killer's playground; a wide field crammed with an unsuspecting enemy. Twenty thousand French infantry had crossed the valley and two and a half thousand cavalry would now charge at their exposed flank. The horsemen spurred into a canter, their plumes tossing wild in the smoky wind. Sabretaches and empty scabbards flapped at their sides. A guidon embroidered in gold thread led them down the slope. The troopers' ranks were already ragged for each man only wanted to close on the enemy, while their officers, not wanting to be outrun, raced ahead as though they rode on a hunting field and feared to miss the kill.

Then, at last, the trumpeters sounded the full charge. The ten notes, rising in triplets, pierced to the final high and brilliant tone which threw the horsemen on. Damn caution. Damn the slow approach and the final steady charge that would bring the horses home as one cohesive mass. This was war! This was the hunting field with a human quarry, and glory did not wait for the last man to form line, and so the trumpet shivered the blood with its madman's call. Charge home, and the devil bugger the hindmost.

They made a glorious charge of bright horse that slanted across the face of the ridge's forward slope like a flood. Ahead of them were the Cuirassiers, and beyond the breast-plated enemy horsemen were the infantry who were neither in column nor in line. None of the French was expecting the attack.

The Cuirassiers' horses were blown. They were still forming their lines after the slaughter of the Red Germans, and now they stood no chance. They were broken in an instant. Lord John, racing behind the Life Guards, heard the blacksmith sound of swords clashing on breast-plates; he had a glimpse of unhorsed men, of horses thrown to the ground, then of a sword rising high and bloody. The Cuirassiers, hugely outnumbered, were obliterated in the time it took for a trooper on a galloping horse to hack down once. An Irish horseman screamed, not in pain, but from the sheer joy of killing. Another man was drunk on rum, his sword was wet with blood, and his horse bleeding from the spur wounds as he hurled it on to yet more slaughter.

A few British riders were down, their horses tripped by the broken Cuirassiers, but most of the charge simply flowed around the fallen horses and wounded Frenchmen. The horsemen could see the infantry milling like sheep brought to the wolf's den. A bugle, its notes wavering because they were being blown from a galloping horse, tore its bright challenge to glory.

Lord John was screaming as though drunk. He had never, in all his life, known excitement like this. The very earth seemed to shudder. All around him, bright in the day's gloom, a torrent of men and horses flowed at full killing stretch. The horses, teeth bared, seemed to fly across the field. Mud churned up by the hooves ahead flecked and slapped his face. There was a wild music in the air, the sound of banging hoofbeats and shrill shouts, of horses' lungs rasping like bellows, of screams fading behind and warning shouts sounding louder ahead, of the bugle hurling them on, of glory as vivid as the guidon banner that seemed to drive straight at the heart of the doomed French column.

Then the horsemen hit.

And the French, still half manoeuvring out of column, were helpless.

The big horses and their towering riders crashed home all along the column's broken flank. Cavalry drove great wedges into the very centre of the French infantry. The swords slashed down, rose, then slashed again. Horses reared, lashing with their hooves to break skulls. The troopers, revelling in the slaughter, wheeled in the middle of the breaking column to break it yet further apart and thus make it easier to kill its constituent parts. They lashed the French with steel, and still more horsemen came to drive yet further lanes of death and horror into the shattered mass.

'Fix bayonets!' The redcoats on the ridge top fumbled at their scabbards, dragged the long blades free, then slotted the bayonets onto the hot smoking muzzles of the guns.

'Forward!'

There was a hurrah along the ridge, then the redcoats ran to join the killing.

The French broke. No infantry could have stood. The French columns broke and fled, and that made the horsemen's task even easier. It was no trouble to kill a running man and so the cavalrymen slaked themselves on killing and wanted even more. They were drunk on the slaughter, drenched in it, glorying in it. Some of the riders were properly drunk, soused in rum and lust, and killing like fiends. The bugles screamed at them, encouraged them until the sword blades were so thick with blood that the cavalry's hands and wrists were sopping with it.

A Scots sergeant, six feet four inches tall and on a horse to match, took the first Eagle. He did it alone, riding his great warhorse deep into a thicket of desperate Frenchmen who were ready to die for their standard. They did die. Sergeant Ewart was strong enough to use the clumsy thirty-five-inch sword. He cut the first defender down through the head. A French sergeant, armed with one of the spears issued to protect the precious Eagles, drove its point at Ewart, but the Scotsman's blade drove up through the Sergeant's jaw. He wrenched the sword free, spurred his horse on, felt a musket-ball blaze past his face and hacked down at the man who had fired, breaking the man's skull apart with the vicious blade. Ewart wheeled his horse, reached for the Eagle, snatched it, and his heels went back as he lifted the golden trophy high over his head. He was shouting so all the world would see what he had done, and his horse, as if it shared the triumph, rode across the path of dead with its bloody head high and its flanks sheeted scarlet.

'You've done enough for one day!' The Scots Greys' Colonel offered Sergeant Ewart a salute. 'Take it to the rear!'

Ewart, holding the Eagle high, and punching it at the sky to show the gods what he had achieved, cantered back towards the British ridge. He passed a Highland infantry regiment that cheered him hoarse.

The other horsemen drove on. The field was wet with blood and rain, and treacherous underfoot with the fallen dead and pitiful with the wounded, yet still the horses streamed their ribbons of steel and bone into the fleeing, panicked Frenchmen. A drum was splintered by a horse's hooves. The drummer boy, just twelve years old, was dead. Another boy, screaming in terror, was ridden down by a white horse that broke his skull with the blow of a hoof. Some of the French infantry just ran to the charging British infantry and threw themselves onto the redcoats' mercy. The British infantry, checked by the slaughter in their path, stopped their charge and gathered in the terrified prisoners.

The cavalry knew no such mercy. They had dreamed of such a field, filled with a broken enemy to be broken further. Captain Clark of the Royals took the second Eagle, hacking its defenders apart with his sword, snatching the trophy, defending it, then carrying it clear of the pathetic French survivors who, hearing their death in the big hooves, still tried to run, but there was nowhere to run as the Irish and Scots and English horsemen ravaged about the valley. Even the horses were trained to kill. They bit, they lashed with their hooves, they fought like the crazed men who rode them.

Lord John at last learned how to kill. He learned the joy of losing all restraint, of absolute power, of riding into shattered men who turned, screamed, then disappeared behind as his sword thumped home. He found himself picking a target, and stalking the man even if it meant ignoring closer Frenchmen, then choosing the manner of his victim's death. One he skewered through the neck, almost losing his sword because it pierced so far. He practised the lunge, learning to control the heavy point of the blade. He soaked the steel in blood, spraying droplets into the air after each victory, then lowering the point for more. He saw a fat French officer clumsily running away, and Lord John spurred through the closest Frenchmen, stood in his stirrups, and slashed down with the sword. He felt the skull crumple like a giant boiled egg and he laughed aloud to think of such a comparison at such a moment. The laugh sounded more like a demonic screech, a fit accompaniment to the screams of the other death-drunk troopers about him. He wheeled, sliced a Frenchman in the face, and spurred on. He saw Christopher Manvell parry a desperate bayonet lunge then stab down. A knot of Inniskillings thundered past Lord John, their horses sheeted with enemy blood and their voices ululating a paean to massacre. A drunk trooper of the Scots Greys was ahead of Lord John, hacking and hacking at a French sergeant who twitched on the ground in a pool of spreading blood. The Scotsman's face was a mask of laughing blood.

'On to Paris!' a major of the Life Guards shouted.

'The guns! Kill the bastard gunners!'

'To Paris! On to Paris!'

The charge had done its job magnificently. It had

finished the battalion of Cuirassiers, then destroyed the best part of a French corps of infantry. The charge had filled a valley with bodies and blood, it had taken two Eagles, but these were the British cavalry, the worst led in all the world, and now they thought themselves immortal. They had swamped their souls with the glory of war, so now they would make their names immortal in the halls of war. The bugles screamed the call to rally and the Earl of Uxbridge shouted at the troopers nearest him to withdraw and reform behind the ridge, but other officers, and other buglers, wanted more blood. They were the cavalry. On to Paris!

So the spurs slashed back, the red swords lifted high, and the charge swept on.

The battlefield had a new smell now. Blood, fresh and cloying, mingled its odour with the acrid stench of burnt powder. The British guns fell silent, their barrels hot and smoking, their muzzles blackened. There were no more targets, for the French attack, one minute so overwhelming, had been broken into blood and bones and weeping men. The surviving French infantry, many with hideous slash wounds from the heavy swords, wandered in a daze about the crushed corn. The German Riflemen who had retreated from La Haye Sainte's garden and orchard ran back to their positions, while the 95th Rifles re-occupied the sandpit.

Close to the sandpit a Cuirassier crawled from underneath his dead horse. He stared at the Riflemen, then slowly unbuckled his heavy armour and let it fall. He gave the Greenjackets one last scared look, then limped back towards La Belle Alliance. The Rifles let him go.

The Prince of Orange, the death of his Hanoverians forgotten, clapped his hands with delight as the British heavy cavalry turned south to complete their charge. 'Aren't they fine, Rebecque? Aren't they simply fine?'

The Duke, further along the ridge, also watched the horsemen swerve south in disarray. He looked momentarily sickened, then turned and ordered his infantry back to the shelter of the ridge's reverse slope. French prisoners, stripped of their packs, pouches and weapons, filed towards the forest as the Duke spurred back towards the elm tree.

Sharpe and Harper had found a park of four-wheeled ammunition wagons at the edge of the forest, all under the guard of a plump officer of the quartermaster's staff who refused to release any of the wagons without proper authority.

'What is proper authority?' Sharpe asked.

'A warrant signed by a competent officer, naturally. If you will now excuse me? I'm not exactly underemployed today.' The Captain offered Sharpe a simpering smile and turned away.

Sharpe drew his pistol and put a bullet into the ground between the Captain's heels.

The Captain turned, white-faced and shaking.

'I need one wagon of musket cartridge,' Sharpe said in his most patient voice.

'I need authorization, I'm accountable to –'

Sharpe pushed the pistol into his belt. 'Patrick, just shoot the fat bugger.'

Harper unslung his seven-barrelled volley gun, cocked and aimed it, but the Captain was already running away. Sharpe spurred after him, caught the man's collar, and dragged his face up to the saddle. 'I'm a competent officer, and if I don't get the ammunition I want in the next five seconds I shall competently ram a nine-pounder up your back passage and spread you clear across Brussels. Do you understand me?'

'Yes, sir.'

'So which wagon do we take?'

'Any one you wish, sir, please.'

'Order a driver to follow us. We want musket ammunition, not rifle ammunition. Do you understand that?'

'Yes, sir.'

'Thank you.' Sharpe dropped the man. 'You're very kind.'

The French skirmishers were still sniping at the château's walls, and more enemy infantry were massing in the woods for another assault on Hougoumont as the wagon thundered down the rough track and past the haystack at the gate. The French had turned a battery of howitzers on the farm, and some of their shells had set fire to the farmhouse roof, but Colonel MacDonnell was remarkably sanguine. 'They can't burn stone walls, can they?' A shell crashed onto the stable roof, bounced in a shower of broken slates and landed on the yard's cobbles. Its fuse hissed smoke for a second, then the shell exploded harmlessly, but the sight of the bursting powder acted as a spur to the Guardsmen who were unloading the cartridge boxes from the newly arrived wagon. MacDonnell, turning to go back into the farmhouse, stopped and cocked his head. 'Unless I miss my guess, which I rather doubt, our cavalry are earning their pay for a change?'

Sharpe listened. Through the crack of musketry and the boom of heavy guns, the ten trumpet notes of a cavalry charge sounded thin and clear. 'I think you're right.'

'Let's hope they know which side they're fighting for,' MacDonnell said drily then, with a wave of thanks, he went back to the house.

Sharpe and Harper followed the empty wagon back to the ridge where they turned eastwards towards the line's centre. They passed what was left of Captain Witherspoon who had been killed when a common shell had skimmed the ridge and exploded in his belly. His watch, miraculously unbroken, had fallen into a nettle patch where, unseen and hidden, it ticked on. The hands of the watch now showed twenty-seven minutes past two on the afternoon in which the Prussians were supposed to arrive, and had not come.

Lord John galloped clear of the broken French infantry. Ahead and around him were knots of other horsemen; all galloping across the valley to assault the main French battle line on the southern ridge.

The British charge had been scattered by the fighting among the infantry, so now the horsemen galloped in small groups like a field split apart by a long run after a fox. The troopers were still crazed by victory, confident that nothing could stand against their long and bloody swords.

A hedge of holly, broken and trampled by the advance of the French columns, barred Lord John's path. His horse soared over it, stumbled on the plough ridges beyond, then caught its footing and galloped on. Three men of the Inniskillings charged to his left and Lord John veered towards them, seeking company. An explosion of smoke and earth gouted to his right, then was snatched behind as he galloped on. A ragged line of Scots Greys were just ahead, their horses' flanks sheeted with blood and sweat. Lord John looked for Christopher Manvell, or any other of his friends, but saw none. Not that it mattered, for today he felt that every trooper was his friend.

All across the western half of the valley the cavalry charged. Their big horses were blowing hard, and the ground was soaked and heavy, but the horses were strong and willing. The men had stopped screaming with blood-lust, so the sound of the charge had now become the thrash of the hooves, the creak of saddles, and the rasp of breath.

The French gunners on the southern ridge loaded their twelve-pounders with canister. They spiked the charge bags and pushed the quills into the vents.

The horses thundered across the valley floor. They were closing on each other now, drawn together by the need for companionship and the realization of danger.

The French gunners gave their gun-trails a last adjustment. The gunners crouched with the next round ready in their arms. The officers judged the distance, then shouted the order: '*Tirez!*'

A blast of canister scoured down the forward slope. Two of the Scots Greys ahead of Lord John tumbled in blood and muddy confusion. He galloped between the two men, watching the smoke of the guns roll towards him. A riderless horse with flapping stirrups raced up on his right side. One of the Irish riders on Lord John's left had been hit by canister in his right arm. He put the reins between his teeth and took his sword into his left hand.

The guns fired again; another thunder of smoke in which the sudden flames stabbed, and out of which another blast of canister tore huge gaps in the charging line, but still hundreds of men stayed in their saddles. A Life Guard's dying horse crashed into a Scots Grey and both men and their horses ploughed screaming into the field. An officer behind jumped the dying mess and shouted the mad challenge that had begun the insane charge: 'To Paris!'

The voice seemed to release a thousand others. The screams began again, the screams of men too frightened to recognize their fear, too exhilarated to believe in death, and too close to the guns to turn back.

The leading horses cleared the gun-smoke to see the French artillerymen running desperately for the safety of the infantry behind. The swords began their work again. A gunner swung his heavy rammer at a Life Guard, missed, and died with a sword blade rammed down his open mouth.

The infantry, two hundred yards behind the guns,

and protected by a thick hedge, had formed square. The horsemen, on tired horses that wanted to draw breath, swerved away from the threat of the close-packed muskets. They sought other targets, galloping in a useless mêlée between the abandoned guns and the infantry's invulnerable squares. Some of the horses slowed to a walk. No one had thought to bring the hammers and soft copper nails that were needed to spike the captured guns, so the worst they could do was slash their swords at the Emperor's wreathed initial that was embossed on each gun barrel. Some of the French gunners had been too slow to escape and had taken refuge under their weapons, or between the wheels of the limbers, and those men at least could be hunted down. Horsemen leaned clumsily from their saddles to lunge at men who crouched and dodged under the gun axles.

More British horsemen arrived, thudding up through the cannon-smoke to find the guns captured, the gunners dead or dying, and a mass of cavalry wheeling impotent among the limbers. They had charged to glory, and reached nowhere. The French infantry barred the promised road to Paris, and now that infantry began firing volleys that, even at two hundred yards, found targets.

'Time to go home, I think.' A Scots Grey captain, his sword bloody to the hilt, walked his horse past Lord John whose tired horse cropped at a patch of grass behind a gun. Lord John was staring at the nearest infantry and wondering when the charge would resume.

'Go home?' Lord John asked in surprise, but the Scotsman had already spurred northwards towards the British ridge and safety.

'Withdraw!' another officer shouted. A Scottish trooper, his horse killed by a musket-ball, ran among the guns to find a riderless horse that he managed to corner and mount. He wrenched the beast's head towards the valley and spurred hard for safety.

Lord John looked back to the enemy infantry again, and this time a shredding wind thinned the veil of smoke and he saw the whole French army spread in front of him. He felt an eruption of fear and pulled on his reins. His horse, tired and heaving for breath, turned reluctantly. The British charge was over.

The French charge was about to begin. Their cavalry rode out from the right of their line. They were all fresh horsemen; Lancers and Hussars, the light cavalry of France whose officers knew their grim business to perfection.

They did not charge the mass of broken British horse on the ridge, instead they cantered into the valley to cut off the troopers' retreat.

The British, riding back from the undamaged guns, cleared the smoke and saw the waiting enemy. 'Shit!' A Life Guard raked back with his spurs and his horse lumbered into an unwilling canter. It was a race that the heavy British cavalry was doomed to lose. In ones and twos, in scattered groups, in panic, they fled northwards to the far crest where their own infantry waited.

The French trumpets sounded.

The Red Lancers led the charge. Some were Poles, still faithful to the Emperor, but most were Dutch-Belgians, fighting for the flag they loved, and now they lowered their swallow-tailed pennants and flung their fresh horses at the panicked British.

'Run! Run!' The panic among the British was absolute now. Men forgot the glory and sought only the far shelter, but they were too late.

The Lancers crashed into the flank of the fleeing mass. The lances, held rigid against the body by the pressure of the Lancers' right elbows, drove home. Men fell screaming from horses. The Lancers rode over their victims, tugged the blades free, then brought them forward as they spurred after other fugitives. Behind the Lancers came Hussars with sabres so that any man who escaped the lance was cut down by the curved blades.

Lord John saw the slaughter to his right, but his horse was still running free. A riderless horse galloped past him and his own horse seemed to match its stride. The holly hedge was a hundred yards in front of him. He could see British light cavalry coming from the ridge, riding to rescue the remnants of the heavy brigade.

'Go on!' He slashed back with his sword as though it was a whip. A Scots Grey was over the hedge. A Lancer chased the man, lunged, but the Scot swerved, backswung, and the Lancer reeled bloodily away. Lord John looked behind and saw two of the red devils pursuing him. He savaged his horse with his spurs. Fear was in his throat like a sour vomit. There was to be no glory, no captured Eagle, no radiant moment of heroism that would make his name famous; there was just a desperate scramble for life across a muddy field.

Then, from his right, he saw a slew of the Red Lancers charging at him. Their horses' teeth were bared yellow, while the riders seemed to leer at him above the bright wickedness of their spears. Lord John was pissing himself with fear, but he knew he must not give up. If he could just charge through their line and jump the hedge, they might abandon their pursuit.

He screamed in defiance, gripped his sword rigid at the end of his right arm, and touched the reins to swerve his horse to the right. The sudden change of direction threw the Lancers off their own intercepting course. They had to wheel slightly, their lances wavered, and Lord John was suddenly crashing through them. His sword, held at arm's length, parried a lance to splinter a great shard of bright wood from the shaft. He was past the lance points! The realization made him shout in triumph. His horse cannoned off a smaller French horse, but kept its footing. Two Hussars were in front of him. One of the two lunged at Lord John, but the Englishman was swifter and his sword rammed hard into the Frenchman's belly. The blade was gripped by the contracting muscles of the dying man, but Lord John somehow ripped it free of the suction and swept it across his body to slice down at the second Hussar who parried desperately and wrenched his horse away.

Lord John's fear was turning to exultation. He had learned to fight. He had killed. He had survived. He had beaten his pursuers. He held his bloodied borrowed sword high like a trophy. Last night he had lied about his prowess, yet today the lies had come true; he had been tested in combat, and he had rung true. Happiness welled and seethed in Lord John as his horse crashed through the holly hedge and he saw only the long empty slope in front of him. That slope meant freedom, not just from his pursuers, but from the fear that had dogged him all his life. He suddenly knew just how frightened he had been, not just of Sharpe, but of Jane's anger. Then damn her! She would learn that her anger could no longer frighten Lord John, for he had conquered fear by riding to the enemy's gun line and coming home. He shouted his triumph just as a riderless grey horse galloped across his front.

Lord John's shout turned to alarm as his horse baulked and swerved. The horse staggered into a patch of deep mud and, as it tried to find its balance, stopped dead.

Lord John screamed at the horse to move. He sliced the spurs savagely back.

The horse tried to pull its hooves out of the glutinous mud. It lurched forward, but with painful slowness, and the first of the two Lancers who still pursued Lord John caught up with his lordship.

The first lance point went into the small of Lord John's back.

He arched his spine, screaming. He dropped his sword

as his hands groped behind to find the blade that twisted like a flesh hook in his belly. The second Lancer grunted as he lunged. His spear struck Lord John in the ribs, but glanced off the bone to slice into his right arm.

Lord John was screaming and falling. The surviving Hussar, whose friend Lord John had killed, rode in on the Englishman's left and gave his lordship a vicious backswing of his sabre which, like many of the French weapons, had only a sharpened point to encourage the trooper to lunge and not slash. The blunt steel edge thudded into Lord John's face, breaking the bridge of his nose and bludgeoning his eyes to instant blindness. His left foot slid from the stirrup, his right, trapped by the iron, dragged him through the mud as his horse struggled free. The lance was ripped out of his back. He fell onto his belly, screaming and crying as his stirrup leather broke. He tried to turn over to face his tormentors and he scrabbled for the sword that was still hanging from its wrist strap, but another lance thrust ripped down into his right leg, this blade thrust with all the weight of man and horse, and Lord John's thighbone snapped. The lance point broke off in the wound. Lord John wanted to plead with his attackers, but the only sound he could make was a babbling and childlike cry of terror. His fingers fluttered uselessly as though to ward off any more blades.

The three French horsemen stood round the twitching, bleeding Englishman.

'He's finished,' one of the Lancers said, then slid out of his saddle and knelt beside the Englishman. He unsheathed a knife and cut at the straps of Lord John's sabretache that clinked with coins. He tossed the pouch up to his companion, then slit open the Englishman's pockets, starting with his breeches. 'The dirty *bougre* pissed himself, see?' The Lancer spoke with a Belgian accent. 'Rich as a pig in shit, this one. Here!' He had found more coins in the pockets of Lord John's breeches.

The Lancer ripped away Lord John's silk stock and tore at his shirt. Lord John tried to speak, but the Lancer slapped his face. 'Quiet, shitface!' Under Lord John's shirt he found a golden chain with a golden locket. He snapped the chain with one jerk of his hand, clicked the locket lid open with his bloody thumb, and whistled when he saw the golden-haired beauty whose picture lay inside. 'Have a look at that piece of meat! Last time he'll screw her, eh? She'll have to find someone else to warm her up.' He tossed the locket to his companion, pulled the watch from Lord John's fob, then rolled the wounded man onto his belly to get at the pockets in his coat's tail. He found a folding spyglass that he shoved into his own pockets. The Hussar who had blinded Lord John was searching the Englishman's saddlebags, but now shouted a warning that the enemy's light cavalry was getting dangerously close.

The Lancer stood, put his right boot on Lord John's back and used his lordship as a makeshift mounting block. He and his companion wheeled away. So far it had been a good day; the two Belgians had set out on their charge with the idea of hunting down a richly dressed officer and, by finding Lord John, they had taken at least a year's pay in plunder. The Hussar took Lord John's horse.

Lord John slowly, slowly twisted his burning, bleeding, blinded eyes from the mud. He wanted to cry, but his eyes were like bars of fire that annealed his tears. He moaned. The glory had turned obscene, to an agony that filled his whole universe. The pain burned and racked at his back and leg. The pain tore and filled him. He screamed, but he could not move, he cried but no help came. It was over, all the honour and the excitement and all the gold-bright future, all reduced to a bleeding blind horror face down in the mud.

The survivors of the British charge came home slowly. There were not many. A few riderless horses formed ranks with the survivors as the rolls were taken. One regiment had charged with three hundred and fifty troopers, of whom only twenty-one came home. The rest were dead, or dying, or prisoners. The British heavy cavalry had broken a whole French corps, and themselves with it.

Steam rose from the wet fields. The day was hot now. The Prussians had not come.

CHAPTER 17

'There.' Rebecque pointed at the bodies which lay in the grass east of La Haye Sainte. They were scattered in a fan shape, like men killed as they spread out from a single point of attack. At the centre of the fan, where men had bunched together in desperate defence, the bodies were in heaps. Sharpe glowered while Harper, a few paces behind the Prince's staff, crossed himself at the horrid sight.

'They were Hanoverians. Good troops, all of them.' Rebecque spoke bleakly, then sneezed. The drying weather was bringing back his hay fever.

'What happened?' Sharpe asked.

'He advanced them in line, of course.' Rebecque did not look at Sharpe as he spoke.

'There were cavalry?'

'Of course. I tried to stop him, but he won't listen. He thinks he's the next Alexander the Great. He wants me to have an orange banner made that a man will carry behind him at all times . . .' Rebecque's voice tailed away.

'God damn him.'

'He's only twenty-three, Sharpe, he's a young man and he means very well.' Rebecque, fearing that his previous words might be construed as disloyal, found excuses for the Prince.

'He's a Goddamned butcher,' Sharpe said icily. 'A butcher with pimples.'

'He's a prince,' Rebecque said in uncomfortable reproof. 'You should remember that, Sharpe.'

'At best, Rebecque, he might make a half-decent lieutenant, and I even doubt that.'

Rebecque did not respond. He just turned away and stared through tearful eyes at the western half of the valley that was a mangled ruin of dead infantry, dead cavalrymen and dead horses beneath the skeins of cannon-smoke. He sneezed again, then cursed the hay fever.

'Rebecque! Did you see it? Wasn't it glorious?' The Prince spurred his horse from the knot of men who marked Wellington's position at the elm tree. 'We should have been there, Rebecque! My God, but the only place for honour is in the cavalry!'

'Yes, sir.' Rebecque, still unnaturally subdued, did his best to match his monarch's high spirits.

'They took two Eagles! Two Eagles!' The Prince clapped his hands. 'Two! They've brought one to show the Duke. Have you ever seen one close up, Rebecque? They're not gold at all, just tricked out to look like gold. They're just a shabby French trick, nothing else!' The Prince noticed Sharpe's presence for the first time and generously included the Englishman in his excitement. 'You should go and take a look, Sharpe. It's not every day you see an Eagle!'

'Sergeant Harper and I once captured an Eagle,' Sharpe's voice was filled with an unmistakable loathing. 'It was five years ago when you were still at school.'

The Prince's happy face changed as though someone had just struck him. Rebecque, startled by Sharpe's egregious rudeness, tried to drive his horse between the Rifleman and the Prince, but the Prince would have none of his Chief of Staff's tact. 'What the hell are you doing here?' he asked Sharpe instead. 'I told you to stay in Hougoumont.'

'They don't need me there.'

'Sir!' The Prince shouted the word, demanding that Sharpe use the honorific. The other staff officers, Doggett among them, backed away from the royal anger.

'They don't need me there,' Sharpe said stubbornly, then he could no longer resist his dislike and derision of the Prince. 'The men at Hougoumont are proper soldiers. They don't need me to teach them how to unbutton their breeches before they piss.'

'Sharpe!' Rebecque yelped helplessly.

'So what happened to them?' Sharpe pointed at the Red Germans but looked at the Prince.

'Rebecque! Arrest him!' the Prince screamed at his Chief of Staff. 'Arrest him! And his man. What the hell are you doing here anyway?' The question was screamed at Harper, who gazed placidly back at the Prince without bothering to offer any answer.

'Sir –' Rebecque knew he had neither the authority nor the cause to make any arrests, but the Prince did not want to listen to any reasoned explanations.

'Arrest him!'

Sharpe raised two fingers into the Prince's face, added the appropriate words, and turned his horse away.

The Prince screamed at the Riflemen to come back, but suddenly the French cannons, which had paused while the British cavalry were being slaughtered in the valley, opened fire again, and it seemed to Sharpe as though every gun on the French ridge fired at the same instant, making a clap of doom fit to mark the world's ending and even sufficient to divert a prince's outrage.

The shells and roundshot raged at the British ridge. Explosions and fountains of earth shook the whole line. The noise was suddenly deafening; a melding of cannon-fire into one long thunderous roll that hammered at the sky. The Prince's staff instinctively ducked. A gunner officer, not ten paces from where Sharpe was cantering away from the Prince, disappeared in an explosion of blood as a twelve-pound ball struck him clean in the belly. One of his guns, struck full on the muzzle, bucked backwards into the deep wheel ruts made by its own recoil. The French were serving their guns with a frenetic and desperate speed.

Which could only mean one thing.

Another assault was coming.

It was two minutes past three, and the Prussians had not come.

Belgian soldiers, fugitives from the battle, streamed into Brussels. This was not their war; they had no allegiance to a Dutch Stadt-holder made King of the French-speaking province of Belgium, nor did they have any love for the British infantry that had jeered their departure.

Once in the city they were besieged for news. The battle was lost, the Belgians said. Everywhere the French were victorious. The streams in the forest of Soignes were running with English blood.

Lucille, walking through the streets in search of news, heard the tales of dead men strewn across a forest floor. She listened to accounts of vengeful French cavalry hunting down the last survivors, but she could still hear the gun-fire and she reasoned that the cannons would not be firing if the battle had already been won.

She called on her acquaintance, the Dowager Countess of Mauberges, who lived in the fragile gentility of a small house behind the rue Montagne du Parc. The ladies drank coffee. The Countess's house backed onto the kitchen yard of Brussels' most fashionable hotel. 'The hotel kitchens are already cooking tonight's dinner,' the Countess confided in Lucille.

'Life must go on,' Lucille said piously. She supposed that the Countess was obliquely apologizing for the smell of cooking grease that permeated the dusty parlour.

Above Lucille's head the crystal drops of a candelabra shivered to the guns' sound.

'No! You mistake me! They're cooking the celebratory dinner, my dear!' The Countess was elated. 'They say the Emperor is very fond of roast chicken, so that is what they are cooking! Myself, I prefer duck, but I shall eat chicken tonight most gladly. It's being served with bread sauce, I believe, or so the servants tell me. They gossip with the hotel staff, you see.' She sounded rather ashamed of betraying that she listened to servants' gossip, but nevertheless the cooking was an augury of French victory so the Dowager Countess could not keep the good news to herself.

'They're cooking for the Emperor?' Lucille sounded dubious.

'Of course! He'll want a victory dinner, will he not? It will be just like old times! All the captured Generals being forced to eat with him, and that nasty little Prince slobbering over his food! I shall enjoy that sight, indeed I shall. You'll come, will you not?'

'I doubt I shall be invited.'

'There will be no time to send invitations! But of course you must come, all the nobility will be there. You shall have dinner with the Emperor tonight and you shall watch his victory parade tomorrow.' The Countess sighed. 'It will all be so enjoyable!'

Upstairs in the hotel the windows shivered under the impact of the gun-fire. Jane Sharpe lay in bed, the curtains closed and her eyes shut. She felt sick.

She listened to the guns, praying that one small part of their appalling violence would free her by killing Sharpe. She prayed passionately, nagging God, beseeching him, weeping at him. She did not ask for much. She only wanted to be married, and titled, and mother of Lord John's heir. She thought life was so very unfair. She had taken every precaution, yet still she was pregnant, so now, as the guns echoed, she prayed for a death. She must marry Lord John, or else he might marry elsewhere and she would be left a whore, and her child a whoreson. That child felt sour in her belly. She turned on her side in the darkened room, cursed the kitchen smells that made her want to vomit, and wept.

The guns fired on, and Brussels waited.

Peter d'Alembord was resigned to death. The day's only miracle so far was that his death had not yet come.

It seemed certain to come now for a sudden torrent of metal was being poured at the ridge. The French guns were in fury, and the soil about d'Alembord was being churned to ragged turmoil by roundshot and shell. His horse had been killed in the bombardment that had opened the battle, so now d'Alembord was forced to stand quite still while the air hummed and quivered and shook with the passage of the missiles, and as the ground thumped and trembled and spewed up great gobs of mud and stone.

He stood in front of the battalion, which in turn was a few hundred paces to the right of the elm tree. Not that the tree could be seen any more, for gun-smoke had settled over the British ridge to hide anything more than a hundred yards away. D'Alembord had earlier watched the attacks on Hougoumont, then seen the Hanoverians march to their deaths, but the great cavalry charge had been hidden from him by the smoke of the cannons firing from the British centre. He wished he could see more of the battle, for at least that would be a diversion while he waited for death. He had accepted that he would die, and he was determined that he would do it with as much grace as he could muster.

Which was why he had gone to the front of the battalion to stand in the place of greatest danger at the crest of the ridge. He could have stayed with the colour party where Colonel Ford fretted and continually polished his eyeglasses with his officer's sash, or he could have taken his proper post at the rear right flank of the Prince of Wales's Own Volunteers, but instead d'Alembord had gone a few paces ahead of the company officers and now stood, quite still, staring into the cannon-smoke across the valley. Behind him the men were lying flat, but no officer could thus take shelter. An officer's job was to set an example. An officer's duty was to stand still; to show insouciance. The time would come when the men would have to stand up in the face of the French fire, and therefore the officers must set an example of absolute stoicism. That was an infantry officer's prime task in battle; to set an example, and it did not matter if his belly was churning with fear, or that his breath sometimes came with a whimper, or that his brain was cringing with terror; he must still show utter calmness.

If an officer had to move under fire, then it had to be done very slowly and deliberately, with the air of a man distractedly taking a meditative stroll in the country. Captain Harry Price so moved, though his deliberate gait was somewhat spoilt when his new spurs caught in a tangle of crushed rye and almost tipped him arse over heels. He caught his balance, tried to show dignity by plucking at his new pelisse, then stood at ease alongside Peter d'Alembord. 'A bit of heat in the day now, Peter, wouldn't you say?'

D'Alembord had to control his breathing, but managed a creditable response. 'It's definitely become warmer, Harry.'

Price paused, evidently seeking some observation that would keep the conversation going. 'If the clouds cleared away, it might become a rare old day!'

'Indeed, yes.'

'Good cricketing weather, even.'

D'Alembord looked sideways at his friend, wondering

for a second whether Harry Price had gone quite mad, then he saw a muscle quivering in Harry's cheek and he realized that Price was just trying to hide his own fear.

Price grinned suddenly. 'Speaking of cricket, is our brave Colonel happy?'

'He's not saying very much. He's just polishing those damned spectacles of his.'

Harry Price dropped his voice as though, in the maelstrom of shells and roundshot, he might yet be overheard. 'I put some butter on the tails of his sash this morning.'

'You did what?'

'Buttered his sash,' Price said gleefully. He looked warily upwards as a shell made a curious fluttering noise overhead, then relaxed as the missile exploded far to the rear. 'I did it this morning, while he was shaving. I only used a spot of butter, for one doesn't wish to be obvious. It isn't the first time I've buttered his eyeglasses, either. I did it the last time he insisted we play cricket. Why do you think he couldn't see the ball?'

D'Alembord wondered how anyone could play such a schoolboy trick on a morning of battle, then, after a pause, he spoke with a sudden passion. 'I do hate bloody cricket.'

Price, who liked the game, was offended. 'That's not very English of you.'

'I'm not English. My ancestry is French, which is probably why I find cricket such a bloody tedious game!' D'Alembord feared that he was betraying a note of hysteria.

'There are more tedious games than cricket.' Price spoke very earnestly.

'You really believe so?'

A cannon-ball slammed into Number Four Company. It killed two men and wounded two others so badly that they would die before they could reach the surgeons. One of the two men screamed in a tremulous,

334

nerve-scraping voice until Regimental Sergeant Major McInerney shouted for the wounded man to be quiet, then ordered that the dead men be thrown forward to where the corpses were being stacked into a crude barricade. A shell exploded in midair, drowning the RSM's voice. Harry Price looked up at the drifting billow of smoke left by the shell's explosion. 'One of the Crapaud batteries is cutting its fuses a bit brief, wouldn't you say?'

'You claim there's a more tedious game than cricket?' D'Alembord did not want to think about fuses or shells.

Price nodded. 'Have you ever seen men play golf?'

D'Alembord shook his head. Off to his left he could see French skirmishers advancing among the Hanoverian dead towards La Haye Sainte. The distinctive sound of rifle-fire betrayed that the farm's garrison had seen the danger, then the French muskets began to add their own smoke to the battle's fog. 'I've never seen golf being played,' d'Alembord said. The effort of controlling his fear made his voice sound very stilted, like a man rehearsing a strange language. 'It's a Scottish game, isn't it?'

'It's a bloody weird Scottish game.' Price blinked and swallowed as a roundshot went foully close, fanning both men with the wind of its passing. 'You hit a small ball with a bent stick until you get it near a rabbit hole. Then you tap it into the hole, fish it out, and hit it towards another hole.'

D'Alembord looked at his friend who was keeping a very straight face. 'You're inventing this, Harry. You're making it up just to make me feel better.'

Harry Price shook his head. 'God's honour, Peter. I might not have mastered the finer points of the game, but I saw a man with a beard playing it near Troon.'

D'Alembord started to laugh. He did not quite know why it was so funny, but something about Harry's solemnity made him laugh. For a few seconds his laughter rang loud across the battalion, then a shell cracked apart with what seemed unusual violence, and Sergeant Huckfield was shouting at his men to stay down. D'Alembord turned and saw three of his old light company men had been turned into blood-stained rag dolls. 'What were you doing in Troon, for God's sake?'

'I have a widowed aunt who lives there, the childless relict of a lawyer. Her will is not yet decided and the lawyer's fortune was far from despicable. I went to persuade her that I am a godly, sober and deserving heir.'

D'Alembord grinned. 'She doesn't know you're a lazy, drunken rogue, Harry?'

'I read her the psalms every night,' Price said with a very fragile dignity.

A thudding of hooves turned d'Alembord round to see a staff officer galloping along the ridge crest. The man slowed his horse as he neared the two officers. 'You're to pull back! One hundred yards, no more!' The man spurred on and shouted the order over the prone battalion to Colonel Ford. 'One hundred yards, Colonel! Back one hundred yards! Lie down there!'

D'Alembord faced the battalion. Far in the rear a shell had exploded an ammunition wagon that now burned to send a plume of boiling smoke up to the low clouds. Colonel Ford was standing in his stirrups, shouting his orders over the din of shells and guns. The Sergeants rousted the men to their feet and ordered them to pace back from the crest. The men, glad to be retreating from the cannonade, went at the double, leaving their bloodied dead behind.

'We walk, I think.' D'Alembord heard a shakiness in his voice, and tried again. 'We definitely walk, Harry. We don't run.'

'I can't run in these spurs,' Price admitted. 'I suppose the thing about spurs is that you need a horse to go with them.'

The small retreat took the leading companies away from the lip of the ridge onto the hidden reverse slope, yet even so, and even lying flat in the trampled corn, the shells and roundshot still found their marks. The wounded limped to the rear, going to the forest's edge where the surgeons waited. Some men, unable to walk, were carried by the bandsmen. A few shrunken bands still played, but their music was overwhelmed by the hammering of the massive bombardment. More ammunition wagons were struck, their fire and smoke thickening until the forest's edge looked like a giant crucible in which the flames spat and flared. Frightened horses, cut from the traces of the burning wagons, galloped in panic through the wounded who limped and crawled to the surgeons.

On the southern ridge the French general officers sought vantage points from where their guns' smoke did not obscure the view and from where they could search the British lines for clues to the effectiveness of their bombardment.

They saw the turmoil of burning ammunition. They saw the wounded limping back; so many wounded that it looked like a retreat. Then, quite suddenly, they saw the battalions that had lined the crest pull back from the crest and disappear.

French infantry still assaulted Hougoumont, and more men had just been sent to capture the awkward bastion of La Haye Sainte, but perhaps neither attack would need to be successful, for it was clear that the vaunted British infantry was beaten. The Goddamns were retreating. Their ranks had been shredded by the Emperor's *jeune filles*, and the redcoats were fleeing. The Emperor had been right; the British would not stand against a real assault. The guns still fired, but the ridge seemed empty, and the French smelt glory in the powder smoke.

Marshal Ney, bravest of the brave, had been ordered by the Emperor to finish the British quickly. He gazed through his telescope at the enemy ridge and saw a shining chance of swift victory. He slammed his spyglass shut, turned in his saddle, and beckoned to his cavalry commanders.

It was half-past three, and the Prussians had not come.

Sharpe and Harper had instinctively returned to the ridge above Hougoumont where Captain Witherspoon's body lay. It was the place their battle had started, and where they felt a curious sense of safety. The French bombardment was concentrating on the ground to their left, leaving the slope above the beleaguered château in relative peace.

They reined in close to Witherspoon's disembowelled corpse. A glossy crow noisily protested their arrival, then went back to its feeding. 'There goes my colonel's pay,' Sharpe said after staring in silence at the shifting smoke above the valley.

Harper was frowning at the corpse, wondering if it was that of the pleasant young Captain who had been so friendly at the beginning of the battle.

'Worth it, though, just to tell that poxy little Dutch bastard one home truth,' Sharpe continued. He was staring at Hougoumont. The roof of the château was burning fiercely, spewing sparks high and thick into the smoky sky. The western end of the house had already been reduced to bare walls and blackened beams, though, judging from the amount of musket smoke which ringed the château, the conflagration had not diminished the defenders' resistance. The French attacks still broke to nothing on the château's walls and musketry.

'So what do you want to do?' Sharpe asked Harper.

'We can go, you mean?' Harper sounded vaguely surprised.

'There's nothing to keep us here, is there?'

'I suppose not,' Harper agreed, though neither man

moved. To the left of the château the valley was still oddly unscarred by the battle. The only French attack on the main British line had come in the east, not here in the west, and the only scars in the patchy field of wheat and rye were black marks where some shells had fallen short and scorched the damp and rain-beaten crops. French infantry was thick about Hougoumont, and a mass of men were closing on La Haye Sainte, yet between those bastions the valley lay empty beneath the screaming passage of the French bombardment.

'So where the hell are the bloody Prussians?' Harper asked irritably.

'God knows. Gone to a different war, perhaps?'

Harper turned to stare at the British infantry who lay patient and unmoving beneath the flail of the French guns. 'So where will you go?' he asked Sharpe.

'Fetch Lucille and go back to England, I suppose.' Lucille would have to wait to go home and, Sharpe thought, the wait could prove a very long one for if this battle was lost the Austrians and Russians might make peace with Napoleon and it could take years to forge another alliance against France. Even if today's battle was won it could still take months for the allies to destroy what remained of the Emperor's armies.

'You could wait in Ireland?' Harper suggested.

'Aye, I'd like that.' Sharpe took a piece of hard cheese from his saddlebag and tossed a lump of it to Harper.

A shell bounced off the ridge nearby and whirled its fuse crazily in the air to leave a mad spiral of smoke. The shell landed, spun in a mud bowl for a second, then simply died. Harper watched it warily, waiting for the explosion that did not come, then he looked back to the French-held ridge. 'It seems a shame to leave right now.' Harper had come to Belgium because the British army and its war against an Emperor had been his whole adult life and he could not relinquish either the institution or its purpose. He might be a civilian, but he thought of himself as a soldier still, and he cared desperately that this day saw victory.

'You want to stay here, then?' Sharpe asked, as though he himself did not much care either way.

Harper did not answer. He was still staring across the valley, staring through the scrims of smoke, and as he stared his eyes grew wide as gun muzzles. 'God save Ireland!' His voice was full of astonishment. 'Christ in his cups, but will you just look at that?'

Sharpe looked and, like Harper, his eyes widened in amazement.

All the damned cavalry in all the damned world seemed to be spilling down the far side of the gentle valley. Regiment after regiment of French horse was threading the spaces between the enemy's artillery batteries to form up in the undisturbed fields of rye and wheat. The sun was breaking through the shredding clouds to glint on the breastplates and the high-crested helmets of the Cuirassiers. Behind the Cuirassiers were Lancers, and behind them were even more horsemen. Every cavalry uniform in the Empire was there: Dragoons, Carabiniers, Hussars, Chasseurs, all forming their long lines of attack behind the Lancers and Cuirassiers.

Sharpe trained his telescope on the far ridge. He could see no infantry. There had to be infantry. He searched the smoke clouds, but still found none. A charge by horse alone? And where were the French gunners? The cavalry, after all, would force the British infantry to form squares which made wonderful targets for gunners and infantrymen, but the cavalry could not hope to destroy the squares by itself. Or did the French believe this battle already won? Had the Emperor reckoned that no troops, so battered by gun-fire, would stand against his prized cavalry? 'There's no infantry!' Sharpe said to Harper, then turned to shout a warning of cavalry to the nearest

British battalion, but their officers had already seen the threat and all along the British line the battalions were climbing to their feet and forming squares.

While on the far side of the valley the Cuirassiers drew their swords. The sun rippled down the long line of steel. Behind them the red and white flags of the Lancers pricked the smoke scrims. Harper was entranced by the sight. It was like something from a saga, a legend of old battles come to flesh and steel. Half a battlefield was filled with the glory of cavalry; with plumes and crests and leopard skins and flags and blades.

Brigade officers were galloping among the newly formed British squares, ordering some battalions further back so that the unwieldy formations were staggered like a draught board. Now the flank of one square could not fire on the face of another, and wide spaces were left between the battalions so that the enemy horse could flow freely between the squares. Batteries of the Royal Horse Artillery placed their cannon in the wide spaces and loaded with roundshot. They would have preferred to have double-shotted their cannon, but the lighter guns of the horse artillery would not survive the extra strain. The gunners' horse teams were taken far behind the squares to where British and Dutch light cavalry waited to tackle any French horsemen who survived the passage through the wicked maze of men, muskets and cannon-fire.

The French gun-fire was undiminished and, because the British were now standing in square, the shells and roundshot which streaked across the ridge's rim were finding targets. Sharpe watched a cannon-ball strike savagely down one side of a square of Highlanders. At least ten men fell, perhaps more. Another ball struck the face of the square, driving a bloody hole that was instantly filled as the files shuffled together.

'The buggers are coming!' Harper warned.

The Cuirassiers walked their heavy horses forward.

Behind them were the Red Lancers in their square czapka headgear and the Horse Grenadiers in their tall black bearskins. Further back were the Carabiniers in their dazzling white uniforms, and squadrons of green Dragoons and troops of plumed Hussars. The horsemen covered the far slope, obliterating the dull wet crops with a gorgeous tapestry of shifting colours, nodding plumes, sun-brightened helmets and gold-fringed flags. It was a sight Sharpe had never seen before, not in all his years of soldiering. Even the mounted hordes in India had not matched the splendour of this sight. This was the massed cavalry of an empire assembled on one battlefield. Sharpe tried to count them, but there were just too many men and horses flowing through the filmy drifts of gun-smoke. The sun glittered from thousands of drawn swords, raised lances, polished armour, and curved sabres.

The cavalry advanced at a walk. This was how cavalry should attack; not in some madcap rush to glory, but with a steady slow approach that was gradually quickened until, at the last moment, the heavy horses with their steel-clad riders should crash home as one unit. If a horse was shot in its last few galloping strides, then man and horse could slide as dead meat to crumple a square's face. Sharpe had seen it happen; he had ridden behind the Germans at Garçia Hernandez and watched as a dead horse and dying rider smashed in blood and terror through the face of a French square. All the French were dead at that moment as the following horsemen streamed through the gap to gut the square from its inside outwards.

Yet, if the square was steady and shot at the right time, it should not happen. Each side of a square was formed of four ranks. The two front ranks knelt, their bayonet-tipped muskets driven hard into the ground to make a hedge of steel. The two ranks behind stood with muskets levelled. Once the front two ranks had fired, they did not reload but just held their bayonets hard and steady. The rear ranks could load and fire, load and fire, and the attacking horses, unwilling to charge such an obstacle, would swerve away from the face of the square to be raked by the fire of the square's flanks.

Yet one dead horse, slithering in mud and blood, could break that theory. And when one square broke its men would run for shelter to another square, fighting their way inside, and the horsemen would ride with them, letting the panicked infantry break the second square's ranks apart. Then the butchery could continue.

'The daft bugger misjudged!' Harper said with undisguised glee.

The French cavalry commander had formed his attack into a succession of long lines, but too long, for the flanks were approaching the fields of fire from Hougoumont and La Haye Sainte. Those bulwarks that lay like breakwaters ahead of the British line were being besieged by infantry, but their defenders had muskets and rifles enough to fire on the tempting target of the cavalry which was thus forced to contract its line. The wings of the cavalry trotted inwards, thickening the centre of the attack, but also compressing it so that as the horsemen began to climb the British ridge they looked more like a column of horsemen than a charging line. The compression became worse as the horsemen neared the crest and squeezed yet further inwards from the threat of the flanking batteries. The horses were so tightly packed that some were lifted clean off the muddy ground and carried along by their neighbours. The air was filled with the chink of curb chains, the slap of scabbards on leather, the thump of hooves, and the whipping sound of lance pennants flapping.

The British cannons drowned the cavalry's noise. The first volley came from the nine-pounder batteries on the ridge's crest. The guns smashed roundshot deep

343

into the compressed formation. The second volley was double-shotted and Sharpe, in the deafening echo of the guns' reports, heard the clatter of the musket-balls striking the Cuirassiers' breastplates. The gunners reloaded frantically, ramming a last charge of canister down the hot barrels as the French trumpets threw the attack into a canter.

'Fire!' A last volley was fired from the threatened guns. Sharpe had a tangled impression of horsemen flailing inwards from the canister's strike, then he and Harper turned their horses and raced for the safety of the nearest square. Staff officers who had been positioned on the crest were similarly galloping to safety.

Sharpe and Harper thudded through an opening in a square of Guardsmen that immediately closed ranks behind the two Riflemen. Thirty yards in front of the square a battery of horse artillery waited for the enemy.

The French horsemen were close, but still hidden by the fall of the forward slope, and there followed one of the odd moments of apparent battlefield silence. The French gunners, fearful of hitting their own cavalry, had ceased fire, while the closest British gunners had yet to be given their target. It was not a true silence, for the enemy infantry still snarled and fired around Hougoumont and La Haye Sainte, and the guns in the eastern part of the valley still fired, while closer, much closer, there was the thunderous shaking of uncountable hooves, yet the absence of the murderous enemy bombardment made the moment seem very like silence. There was even a palpable relief that the shells and roundshot had stopped their slaughter. Men drew breath as they waited and watched the empty crest which was topped with dirty smoke.

Somewhere beyond the smoke a trumpet screamed.

'Hold your fire when you first see Monsewer!' A mounted Guards major walked his horse behind the face of the square where Sharpe and Harper had taken refuge. 'Let the bastards get close enough to smell your farts before you kill them! Take that smile off your face, Guardsman Proctor. You're not here to enjoy yourself, but to die for your King, for your country, and above all for me!'

Harper, liking the Guards officer's style, grinned as broadly as any of the Guardsmen. The Major winked at Sharpe, then continued his harangue. 'Don't waste your powder! And remember you are Guardsmen, which is almost like being gentlemen, so you will behave with good manners! Permit the little darlings to lift their skirts before you give them your balls!'

And suddenly the little darlings were there as the ridge filled with a horde of horses. One moment the skyline was empty, then the world was dominated by cavalry and the sky was pierced by the last fine notes which hurled the Cuirassiers into their gallop.

The close support artillery, exposed in the spaces between the squares, opened fire. The guns slammed back on their trails, spewing mud from their bucking wheels.

Sharpe saw a cannon-ball split the mass of horsemen apart as though an invisible cleaver had chopped through the formation. The gunners were clearing the gun's barrel, ramming a canister onto a powder charge, and hurling themselves away from the coming recoil.

'Fire!' This time a blast of canister flailed a dozen tight-packed horses to the ground, then the artillerymen were abandoning their cannon to seek safety inside the squares. The gunners carried their rammers and portfires with them.

The Cuirassiers could not be stopped by cannon-fire. They flowed round their dead and dying and threw themselves at the squares in a desperate, brave charge. They had believed themselves to be pursuing a broken and fleeing enemy, and their General had promised

345

that the only obstacles between them and the whores of Brussels were a few demoralized Goddamn fugitives, yet now the horsemen discovered they had ridden to a bitter trap. The squares had been hidden behind the crest, the enemy was not broken and running, but instead standing and waiting to fight.

Yet these were the Emperor's Cuirassiers, his 'big brothers', and glory would be theirs if they broke these squares. High above each British battalion hung the colours that, if captured, would give a man eternal fame in an empire's heaven, and so the horsemen screamed a challenge and lowered the points of their heavy swords.

'Number One and Two Companies!' The Guards Major eschewed his jesting as the enemy came close. 'Wait for my word!' He paused. Sharpe could hear the horses' breathing, see the distorted Cuirassiers' faces beneath their steel visors, then, at last, the Major shouted, 'Fire!'

The forward face of the square disappeared in white smoke. Musket flames stabbed bright and somewhere a horse squealed in awful, gut-wrenching pain. The two front ranks, not bothering to reload, rammed their musket butts into the ground so that their bayonets made a savage hedge of sharpened steel. The rear two ranks reloaded with the speed of men whose lives depended on their musketry.

There was a pause of a heartbeat while the Guardsmen wondered whether a dead horse would slide in hoof-flailing horror to smash their square's southern face, then, beyond the fringes of the smoke, the horsemen appeared. They had swerved apart, dividing into streams either side of the square. The horses would not crash home, instead the survivors had veered away to gallop between the squares.

'Fire!' That was an officer on the flank of the Guards' square. A Cuirassier's horse was hit in the chest to pump obscenely bright blood as its legs crumpled. The rider, mouth wide open in silent terror, was thrown over its head. Another Cuirassier was being dragged by his stirrup in a spray of blood.

'Fire!' The front face of the square volleyed again, and this time the bullets threw back four Red Lancers. The Lancers had been following the Cuirassiers and seeking the safety of the open ground between the squares, which was not safe at all, but a killing ground that led to the volley fire of yet more squares. The horsemen had been beguiled into the maze of death, yet they were brave men and they still dreamed of carrying the Emperor to victory on their lance points. 'Thrust home! Thrust!' Sharpe heard a Lancer officer shout at his men, then saw a group of the red-uniformed horsemen swerve towards the square with their weapons held low. 'Thrust hard!'

'Fire!' The Guards Major snapped the command, a blast of smoke blotted out the charging Lancers so that the only evidence of their existence was a terrible high-pitched scream of either man or horse, and as the smoke cleared Sharpe saw only the butchered horse, and a man crawling away, and a lance shaft quivering with its point buried in the mud and a horse shaking as it tried to stand.

'Platoon fire!' the Guards Colonel called.

'Aim for the horses!' A sergeant strolled behind the square's face. 'Aim for the horses!'

'Number One Platoon!' another major shouted. 'Fire!'

Now the platoons in the faces of the square fired one after another so that the blasts of smoke and flame seemed to be driven like the hand of a clock. Each volley thickened the smoke about the square's faces so that the compass of the battle shrank to the few yards visible through the choking white cloud. The other squares were invisible, hidden behind their own banks of fog. Sharpe could hear their volleys, and hear a piper playing some skirling weird music somewhere to the west. The stream of horsemen galloped through the smoke, and sometimes a brave man would hurl himself at the Guards' square in a suicidal attempt to force victory out of stalemate. A Lancer tried to ride obliquely at a square's flank, but a corporal shot him down three paces before his blade would have struck home. Two young Guards Lieutenants competed with their pistols, wagering a month's pay on who could kill more Frenchmen. A sergeant spotted a Guardsman surreptitiously discarding part of the powder from his cartridge to lessen the pain of the musket's recoil and the Sergeant struck the man with his cane and promised him real punishment when the battle was over.

Still the horsemen came, the uniforms changing as the rear ranks of the charge followed in the bloody path of the Cuirassiers and Lancers. Carabiniers and Dragoons raced madly through the corridors of slaughter. The attacking streams divided and subdivided as they sought safer passages between the squares.

'Aim at the horses!' the Guards Major called to his men. 'Aim at the horses!'

Harper had his rifle at his shoulder. He tracked a French officer's horse, fired, and watched man and beast tumble down. A horse was an easier target to hit, and a wounded or dead horse removed a cavalryman just as effectively as shooting the man.

'Fire!' Another frontal volley. A horse reared in the smoke between two of the abandoned cannon. Its rider fell backwards and his helmet struck a gun-wheel with a sickening crack. A dying horse drummed the turf with its hooves. An unhorsed Cuirassier scrabbled at his buckles to remove the weight of his armour. Another Cuirassier, fallen on his back, jerked to twist his huge weight of steel out of the cloying mud. A musket bullet spurted mud beside the struggling man. 'Leave those lobsters alone!' the Guards Major shouted. 'They're out of it! Go for the live 'uns!'

Sharpe watched a cavalryman beating impotently at a captured gun with his sword. The French, like the British cavalry earlier, had brought no implements to disable the guns. A French Hussar officer fired a pistol at a flank of the Guards' square and was hit by a full platoon's volley in revenge.

'Cease fire! Front ranks reload!' The charge had streamed clear past these foremost squares; all except for a few timid horsemen who were reluctant to risk the fatal corridors and had therefore hung back at the ridge's crest. The bravest and luckiest horsemen had already succeeded in riding clean right through the staggered squares, only to be faced by a line of British and Dutch cavalry. The French troopers, scattered and broken, knew they would be cut down by the waiting sabres, so turned to race back towards the safety of the valley. Like a great wave the cavalry had broken and divided about the squares, now it must ebb back before reforming. The smoke began to shred and clear, revealing that the other squares were unbroken. Dead men and horses littered the spaces between the squares. An unhorsed Lancer, reeling with concussion or weakness, staggered like a drunk towards the ridge crest.

'Present!' The Guards Colonel had seen that the French charge was now returning, and he would give the horsemen more fire as they tried to regain their own lines. The thunder of their hooves became louder, then the first frightened men appeared. 'Fire!' A white Carabinier's uniform seemed to turn instantly red. A horse collapsed, rolled and broke its rider's leg. Another wounded man was clinging to the mane of his horse, his face white with terror as he desperately ran through the staggered walls of fire. The unhorsed Lancer was ridden over by his own men. He screamed as he fell and as the hooves pounded his flesh to jelly.

'Fire!' a Guards Lieutenant called.

The flood of horsemen flowed past, this time retreating, and Sharpe had a glimpse of a red-haired man in the gorgeous uniform of a Marshal of the Empire, his hat gone, screaming at his troops. Riderless horses had joined the fleeing mob. A few cavalrymen ran among the horses, some of them trying to grab the reins of a free horse.

'Fire!' A pigtailed Dragoon with a broken sword slumped over his horse's neck, but somehow clung on. Sharpe could smell blood and leather and horse-sweat. The uniforms were flecked with mud. The horses' eyes rolled white as they galloped and their breath pumped loud and harsh.

The horsemen went as they had come. As soon as the last Frenchmen had passed, the British gunners sprinted out of the squares to regain their undamaged guns. A few cannon had been left loaded with canister and the portfires touched the quills to send barrels of the killing musket-balls at the rumps of the fleeing cavalry. The ground between the squares was a slaughteryard where the dead and the dying lay among rye stalks hammered into the mud that was thick with hoofprints and horse dung.

'Sad, really.' The Guards Major offered Sharpe a pinch of snuff.

'Sad?'

'Wonderful looking horses!' The Major, who was clearly so popular with his men, proved to have a rather melancholy demeanour when he was no longer performing for them. 'A damned pity to throw good horseflesh away, but what can one expect of a paltry gunner like Bonaparte? Do you care for snuff?'

'No. Thank you.'

'You should. It clears out the lungs.' The Major

snapped his box shut, then vigorously sniffed the powder off his hand. Some of his Guardsmen had run forward to plunder the French corpses and the Major shouted at them to put the wounded horses out of their misery before they robbed the dead. A Cuirassier with a musket bullet in his thigh was dragged back into the square. A Guardsman picked up the wounded man's glittering helmet with its long horsehair plume and, replacing his shako with the gaudy headgear, pranced along the square's face in a grotesque parody of a barrack gate whore. His comrades cheered him.

'I suppose', the Major smiled at the soldier's mockery, 'that Monsewer's damned guns will start up again?'

But instead it was the British guns on the crest that fired. The sound of the volley told Sharpe that the cannon had been double-shotted and the frantic speed with which the crews reloaded was a warning that the cavalry were again approaching up the ridge's front slope.

'My God! The bastards haven't had enough!' the Major said incredulously, then cheered up as he realized he would have another chance to encourage his men. 'Mademoiselle Frog is coming back for more, boys! You must have treated her well last time, so give her the same treatment again!'

The cavalry was indeed returning, and this time there were even more horsemen. Reinforcements must have been sent across the valley and it now seemed as though all the cavalry of France was to be hurled in one desperate charge at the British squares. The horsemen streamed over the ridge, and the guns by the squares gave them a greeting of canister before the gunners again ran with their precious implements to the square's safety.

'Hold your fire!' The Guards Major peered through the cannons' smoke. 'Wait for it, lads! Wait for it! Fire!'

The muskets could not miss. The heavy balls thudded into men and horses, piercing breastplates and helmets, turning the majesty of plume and pelisse into screaming pain. There was also pain inside the squares, where those men wounded by the cannon-fire and not given time to retreat to the forest's edge, still sheltered. The battalion officers rode between the wounded, shouting encouragement to each face of their square as the French horsemen flowed past.

The cavalry had returned full of resolve to charge home, but the horses could not be forced to charge the squares that were now given the further protection of makeshift bastions formed of dead and dying horses and men. The new attack flowed about the squares just like the first, except this time the attack went more slowly because the horses were tiring. Those horses that had lost their riders during the first charge dutifully attacked with the second, dumbly obedient to their herd instincts even though those instincts took them up into the storm of canister and musket-fire.

Once again some Frenchmen pierced through the whole depth of arrayed squares, but only to discover the screen of waiting cavalry. This time, instead of risking the return journey through the alleys of musket-fire, some Cuirassiers swerved to their left to find another route back to the valley. They discovered a lane which ran behind the ridge and spurred along it, aiming for the open flank. The lane dropped into a deep cutting, its banks too steep and wet for any horse to climb, and at the cutting's end was a barricade of felled trees put there to check any French attempt to attack in the other direction. The horsemen reined in and shouted at the men behind to turn back and find another way around the sunken lane.

Then British infantry appeared at the top of the embankments. These redcoats were fresh, posted to guard against a flank attack that had not happened, and now they found a helpless enemy under their muskets.

They opened fire. Volley after volley plunged down into the steep-sided cutting. They fired without pity, firing until not a man nor horse was left whole, and only then did the infantry clamber down through their smoke to the heaps of stirring, crying, whimpering horror. They did not go to help their victims, but to plunder them.

The second charge died as the first had died, but the French were brave, and led by the bravest of the brave, and so they returned. The guns fired a last volley before the charge reached the squares, and this time a vagary of the shifting smoke let Sharpe see a group of charging horsemen blown apart like crops struck by a monstrous scythe. The gunners ran to safety with their rammers as the horses were spurred again at the squares' faces. Again the muskets threw them back, and again the cavalry swerved away. It was sheer madness. Sharpe, not even bothering to unsling his rifle, watched in disbelief. The French were slaughtering their own cavalry, hurling them again and again at the unbroken squares of infantry.

Again the cavalry retreated, allowing the British gunners to reoccupy their undamaged batteries. Some French skirmishers had climbed the ridge either side of the cavalry's path, but there were not enough Voltigeurs to trouble the squares. Some French gunners opened fire in the pause between cavalry charges and their rounds did more damage than all the horsemen had achieved. The gunners were forced to stop their cannonade as the stubborn cavalry wheeled back to charge the squares again. Between each charge a few redcoats were allowed out of the squares to bring back plunder: an officer's gilded sword, a handful of coins, a silver trumpet with a gorgeously embroidered banner. One sergeant unstrapped a dead Dragoon's leopard-skin helmet, only to throw it down with disgust when he saw the leopard skin was merely dyed cloth. Another man laughed to find a small and bedraggled bunch of faded violets stuck in the buttonhole of a dead Dragoon General whose white moustache was splashed with blood.

Sharpe and Harper used one of the pauses between the French charges to canter out from the Guards' square. It was partly curiosity which drove them. Other staff officers similarly rode between the formations and past the heaps of French dead to discover how other battalions were faring. Sharpe and Harper sought their old battalion and finally spotted the yellow regimental colour of the Prince of Wales's Own Volunteers above the lingering musket smoke. The colour bore the badge of a chained eagle to commemorate the trophy that Sharpe and Harper had captured at Talavera. The redcoats cheered as the two Riflemen trotted out of the misting smoke and into the square's embrace.

'You don't mind if we shelter here, do you?' Sharpe politely asked Ford.

Ford was clearly nervous of Sharpe's motives in seeking out his old battalion, but he could hardly refuse his hospitality and so nodded his reluctant consent. The Colonel nervously plucked off his glasses and scrubbed at their lenses with his sash. For some reason the spectacles seemed misted and he wondered if it was some strange effect caused by the thickness of powder smoke. Major Vine glared at the Riflemen, fearing that Sharpe had again come to take command as he had at Quatre Bras.

Peter d'Alembord, dismounted, was still unwounded. He smiled at Sharpe. 'I don't mind this malarkey! They can try this nonsense all day and night!'

The French tried the nonsense again, and again achieved nothing. They had been lured to the attack by the mistaken apprehension of a British withdrawal, yet, though they had learned their mistake, they seemed incapable of abandoning the suicidal attacks. Again and again they attacked, and again and again the muskets flamed and smoked and the tired horses fell screaming and quivering.

Close to Sharpe, between the Prince of Wales's Own Volunteers and a square of the King's German Legion, a French Hussar officer struggled to unbuckle his expensive saddle. Both squares left him undisturbed. The girth of the saddle was trapped by the horse's dead weight, but at last the officer tugged it free and the Germans gave him an ironic cheer. The Frenchman trudged away with his burden. Two riderless horses trotted down the rear face of Ford's square, but none of his men could be bothered to retrieve the trophies, even though a reward was offered for captured horses. A wounded Cuirassier, divested of his armour, limped southwards. 'Hey! Frenchie! Get yourself a horse, you silly bugger!' Private Clayton shouted at him.

'Why are the bloody fools persisting?' Harry Price asked Sharpe.

'Pride.' Sharpe did not even have to think about his answer. These were the horsemen of France and they would not limp back to their own lines to confess failure. Sharpe remembered moments like this from his own experience; at Badajoz the French had filled a stone-faced ditch with British dead, yet still the infantry had attacked the breach. In the end that obstinate pride had brought victory, but these blown horses with their tired riders were now incapable of breaking a square.

Sharpe edged his horse close behind his old light company. Weller was still alive, so was Dan Hagman and Clayton. 'How is it, lads?'

Their mouths were dry from biting into the cartridges, their lips were flecked with unburned powder, and sweat had carved clean rivulets down their faces which were blackened by the smoke and smuts from the powder exploding in their musket pans. Their fingernails were bleeding from dragging back the heavy flints, yet they grinned and gave an ironic cheer when Sharpe handed down a canteen of rum from his saddle. Colour Sergeant

Huckfield had a pocket of spare flints which he doled out to those men whose old ones had been chipped away by repeated firing.

'I know how the gentry feel now,' Dan Hagman said to Sharpe.

'How come, Dan?'

'When all the game is driven towards them, and all the rich buggers have to do is aim and fire? It's just like that, innit? Not that I mind. Silly buggers can line up all day to be shot so far as I care.' Because so long as the French cavalry were around the squares, so long the dreaded French artillery could not fire at the redcoats.

The horsemen came again, though by now men and beasts were too tired and too wary to charge home. A mass of enemy cavalry walked their horses to within sixty yards of the Prince of Wales's Own Volunteers and stopped beside a battery of abandoned guns. The horses were sweating and their ribs heaving, yet the cavalry had still not given up hope of breaking the infantry. If brute force would not work, then subtlety might, and every few minutes a group of the cavalry would spur forward in an attempt to provoke a volley from the square's face. If such feint attacks could empty the deadly muskets there was a chance that the remaining horsemen could hack their way through the unloaded ranks with their heavy swords. Lancers, with their long and deadly reach, could easily break a square from a standing horse, but not if the muskets were loaded.

But the battalion was too canny to take the bait. Instead they jeered insults at the French. Some of the horsemen trotted away to find another square, hoping their discipline would be poorer. The great cavalry assault had reached stalemate. The cavalry, too proud to retreat, were unable to charge, and so they stood their horses just out of effective volley range and tried to bluff the infantry into firing. Hundreds of Frenchmen were dead or dying, yet thousands remained in the saddle, enough to keep alive the desperate hope of victory. Sometimes an officer managed to spur a group into a full-blooded charge and the muskets would spit their flames again, more horses would go down again, and then the stalemate resumed.

'Hold your fire! Hold it!' d'Alembord was suddenly shouting at the square's rear face. 'Open ranks!'

Three horsemen had spurred across the field and now took shelter among the Prince of Wales's Own Volunteers. Sharpe, turning in his saddle, saw the Duke of Wellington nodding a curt greeting at Ford who frantically began polishing his lenses. Sharpe looked back to the front where the horsemen still stood threateningly, but did not charge. Two of the Lancers, frustrated and embittered by the stalemate, threw their lances like javelins, but the missiles fell harmlessly short of the front rank. The redcoats jeeringly invited the horsemen to come and get their toys back. Another Lancer jabbed his lance point at a cannon's blackened vent, and achieved nothing.

'Wasting their time.' The Duke's voice sounded just behind Sharpe.

Sharpe turned to see that the Duke was talking to him. 'Yes, sir.'

The Duke's face betrayed neither hope for his army's survival, nor despair for its defeat. He had lost most of his cavalry to a foolish charge, many of his allies had run away, and he was left with scarce half the men he had paraded at the day's beginning, but he looked calm, even detached. He offered Sharpe the ghost of a smile; an acknowledgement of how many battlefields the two men had shared across the years. A more perceptive man than Sharpe might have read some message in the Duke's seeking the companionship of a veteran soldier, but Sharpe merely felt his usual awkwardness when he was in the company of his old commanding officer. 'So what do you make of the man?' the Duke asked.

'The man' was clearly the Emperor. 'I'm disappointed,' Sharpe answered shortly.

The reply amused the Duke. 'He might please you yet. He's throwing bits and pieces at us to see what we're made of, but doubtless he'll put a real attack together sooner or later.' The Duke looked at the closest enemy horsemen, a mix of Cuirassiers, Hussars and Lancers. 'Fine-looking devils, aren't they?'

'They are, sir.'

The Duke suddenly astonished Sharpe by giving his great whoop of a laugh. 'I was in another square over there and a major was telling his men to make faces at the rogues! "Pull faces," he shouted! Can you believe it? Pull faces! We shall have to add that order to the drillbook.' He laughed again, then shot a look at Sharpe. 'Is Orange keeping you busy?'

'He's dismissed me, sir.'

The Duke stared disapprovingly for a heartbeat, then gave another neighing laugh which made the nearest red-coats look round in astonishment at their Commander-in-Chief. 'I always thought he was a fool to pick you. I told him you were an independent-minded rogue, but he wouldn't listen. At his age they always think they know best.' The Duke looked back to the French horsemen who still showed no inclination to close on the square. 'If those rascals don't intend to charge, I might make a run for it.'

'Your Grace?' Sharpe could not resist a question as the Duke turned his horse away. 'The Prussians, sir?'

'Their cavalry picquets are in sight.' The Duke spoke very calmly, as though he had not been racked all day by fears of a Prussian betrayal. 'I fear it will be some time before their infantry can close on us, but at least their picquets are in sight. We just need to hold fast.' The Duke raised his voice so that the whole square could hear his confidence. 'We just have to hold fast now! I thank you for your hospitality, Ford!'

He galloped from the rear of the square, followed by the two staff officers who had managed to keep up with his progress. Some of the French horsemen spurred after the Duke, but gave up the chase when it was clear that his horse was a far better animal.

''Ware right! Present!' That was d'Alembord, warning of the approach of another mass of enemy cavalry who were making a final and hopeless attempt to justify the slaughtered men and horses who lay in bloody heaps about the stubborn squares.

The muskets flamed again, the ramrods clattered in hot barrels, and the volleys flickered red in the smoke. Somewhere a dying Hussar cried his woman's name aloud. A horse limped towards home, dragging a rear leg dripping with blood. The horse's saddle-cloth was decorated with an Imperial 'N' embroidered in blue and golden threads. Beside the horse, and howling with pain though apparently unwounded, a dog loped southwards to seek its master among the retreating French cavalry. A Cuirassier, his face bitter with failure, slammed his sword down onto a British cannon's barrel. The steel rang like a hammer's blow on an anvil, but achieved nothing. The Cuirassier wrenched his horse around and spurred southwards.

The French cavalry had been beaten and, like a last exhausted wave that had failed to breach a sea wall, the horsemen ebbed back into the valley. They went slowly, bloodied and muddied, a golden horde turned into a defeated mob.

And the Emperor's guns, this day's best killers for the French, began to kill again.

CHAPTER 18

Prussian cavalry scouts reached Plancenoit, a village that lay just a cannon-shot behind the French right flank. Far to the east of Plancenoit, yet clearly visible to the French staff officers, were columns of Prussian infantry.

The presence of Blücher's men spelt the failure of the Emperor's strategy; the two armies had not been prised apart, yet their new conjunction was tenuous and the Prussians were not yet advancing in overwhelming force, but only in a fragile line of march. It would take hours for them to assemble an attack, and in those hours the Emperor knew he could break the British before turning on the Prussians.

The destruction of the British needed to be absolute and certain. An attack by a corps of infantry had failed, and Marshal Ney had broken the cavalry in futile onslaughts on the British squares, so now the Emperor stirred himself to bring order to the chaotic assaults. The greatest part of his infantry was still uncommitted, and among them was the élite of his army. The Emperor's own Imperial Guard was waiting.

No man but a veteran who had displayed uncommon valour in the Empire's battles could join the Guard. Guardsmen were paid more than other troops, and uniformed in more splendour. In return, more was expected of them, yet the Guard had always given it. The Guard had never been defeated. Other French troops might grumble at the Guard's privileges, but when the bearskins and long coats marched, victory was certain. The Guards wore side-whiskers and moustaches, ear-rings and powdered pigtails as marks of their prowess. To be a Grenadier of the Guard a man had to be six feet tall, an élite of an élite.

The Guard were the Emperor's 'immortals', passionate in their loyalty to him, and fearsome in battle for him. When Bonaparte had been defeated and sent to Elba the Guard had been ordered to disband, but rather than surrender their colours they had burned the silk flags, crumbled the ash into wine, and drunk the mixture. Some of the immortals had gone into exile with their Emperor, but now they had returned and been reunited with their old comrades and been given new colours to fly beneath new Eagles. The Guard was the élite, the undefeated, the immortals of the Empire, and the Guard would deliver the final lethal blow that would obliterate the British.

But not yet. It was only six o'clock, there were more than three hours of daylight left, and the Prussians were far from ready to fight, so there was time for the Emperor to wear the British down yet further. He ordered the Guard to prepare itself for battle, but not to advance beyond La Belle Alliance. Then, contemplating the smoking ruin that had been a valley of farmland, he stared fixedly at La Haye Sainte. That farm was the bone sticking in the French craw. The Riflemen behind its walls were raking the flank of every French attack, and protecting the batteries at the centre of the British line. The farm must be taken so the British line would be stretched ever more thinly, and then the Guard would ram home the victory.

The Emperor had stirred himself, and now the British would learn just how he could fight.

All along the British line the flail of the cannon-fire

struck and killed. The British battalions were ordered to lie down, but the French gunners had the range to perfection now and their roundshot skimmed the ridge to plough bloody furrows through the prone ranks. British guns were shattered; their barrels blasted off carriages and their wheels splintered. Shells exploded on the ridge to add their burden of smoke to the thickening air. Burning ammunition wagons added their stench to the sour smell of blood.

This was how an emperor fought. He would kill and kill and kill with his guns, and when the British were screaming to be released from the torrent of death he would send their quietus in the hands of his immortals.

The air quivered with the impact of the guns. Sharpe, abandoning his mare into Harper's care, walked forward from the Prince of Wales's Own Volunteers as far as the ridge's crest where the percussion of the heavy French artillery was like a succession of physical punches in the belly. The roundshot plucked at the thick skeins of smoke, grazed the ridge to fleck the sky with mud, then screamed and whined and hummed and crashed home behind him. In twenty-two years Sharpe had never known a cannonade like it, nor had he ever breathed air so heated and thickened by smoke and flame that to stand at the valley's rim was like facing the open door of some gigantic and red-hot kiln. The rye crop on the crest, where it had not been obliterated into quagmire, had been trampled to the consistency of the woven mats he remembered from India.

A shell traced its trail of smoke over his head. A roundshot ricocheted up from the ridge a dozen yards to his left. To his right, where the cavalry had advanced to their vain attacks, the slope was a horror of dead horses and men. A yellow dog dragged a length of gut from a corpse, though whether it was of man or beast Sharpe could not tell.

Beyond the slaughtered cavalry Sharpe could see the smoke illuminated by the flaring glow made by the burning château of Hougoumont. He could see nothing in the smoke to his left. Behind Sharpe the red-coated battalions had been deployed into line again, but all were lying flat so that for a strange moment he had the impression that he was the only man left alive on all the battlefield.

Then, in the valley's smoke in front of him, he saw more live men; thousands of live men, skirmishers, Frenchmen, a swarm of Voltigeurs running forward in loose order and Sharpe knew that added to the ordeal of cannon-fire the battalions must now endure an onslaught of musketry. He turned and shouted a warning. 'Skirmishers!'

The British light companies ran forward to take their places on the forward slope, but they were horribly outnumbered. Peter d'Alembord persuaded Ford to release a second company, and sent Harry Price's men to face the Voltigeurs. Price had been a skirmisher himself once, and understood what was needed, but not all the skirmishers in Wellington's army could have defeated such an overwhelming number of French Voltigeurs. Behind the French skirmishers were the remnants of their cavalry who had been advanced to check any British cavalry charge that might threaten the loose formation of Voltigeurs.

Peter d'Alembord had brought the two companies forward himself and, once they were deployed, he crossed to Sharpe's side. The two officers strolled half-way down the forward slope, then stopped to stare at the vast spread of enemy troops. 'Not a very encouraging sight,' d'Alembord said quietly.

The first muskets spat, yet for every British shot, two or three French muskets replied. To Sharpe's left some Riflemen held up the French advance for a few moments, but the French overwhelmed them with musketry and the

Greenjackets were forced back, leaving three men dead in the mud.

D'Alembord's men were similarly suffering. 'We're going to have to let them take the slope!' he said to Sharpe, instinctively seeking the Rifleman's approval.

'You haven't much choice, Peter.' Sharpe was on one knee, his rifle at his shoulder. He fired at a French sergeant, but the muzzle smoke prevented him from seeing whether the bullet hit. He began to reload. A hundred yards to his right a line of Frenchmen was already near the ridge's crest. Peter d'Alembord's two companies were temporarily holding the skirmishers in their front, but they would soon be outflanked, and even as Sharpe rammed his next bullet home he saw a rush of blue-uniformed men force back a section of Harry Price's company. Bullets were hissing and thrumming near Sharpe, presumably attracted by the sight of the two officers so close together.

Sharpe, his rifle reloaded, ran a few paces to his right, dropped to his knee, and looked for an enemy officer.

D'Alembord gave the smallest gasp. 'Oh, God!'

'What is it?'

'Jesus Christ!' The blasphemy was uttered more in anger than in pain. D'Alembord had been hit, and the force of the blow had knocked him backwards, but he had somehow kept his footing even though the bullet had struck his right thigh. Now he staggered with his right hand clamped over the wound. Blood was seeping through his fingers. 'It's all right,' he said to Sharpe, 'it doesn't hurt.' He tried to take a pace forward, and almost fell. 'It's all right.' His face had gone pale with shock.

'Here!' Sharpe put an arm under d'Alembord's shoulder and half carried him and half walked him up the slope.

D'Alembord was hissing with every step. 'I'll be all right. Leave me!'

'Shut up, Dally!'

Harper saw them as they crossed the ridge's crest and galloped forward with Sharpe's horse. 'Take him back to the surgeons!' Sharpe called up to the Irishman, then gave d'Alembord a mighty heave that swung him painfully into the empty saddle. 'Wrap your sash round the wound!' Sharpe told d'Alembord, then slapped the mare's rump to speed her out of range of the skirmishers' fire.

Sharpe turned back to the heated, choking air in the valley. The French were pressing everywhere. More frightening still, a column of enemy troops was marching towards La Haye Sainte, but that was not Sharpe's business. His business was the enemy immediately in front and, reduced to being a Rifleman again, he knelt and searched for an officer or sergeant. He saw a man with a scabbard not a hundred yards away and fired. When the smoke cleared, the man was gone.

Harry Price backed nervously up the slope. 'Where's Peter?'

'He got one in the leg! It's not serious.'

'This is bloody serious, sir! I've lost ten men, probably more.'

'Pull back. What's the name of the new light company man?'

'Matthew Jefferson.'

Sharpe cupped his hands. 'Captain Jefferson! Pull back!'

Jefferson waved a hand in reply, then ordered Huckfield to sound the whistle that recalled the skirmishers. The redcoats ran back to the crest, dropped again, and fired a last feeble volley at the French Voltigeurs. A shell exploded behind the crest, showering Jefferson with earth. A roundshot crashed past Sharpe, its sound like a sudden overwhelming wind. Musket-balls whip-cracked too close. Sharpe waited till Harry Price's company was safely past him, then shouted at Price to run.

They ran back together, but Price tumbled, then gasped as the breath was knocked out of him by his fall. Sharpe twisted back to help him, but it was only a pair of ridiculous spurs that had tripped the younger man. 'Take the damn things off, Harry!'

'I like them.' Price stumbled on. To their right and left other battalions were reluctantly climbing to their feet, then forming lines of four ranks. They could not fight off skirmishers lying down, nor did they dare risk a charge of the French cavalry that had reached the bottom of the slope, and a four rank line offered more protection against horsemen than a two rank formation. It also meant that every cannon-ball that hit could take as many as four men with it.

But there was nothing to be done, except suffer.

The French skirmishers, thick along the crest of the ridge, raked the battalions with musket-fire. The surviving British cannons hammered canister at the Voltigeurs, but their scattered formation saved the French from heavy casualties. The enemy Voltigeurs now ruled the ridge's crest, while the British skirmishers, overwhelmed by the French mass, could only form on their battalions. Every few moments, when the enemy skirmishers became too insistent or advanced too far, a battalion would charge forward and drive them back. A single battalion volley also had the effect of clearing the enemy skirmishers off the crest, but they always returned, their losses made up from reinforcements despatched from the valley.

Cavalry could scour the Voltigeurs away, but the Duke had lost his heavy cavalry and was keeping his best remaining horsemen, the Germans and British light cavalry, to cover his retreat if disaster struck. He still had a Dutch cavalry brigade and the Prince of Orange was ordered to bring it forward. They came, curb chains jingling and sabres drawn. 'They're just to clear the ridge face!' the

Duke's aide ordered. 'No damned heroics. Just gallop along the face and sabre the skirmishers!'

But the Dutch horsemen refused to charge. They sat lumpen in their saddles, their doughy faces stubborn and sullen. They stared blankly at the churning strike of shot and shell and no words would persuade them to spur into the quagmire of mud, fire and iron. The Prince, told of their cowardice, pretended not to hear. Instead he just stared at the farm of La Haye Sainte that was now besieged by an overwhelming throng of French infantry. The British cannons on the crest by the elm tree were pouring roundshot into the French ranks, and a battery of howitzers was lobbing shrapnel into the valley, but the French infantry seemed to soak up the punishment as they edged ever closer to the beleaguered farm. La Haye Sainte's orchard was already captured, and the French had brought cannon down the road to pour shot after shot into the besieged farm buildings.

The Prince knew that the centre of the Duke's line would be open to disastrous attack if the farm fell. Suddenly he knew he must save the farm. The glory of the idea blossomed in his mind. Fulfilment of the idea would utterly obliterate any shameful memory of the Red Germans, or of the sullen Dutch cavalry. The Prince saw his chance of glory and renown. He would rescue the farm, hold the line's centre, and win the battle. 'Rebecque!'

In the eastern half of the valley, in the dangerous re-entrant from where the Dutch-Belgians had fled at the first approach of the French, the First Battalion of the 27th Regiment of the Line now stood in square and suffered. They were the Inniskillings, and their only shelter was the screen of smoke that the French gunners created before their own cannon, but the enemy artillery had the Inniskillings' range and, even though fired blind, roundshot after roundshot crashed into the Irish ranks. Their Colonel ordered another issue of rum and the Sergeants doggedly closed the thinning ranks, but there was nothing else anyone could do except stand and die, and that the Irish did.

They might have deployed out of square, but the Emperor made sure his cavalry was always threatening and so the Irish were forced to stay in their vulnerable square like a great fat target for the gunners and the Voltigeurs who infested the eastern half of the valley as thickly as they swarmed in the west.

Some of those Voltigeurs, fearful that a French victory and pursuit might take them away from the rich plunder of the battlefield, took care to enrich themselves before the British line shattered. The dead and injured of the British heavy cavalry littered the valley floor and, though the pockets of many of the casualties had been hastily searched already, the Voltigeurs had the luxury of time in which they could slit the uniform seams or tear out the greasy helmet liners where men liked to hide their precious gold coins. Some of the French skirmishers carried pliers which they used to extract fine white teeth that Parisian dentists would buy to make into dentures.

One fortunate Frenchman found a cavalryman's body that sported a fine pair of brown-topped, silk-tasselled boots. He first took the spurs off the heels, then tugged at the right boot. The body jerked, cried aloud, and a horrid face in which the eyes were nothing but crusts of blood stared wildly and blindly towards the Frenchman.

'You frightened me!' the Voltigeur chided the wounded man cheerfully.

'For God's sake, kill me.' Lord John Rossendale, half-crazed with pain, spoke in English.

'You just stay still,' the Voltigeur said in French, then dragged off his lordship's expensive boots. He noted that the Englishman's breeches were made of the finest whipcord and though the right thigh had been slashed by a blade the breeches would doubtless mend well, and so the Voltigeur undid the waist buttons and dragged the breeches free. Lord John, his broken thigh grating with each tug, screamed foully.

'Noisy bugger!' The Voltigeur rolled the breeches into a ball that he thrust inside his jacket. Then, fearing that Lord John's scream might have attracted the untimely attraction of his Sergeant, the Frenchman ostentatiously loaded his musket and, pretending to be merely doing his job, used Lord John as a rest for the barrel that he aimed towards the beleaguered Inniskillings. 'Mind the bang!' the Voltigeur said happily, then fired.

'Kill me! Please!' Lord John spoke in French. 'Please!'

'I'm not going to kill you!' the Voltigeur protested. 'I can't do that. It wouldn't be right! I won't even take your teeth!' He gave his lordship's shoulder a sympathetic pat, then went to find more plunder.

And Lord John, lost in a universe of unjust pain, moaned.

Peter d'Alembord lay on the unfolded backboard of a cart that was serving as a surgeon's table. The wooden boards of the cart were soaked with blood, while the surgeon's hands were so steeped in it that the skin of his fingertips had gone soft and wrinkled. 'Are you ready, Major?' The surgeon had a strong West Country accent.

'I'm ready.' D'Alembord had refused to drink any rum to dull the agony of the surgery, nor would he accept the leather gag to bite on. It was important that he showed no reaction to the pain, for such stoicism was expected of a soldier.

'There are no bones broken,' the surgeon said, 'and there's not even a major blood vessel cut, so you're a lucky man. Hold his leg, Bates!' The orderlies had already cut away the sash d'Alembord had used as a bandage and slit open the expensive breeches which he had worn to the Duchess's ball. The surgeon wiped away the welling blood from the lips of the wound with his fingers. 'This won't be half as bad as having a baby, Major, so be grateful.' He thrust a cigar into his mouth and picked up a blood-stained probe.

A pain like a lance of fire streaked up d'Alembord's thigh and into his groin. The surgeon was probing for the bullet with a long thin metal rod. D'Alembord dared not cry aloud, for he had watched a man of his own battalion lose a leg not a moment since, and the man had uttered not a sound as the bone-saw ground away at this thigh bone. Besides, Patrick Harper was close by and d'Alembord would not shame himself by making any noise in front of Harper.

'I've got the little bastard!' the surgeon mumbled past the wet cigar stub. 'Can you hear the little devil, Major?'

D'Alembord could hear nothing but the thud of gunfire and the crash of shells exploding and the splintering roar of burning ammunition, but the surgeon was evidently scraping the edge of the musket-ball with his probe. 'I won't be long now,' the surgeon said cheerfully, then fortified himself with a long swig of rum. 'This next moment might be slightly uncomfortable, Major, but be glad you're not whelping a child, eh?'

'Jesus!' D'Alembord could not resist whimpering the imprecation, but he still managed to lie motionless as the pain gouged and routed about inside his leg. A shell exploded nearby and a fragment of its casing whistled and smoked overhead.

'Here it comes!' The surgeon had succeeded in gripping the bullet with his narrow-bladed tongs. 'Your hand! Hold out your hand, man! Quick!' D'Alembord dutifully held out his hand and the surgeon dropped the bloody little bullet into his palm. 'I'll just extract what's left of your dancing togs, Major, then you'll be as quick as a trivet again.'

There was another minute's excruciating pain as the shreds of cloth were picked from the wound, then something cool and soothing was poured onto d'Alembord's thigh. Sweat was beaded on his forehead, but he knew the worst was over. He wiped the bloody bullet on his jacket and held the small missile before his eyes. Such a small thing, no bigger than his thumbnail.

The orderlies bandaged his thigh, then helped him down from the cart. 'You should rest for a time.' The surgeon wiped his hands on his apron which was already drenched in blood. 'Go back into the trees, Major. There's some tarpaulins there to keep the damp out.'

'No.' D'Alembord tried to walk and found he could hobble without too much pain. 'Thank you, but no.'

The surgeon had already forgotten him. A man with an arm blown away and three ribs exposed was being lifted onto the cart. Harper brought the horses forward. 'Shouldn't you rest, Mr d'Alembord?'

'I'm going back to the battalion, Harper.'

'Are you sure, now?'

'It was a flesh wound, nothing else.'

'But painful, eh?'

D'Alembord almost screamed with agony as Harper heaved him up into Sharpe's saddle. 'You should know,' he managed to reply with admirable self-restraint.

'Funnily enough,' the Irishman said, 'I've never had a bad wound. Mr Sharpe, now, he's different, he's always getting bits chopped out of him, but I must be lucky.'

'Don't tempt fate,' d'Alembord said fervently.

'Considering what fate's done to Ireland, Major, what the hell more can it do to me?' Harper laughed. 'Back to duty, eh?'

'Back to duty.' D'Alembord knew he could have ridden away from the battlefield, and no one would have blamed him, but in his time he had seen more than one officer lose an arm and still go back to the battle line after the surgeon had chopped and sawed the stump into shape. So d'Alembord would go back, because he was an officer and that was his duty. He hid his terror, tried to smile, and rode to the ridge.

Major Vine was shot through his left eye by a skirmisher. He gave a last bad-tempered grunt, fell from his saddle, and lay stone-dead beside Lieutenant-Colonel Ford's horse. The Colonel whimpered, then stared down at the fallen Major whose face now appeared to have one vast red Cyclopean eye. 'Major Vine?' Ford asked nervously.

The dead man did not move.

Ford tried to remember Vine's Christian name. 'Edwin?' he tried, or perhaps it was Edward? 'Edward?' But Edwin Vine lay quite still. A fly settled next to the fresh pool of blood that had been his left eye.

'Major Vine!' Ford snapped as though a direct order would resurrect the dead.

'He's a gonner, sir,' a sergeant from the colour party offered helpfully, then, seeing his Colonel's incomprehension, made a more formal report. 'The Major's dead, sir.'

Ford smiled a polite response and stifled an urge to scream. He did not know it, but a quarter of the men who had marched with him to battle were now either dead or injured. RSM McInerney had been disembowelled by a roundshot that had killed two other men and torn the arm off another. Daniel Hagman was bleeding to death with a bullet in his lungs. His breath bubbled with blood as he tried to speak. Sharpe knelt beside him and held his hand. 'I'm sorry, Dan.' Sharpe had known Hagman the longest of all the men in the light company. The old poacher was a good soldier, shrewd, humorous and loyal. 'I'll get you to the surgeons, Dan.'

'Bugger them surgeons, Mr Sharpe,' Hagman said, then said nothing more. Sharpe shouted at two of the bandsmen to carry him back to the surgeons, but Hagman was dead. Sergeant Huckfield lost the small finger of his left hand to a musket-ball. He stared in outrage at the wound, then, refusing to leave the battalion, sliced once with his knife then asked Captain Jefferson to wrap a strip of cloth round the bleeding stump. Private Clayton was shaking with fear, but somehow managed to stand steady and look straight into the eyes of the French skirmishers who still roamed the ridge crest with apparent impunity. Next to him Charlie Weller was trying to remember childhood's prayers, but, though childhood was not very far in his past, the prayers would not come. 'Oh, God,' he said instead.

'God's no bloody help,' Clayton said, then ducked as a skirmisher's bullet almost knocked the crown off his shako.

'Stand still there!' Sergeant Huckfield shouted.

Clayton pulled his shako straight and muttered a few curses at the Sergeant. 'We should be bloody attacking,' he said after he had exhausted his opinion of Huckfield's mother.

'In time we will.' Charlie Weller still had a robust faith in victory.

Another musket bullet went within inches of Clayton's head. He shivered helplessly. 'If I'm a dead 'un, Charlie, you'll look after Sally, won't you?' Clayton's wife, Sally, was by far the prettiest wife in the battalion. 'She likes you, she does,' Clayton explained his apparent generosity.

'You're going to be all right.' Charlie Weller, despite the hiss and crash of bullet and shell, felt a frisson of excitement at the thought of Sally.

'Sweet God, I've had enough of this!' Clayton looked round to see what officers still lived. 'Bloody hell! Major Vine's a dead 'un! Good riddance to the bastard.'

'Look to your front, Private Clayton!' Sergeant Huckfield touched the New Testament in his top pocket, and prayed that the damned French skirmishers would soon run out of ammunition.

Colonel Joseph Ford almost vomited as he tried to wipe away the globules of Major Vine's brains that smeared his breeches. Ford was feeling horribly alone; one major was dead, the other was wounded and gone to the surgeons, and all around him his precious battalion was being chewed to pieces by the guns and the skirmishers. He took off his spectacles and rubbed frantically at the lens, only to discover that his sash was thickly smeared with scraps of Major Vine's brains. Ford gasped for horrified breath and knew he was going to vomit helplessly.

'It's nothing to do with me!' a harsh voice suddenly spoke from beside Ford's horse, 'but I'd suggest a fifty-pace advance, give the bastards one good volley, then retire.'

Ford, his impulse to vomit checked by the voice, frantically pulled on the smudged eyeglasses and found himself staring into the sardonic face of Lieutenant-Colonel Sharpe. Ford tried to say something in reply, but no sound came.

'With your permission, sir?' Sharpe asked punctiliously.

Ford, too frightened to open his mouth, just nodded.

'South Essex!' Sharpe's thunderous voice startled the nearest men. It did not matter that he had inadvertently used the battalion's old name, they knew who they were and who, at last, was giving them direction in the middle of horror. 'Front rank! Fix bayonets!'

'Thank Christ for bloody Sharpie,' Clayton said fervently, then half crouched to hold his musket between his knees as he pulled out his bayonet and slotted it onto his musket.

Sharpe thrust between the files of Number Five Company, placing himself in the very centre of the battalion's front rank. '"Talion will advance fifty paces! At the double! By the right! March!' As the men started forward, Sharpe drew his long sword. 'Come on, you buggers! Cheer! Let the bastards know you're coming to kill them! Cheer!'

The battalion ran forward, bayonets outstretched. And they cheered. They knew Sharpe, they had followed him into battle before, and they liked to hear that voice shouting commands. They trusted him. He gave them confidence and victory. They cheered even louder as the mass of startled skirmishers on the ridge's crest upped and fled from their sudden advance. Sharpe had run ahead of them to stand with his drawn sword on the very lip of the crest.

'Halt!' Sharpe's voice, trained as a sergeant, instantly silenced and stopped the shrunken battalion. Ahead of them the French Voltigeurs were dropping into new firing positions.

Sharpe turned to face the battalion. 'Front rank kneel! Aim at the buggers! Don't throw away this volley! Find your man and kill the bastard! Aim for their bellies!' He pushed his way between two men of the kneeling front rank then turned to look at the French. He saw a Voltigeur's musket pointing directly at him and he knew that the Frenchman was taking careful aim. He also knew he could not duck or dodge, but just had to trust in the French musket's inaccuracy. 'Aim!' he shouted. The Frenchman fired and Sharpe felt the wind of the ball on his cheek like a sudden hot blow. 'Fire!'

The massive volley crashed down the slope. Perhaps twenty Frenchmen died, and twice as many were wounded. 'Light company! Stay where you are and reload! Front rank, stand! No one told you to run!' Sharpe remained on the crest. Behind him a man was lying dead, struck in the head by the bullet intended for Sharpe. 'Light company! Chain formation, quick now!'

The battalion's skirmishers spread along the crest. Their new Captain, Jefferson, jiggled impatiently, wanting to be away from this exposed ridge where the roundshot slashed and thudded, but Sharpe was determined that the Company's volley would have an effect. The men finished reloading their muskets, then knelt. The surviving French skirmishers were creeping forward again, filling the gaps torn by the battalion volley. 'Wait for the order!' Sharpe called to his old Company. 'Find your targets! Clayton!'

'Sir?'

'There's an officer on your right. A tall bugger with a red moustache. I want him dead or I'll blame you for it! Company!' He paused a second. 'Fire!'

The smaller volley did more damage, though whether the moustached officer was shot, Sharpe could not tell. He shouted at the men to retire to battalion. The manoeuvre had gained a few moments' respite, nothing more, but it was better to hit back than simply endure the galling punishment of the enemy skirmishers.

Sharpe lingered at the crest a few more seconds. It was not bravado, but rather curiosity because, five hundred paces to his left, he could just see two red-coated infantry battalions of the King's German Legion advancing in column. They marched towards La Haye Sainte with their colours flying, presumably to drive away the French infantry who clustered about the farm.

He would have liked to have watched longer, but the enemy was creeping back towards the crest, and so Sharpe turned and walked back to the battalion. 'Thank you for the privilege, Colonel!' he shouted to Ford.

Ford said nothing. He was in no mood to appreciate Sharpe's tact, instead he felt slighted and diminished by the Rifleman's competence. Ford knew that he should have given the orders, and that he should have taken the battalion forward, but his bowels had turned to water and his mind was a haze of fear and confusion. He had fought briefly in southern France, but he had never seen a horror like this; a battlefield where men were dying by the minute, where his battalion shrank as the files closed over the gaps left by the dead, and where it seemed that every man must die before the field's appetite for blood was slaked. Ford snatched off his fouled spectacles and scrubbed their lenses on a corner of his saddle-cloth. The white smoke and cannon's glare melded into a smear of horror before his eyes. He wished it would end, he just wished it would end. He no longer cared if it ended in victory or defeat, he just wanted it to end.

But the Emperor had only just started to fight.

The Duke of Wellington no longer troubled himself about the Prince of Orange. At the battle's commencement, when some niceties of polite usage persisted, the Duke had taken care to inform the Prince of any orders involving those troops nominally under the Prince's command, but now in the desperate moments of pure survival the Duke simply ignored the Young Frog.

Which did not mean that the Prince considered himself redundant. On the contrary, he saw his own genius as the allies' sole hope of victory and was prepared to use the last shreds of his authority to achieve it. Which meant La Haye Sainte must be saved, and to save it the Prince ordered the remnants of the 2nd Infantry Brigade of the King's German Legion to attack the besieging French.

Colonel Christian Ompteda, the brigade commander, formed his two battalions into close column of companies, ordered them to fix bayonets, and then to advance into the suffocating mix of heated air and bitter smoke that filled the valley. The German objective was the field to the west of La Haye Sainte where the French skirmishers were pressing close and thick on the beleaguered farm.

The Germans reached the crest and were about to march down on the French when the Prince of Orange galloped to intercept them. 'In line!' the Prince shouted. 'In line! You must overlap them! I insist you advance in line!'

Colonel Ompteda, his battalions halted on the very edge of the valley and under fire from the French guns, protested that there were enemy cavalry patrolling the valley floor. The Prince turned sarcastic eyes towards the smoke. 'I see no cavalry.'

'Your Highness, I must insist that –'

'You cannot insist! You will form line! Damn you!' The Prince was ebullient, feeding off the crash and hammer of the guns. He felt himself born to this heated chaos of battle. He did not give a fig that Ompteda was a man who had spent a lifetime soldiering; the Prince had the passionate certainty of his convictions and not even his experiences with Halkett's brigade at Quatre Bras nor the massacre of the Red Germans would sway him. 'I order you into line! Or do you wish me to appoint another brigade commander?' he shouted into the Colonel's face.

Ompteda, in whom obedience was deeply ingrained, reluctantly deployed his two battalions into line. The Prince, scornful of Ompteda's timidity and certain that he had just given the orders necessary to bring glowing victory, watched triumphantly as the German bayonets marched into the valley.

Fifty paces from the edge of the skirmishers, Ompteda ordered his men to charge.

The Germans ran forward, their bayonets bright in the gloom under the smoke. The French infantry, taken utterly by surprise, fled from the appalling threat of the seventeen-inch blades. The German colours swirled forward into the musket smoke left by the skirmishers.

'There!' The Prince, happy on his hill, exulted in the success.

'Let me congratulate Your Highness,' Winckler, one of the Prince's Dutch aides, smirked at his master's side.

Lieutenant Simon Doggett, who was a few yards to the Prince's right, stared beyond the infantry and could have sworn he saw a file of cavalry trotting across the valley. Or at least he was sure he saw the glint of helmets and the swirl of horsehair plumes in a rift of the smoke. 'Sir? There's cavalry out there, sir!'

The Prince turned furiously on the Lieutenant. 'That's all you British ever see! Cavalry! You're nervous, Doggett. If you can't endure the rigours of battle, you shouldn't be a soldier. Isn't that right, Winckler?'

'Entirely right, Your Highness.'

Rebecque listened to the conversation and said nothing. He just stared into the shifting white scrims where the muskets crackled like burning thorns.

'You see!' The Prince made a great play of peering into the valley, shading his eyes and gaping like a village idiot. 'No horses! Lieutenant Doggett? Where are your gee-gees?'

Simon Doggett was no longer certain that he had seen any cavalry, for the valley was thick with smoke and he feared that nervousness had played tricks with his perception, but he stubbornly held his ground. 'I'm fairly sure I saw them, sir, in the smoke. They were Cuirassiers, off to the right there.'

But the Prince had taken enough from pusillanimous Englishmen. 'Get rid of the boy, Rebecque! Just get rid of him. Send him back to his nursemaid.' The Prince's horse shied sideways as a cannon-ball slashed close past. 'There!' the Prince cried triumphantly as the smoke drifted aside to reveal that the KGL infantry had scoured the last Frenchmen away from the farm's western walls. 'You see? No cavalry! Boldness wins!'

'Your Highness's boldness wins,' Winckler hastened to correct his master.

A trumpet interrupted the Prince's next words. The trumpet call sounded from the valley, from inside the smoke where the Prince had insisted no cavalry lurked, but out of which, like avenging furies, the troop of Cuirassiers now led the charge.

Rebecque groaned. In almost the exact same place as the Hanoverians had been slaughtered, the KGL now suffered. The cavalry, a mixture of Cuirassiers, Lancers and Dragoons who had survived the slaughter of the horsemen among the British squares, now struck the flank of Ompteda's right-hand battalion. To Rebecque it seemed that the red-coated infantry simply disappeared beneath the swarm of mounted killers. To the French horsemen this was a blessed moment of revenge on the infantry who had made them bleed and suffer earlier in the day.

The Prince just stared. He had gone pale, but he made no move to help the men he had just doomed. His mouth opened slackly and his fingers twitched on his reins.

The Germans stood no chance. The horsemen sabred and stabbed from the open flank. The men of the right-hand KGL battalion broke into hopeless flight and were run down by the horses. The left-hand battalion formed a rally square to protect its colour, but the right-hand battalion was destroyed. The Prince turned away as a French swordsman captured a KGL colour and hefted it aloft in a gesture of triumph. Colonel Ompteda died trying to save the flag. The French infantry ran to add their bayonets to the horsemen's blades. The German survivors, pitifully few, inched in their rough square back towards the ridge. They too might have been doomed, but some of their own cavalry streamed down from the elm tree to drive the enemy back.

A French cavalry trumpeter sounded a derisive flurry as the remnants of the King's German Legion limped back up the slope. A Cuirassier brandished the captured colour, taunting the suffering British ridge with this foretaste of French victory.

The Prince did not look at the Germans nor at the exultant French. Instead he stared imperiously towards the east. 'It isn't my fault if men won't fight properly!'

None of the staff answered. Not even Winckler was minded to soften the disaster with flattery.

'We gave the garrison a breathing space, did we not?' The Prince gestured at La Haye Sainte that was once more ringed with smoke, but again no one answered and the Prince, who believed he deserved loyalty from his military family, turned furiously on his staff. 'The Germans should have formed square! It wasn't my fault!' He looked from man to man, demanding agreement, but only Simon Doggett was brave enough to meet the Prince's petulant and bulging eyes.

'You're nothing but a silk stocking full of shit,' Doggett said very clearly, and utterly astonished himself by so repeating Patrick Harper's scornful verdict on the Prince.

There was an appalled silence. The Prince gaped. Rebecque, not quite sure whether he had heard correctly, opened his mouth to protest, but could not find adequate words.

Doggett knew he had just seconds to keep the initiative. He tugged at his horse's reins. 'You're a bloody murderer!' he said to the Prince, then slashed back his spurs and galloped away. In a few seconds the smoke hid him.

The Prince stared after him. Rebecque hastened to assure His Highness that Doggett's wits had clearly been loosened by the stress of battle. The Prince nodded acceptance of the facile explanation, then turned furiously on his staff again. 'I'm surrounded by incompetents! That bloody man should have formed square! Is it my fault if a damned German doesn't know his job?' The Prince's indignation and anger spilled out in furious passion. 'Is it my fault that the French are winning? Is it?'

And in that, at least, the Prince spoke true. The French, at last, were winning the battle.

CHAPTER 19

French victory became a virtual certainty when La Haye Sainte fell. The farm's German defenders ran out of rifle ammunition and the French attackers tore down the barricaded doors and flooded into the farm buildings. For a time they were held off by bayonets and swords as the defenders fought furiously in the corridors and stables. The Germans made barricades of their own and the French dead, then rammed their sword-bayonets over the piled bodies, and for a time it seemed as if their steel and fury might yet hold the farm, but then the French musket volleys tore into the Riflemen and the French musket wadding set fire to the stable straw, and the defenders, choking and decimated, were forced out.

Those Riflemen who escaped from La Haye Sainte ran up the ridge's slope as the victorious French swarmed into the farm buildings. The Riflemen of the 95th had long been driven from the adjacent sandpit, so now the centre bastion of the Duke's line was gone. The French brought cannon into the farm's kitchen garden and, at perilously short range, opened fire on the ridge. Voltigeurs, given a new territory to exploit, spread up the forward slope to open a killing fire on the troops nearest to the elm tree.

An immediate counter-attack could have recaptured the farm while the French hold on its buildings was still new and tenuous, but the Duke had no reserves left. Every man who could fight in the Duke's army was now committed to defend the ridge, while the rest of his troops had either fled, were wounded, or were dead. What was left of the Duke's army was a thin line of men stretched along a blood-soaked ridge. The line was two ranks deep, no more, and in places the ridge seemed empty where the battalions had been forced to shrink into four ranks as a precaution against the cavalry that still lurked in the smoke that drifted at the slope's foot.

The French were winning.

The Duke, hardly a man given to despair, muttered a prayer for the coming of either the Prussians or the night. But both, this day, came painfully slowly.

The first French attacks on the British ridge had failed, but now their gunners and their skirmishers were grinding down the British defence. Men died in ones and twos, but constantly. The already truncated battalions shrank as the surviving Sergeants ordered the files to close the gaps. Men who had started the day four files apart became neighbours, and still the gun-fire shredded the ranks and still the Voltigeurs fired from the smoke and still the Sergeants chanted the litany of a battalion's death, 'Close up! Close up!'

Victory was a mere drumbeat away because the British line had been scraped thin as a drumskin.

The Emperor felt the glorious certainty of victory. His will now stretched clear across the battlefield. It was seven o'clock on a summer's evening, the sun was slanting steeply through the remnants of cloud and skeins of smoke, and the Emperor held the lives and deaths of all three armies in his hand. He had won. All he now needed to do was fend off the Prussians with his right hand, and annihilate the British with his left.

He had won. Yet he would wait a few moments before savouring the victory. He would let the guns in the newly captured La Haye Sainte finish their destruction of the British centre, and only then would he unleash his immortals.

To glory.

The bombardment ground on, but slower now for the French gun barrels were degrading from their constant fire. Some guns shot their vents, leaving a gaping hole where their touchholes had been, while others broke their carriages, and one twelve-pounder exploded as an air bubble in its cast barrel finally gave way. Yet more than enough French cannon remained in service to sustain the killing. The surviving British infantry was numbed and deafened by the fire. Less than half of Wellington's army was still capable of fighting. Their faces were blackened by battle and streaked white with sweat, while their eyes were reddened from the irritation of the powder residues that had sparked from their musket pans.

Yet, battered and bleeding, they clung to the ridge beneath the dwarfing pall of churning smoke that belched from the burning ammunition wagons. The French cannonade had long assumed an inhuman inevitability; as though the gunners had sprung free some malevolent force from within the earth itself; a force which now dispassionately ground the battlefield into blood and embers and ragged soil. No humans were visible on the French-held ridge; there was just the bank of smoke into which the guns flashed fire that was diffused into lurid flares that erupted bright, then slowly faded into gloom.

Sharpe, standing a few feet to one side of his old battalion, watched the ominous bursts of red light ignite and die, and each unnatural glow marked a few more seconds survived. The fear had come with inactivity, and each minute that Sharpe waited motionless on the ridge made him feel more vulnerable as though, skin by skin, his bravery was peeling away. Harper, crouching silent beside Sharpe, shivered as he stared wide-eyed at the strange inhuman fires that pulsed amidst the smoke.

This was unlike any battlefield that either man had known before. In Spain the fields had seemed to stretch away to infinity, but here the combat was held tight within the cockpit of the small valley above which the smoke made an unnatural early dusk. Beyond the battle's margin, out where the crops stood unharmed and no blood trickled in the plough furrows, the sunlight shone through ragged clouds on peaceful fields, but the valley itself was a piece of hell on earth, flickering with flame and belching smoke.

Neither Sharpe nor Harper spoke much. No one was speaking much in the British line any more. Sometimes a sergeant ordered the files to close, but the orders were unnecessary now. Each man was simply enduring as best he could.

The French skirmishers were falling back as their ammunition became exhausted. That, at least, gave some relief, and let the British battalions lie down on the crushed mud and straw. The Voltigeurs did not retire all the way to their own ridge, but waited on the valley floor for a fresh supply of cartridges to be brought forward. Only in the British centre, in front of the newly captured La Haye Sainte, were newly committed skirmishers advancing up the slope beneath the raking canister fire of the two eight-pounder guns that the French had placed in the farm's kitchen garden.

Peter d'Alembord, insisting that he was well, had returned to Colonel Ford's side. He still rode Sharpe's horse that he now stood beneath the battalion's colours, which had been torn to yellow shreds by the skirmishers' bullets. Colonel Ford's ears were so dulled by the incessant percussion of the guns that he could hardly hear the small remarks d'Alembord made. Not that Ford cared.

He was clutching his horse's reins as though they were his last hold on sanity.

A single horseman rode slowly in the emptiness behind the British battalions. His horse picked a slow path through the broken gun carriages and past the rows of red-coated dead. Shell fragments smoked on the scorched and trampled crops. The horseman was Simon Doggett who now sought his own battalion of Guardsmen, but as he rode westwards he saw the two Riflemen crouching close to the ridge's crest. Doggett turned his horse towards the Greenjackets and reined in close behind them.

'He did it again, sir. He damn well did it again,' Doggett's outraged indignation made him sound very young, 'so I told him he was a silk stocking full of shit.'

Sharpe turned. For a second he blinked in surprise as though he did not recognize Doggett, then he seemed to snap out of the trance induced by the numbing gun-fire. 'You did what?'

Doggett was embarrassed. 'I told him he was a silk stocking full of shit.'

Harper laughed softly. A shell whimpered overhead to explode far in the rear. A roundshot followed to strike the ridge in front of Sharpe and spew up a shower of wet earth. Doggett's horse jerked its face away from the spattering mud.

'He killed them,' Doggett said in pathetic explanation.

'He killed who?' Harper asked.

'The KGL. There were two battalions, all that was left of a brigade, and he put them in line and sent them to where the cavalry were waiting.'

'Again?' Sharpe sounded incredulous.

'They died, sir.' Doggett could not forget the sight of the swords and sabres rising and falling. He had watched one German running from the slaughter; the man had already lost his right arm to a sabre's slice, yet it had seemed that the man would still escape, but a Cuirassier had spurred after him and chopped down with his heavy blade and Doggett could have sworn that the dying man threw one hateful look up the slope to where his real killer was. 'I'm sorry, sir. There's no point in telling you. I tried to stop him, but he told me to go away.'

Sharpe did not respond, except to unsling his rifle and probe a finger into its pan to discover whether the weapon was still primed.

Doggett wanted Sharpe to share his anger at the Prince's callous behaviour. 'Sir!' he pleaded. Then, when there was still no reply, he spoke more self-pityingly. 'I've ruined my career, haven't I?'

Sharpe looked up at the young man. 'At least we can mend that, Doggett. Just wait here.'

Sharpe, without another word, began walking towards the centre of the British line while Harper took Doggett's bridle and turned his horse away from the valley. 'There are still a few skirmishers who wouldn't mind making you into a notch on their muskets,' the Irishman explained to Doggett. 'Did you really call the skinny bastard a silk stocking filled with shit?'

'Yes.' Doggett was watching Sharpe walk away.

'To his face?' Harper insisted.

'Indeed, yes.'

'You're a grand man, Mr Doggett! I'm proud of you.' Harper released Doggett's horse a few paces behind the colour party of the Prince of Wales's Own Volunteers. 'Now just wait here, sir. The Colonel and I won't be long.'

'Where are you going?' Doggett shouted after the Irishman.

'Not far!' Harper called back, then he followed Sharpe into a drifting bank of powder smoke and disappeared.

*　　*　　*

Sharpe was half-way to the elm tree when Harper caught him. 'What are you doing?' the Irishman asked.

'I'm sick of the royal bastard. How many more men will he kill?'

'So what are you doing?' Harper insisted.

'What someone should have done at his bloody birth. I'm going to strangle the bugger.'

Harper put a hand on Sharpe's arm. 'Listen –'

Sharpe threw the hand off and turned a furious face on his friend. 'I'm going, Patrick. Don't stop me!'

'I don't give a bugger if you kill him.' Harper was just as angry. 'But I'll be damned if you hang for it.'

'Damn the bloody rope.' Sharpe walked on, carrying his rifle in his right hand.

The ridge's centre was more thickly smothered with smoke than its flanks. The muzzle blast of the two cannon that the French had placed in La Haye Sainte's kitchen garden carried almost to the ridge's summit, and every shot pumped a filthy stinking fog to blanket the slope. The French were firing canister, punching a massive weight of musket-balls into the heart of the British defences. The British gunners, exposed on the skyline as they tried to return the fire, had been killed or wounded, allowing the enemy skirmishers to creep ever closer to the bullet-scarred elm tree from which every leaf and most of the bark had been blasted away.

Those staff officers who still lived, and they were not many, had sensibly retreated from the ravaged tree and now stood their horses well back from the ridge's summit. Sharpe could not see the Duke, but he found the Prince in his fur-edged uniform. The Prince was two hundred paces off, close to the highway and surrounded by his Dutch staff. It was a long shot for a rifle loaded with common cartridge instead of the extra-fine powder, and it would be a tricky shot because of the men who crowded close to the Prince.

'Not here!' Harper insisted.

A shattered gun limber and two dead horses lay not far away and Sharpe crouched in the wreckage to see whether it gave him the cover he needed.

'You'll never hit the bastard from this distance,' Harper said. 'They don't call him Slender Billy for nothing.'

'I will if God's on my side.'

'I wouldn't rely on God today.' The Irishman stared about the ridge top, seeking an idea, then saw a file of green-jacketed Riflemen running towards the valley. The Prince had spurred his horse to follow the Riflemen, thus taking himself closer to the embattled crest of the ridge.

'Where are those lads going?' Harper asked.

Sharpe saw the Greenjackets, and understood. The Duke must have gathered the remnants of his Riflemen and ordered them to stop the French guns firing from La Haye Sainte. It was a desperate throw, but Riflemen alone might succeed in silencing the murderous guns. Fifty Greenjackets were preparing to charge over the crest, and the Prince, who had never lacked bravery, could not resist going forward to watch their fight.

Sharpe suddenly upped and ran towards the Riflemen who had stopped just short of the crest and now crouched in a group as they fixed their long, brass-handled sword-bayonets onto their rifle muzzles. 'You're not coming,' he shouted at Harper who had begun to follow him.

'And how will you stop me?'

'You bloody deserve to die.' Sharpe dropped at the back of the squad of Riflemen, all of whose faces were blackened by the powder scraps exploded from their rifles' pans. Their commanding officer was Major Warren Dunnett whose face showed understandable resentment when he recognized Sharpe. 'Are you taking over?' he asked stiffly.

'It would be a great honour to serve under your command once again, Dunnett.' Sharpe could be very tactful when he wished.

Dunnett, pleased with the compliment, smiled grimly. 'We make this very quick!' he spoke to his fifty men. 'Use the blades to clear the slope, then make your shots count! Once you've fired, tap reload and hold off the Voltigeurs. You understand?' The men nodded, and Dunnett waited. He waited so long that Sharpe wondered whether Dunnett had lost his nerve, but instead it seemed that there was another identical group of Riflemen who were attacking from the far side of the highway and Dunnett's men merely waited for their signal so that the two groups crossed the ridge crest at the same moment.

Sharpe looked behind him. The Prince was fifty yards away, but staring over the Riflemen's heads towards La Haye Sainte. Sharpe, to lessen his chances of being recognized, smeared mud on his scarred face and shoved his tricorne hat into his belt.

From somewhere beyond the high road a bugle called the familiar running triplets of the order to open fire. 'That's the signal, my boys! Let's go!' Dunnett had waited six years to avenge himself on the French and now, his sabre drawn, he led the Riflemen over the crest.

The appearance of the Rifles was so sudden that the closest French skirmishers were trapped. The sword-bayonets rammed down, were kicked free, then carried on. Dunnett shouted an incoherent challenge and slashed madly with his sabre, not striking anyone, but hissing the blade so fiercely through the smoky air that the French scrambled to escape such an apparent maniac. The fifty Riflemen on the far side of the road attacked with the same sudden and vicious desperation, driving the panicked Voltigeurs down the long slope. The mad charge stopped a hundred yards short of La Haye Sainte as the Riflemen abandoned the pursuit of the French to take up their firing positions. First, before aiming, they unclipped their sword-bayonets so that the heavy blades would not unbalance their rifles.

Each man had loaded carefully. They had cleaned their rifle barrels by the old expedient of pissing down the barrels, sluicing the caked powder deposits loose, then pouring out the fouled liquid. Then, when the barrels had dried, and using the extra-fine powder they carried in their horns, the Riflemen had charged their rifles. They had wrapped their bullets in a scrap of greased leather that not only helped the bullet grip the spiralling lands in the barrel, but, when the weapon was fired, expanded to block any of the exploding gas escaping past the bullet through the barrel's grooves. It took over a minute to load a rifle so meticulously, but the resultant shot would be as accurate as any weapon in the world.

Now, in the brief space and time they had won, the Riflemen aimed at the gunners who were visible above the hedge of La Haye Sainte's kitchen garden. The range was a hundred yards; a simple rifle shot, but misted by the drifting smoke. The gunners in the garden were too busy serving their guns to be aware of the threat.

Dunnett did not hurry his men. He must have been tempted to urge them to fire quickly, for the French skirmishers were regrouping at the foot of the slope, but instead he trusted his men and they did not disappoint him.

The first rifles crashed their brass butts into shoulders bruised raw by a day's fighting. White smoke spurted across the slope. The French skirmishers began firing uphill and two Greenjackets lurched backwards. Other Riflemen still took careful aim. A gunner stared over his rammer at the slope and a bullet took him in his open mouth. A French artillery officer spun backwards, half clambered up, then began crawling under his gun's trail. More rifles fired. The officer slumped flat. A handful of gunners fled to the farmhouse where they crowded and obstructed each other in the narrow door, and where they were struck by a flail of rifle-fire. Those Greenjackets who had already fired reloaded, not with the fine powder and wrapped bullet, but by tap loading with a normal cartridge. Then they turned their weapons on the skirmishers.

'Withdraw!' Dunnett, the executions neatly carried out, shouted at his men.

'Got the bastard!' Harper shouted.

'Where?'

'Look at the tree, then left thirty yards.'

Sharpe was downhill of Harper. 'Kneel down. Aim your rifle at the farm.'

Harper, bemused, obeyed. He braced his left leg forward, knelt on his right knee, and aimed his rifle at the kitchen garden which seemed to be filled with dead artillerymen. The first Riflemen were already running uphill. 'Hurry, for Christ's sake!' Harper muttered.

Sharpe lay flat on the ground and thrust his rifle between Harper's right thigh and left calf. Now Sharpe was effectively hidden from the staff officers close to the Prince who were all staring at the slaughtered gunners in the farm's garden. The Prince's horse was sideways on to the valley, presenting the Prince's left shoulder to Sharpe's rifle sights.

Sharpe had not had time to load with the good powder, or wrap a ball in leather. Instead he was using the commonplace coarse-powder cartridge, but if God was good this evening then an ordinary musket cartridge would suffice to avenge a thousand dead men and perhaps to save the lives of a thousand more.

'God save Ireland,' Harper hissed, 'but will you bloody hurry yourself?'

'Don't fire till I do,' Sharpe said calmly.

'We'll bloody die together if you don't hurry!' Sharpe

and Harper were almost the last Riflemen on the slope. The rest were sprinting back to safety, while the enraged Voltigeurs were hurrying after them. Harper changed his aim to point his rifle at a French officer who seemed particularly lively.

Sharpe aimed at the Prince's belly. The Young Frog was no more than a hundred paces away, close enough for Sharpe to see the ivory hilt of his big sabre. The rifle bullet would fall a foot over a hundred paces, so Sharpe raised the muzzle a tiny fraction.

'For the love of Ireland, will you bloody kill the bastard?'

'Ready?' Sharpe said. 'Fire!'

Both men fired together. Sharpe's rifle hammered his shoulder as smoke gouted to hide the Prince.

'Let's get out of here!' Harper saw his target plucked backwards, and now he hauled Sharpe to his feet and both men sprinted away towards the crest. Sharpe had just staged an assassination in full view of an army, but no one shouted at him and no one gaped in astonishment because no one, it seemed, had noticed a thing. A French roundshot screamed low overhead. A Voltigeur's bullet clipped Sharpe's sword scabbard and thudded into the ground.

Sharpe began laughing. Harper joined him. Together they reeled over the crest, still laughing. 'Right in the bloody belly!' Sharpe said with undisguised glee.

'With your bloody marksmanship, you probably killed the Duke.'

'It was a good shot, Patrick.' Sharpe spoke as fervently as any young Rifleman first mastering the complex weapon. 'I felt it go home!'

Major Warren Dunnett saw the two Riflemen grinning like apes and assumed they shared his pleasure at a task well done. 'A successful venture, I think?' Dunnett said modestly, but he was clearly eager for praise.

Sharpe gave it gladly. 'Very. Allow me to congratulate you, Dunnett.' The efficient Greenjacket foray had taken the French cannon at La Haye Sainte out of the battle. Their gunners were dead, cut down by the best marksmen in either army.

Sharpe led Harper to the rear of a British battery from where he could see Rebecque and a group of other Dutch officers helping the Prince away. The Prince had slumped sideways, and was only being held in his saddle by the support of his Chief of Staff. 'Harry!' Sharpe shouted at Lieutenant Webster, the Prince's only remaining British aide. 'What happened, Harry?'

Webster spurred across to Sharpe. 'It's bad news, sir. The Prince was hit in the left shoulder. It isn't too serious, but he can't stay on the field. One of those damned skirmishers hit him, I'm afraid.'

'Oh, shit,' Sharpe spoke with obvious remorse.

'It is indeed bad news, sir.' Webster offered sympathetic agreement. 'But his Highness will live. They're taking him to the surgeons, then back to Brussels.'

Harper was trying not to laugh. Sharpe scowled. 'A pity.' His voice was fervent. 'A damned bloody pity!'

'It's decent of you to be so upset, sir, especially after the way he's treated you,' Webster said awkwardly.

'But you'll present my regards, Lieutenant?'

'Of course I will, sir.' Webster touched his hat, then turned to ride after the wounded Prince.

Harper grinned and mocked Sharpe with imitation. 'It was a good shot. I felt it go home.'

'The bugger's gone, hasn't he?' Sharpe said defensively.

'Aye,' Harper admitted, then looked ruefully along the British line. 'And it won't be long before we're all gone either. I've never seen the like, nor have I.'

Sharpe heard the Irishman's despair of victory and was tempted to offer agreement, except that a small part of

Sharpe refused to give up hope even though he knew victory would need a miracle now. The British army was reduced to a ragged line of shrunken, bleeding battalions who crouched in the mud near to the ridge's crest that was crowned with smoke and riven by the explosions of mud thrown up by the continuing cannonade. Behind the battalions the rear of the ridge was empty but for the dead and the dying and the broken guns. At the edge of the forest the ammunition wagons burned to ash. There were no reserves left.

The two Riflemen trudged through the smoke towards the Prince of Wales's Own Volunteers while the French cannon, all but for the two that had been emplaced in La Haye Sainte's garden, fired on. The valley was shrouded by the cloud of smoke which flickered with the unearthly light of the guns.

By La Belle Alliance a tentative drum tap sounded. There was a pause as the drummer rammed the leather rings down the white ropes to tighten his drumskin, then the sticks sounded a jaunty and confident flurry. There was another pause, a shouted order, and a whole corps of drummers began to beat the *pas de charge*.

To tell the French that the Imperial Guard was about to fight.

The Emperor left La Belle Alliance, deigning to ride his white horse down the high road almost as far as La Haye Sainte. He stopped a few yards short of the captured farmhouse and watched his beloved Guard march past. To Napoleon's immortals would go the last honour of this day. The undefeated Guard would cross the pit of hell and break the final remnants of a beaten army.

The Guard marched with bayonets fixed. The flash of French cannon-fire reflected off the thicket of steel blades and from the glossy black sheen of their bearskin hats. The Guard wore the bearskins undecorated for battle, but each man had a waxed canvas sheath, eighteen inches long, strapped to his sabre-briquet, and in the sheaths were the plumes which they would fix to the bearskins for their victory parade in Brussels.

Seven battalions of the Guard marched past the Emperor. With them went the light and powerful horse-drawn eight-pounder cannon that would give the Guard close support when they reached the ridge.

The Guard's drummers drove the column on. Above them, bright in the valley's gloom, the spread wings and hooked claws of the Eagles glistened. The Guard carried their colours attached to the Eagles and the stiff silk flags made bright spots of colour against the black bearskins. The Guard were equipped with the finest muskets from the French armouries, their cartridges were packed with the best powder of the Paris mills, and their bayonets and short sabres were sharpened like razors. These were the unbeaten heroes of France marching to victory.

Yet the Guard had never fought Wellington's infantry.

They cheered as they passed their Emperor. He nodded pleased recognition at men deep in the marching ranks, and raised a hand in benediction to them all. Not an hour before this moment two battalions of the Guard had driven a whole Corps of Prussians out of Plancenoit, now seven full battalions would march against an enemy abraded to breaking point. The last of the Empire's cavalry rode on the Guard's flanks and, as the huge column headed deep into the smoke and heat on the valley's floor, the skirmishers flocked towards it and formed ranks to follow the Guard. Fifteen thousand infantry would make this last triumphant attack.

And it would be a triumph, for the Guard had never failed. But the Guard had never fought the redcoats either.

The Guard left the highway and slanted to their left after they had passed the Emperor. They would cross the fields and climb the slope midway on the British right, following the path made by the cavalry. The drums beat them on. They were led by Marshal Ney, bravest of the brave, who had already had four horses shot from beneath him this day, but who now, on his fifth horse, drew his sword and took his place at the column's head.

The Guard marched across the field of dead, beneath the gun-smoke, to seek the scarred and blackened ridge where the scum of Britain waited. The battle had come to its moment of truth, and the Emperor, his Guard gone to war, turned slowly back to wait for victory.

The Duke galloped along the right of his line. He could see French cavalry at the foot of the slope, but he dared not form his infantry into square for he had seen the approaching Guard and knew he must meet it in line. 'Form into four ranks!' he shouted at the remains of Halkett's brigade. 'Then lie down again! Four ranks! Lie down!'

The French cannon-fire was fitful now. The redcoats lay down, not to escape the sporadic cannonade, but so they would stay hidden till the very last moment of the Guard's attack. Only the British officers could see over the ridge's crest to where the French infantry was a dark shadow slashed by the slanting brightness of their bayonets. The column crept across the valley floor, seemingly propelled by the massive array of drums that beat the *pas de charge* and only paused to let the Guard give the great shout of the Empire at war: '*Vive l'Empereur!*'

Colonel Joseph Ford gazed with despair at the great assault. Next to him, and still mounted on Sharpe's horse, Peter d'Alembord gripped the saddle's pommel. The right side of his saddle-cloth was soaked with blood that had seeped from his bandaged wound. The leg throbbed hugely. He felt weak, so that the shadow of the advancing Guard under the smoke's shadow seemed to swim before his eyes. He wanted to call out for help for he knew he was losing strength and he suspected the surgeon had cut a blood vessel, but he would not give in; not now, not at this desperate moment when the enemy infantry was at last making its final assault.

'Sir! Colonel Ford, sir!' A staff officer from brigade, mounted on a limping horse, came to the rear of the battalion. 'Colonel Ford, sir?'

Ford turned dully to face the officer, but said nothing.

'What is it?' d'Alembord managed to ask.

'Colours to the rear,' the staff officer said.

For a few seconds d'Alembord forgot his wound and his nausea and his weakness. He forgot his fears because he had never heard of such an order, not once in all his years of fighting. 'Colours to the rear?' he finally managed to ask in a shocked voice.

'General's orders, sir. We're not to give the Crapauds the satisfaction of capturing them. I'm sorry, sir, I really am, but it's orders.' He gestured to the rear area where the colours of other battalions were already being carried away. 'Colour parties are to assemble behind our light cavalry, sir. Quickly, please, sir.'

D'Alembord looked to where two sergeants held the battalion's silk colours that had been riddled with musket-fire, blackened by smoke, and stained with blood. Seven men had died this day while holding the colours, but now the bright flags were to be rolled up, slid into their leather tubes, and hidden. D'Alembord thought there was something shameful in the gesture, but he supposed it was preferable to letting the French capture the colours of a whole army, and so he gestured the Sergeants to the rear. 'You heard the order. Take them away.'

D'Alembord's voice was resigned. Till this moment he had harboured a shred of optimism, but the order to take the colours to safety proved that the battle was lost. The French had won, and so the colours would begin the British retreat. The Emperor might have his victory, but he would not be given the satisfaction of piling the captured colours amidst the jubilant crowds of Paris. The great squares of heavy fringed silk were carried away, going back to where the last British cavalry waited to gallop them to safety. D'Alembord watched the flags disappear into the smoke and felt bereft.

Sharpe also saw the flags being carried to the rear. He had come back to the Prince of Wales's Own Volunteers, but, not wanting to interfere with either Ford or d'Alembord's command, he deliberately posted himself fifty paces from the battalion's left flank. He loaded his rifle.

Harper, his rifle already reloaded, watched the Imperial Guard and crossed himself.

Lieutenant Doggett saw the two Riflemen return and rode his horse to join them. Sharpe looked up at him and shrugged. 'I'm sorry, Lieutenant.'

'You're sorry, sir?'

'The Prince wouldn't listen to reason.'

'Oh.' Doggett, seeing the ruin of his career, could say nothing more.

'I hit the bugger in the shoulder, you see,' Sharpe explained, 'instead of in the belly. It was just plain bad marksmanship. I'm sorry.'

Doggett stared at Sharpe. 'You . . .' He could not finish.

'But I wouldn't worry,' Sharpe said, 'the bugger's got enough to worry about without pissing all over your commission. And if you fight with us now, Lieutenant, I'll make sure your Colonel gets a glowing report. And I don't want to sound cocksure, but maybe my recommendation is worth more than the Prince's?'

Doggett smiled. 'Yes, sir.'

It seemed cocksure to even surmise survival. Doggett turned to look into the smoke-shot valley that was filled with the overwhelming enemy attack. An errant shaft of sunlight glinted brilliant gold from an Eagle. Beneath the gold the long dark coats and the tall black bearskins made the attackers seem like sinister giants. Cavalry, pennons and lances high, followed the huge column, while further back a shifting mass of shadows betrayed the advance of the rest of the French infantry. The drums were clearly audible beneath the louder percussion of the remaining French guns. 'What happens now?' Doggett could not help asking.

'Those bastards in front are called the Imperial Guard,' Sharpe said, 'and their column will attack our line, and our line ought to beat the hell out of their column, but after that?' Sharpe could not answer his own question, for this battle had already gone far outside his own experience. The British line should beat the French column, for it always had and it was an article of an infantryman's faith that it always would, but Sharpe sensed that this column was different, that even if it initially recoiled from the volley fire it would somehow survive and bring on all the other enemy behind in one last cataclysmic attack. An empire and an emperor's pride rode on this drum-driven attack.

'You don't worry about what happens, Mr Doggett.' Harper's voice was sombre as he rammed the last half-inch bullet into his seven-barrelled gun. 'Once you hear the Old Trousers you just kill as many of the bastards as you can. Because if you don't, then sure as eggs the bastards will kill you.'

Sharpe looked at Harper as the Irishman primed the big gun and tested the seating of its flint. 'You shouldn't be here,' he said.

'A bit bloody late to tell me that,' Harper smiled.

'You promised Isabella,' Sharpe said, but not forcefully. The truth was that he did not want Harper to leave. Bravery was not something that was inspired by king or country or even by battalion. Bravery was what a man owed his friends. It was keeping pride and faith in front of those friends. For Sharpe and Harper it was even habit; they had fought side by side for too long for either man to turn aside at the end.

And this moment seemed like the end. Sharpe had never seen a British army so worn down to fragility, nor an attack like the monstrous drum-driven column that now took shape in the gloom below. He tried to smile, as though to show Doggett that there was no real need to be frightened, but his lips had been cracked by the powder-dried air and all he achieved was a bloody grimace.

Harper stared at the column and cocked his gun. 'God save Ireland.'

The surviving gunners of the British line rammed canister on top of roundshot, stabbed the spikes to break the powder bags, and rammed quills into blackened vents. The guns, and the redcoats, were ready.

And the Guard cheered.

CHAPTER 20

'Cheer, you bastards!' Marshal Ney raised his sword to catch the dying light.

The Guard cheered. They were the Emperor's best.

Ney's sword dropped to point towards the left and the great column split smoothly into two parts. The larger of the two newly formed columns would attack close to Hougoumont while the smaller would assault the ridge straight in front. The cavalry would follow the twin assaults, ready to pursue the broken enemy, while the great mass of other infantry would march at the rear of the attack to hold the ground the Guard captured.

The leading Guard battalions looked up, seeing nothing but a few mounted officers and a handful of guns at the top of the ridge.

They had begun their climb to victory. The slope was not steep. A man could run the slope without catching breath. Some men stumbled because the soil had been churned by the cavalry, but the ground was not so broken that the long ranks could not keep their order. Those ranks advanced slowly, even ponderously, as if to suggest that their victory was inevitable. And so, for them, it was. They were the immortals; the unbeaten. They were the Guard.

'Fire!'

The glowing slow-matches of the portfires touched

the quills and the nine-pounders crashed back on their trails. The six-pounders, their barrels too light for double shotting, fired canister or roundshot alone.

The guns pierced their missiles deep into the two columns. Gunners swabbed and rammed, and when they looked up again the columns had closed ranks and were still marching forward, almost as though no men had died. The drums still sounded, and the French cheer was still as confident and just as menacing as before. The next quills were shoved into the vents, the gunners ducked aside, and the guns hammered back.

Colonel Ford watched in horrified disbelief. The smaller French column was marching to strike the ridge just to the right of his battalion, and he could see that the column was quite unstoppable. He saw the roundshot plunge into the long blue coats, and the cannon-balls seemed to do no damage at all. The Guard just soaked up the fire, sealed its ranks, stepped over its dead and injured, and marched stolidly on.

Sharpe had seen such columns before. He had seen them more times than he could remember, but once again, as on all those other times, he marvelled at how the French infantry could take such punishment. With each strike of roundshot and canister the column seemed to quiver, but then it sealed up its ranks and kept on marching. Gun-fire would not stop these huge men, only musketry could do that. It would have to be volley fire, calm and fast; musketry that killed in bloody droves to pile the column's leading ranks in rows of corpses.

The cannon fired again, pouring shot at pistol range into the closest column. Sixty Guardsmen marched in each rank. The foremost ranks were almost at the ridge's crest while the rear ranks had yet to clear the obscuring smoke on the valley's floor. Far to Sharpe's right, where the British Guards waited, the larger column filled the whole slope with its dark menace, then Sharpe looked back to the nearer column as he waited for Ford to give the battalion the orders to stand and fire.

'*Vive l'Empereur!*' the Guard shouted, their voices close enough to sound hoarse and overwhelming.

D'Alembord glanced expectantly at Ford, but the Colonel had taken off his spectacles and was furiously rubbing them on the tail of his sash.

'For God's sake, sir!' d'Alembord pleaded.

'Oh, my God!' Ford had suddenly realized that he was smearing Major Vine's brains all over his spectacles. He whimpered and let the eyeglasses fall as though they were white hot. He whimpered again as the precious spectacles dropped into the mud.

'Sir!' d'Alembord swayed in the saddle.

'Oh, no! No!' Ford had evidently forgotten all about the Guard, but was instead leaning far out of his saddle in an attempt to reach his eyeglasses. 'Help me, Major! My spectacles! Help me.'

D'Alembord took a deep breath. 'Stand up!' His voice sounded weak, but the battalion had been waiting for the command and scrambled eagerly to their feet to see the enemy on their right front. Peter d'Alembord filled his lungs to shout the next order, but instead, in a gasp of pain, he toppled senseless from the saddle. His right leg was a mess of blood. The remnants of his breeches, his silk stocking, the bandage and his dancing shoe were all soaked in a slippery mess of blood. He fell on top of Colonel Ford's spectacles, breaking them.

'No! No!' Ford protested. 'My glasses! Major, please! I must insist! You'll destroy my eyeglasses. Move, I beg you! My spectacles!' He screamed the last word in sheer despair, betraying his horror at this last tragedy in a day of madness.

The battalion gaped at the Colonel, then looked back to see a French eight-pounder gun slewing violently round behind its team of horses half-way down the slope. The gun's wheels spewed mud ten feet into the air as the weapon slid to a halt. The gunners spiked the trail round as the horses were led away. Ford looked up from d'Alembord to see the vague shape of the cannon, its muzzle huge and black. The French column was a hundred paces to Ford's right, its men's faces visible to him as pale blurs in the smoke. Worse, the column was beginning to unfold, its rear ranks marching outwards to form a broad line that would challenge and crush the British muskets.

The French cannon fired.

The canister crashed into the battalion's four ranks. Seven men went down. Two screamed foully until a sergeant told them to stop their damned noise. Ford, racked by the screams, could take no more. His tongue clove to the roof of his mouth and his hands were shaking. He tried to speak, but no sound came. The nearest Frenchmen were just fifty yards away and, even without his spectacles, he could see their moustaches and the bright streaks that were their bayonets. He saw their mouths open to shout their war cry. '*Vive l'Empereur!*'

The battalion to Ford's right was edging backwards. They, like Ford's men, were survivors of Halkett's brigade who had so nearly died with the men of the 69th at Quatre Bras. Now, their nerves shredded and their officers mostly dead, they gave ground. The French were just too huge, too threatening, and too close.

'*Vive l'Empereur!*'

Ford's men smelt their neighbours' panic. They too shuffled backwards. They looked for orders, but their Colonel could not stop them. His saddle was wet, his bowels were churning and his muscles twitching helplessly. He could see death coming at him in a myopic blur of long blue coats. He wanted to cry, because he did not want to die.

While for the Guard, for the Emperor's immortal undefeated Guard, victory was so sweet. '*Vive l'Empereur!*'

'Now, Maitland! Now's your time!' The Duke had stationed himself behind the survivors of the British Foot
Guards who faced the larger of the two French columns.
The Duke, who had learned his trade as a battalion
officer, could not resist giving the orders himself. 'Stand
up, Guards!'

To the French Guardsmen it seemed as though the line
of redcoats rose out of the mud like the reviving dead.
They suddenly stood to make a barrier across the path of
the larger French column which, instinctively, checked.
One moment the ridge had appeared empty, now, suddenly, an enemy had risen from the ravaged earth.

'Forward!' the French officers shouted, while at the
back of the Imperial Guard's column the battalions began
to spread outwards to form the musket line which would
overpower the handful of men who dared to oppose
them.

'Make ready!' It had been many years since the Duke
had handled a single battalion in battle, but he had lost
none of his skills and had judged the moment to perfection. The British muskets were suddenly raised, making it
seem to the approaching Frenchmen as if all the waiting
redcoats had made a quarter turn to the right. The Duke
looked grim, waited a second, then shouted 'Fire!'

The British muskets flamed. They could not miss at fifty
paces and the leading ranks of the French column were
cut down in blood and screams. The dead were numbered
in scores, making a barrier of blood and meat to block the
following ranks.

More muskets crashed flame and smoke to fill the
ridge with the sound of infantry volleys. On either flank
of Maitland's Guards other British battalions were closing on the deploying French. The 52nd, a hard and

bloody-minded battalion that had learned its trade in Spain, was wheeling out of line and advancing to take the wounded column in its flank. They raked the French Guards with a lethal and practised volley fire. Fifteen thousand Frenchmen might have crossed the valley, but only the handful of men at the head of each column could use their muskets, and that handful was faced by the rippling volleys of the red-coated battalions. Column had met line again, and the line was swamping the heads of the columns with fire. The rear flanks of the column tried but could not deploy into line; instead they shrank back from the relentless musketry.

The Imperial Guard could not go forward, nor could it form its own musket line, it could only stand stock still while its face and flanks were mauled by the redcoats' fire. The French officers shouted at the ranks to advance, but the living were obstructed by the dead and under a lashing fire that made each new front rank into a barricade of corpses. The Emperor's dream had begun to die.

The British Guards facing the column's head reloaded. 'Make ready! Fire!' The Guards of either nation were close enough to see each other's faces clearly, close enough to see the pitiful agony in a wounded man's eyes, to see the bitter anger of an officer's broken pride, to see a man spit tobacco juice or vomit blood, to see resolve turn swiftly to fear. The undefeated, immortal, Imperial Guard was beginning to falter, beginning to edge backwards, though still the drummer boys tried to beat them on with their desperate sticks.

'Make ready!' The voice of a British Guards officer rose cool and mocking. 'Fire!'

The splintering, ripping sound of a battalion volley filled the sky as the musket-balls thudded home through the twitching smoke. The British Guards had stopped the French advance, while the 52nd had closed on the column's flank and was now turning it bloody with their pitiless and murderous fire. Hours of practice had gone into this column's death; tedious hours of loading and ramming and priming and firing until the redcoats could perform the motions of firing a musket in their rum-sodden sleep. Now they grimaced with powder-blackened faces as their brass-bound musket butts crashed back into their bruised shoulders. They were the scum of the earth and they were turning the Emperor's pampered darlings into bloody offal.

'Now's your time!' The Duke's voice pierced the noise. 'Fix bayonets!'

The Imperial Guard had been stopped. Now it must learn defeat.

Then Wellington glanced to his left, and saw his own defeat.

The last of the British light cavalry had been drawn up in line a hundred yards behind Halkett's brigade. They had been posted there in case of disaster. Some would escort the colours of the defeated army to safety, while the rest would protect the retreat of the surviving British infantry with a last suicidal charge.

They believed that suicidal charge was imminent for they could see the battalions of Halkett's brigade edging back towards them. Beyond those scared troops, and dark on the crest, a column of French infantry was appearing from the smoky darkness of the valley. Far off to the right the British Guards were standing firm and pouring musket-fire at another enemy column, but here, closer to the centre of the British line, the redcoats were giving ground and the Emperor's men were pounding relentlessly forward.

'Stop them!' a cavalry colonel shouted. He pointed, not at the French, but at the British infantry.

Sabres rasped from scabbards and the horsemen spurred forward to threaten their own infantry.

The redcoats were shuffling backwards. The wounded begged their comrades not to leave them. Some officers and men tried to staunch the spreading panic, but the battalions were leaderless and they knew this battle was lost for their colours had been taken away, and they knew that in a moment the long French bayonets would sear forward. The men of the Prince of Wales's Own Volunteers looked to their rear, searching for orders, and all they saw was their own terrified and half-blind Colonel riding backwards. Beyond the Colonel was the cavalry. The redcoats looked left towards the open space on the ridge where flight was still possible. They were no longer soldiers; they were a mob on the teetering edge of panicked flight, and then, above the noise of the drums and above the sound of the cavalry's hooves and above the crash of the British Guards' volleys and above the French cheers for their Emperor, one huge voice stilled the battlefield.

'South Essex! Halt!' The voice filled the space between the blood-reeking mud and the smoke. 'Sergeant Harper!'

'Sir!' Harper's voice answered from the rear of the battalion.

'You will kill the next man who takes a step backwards, and that includes officers!'

'Very good, sir!' Harper's voice held a convincing edge of anger as an implicit promise that he would indeed murder any man who took another backwards pace.

Sharpe stood in front of the battalion and with his back to the French column. His horse, which d'Alembord had been riding, was being held by a sergeant in the Grenadier Company. Sharpe suspected the man had been ready to mount and flee from the expected defeat, and now the Sergeant stared with fear and defiance at Sharpe. 'Bring the horse here!' Sharpe called to the Sergeant, but not angrily, instead keeping his voice almost matter-of-fact as though there was not a damned great column of victorious French infantry storming across the ridge's crest not a pistol's shot behind him. 'Bring the horse here! Quickly now!' Sharpe wanted to be on horseback so that every man in the battalion could see him. These soldiers had no colours any more, they had precious few officers any more, so they must be able to see who led them and see that he was not flinching from the drum-driven threat which pounded so close.

'Form ranks! Hurry now!' Sharpe dropped his rifle into the saddle holster, then pulled himself awkwardly into the saddle. He was secretly flinching because he expected a volley of French musketry to chop him and the horse brutally down, but he had to show calmness in front of the frightened battalion. They knew him, they trusted him, and Sharpe knew they would fight like the gutter-born bastards they were if they were just given a chance and given leadership. He thanked the Sergeant for bringing the horse, then, as he fiddled his left foot into the stirrup, he turned to stare at the four shaken ranks. 'Make sure you're loaded!' He turned the horse so he could see the enemy. Christ, but they were close! They were marching towards the open space to the right of the Prince of Wales's Own Volunteers, a space left by a panicking battalion that had evidently fled. Sharpe toyed with the idea of marching his own men into that gaping hole, but he knew he was too late. The French had almost pierced the British line, so now they must be attacked on their open right flank.

A mounted French officer was riding on that open flank and he pointed with his sword at Sharpe, doubtless showing his men a target, and the sight of the French officer's confident expression angered Sharpe who, to show his utter disdain, turned away from the enemy to face his own men. 'We're going to advance! Then we're going to give those poxy bastards some volley fire!' He looked along the apprehensive ranks; powder stained, bloodied and ashamed, but they were steady now and had their muskets loaded. This might be a shrunken and half defeated battalion, but to Sharpe it was a weapon that he could fight with a lethal precision. He blinked as a musket bullet slapped close past his face, then grinned as he drew his long sword. He wanted the men to see his pleasure, because this was the moment when a soldier had to take a perverse delight in killing. Remorse and pity could come later, for they were the luxuries of victory, but now these scum must kill and the enemy must fear the joy of their killing. Sharpe held the sword high, then dropped its point towards the enemy. ''Talion will advance! Sergeant Harper! If you please!'

''Talion!' the Irishman's voice was huge and confident, the voice of a man unworriedly doing his job, ''Talion! Forward! March!'

They marched. It was only seconds since they had been retreating and their ranks had been shaking loose into chaos, but now, given leadership, they went towards the conquering Guard. Sharpe stood his horse still to let the battalion divide either side of him, and only then did he walk forward, a horseman advancing in the centre of the marching battalion. He saw that a Brunswick infantry battalion was raking the far flank of the French column, but the fire was not sufficient to stop the Guard, only to deflect it towards the Prince of Wales's Own Volunteers. There were still no troops facing the column's head, while the rear ranks of the great formation were clumsily spreading outwards to form a musket line that was designed to drown the ridge's shaken defenders with volley fire. Behind the Guard a swarm of cavalry and lesser infantry was pressing up the lower slope, ready to turn a British defeat into rout and slaughter.

'Grenadier Company! Halt! 'Talion will wheel to the right! Right wheel!' Sharpe was taking a risk that his men would understand and obey the difficult order in the noise and heat and fear. It would have been simpler just to halt the battalion and to fire obliquely at the French column, but such a compromise would have stranded the left half of the battalion a long way from the enemy. Yet if the battalion wheeled in good order they would sweep round like a swinging gate to face the enemy's unfolding flank. The Grenadier company, on the right of the line, stayed still as the remaining companies hinged on them. 'At the double!' Sergeant Huckfield hurried the light company who had the furthest to go.

The wheeling line was ragged, but that did not matter. They were carrying their muskets to face the French, and Sharpe felt the exultation of handling a battalion in battle. He could see apprehension on the face of the mounted French officer who understood exactly what horror was about to be unleashed on his men.

'Halt!' Sharpe stopped the swinging battalion fifty paces from the column's flank. The whole battle was now reduced to a few dirty paces of smoke-fogged air. 'Present!' The battalion's heavy muskets came up. Sharpe waited a heartbeat. He saw the Guards' mouths open to chant their litany of praise for the Emperor, but before they could make a sound, Sharpe at last gave the order. 'Fire!'

He heard the old sound, the blessed sound, the splintering crash of a battalion's muskets spitting bullets, and he saw the deploying wing of the column jerk as the bullets struck home. A few Frenchmen fired back, but they were still marching and their muskets were unbalanced by the fixed bayonets and so their fire went wild. The mounted officer was down, his horse thrashing on the ground as he crawled away. Harper was shouting at the battalion to reload. Simon Doggett, still on horseback, was firing a pistol over the battalion's head. Ramrods rattled in musket barrels as the men desperately thrust bullets down onto powder.

Sharpe's battalion threatened the Imperial Guard's right, while on their left flank the Brunswickers fired another volley, but directly in front of the column was nothing but a broken mass of redcoats. The British cavalry closed on the frightened men, but, before the sabres could be used on the redcoats, the Duke was suddenly among them, and somehow the redcoats were stopped and turned by his confident voice. Staff officers rode among the fugitives, order was shaken out of their chaos, muskets were levelled, and a ragged volley sheeted flames at the column's head. The Guard, assailed on three sides, halted and shrank away from the musketry.

Sharpe watched the central ranks of the column pushing against the motionless men ahead. 'Fire!' Sharpe gave the French right flank another bellyful of bullets. The column was still trying to advance, and the rearmost ranks were swinging obliquely out to form the musket line, and Sharpe sensed that the whole fate of this battle hung on the next few seconds. If the French could be made to move forward over their own dead then they could flood the ridge with their revenge and the fragile British line would shatter. Yet if this column could be driven backwards then the British line would earn a respite in which night or the Prussians might snatch survival from defeat.

'Forward! Forward! Forward!' a French voice shouted huge and desperately in the column's centre. The drums were still beating their message of victory. '*Vive l'Empereur!*'

'Forward! Forward for the Emperor!'

'Fix bayonets!' Sharpe shouted in response.

The battalion, already reloading, dropped their half-torn cartridges and clawed their bayonets free. They slotted the blades on to blackened muzzles. The French drums sounded desperately close. Sharpe spurred ahead of the battalion. His horse was nervous and slick with sweat, and his long sword was still stained with the blood he had drawn in the yard at Hougoumont. He saw the French column push over the bodies of the men his last volley had killed, and he wondered whether he had enough bayonets to break these confident Frenchmen apart, but there was only one way to discover that answer and Sharpe suddenly felt the old excitement of battle, and the mad joy of it, and he raised his long bloodied blade high and ordered his battalion forward. 'Charge!'

The survivors of the Prince of Wales's Own Volunteers charged with all the fury of bitter men who had taken hell all day and who now faced the pristine, untouched favourites of an Emperor who had been sheltered from death till this moment. They charged with bloodied and powder-stained faces, and they screamed like furies as they carried their long blades forward.

The flank of the column tried to retreat from the charge, but the Frenchmen only pressed against the ranks behind that still tried to advance to the drumbeat. The sound of the drums was menacing, yet even the men sheltered in the very heart of the column knew that something was wrong. Their left flank was dying from the Brunswicker volleys, the Duke had rallied the redcoats in their front, and now Sharpe's men struck home on the right.

Sharpe slashed back with his heels, the horse leaped forward, and his sword crashed down like an axe. The blade drove a long splinter from a parrying musket, then hacked down again to thump through a bearskin and drive a Frenchman to his knees. The horse screamed and reared as a bayonet stabbed its chest, but then the redcoats swarmed past Sharpe to carry their blades at the enemy. The Prince of Wales's Own Volunteers had a score to settle, and so they ripped into the Emperor's immortals with a savagery that only men atoning for a moment's cowardice could show.

Sharpe's horse was wounded, but not fatally. It screamed with fear or pain as he crashed a musket aside with his sword then lunged at the Frenchman's face. The man recoiled from the blade, then went down beneath the bayonets of two snarling redcoats who thrust hard to force their blades through the Frenchman's heavy blue greatcoat. The enemy were sweating and edging back. The column was so closely packed that the French had no space to use their weapons properly. Sharpe's men were keening as they killed, crooning a foul music as they lunged and stabbed and gouged and fought across the dead. Sharpe's horse half stumbled on a corpse and he flailed with the sword to find his balance. The ridge stank of blood and sweat and powder smoke. A vast crash announced that Harper had fired his volley gun point blank into the ranks of the Guard, and now the Irishman threw himself into the space his bullets had made. He widened the space by stabbing with his sword-bayonet, each vicious thrust accompanied by a Gaelic war-cry.

Lieutenant Doggett, still on horseback, shouted at the files to give way then crashed his horse hard into the French ranks and stabbed down with his slim sword. He was screaming madly, covering his terror with a sound mad enough for a smoking field of blood. Ahead of Sharpe an Eagle swayed over the bearskin hats. He slashed his sword towards it, but the French ranks were so close that he could not force a path towards the trophy. He swore at a man as he killed him, then drove the sword into a moustached, sun-tanned face and twisted the steel to flense the man's cheek away. 'The Eagle! The Eagle!' Sharpe screamed, then cursed the men who barred his way. Beneath and beside Sharpe the bayonets stabbed and twisted, but suddenly the enemy's gilded standard vanished, plucked backwards from the ridge top as the Emperor's Guard began their retreat. The drums had fallen silent and the immortal undefeated Guard were running away.

They ran. One moment they had been trying to fight, the next they were shouting that the day was lost and they were scrambling backwards from the bloody bayonets with panic and fear on their moustached faces, and the redcoats, panting and bloodied like hounds at their kill, watched in silence as the enemy élite fled. The Guard had been defeated by a remnant of red-coated killers who had sprung from the mud to maul an emperor's glory.

'Don't give them a chance to stand!' A commanding voice rose clear among the smoke and chaos. The Duke, cantering his horse behind the victorious battalions, was staring intently at the fleeing French. 'Don't let them stand! Go forward now! See them off our land!' Typically there was an edge of impatience in the Duke's voice as though his men, having performed the miracle of defeating the Imperial Guard, had disappointed him by not yet converting that defeat into rout. Yet, equally typically, the Duke's eye had missed nothing and he was not graceless at this moment of salvation. 'Mr Sharpe! I am beholden to you! That is your battalion now! So take it forward!'

''Talion!' Sharpe had no time to savour his reward. Instead he had to straighten his line to face the valley where the French were still massed, and from where their next attack would surely come. 'Light company stand firm! Right flank forward! March!'

The battalion wheeled left to face the enemy again. They had to negotiate the bodies of the French dead and dying. A man called for his mother, wailing foully until the slice of a bayonet stilled his voice. A wounded horse, its rump a mess of blood and torn flesh, galloped across the slope in front of Sharpe. ''Talion will advance!' The Sergeants and Corporals echoed Sharpe's order. Sharpe could not tell if any officers were left, though

417

he saw Simon Doggett was still alive and he heard Patrick Harper's voice, and then the smoke cleared from the ridge's crest and Sharpe advanced his men to the very edge of the valley and, amazingly, miraculously, they saw that there would be no more French attacks for the enemy had not just retreated, but had been broken.

The battle was won and across the whole smoke-wreathed battlefield the enemy infantry was running. The Guard, the immortal undefeated Guard had been beaten, and if the Guard could lose, then no Frenchman thought himself safe and so panic had seized a whole army. There were plenty of French troops left, more than enough to overwhelm the British ridge, but those troops had seen the Imperial Guard running away, and the panic had spread, and so a whole army now ran for safety. A few staff officers galloped among the French and tried to rally them, but victory had been collapsed to nightmare by a few seconds of volley fire and steel, and so the French ran, all but for a few brave men who tried to stand firm in the valley's floor.

The Earl of Uxbridge, who had lost the Duke his cavalry just as Marshal Ney had lost the Emperor his, reined in beside Wellington who was staring hard at those few enemy who still showed defiance. 'Oh damn it!' the Duke said in wonderment. 'In for a penny, in for a pound!' The Duke took off his hat with its four cockades. The sun miraculously found a shaft of clear air between the cloud and smoke and slanted its golden light on the Duke as he brandished the hat forward. He thrust the hat forward again, signalling the whole British line to advance. This time they were not just to clear the French from the ridge, but from the whole battlefield. They had defended their ground all day, but now they could attack the enemy's ground. 'Go on!' the Duke called. 'Go on! They won't stand! Go on!'

And so they went. The battered survivors in their

shattered ranks went forward at last. Somewhere a piper began his wild Scots music as the redcoats marched in a ragged line down to the valley floor to drive a beaten enemy to final ruin. A few last guns fired from the French ridge as a loser's defiance at the hour of defeat.

One of the cannon-balls crashed past the Duke and struck the Earl's right knee. 'My God! I've lost my leg!'

'Have you, by God?' The Duke galloped forward to where his infantry marched down to the valley floor. 'Go on! They won't stand now! Go on!'

Dazed men marched down a slope they had defended all day. Slowly, incredulously, the fact of victory was born in them. They had won, by God, they had won, and to their left, in the east, the sky flickered with new gun-fire and the setting sun shone on dark-uniformed troops who were swarming up the flank of the far French ridge. The Prussians had come at last.

A British regiment of light cavalry, saved to cover the retreat, now trotted forward to exploit the victory. 'Eighteenth!' their Colonel shouted. 'Follow me!'

'To hell!'

The trumpet sounded the ten dizzying notes. The horsemen careered down the slope, splitting the French survivors, sabring the last gunners who had stayed at their weapons, and then they saw a reserve battalion of the Guard formed into square on the enemy ridge. The square was edging backwards; attempting to escape the rout in good order and so be ready to fight for the Emperor another day.

The British sabres broke the square. The horsemen did what all the cavalry of France had failed to do, they broke a square. They died in their scores to do it, but nothing would stop them now. This was victory. This was better than victory, this was revenge, and so the rum-soaked horsemen hacked their sabres down at the bearskins and forced their horses across the dead to cut the living into bloody ribbons with their blades. The Prussians were marching from the left, the British were advancing across the valley, and the Emperor fled into the dusk as his Eagles fell.

The Inniskillings alone did not advance. Those who were not dead were wounded, for the Irishmen had held the weak spot in the Duke's thin line, and they had held it to the end. They had died in their ranks, they had never stopped fighting, and now they had won. Their dead lay in a perfect square and their colours still flew in the shredding smoke as their last living soldiers stared across a valley stinking with blood and palled by fire, a valley plucked from hell; a battlefield.

EPILOGUE

The wounded lay beneath a smoky moon while the living, exhausted, slept.

It was a warm night. A small west wind slowly took the stench of powder away, though the smell of blood would linger in the soil for weeks. Plunderers crept into the darkness. To the Belgian poor every scrap of litter was worth money; whether it was a Cuirassier's bullet-punctured breastplate, a broken sword, a pair of boots, a trooper's saddle, a bayonet, or even a strip of cloth. They stripped the dead naked, and killed the wounded to get their uniforms. Injured horses neighed pitifully as they waited for death in a field which rustled with thieves and murderers. A few fires flickered among the carnage. More than forty thousand men lay dead or wounded in the valley, and the survivors could not cope.

Lord John Rossendale still lay in the valley where he drifted in and out of consciousness. The pain had lessened in the night, but so had his lucidity. He dreamed. At times he was even happy in his dreams, but then hands began pulling at his chest and he moaned and tried to ward off the grasping fingers that were causing him such pain. A woman told him to lie still, but Lord John jerked as the pain stabbed and shrieked at him. The woman, a villager from Waterloo, was trying to drag Lord John's coat from his body. Her child, an eight-year-old girl, kept watch for the few sentries who tried to stop the plundering.

Lord John thought the woman was Jane. He was blind so he did not know it was still the heart of a dark night; instead he thought it was morning and that Jane had found him and he began to sob for joy as he reached up to hold her hand. The woman cursed Lord John, for making her life so difficult, but she was not unprepared for such unco-operative victims. She carried a ten-inch knife that she used to slaughter the pigs she raised in her back yard. 'Lie still!' she told Lord John in French.

'Jane!' he cried desperately, and the woman feared that his noise would bring the sentries so she sawed the knife quick and hard across his moon-whitened throat. Blood jetted black. He choked, jerked once like a landed fish, then was still.

The woman took Lord John's coat with its precious epaulettes, but left his shirt because it was too drenched in blood. In a pocket of the coat she found a ragged length of dirty rope that she used to bind up her bundle of plundered clothing. Beyond the southern ridge a vixen howled at the sky that was suffused with the smoke of the victors' camp-fires.

The Prince of Wales's Own Volunteers slept on the ridge they had defended. Peter d'Alembord's leg had been taken off, so he might yet live. Private Clayton was dead; killed by the Imperial Guard at the very moment of victory. Charlie Weller lived, as did Colonel Ford, though the Colonel had been sent back to Brussels and whether he wanted to stay alive any longer was another matter. Harry Price was the next most senior living officer, so Sharpe had made him into a Major and given Simon Doggett a Captaincy, though he had warned both men that the promotions might not stand up to the scrutiny of the civil servants in Whitehall. Men might fight and bleed and write a chapter of history for Britain, but still the evil-minded soft-bummed bastards of Whitehall would have the last say.

Sharpe slept for an hour, then woke to sit beside a fire that he had made from fragments of lance shafts and the broken spokes from a shattered gun wheel. The first light came early; a sickly grey that dispersed the plunderers and brought the black-winged carrion birds to feast on the dead. The air was already humid, promising a day of stifling heat. In the west the fires of the Prussian bivouacs made thin skeins across the wash of high cloud. Somewhere behind the ridge a bugle called the Rouse and other buglers took up the call that seemed to be echoed by the crowing of cockerels from distant villages.

'Orders, sir?' Harry Price looked red-eyed, as though he had been crying, though it was probably just tiredness.

Sharpe felt tired and emptied, so it took an immense effort to think of even the simplest tasks. 'I want a proper butcher's list, Harry.' That was the list of the dead and wounded. 'Give Sergeant Huckfield a work party to salvage muskets, and see what other equipment you can filch.' The aftermath of battle was a prime time to stock the battalion's equipment needs. 'We need some food. Remind me who's guarding the prisoners?'

'Sergeant Ryan.'

'Tell him to march the buggers back to brigade. If they don't want them, then turn them loose without any boots or belts.'

'We're going to need more sergeants,' Harry Price warned.

'I'll think about it.' Sharpe turned to stare at the newly stripped bodies of the dead which lay so white among the charred stalks of rye. 'And start digging a grave, Harry. A big one.'

'Yes, sir.'

A soldier brought Sharpe a scorching mug of tea that

he drank as he gazed into the valley. Smoke still drifted from the remains of the château of Hougoumont and from the farm of La Haye Sainte. The château had been burnt right out, leaving nothing but blackened roof beams above a scorched stone shell, while the corridors of La Haye Sainte were still choked with dead. At the foot of the slope beneath Sharpe a horse that had survived the night without its back legs sat on its gory haunches and whinnied pathetically for help.

The first soldiers went down from the ridge. Some went to bury the dead while others searched for loot. A man found a French sword knot, its gilt braid beautiful and intricate, and kept it as a gift for his girl. Another man picked a silver-handled shaving brush from a stiff pool of congealed blood. Flies buzzed above the dead. A redcoat carefully collected a pack of playing cards that had been strewn around the body of a French skirmisher. The pages of a blood-stained book riffled in the small wind. Pistol shots sounded flat as men put horses out of their long misery. A group of cavalry officers, their uniforms oddly bright in the dull dawn, cantered down from the ridge to search the slew of bodies that marked the ride of the British horse from glory to defeat.

The first civilians arrived from Brussels. They parked their carriages near the elm tree and walked in horrified silence into the valley where the working parties searched for the wounded. Crows were ripping at the white-skinned dead. A woman found her husband and vomited. A local priest, come to minister to the injured French, reeled hopelessly towards the road with a hand clapped to his mouth.

Simon Doggett's work party came back to the battalion with two tubs of salt beef, a sack of bread, and a barrel of rum. He proudly told Sharpe that he had stolen the food from the cavalry. 'So what happens now?' Doggett asked.

Sharpe found it hard to think. It was as if the battle had deadened his senses. 'We'll go to Paris, I suppose.' He could not imagine the Emperor recovering from this defeat.

'Paris?' Doggett sounded surprised, as though he had not realized till this moment just what Wellington's army had achieved in this valley that stank of smoke and blood. 'You really think we'll go to Paris?' he asked excitedly.

But Sharpe did not reply. Instead he was watching a horseman pick his way up the face of the ridge and across the long dark scars of earth that had been gouged by the French cannonade. He recognized Captain Christopher Manvell and walked to meet him. 'Morning.' Sharpe's greeting was curt.

Manvell touched a gloved hand to his hat. 'Good morning, sir. I was hoping to find you.' He seemed embarrassed and turned to look at Sharpe's men who, muddied and tired, stared malevolently back at the elegant cavalryman. 'He's dead,' Manvell said without any more effort at politeness.

'Rossendale?'

'Yes. He's dead.' Manvell's face showed sadness as he looked back to Sharpe. 'I thought you should know, sir.'

'Why would I need to know?' Sharpe asked brutally.

Manvell seemed nonplussed, but then shrugged. 'I believe he gave you a note? I'm afraid it's worthless, sir. He didn't have a penny of his own money. And then there's –' Manvell stopped suddenly.

'There's what?' Sharpe pressured him.

'There's Mrs Sharpe, sir.' Manvell summoned the courage to say the words. 'Someone will have to tell her.'

Sharpe gave a harsh brief laugh. 'Not me, Captain. She's a Goddamned whore, and she can rot in hell for all I care. Good day to you, Captain.'

'Good day, sir.' Manvell watched Sharpe walk away, then turned his horse towards the road where, unknown to Sharpe, Jane waited in her carriage for news. Manvell sighed, and went to break her heart.

Sharpe went back to the dying fire, took the promissory note from his pocket, and tore it into shreds. There would be no easy way of putting a new roof on the château after all. He scattered the paper scraps to the breeze, then turned towards his men. 'Mr Price!'

'Sir?'

'We've got some bandsmen left alive, don't we?'

'Indeed, sir! We've even got a bandmaster!'

'Then get the idle buggers to play us a tune! We're supposed to be celebrating a bloody victory!'

Somewhere in the valley a woman screamed and screamed, paused to take breath, then screamed again because her husband was dead. Behind the battle line in the farm at Mont-St-Jean the pile of amputated limbs grew higher than the dungheap. A white-faced surgeon came to take the air by the roadside while upstairs, where the wounded officers had been taken to recuperate or die, d'Alembord twitched in his shallow sleep. Mr Little, the rotund bandmaster of the Prince of Wales's Own Volunteers, launched his few musicians into a ragged version of 'Over The Hills and Far Away'. Sharpe ordered the colours, that had been restored to the battalion, to be unfurled and planted above the deepening grave so that the shadows of the silk flags would caress the dead.

A woman wept at the edge of the grave. She was one of the sixty wives who had been allowed to travel with the battalion and, though she was widowed now, she would probably be married again by the month's end, for a soldier's woman never lacked for suitors. Another newly widowed wife, Sally Clayton, sat next to Charlie Weller and Sharpe saw the nervousness with which the young man reached for her hand. 'Make me a mug of tea, Charlie,' Sharpe said, 'and I'll make you into a sergeant.'

'Sir?' Charlie stared up in astonishment.

'Do it, Charlie!' Sally was quicker to understand that Sharpe was offering them a sergeant's wage. 'And thank you, Mr Sharpe.'

Sharpe smiled and turned away as a shout told him that Harper had returned from Brussels. The Irishman had brought Sharpe's dog back with him, and now released Nosey who ran to Sharpe and leaped up to nuzzle and fuss his master. The men of the battalion grinned. Sharpe pushed the dog down, waited for Harper to slide out of the saddle, then walked with his friend towards the lip of the valley.

'She's well,' Harper confirmed. Lucille had wept when she had learned that Sharpe was safe and unhurt, but she had made Harper promise not to reveal her tears. 'And the boy's well, too.'

'Thank you for going for me.'

Harper grunted. He had left for Brussels before dawn and now stared into the battlefield for the first time on this new day. His face showed no reaction to the horror. Like Sharpe he had seen it a hundred times before. They were soldiers; they were paid to endure horror, which is why they understood horror better than other men. They were soldiers and, like the men who dug the nightsoil from the pits of London, or like the women who tended the pestilent dying in the charity wards, they did a distasteful job that more fastidious men and women despised. They were soldiers, which made them the scum of the earth until a tyrant threatened Britain, and then suddenly they were red-coated heroes and jolly good fellows.

'God save Ireland, but we made a right bloody shit-heap of this place,' Harper commented on the valley.

Sharpe said nothing. He was staring beyond the battle-field to where the sunlight glowed on trees unmarked by fire and where the air smelt summer sweet. The cloudless sky promised a day for haymaking, or a day for lovers to stroll through heavy-leafed woods to rest beside the green cool of a streambank. It was a midsummer's day on the borders of France, and the world was at peace.

Historical Note

It was indeed a near run thing; 'the nearest run thing you ever saw in your life,' as the Duke of Wellington confessed on the day after the battle, but Napoleon, as the Duke also said, 'just moved forward in the old style, in columns, and was driven off in the old style.'

The Duke himself would probably have been content to let that stand as a full account of the campaign of Waterloo, for he was a man notorious both for the brevity of his despatches, and for his dislike of authors. He had, he explained later in his life, been too much exposed to authors. One of them, seeking the Duke's assistance for a projected account of the battle, was sternly advised to leave well alone: 'you may depend upon it that you will never make it a satisfactory work'. To another such hopeful scribbler he dismissively remarked that a man might as well seek to write the history of a dance as to write the story of a battle.

Many, though, have defied the Duke's advice, and I must confess my extreme debt to all those whose temerity has produced the vast library on Waterloo. There are too many books to cite here, but I would be shameless if I did not acknowledge two. Even the Duke might have approved of Jac Weller's *Wellington at Waterloo*, the final volume of his impressive trilogy on the Duke's military career. Whenever I found conflict among my sources, and felt unable to clear the matter from my own research,

I relied on Jac Weller's interpretation and I doubt he let me down.

I tremble to imagine what the Duke would have made of a woman writing about his battle, but to my mind the best account of Waterloo is that which concludes Elizabeth Longford's *Wellington, The Years of the Sword*. I used Lady Longford as my source for the Duke's direct quotations, but also for very much more, and I doubt that anyone can ever again write about Wellington or Waterloo without relying on Lady Longford's marvellous book.

Hundreds of contemporary accounts exist of the battle, yet still there is controversy. Even at the time of the battle men did not always see what they thought they saw, which is why Britain now has a regiment called the Grenadier Guards. That is the regiment which defeated the larger column of the Imperial Guard, and they were convinced that they had beaten the Grenadiers of the Guard and, to mark their victory, took their enemy's name. In fact they opposed and beat the Chasseurs of the Guard, but it seems a little late to make the correction now.

There are other mysteries. Did the Prince of Orange really expose infantry in line to cavalry three times? I remain convinced he did, though some say he was not responsible for the débâcle at Quatre Bras. Nor is there agreement about what really happened in front of the smaller column of the Imperial Guard. Undoubtedly some redcoats ran away, but no two accounts agree quite how they were rallied to defeat the Guard, just as no two accounts agree on how many times the French cavalry charged the squares; men who survived those assaults gave figures as various as six or twenty-six. At least one French officer bequeathed historians a fine tale of breaking one of the British squares; riding over and over its remains until it was red ruin, but fine as the account is, there is not a scrap of evidence to support it.

There is, however, much evidence to support the story of the fattest officer in the Prussian army being entrusted with the news of the French invasion, just as it is sadly true that General Dornberg intercepted a despatch to Wellington and refused to forward it on the grounds that he did not believe it. Thus was Wellington humbugged by Napoleon, whose concentration of forces and the speed with which he advanced them across the Dutch border was one of his greatest feats of war.

So who, then, won Waterloo? Or who lost it? The questions are still argued. The Prince of Orange, in a letter to his parents written on the night of the battle, had no doubts: 'My very dear Parents. We have had a glorious affair against Napoleon this day, and it was my troops who bore the brunt of the fighting and to whom we owe the victory.' He then goes on to say that it was the Prussians who really won the battle, thus fuelling the debate between supporters of Blücher and Wellington. The truth is very simple; Wellington would not have fought at Waterloo unless he believed the Prussians to be marching to his aid, and the Prussians, despite Gneisenau, would not have marched unless they believed that Wellington intended to make a stand. In brief it was an allied victory, and Blücher's suggestion of La Belle Alliance as the battle's name was surely more appropriate than the oddly named Waterloo upon which Wellington insisted simply because he slept there on the nights before and after the conflict.

It is an irony that Gneisenau's quite unreasonable distrust of Wellington probably made the victory complete. If the Prussians had come to the field in the early afternoon, when they were expected, Napoleon would undoubtedly have retired behind a tough rearguard action. His army would have been preserved to fight another day among the screen of fortresses that awaited the allies just across the French frontier. As it was, the Emperor's army was so mauled by the evening of Waterloo, and was so deeply committed by the time the Prussians arrived, that Napoleon could not extricate it, and thus his men went down to utter defeat, a defeat so dire that the morale of the fortress garrisons and every other soldier in France collapsed at the news.

If there is fruitless controversy about whether Wellington or Blücher were most responsible for victory, there is even more argument about the generalship of the Emperor. French accounts of the battle describe Waterloo as a glorious French victory that somehow went awry at the last minute. The worst General at the battle, one French historian confidently avers, was Wellington, and he then adduces an impressive list of the Englishman's mistakes; all in aid of proving Napoleon's supremacy. To which we might reply, like General Cambronne of the Imperial Guard when his surrender was demanded at the end of the battle, '*merde*'. Polite French history insists that Cambronne actually said, 'The Old Guard dies, it never surrenders', but that fine defiance was the invention of a newspaperman, and both versions ignore the fact that Cambronne surrendered anyway. The same historians who denigrate Wellington are also the first to plead that the Emperor had piles, or whatever other medical excuse is supposed to have put him off his stroke that day, which makes one wonder why he chose to fight at all. Napoleon did so choose, and he lost, and he spent the next, and last, six years of his life constructing a legend of his glory that is still believed in France.

Nowhere outside France is that glory more visible than at Waterloo itself. The battlefield is a veritable monument to Napoleon and to his army, so much so that an ignorant visitor could be forgiven for thinking they visited the scene of a great French triumph. It is, nevertheless, a battlefield well worth a visit. The greatest change to the scene is, sadly, on the British right, on the ridge where the French cavalry was destroyed and where the Imperial

Guard was defeated. The Dutch scraped four or five feet of soil from the top of that ridge to make their vast lion monument which now dominates the field. More *merde*. Nevertheless, the ridge remains, even though somewhat lower than it was in 1815, and it is now graced with a car park, cafés, museums and shops which sell a variety of the most vulgar, meretricious and shabby souvenirs. The one item worth purchasing is David Howarth's excellent English-language guide to the battlefield. La Belle Alliance is a disco. La Haye Sainte is not open to the public, but if you brave the traffic which now speeds across the battlefield in a matter of seconds, it is possible to stand in the gateway and see into the farmyard. Hougoumont, still with its scars, is more welcoming and well worth visiting; it is signposted 'Goumont', and you can approach it through the gates which Colonel MacDonnell closed on the French intruders, which act, Wellington said, was the bravest done at the battle. In the town of Waterloo the house where the Duke spent the nights before and after the battle is a museum, while the church opposite has some fine memorials. Quatre Bras is worth a visit, and though the wood that was garrisoned by Saxe-Weimar has long disappeared, the field is relatively unchanged and is easily found by driving south from Waterloo.

The campaign produced many heroes. Among the famous are Colonel MacDonnell who closed the gate at Hougoumont, and his immediate enemy, the giant Lieutenant Legros who wielded the axe in his assault on the château. Ensign Christie's defence of his colour at Quatre Bras is memorable, as is Sergeant Ewart's chilling account of how he took the Eagle during the British cavalry charge. Marshal Ney, whose last horse was shot during the attack of the Imperial Guard, raged with a broken sword to rally the defeated French. Ney, truly a brave man, survived only to be executed by a restored Louis XVIII, despite the Duke of Wellington's appeal

433

for clemency. A happy legend has it that the red-headed Marshal escaped that punishment and lived out his days anonymously in South Carolina. I wish that was true.

The war was not ended by the victory at Waterloo, though almost so. Gneisenau, for all his bloody-mindedness during the day of battle, conducted a superb pursuit throughout the short summer night that ended any French hopes of rallying the army's survivors. The allied armies then crossed the frontier and, on 4 July, Paris surrendered. Napoleon left France eleven days later, only to return as a sacred corpse in 1840.

The nineteenth century was not to see comparable slaughter until the American Civil War. Gettysburg was a battle as awful as Waterloo, with similar numbers and casualties. Both battles decided great questions, but at the price of great horror. What made Waterloo so horrid was the smallness of the area into which so many men and killing machines were crammed. Today, standing where the elm tree stood (its remains were reduced to furniture), you can see virtually the whole battlefield. A third of the men who fought in the valley became casualties. No wonder Wellington prayed afterwards that he had fought his last battle.

Not all of the men in the French and British armies fought at Waterloo. Napoleon had detached a whole corps to pursue the Prussians, which corps managed to pursue in the wrong direction and were thus absent from the battle. Their presence would undoubtedly have made a difference, but so would the presence of the 17,000 prime infantry that the Duke sent away to guard his expected line of retreat. Of course, if the French had won at Quatre Bras there would have been no battle at Waterloo and, extraordinarily, one French corps spent the whole of that day marching between Ligny and Quatre Bras. Just when they were about to be committed at Quatre Bras an order summoned them to return to Ligny, and just as they were about to fight at

Ligny another order sent them marching back to Quatre Bras. If that Corps had gone into action against Wellington then I doubt we would have heard so much about the Emperor's haemorrhoids over the last one hundred and seventy-five years.

But, whether because of an emperor's piles or not, Europe's long wars against Revolutionary and Imperial France were at last over. For the Peninsular veterans of the British army it had been a long road from Portugal to Belgium, and finally to Paris, and Sharpe and Harper have now marched its full and bloody length. Perhaps they will march again, but where, or when, neither they nor I yet know.

The Sharpe's Children Foundation

The SCF has been created by actors who took part in the long-running Sharpe television series. Led by Daragh O'Malley (Harper), they are determined to bring a positive change to the lives of the destitute children whom they encountered over the years of filming in India, Turkey and the Ukraine, and in the process to establish a lasting legacy to Sharpe, the charismatic soldier created by Bernard Cornwell in the Sharpe books. Richard Sharpe himself was born in poverty and against all odds rose to high ranks in the British army.

The SCF will establish Sharpe Shelters, residential schools for children aged between 5 and 12 across the developing world, focussing on the areas in which the Sharpe series was filmed.

Bernard Cornwell says:

66 *I hope, like me, you will support the Sharpe's Children Foundation, an amazing initiative by Daragh O'Malley and the superb actors of the Sharpe television series. The Sharpe's Children Foundation fights hard against the immense problems caused by deprived childhoods, but they need our support. Join the Sharpe cast!* 99

If you wish to make a donation, please send payment by cheque or creditcard to : The Sharpe's Children Foundation, 68 Great Eastern Street London EC2A 3JT or check the website.

UK Charity Registration 1129417

To find out more, please visit **www.sharpeschildren.com**